# TALLYING THE TALES
## OF THE
## OLD-TIMERS

✓

# TALLYING THE TALES
## OF THE
# OLD-TIMERS

## Joan Finnigan

GSPH

# TALLYING THE TALES OF THE OLD-TIMERS

**GENERAL STORE PUBLISHING HOUSE**

1 Main Street Burnstown,
Ontario, Canada  K0J 1G0
Telephone (613) 432-7697 or 1-800-465-6072

*Care has been taken to trace the ownership of any copyright material contained in this text. The publishers welcome any information that will enable them to rectify, in subsequent editions, any omitted or incorrect reference or credit.*

Canadian Cataloguing in Publication Data

Main entry under title:

   Tallying the tales of the old-timers

Includes bibliographical references
ISBN 1-896182-95-X

1. Ottawa River Valley (Quebec and Ont.) –
   Oral/Social History. 2.  OttawaValley
   (Quebec and Ont.) – Life stories.
   I. Finnigan, Joan, 1925- .

FC2775.T34 1988   971.3'8   C98-900971-8
F1054.O9T34 1998

Cover Design: Hugh Malcolm
Text Design: Derek McEwen
Printed and Bound in Canada
Custom Printers, Renfrew, ON

Cover photograph by Dr. Jonathan MacKenzie. Some old-timers from the Opeongo Line at Brudenell bean bake, 1970.

Other Ottawa Valley books by Joan Finnigan include:

*I Come from the Valley*
*Giants of Canada's Ottawa Valley*
*Some of the Stories I Told You Were True*
*Laughing All the Way Home*
*Look! The Land is Growing Giants*
*Legacies, Legends and Lies*
*Wintering Over*
*Finnigan's Guide to the Ottawa Valley*
*Tell Me Another Story*
*Down the Unmarked Roads*

The author wishes to acknowledge the support of the Finnigan Foundation for Irish Writers (Ross, Maye, Frank Sr.)

Dedicated to Frank Robert (Bob) Wake,
1914-1993,
Professor Psychology, Carleton University,
1952-80
friend, mentor, supporter
and believer in my work in the oral/social history
of the Ottawa Valley.

# ACKNOWLEDGEMENTS

I wish to acknowledge my gratitude to:

Joan Litke, Burnstown, ON for transcribing, word processing, and all
things beyond the line of duty; Susan Code, Perth, ON for editing;
Betty Corson, Kingston, ON for early editing; Don Taylor, Bancroft, ON;
the McRaes, Whitney, ON; Don Blakeslee, Ottawa, ON; Tom Roney,
Ottawa Room, Ottawa Public Library; Mayfred Dodds, Catherine Horner,
Shawville, QC; the McColgans, Quyon, QC; Hugh MacMillan, Guelph, ON;
Norma Goodfellow, Renfrew, ON.

# PHOTO CREDITS

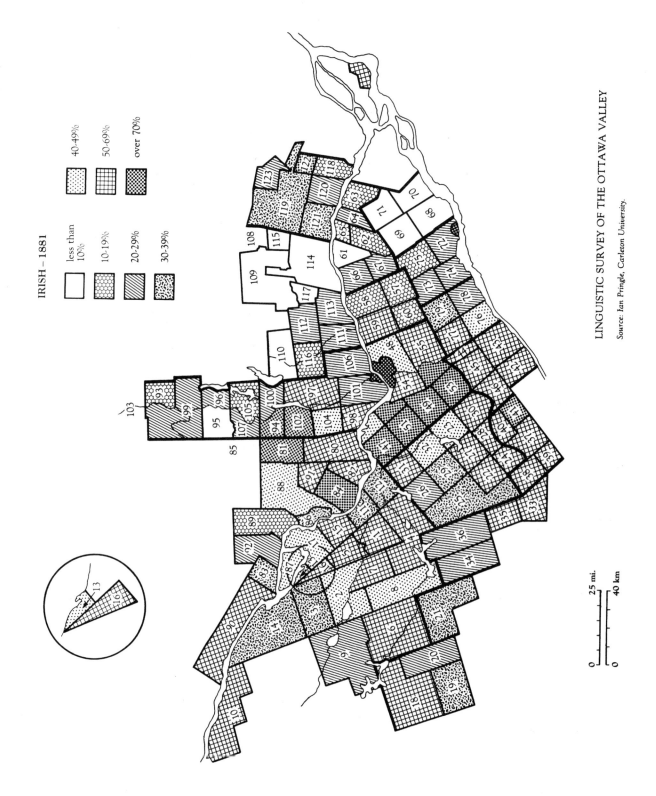

LINGUISTIC SURVEY OF THE OTTAWA VALLEY

*Source: Ian Pringle, Carleton University.*

IRISH – 1881

| | |
|---|---|
| less than 10% | 40-49% |
| 10-19% | 50-69% |
| 20-29% | over 70% |
| 30-39% | |

25 mi.

40 km

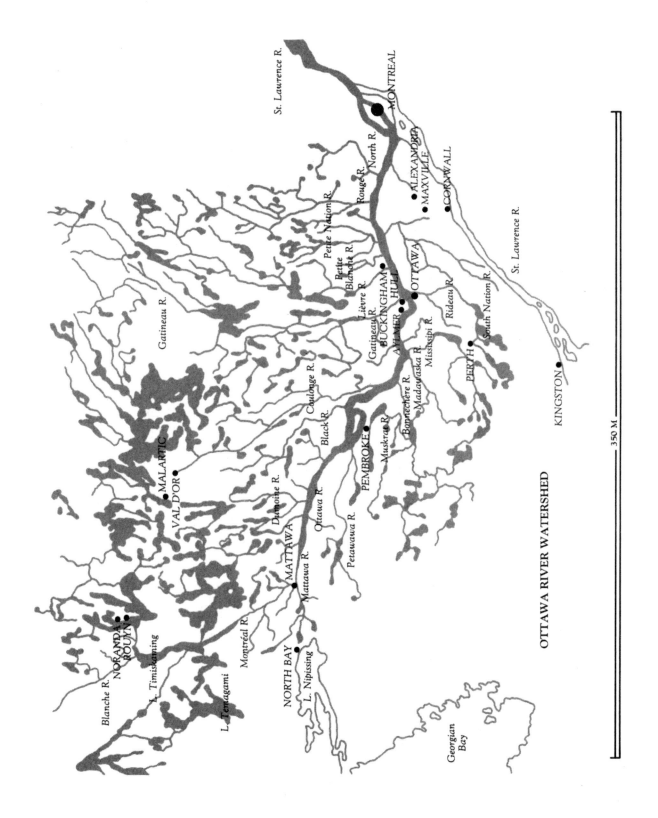

OTTAWA RIVER WATERSHED

350 M

# Table of Contents

# Introduction

1978-1998. Twenty priceless years in the Ottawa Valley on what Jack Yeats called "the moving staircase," travelling thousands of miles down concession roads and up mountain tracks, interviewing and taping approximately four hundred old-timers, most of them in rural kitchens (but only one with a mud floor!)

There are a number of reasons for the predominance of the rural kitchen as the setting for the leisurely unfolding of a life story, and one has been perceptively observed by the Irish writer Benedict Kiely:

"The people of the cities have the machine which is prose and a parvenu. The country people have few events. They can turn over the incidents of a long life as they sit by the fire. With us (in the city) nothing has time to gather any meaning, and too many things are occurring for even a big heart to hold."

Of my twenty-eight books, fourteen of them have been Valley inspired, including this one, my fifth oral/social history of the Valley. It became apparent after my first few years on the road that my work was going to define the identity of the Ottawa Valley in an unique way, on a large scale, and it was therefore incumbent upon me to arm myself with a geographic definition of the Valley. I was already familiar, of course, with the work of the late Professor A.R.M. Lower, who had laid the academic cornerstone of Valley history with his classics on the lumbering trade.

In time and through experience I probably would have defined for myself the Ottawa Valley as the territory covering the watershed of the Ottawa River, including its twenty-seven tributaries, or, even as I do today, as Canada's Eleventh Province. But twenty years ago oral/social history was even more suspect than it is today. So I turned to Professor Lower to "marry the Valley mythology to rock and hill," and to define the geographic parameters for the pragmatists and academics—those who are most frightened by poetic terms like "the Ottawa Valley is a state of mind."

"If Montreal island be taken as lying within the Ottawa Valley, then the population of the whole Valley represents a respectable fraction of all Canada, in rough approximation about twelve per cent. Most of this is concentrated around Montreal and Ottawa, but there are other substantial towns all the way up, such as Hawkesbury, Arnprior, Pembroke, the towns on Lake Temiskaming and the mining towns on the upper waters. Apart from hydroelectricity, the mining region represents the most recent contribution of the Ottawa Valley to Canadian life; within it lie the Kirkland Lake gold mines, the Noranda cluster of copper mines, and lesser centres."

My five oral/social histories place themselves firmly within Lower's definition, but I have also worked within my own definition of the Valley as a metaphoric island with a separate identity that distinguishes it from all other parts of Canada. The Valley accents and idioms; its predominantly Anglo-Celt origins; its geography and ethnography; its history and "frozen economics;" its lumbering saga and log architecture; its folk tales, songs, music, and dance; its "come-all-ye's" and "fiddlin' good times;" its elusively different people; and last, but not least, its astounding network of clans—all have melded together to make the region unlike any other on the Canadian landscape.

Over the past twenty years on the moving staircase I have adhered to definite goals. Lower once said, "The unique identity of the Ottawa Valley is not known to the rest of Canada," and my first goal, in a very general way, was to change that perception, to delineate the Valley's unique identity.

2. Through life story and autobiography to portray the lives of a cross-section of Valley people, and thereby preserve, enhance, and illuminate its history. Quite simply, I did not want "my people" to die and take to the grave that incredibly rich treasure trove of life stories.

3. To preserve the indigenous humour of the Valley. This was done intensively in the two oral history collections of the humour of the Valley, *Laughing All the Way Home*, and *Legacies, Legends and Lies*; but considerable Valley humour is scattered also throughout the other books.

4. To move from oral to written tradition legendary Valley heroes like Mountain Jack Thomson of Portage-du-Fort, Harry McLean of Merrickville; Valley characters like Phoebe McCord of Shawville, Bartley Bohan of Elmdale, Quebec; Valley wits like Dinny O'Brien of the Burnt Lands of Huntley, Billy James of Carleton Place.

5. To put particular emphasis on the history of the Anglo-Celts in Western Quebec, where so much of it is being eroded.

6. To preserve the language. Carleton University's five-year linguistic study of the Valley has separated ten dialects.

7. And, finally, to entertain.

At the turn of the century an American writer named Anson Gard fell in love with the Valley and in 1904 wrote a book entitled *The Hub and the Spokes* thereby creating the metaphor for Ottawa as the wheel's centre with the whole Valley fanning out like spokes, north, south, east, west. In this oral/social history it was my intent to move into the hub for life stories illuminating the Valley history, and this has been done through interviews with people like Joe Gorman, Greg Guthrie, Ted Devlin. It might be said that this oral history has a more urban flavour, but nevertheless we all grow up in the oral tradition.

"No matter how rootless we are, how fractured and transient our clans may be, we all have buried in our subconscious an ancestral chronicle."

This absolute is considerably underlined by John Rolston Saul in *Reflections of a Siamese Twin* when he writes:

"The Canadian relationship to the oral/written tension is relatively different. This is a country built much more through the oral . . . The survival of the animist involves what lies beyond language, but it also favours the oral—the imagination of existence rather than the defined method of existing. Our northern, marginal status legitimizes the oral.

The most obvious element in this orality is the aboriginal community, which remains as one of the three pillars on which the society was originally constructed. If much of the aboriginal culture has been taken into the new complex culture, then the oral must have come with it."

In the Ottawa Valley we are so comparatively young, so close to the original sources of our legends, that we can still collect and document them as I have done with G.A. Howard of Shawville, Quebec, Taddy Haggerty of the Opeongo Line, Tex Maves of Pembroke. If I had not tracked these people up and down the Valley, through themselves if they were alive, and through informants if they were dead, they all would have been lost forever, and gone to the grave taking with them all that humour, wit, language, behaviour, social history.

It has been my observation that after the death the legend fleshes out. And so, in this book, previously encountered great characters and legendary heroes reappear in the process of becoming larger-than-life; the late Carl Jennings, Charlotte Whitton, Harry McLean, George McIlraith, King Clancy, Frank Finnigan, Tom Murray. Destined for exceptional status the new ones come on scene: Willie MacGregor, the drinking judge from Pembroke; Joe Finn, the trickster journalist from Ottawa; George Phillips, bush pilot extraordinaire of Algonquin Park; Henry Taylor, fire ranger, tallyman, still wood-carving and writing for the *Bancroft Times* at the age of ninety-four.

I am deeply grateful to all the people who have contributed to my oral/social histories and to all the powers that be that I was granted the opportunity, yea, the privilege of setting out on this "incredible journey," creatively satisfying and spiritually fulfilling as it has been. But writing an oral/social history is a demanding, exhausting, sometimes emotionally depleting sixteen-stage experience. I could only do it intermittently. Then I would return home to regroup, plan the next foray.

Margaret Atwood has said, "Interviews are an art form in themselves." If this is true—and who am I to question it?—then I have developed over the past twenty years on the moving staircase my own unique style in this art form. I have collected life stories which not only fit into the mosaic of Valley history but often present themselves as short stories or, on occasion, as the makings of a novel. In the final analysis, fundamentally oral/social history as I have developed it provides an important bridge between biography and anthropology, social science and literature.

I consider oral/social history to be the colourful theatre, the human interest additive, the sociological underlay of what is generally termed academic history. My oral/social histories of the Valley are multi-purpose, multi-layered, and have been used in many multi-disciplinary ways by linguists, sociologists, genealogists, writers, storytellers, folklorists, politicians, humorists, psychologists, playwrights, song writers, gerontologists (particularly those studying life stages), librarians, academics, students, doctoral students, and teachers. Indeed, I have seen my books in classrooms worn to tatters with use. One young woman did a university paper on the history of costume using the archival photographs in the oral/social histories. A student from the University of Limerick, Ireland, has used the books in her thesis; another Carleton University student, after hearing me lecture at Ottawa University, was inspired to do my annotated bibliography for her M.A., thesis.

Oral life stories embody a special king of language, often passionate and poetic, told at leisure, usually around the kitchen table, frequently accompanied by comfort food, and always affording for hours on end the luxury of human companionship and communication, and the therapy of laughter.

I like to think of my work collecting the life stories over the past twenty years not only as an antidote to a world of pollution and violence, of despair and dehumanization, but even more as an antidote to the sterility and loneliness of a technological world in which there is "data data everywhere and not a thought to think," or even the time or the place to contemplate in tranquillity.

In a narrow sense my oral/social histories make up a collective autobiography of my beloved people of the Valley, my network of clans who often possess unto their dying days some of the most valuable of human attributes; warmth, pride, wisdom, and a sense of humour about themselves. As the old-timers pass from the Valley stage, taking their talent for storytelling with them, I find myself less and less often now *Laughing All the Way Home*. And it saddens me greatly, for they enriched my life beyond the telling. We were bonded in mysterious human ways that microchips will never fathom.

I have been the recipient of many heart-warming recognitions of my work. But one of the most cherished has come from Ray McGrath, teacher, historian, linguist, storyteller, who, a few years ago returned to his birthplace in Waterford, Ireland.

"A country's social and cultural identity is enhanced when its stock of folklore, legends, tall tales, songs and insights these provide, is preserved. I am reminded of the heroic work done in other times and places by collectors of oral history— Hyde in Ireland, Barbeau in Quebec, Hemister on the Prairies, Creighton in the Maritimes. More recently I feel a great debt of gratitude to Joan Finnigan for preserving so much of what surely would have been lost of our National Heritage."

From the time I was seven I have lived in two worlds, always straddling the Ottawa River, a pattern I seem never to have been able to break. Every Christmas holiday, every fair time, every summer, I left Ottawa with all its urban amenities and exciting turmoils and, with my family in the family car, or by myself on the old Pontiac Push Pull and Jerk, fled to my relatives in their rural world in Western Quebec to bask there among the country people I so loved and respected. Although none of us dreamed it at the time, it was their history I was one day going to record. And that, too, is a kind of loving.

"Whatever happens is as common and well-known as a rose in spring or an apple in autumn— everywhere up and down, ages and histories, towns and families are full of the same stories."

– Joan Finnigan,
  Hambly Lake,
  Hartington, Ont.
  June, 1998.

# 1

# "After the Beer was in the Tubs, All the Labels Came Off"

## CARL and HOWARD CLARK – Norway Bay, Quebec

*I taped Howard and Carl Clark at Howard's home in Norway Bay, Quebec, when Carl was visiting there from Bobcaygeon where he then was living. Unfortunately, both brothers, then seventy-five and eighty-one, died shortly afterwards, before I could return to verify their three hours of transcribed tape. Descendants of Anglo-Celt pioneers in Western Quebec, the Clarks had been living around Eardley-Beechgrove-Quyon area for generations. Before this interview, I was told the Clarks "were full of lumbering stories." But, as usual, their repertoire ranged beyond lumbering into stories of the great characters of the Valley, mostly now passed into legend, who are still remembered and cherished in Western Quebec: Paddy Elliott, Shanty Jack Gilchrist, Bartley Bohan, Frank Finnigan of the Ottawa Senators, Jim Doherty, Austin Gillies. The Clark brothers also contributed to the extraordinary storehouse of Valley humour, passing it from their oral to my written tradition.*

HOWARD: The Clarks have been here for as far back as we can figure things out. Our great-grandfather, Tom Clark, who married Lady Jane Brett, is buried in St. Luke's cemetery at Beechgrove, Quebec. Grandfather George Clark married a Leach from Aylmer, Quebec. Our mother was a Twa[1], her grandmother before her an Armstrong, one of the first settlers on the riverfront in Pontiac County below Shawville, Quebec.

CARL: Uncle Jim (Twa) got tucked away at the foot of the mountain. His wife was Aunt Annie and I used to spend a couple of weeks there every summer. Emerson run the family farm, and then there was Percy in the navy in the First World War. There was another brother and I remember the farmers' excursions he used to go on at fifteen dollars a piece to Winnipeg. Then one time he went and never came back again. So there's Twas in the West related to us.

Who has Indian blood? The Twas, the Roys, the Powells—. Grandpa Twa was a foundling. He was left on the Twas' doorstep, and that is true. They always said he was an Indian and by God he had two granddaughters and if they weren't Indians, I never saw one.

HOWARD: Old Frank Roy. Oh, a real Indian! Every one of those Roys—and there was a lot of them—were carpenters. When I was building this place here I'd get stuck and Leonard Twa would be right up to help me out. He came one night and cut the rafters for me. I can't cut a rafter. I can't keep the right pitch, you know. When they built the Hilton mine down here, he was head carpenter at that mine and the fellow only went as far as Grade 3 in school and he could read blueprints.

1

Then there was Grant Twa. He never went to school and he could count money, but he couldn't read or write. He could build a jumper and it would be perfect. Remember when he built Dad a land roller out of a huge log? Mind you, it would take about twenty team to haul it.

CARL: Our father, Hiram Clark, run camps for years for Gillies[2]. He took over as foreman when Bob Moorehead died in 1922 and Dad died in 1936 and he was with them right up until 1934. He started in cutting roads when he was twelve years old and he worked himself up to be agent. He was born in the Eardley house that we were born in. Our great-grandfather, Tom Clark, married Lady Jane Brett and her brother was the first lieutenant-governor of Alberta[3]. Up in Jasper Park there's a house named after him.

HOWARD: The story is Tom married into the nobility and then her parents chased him out of Ireland. He belonged to the Royal Ulster Constabulary[4] and he was supposed to be the tallest man in the regiment and that's about as much as I know about him, except that he's buried in St. Luke's in a very long casket.

Marion, my sister, with my wife and myself a few years ago went up to my mother's grave at Beechgrove and Marion showed us these coats of arms. She told us the same story about Great-Grandfather being chased out of Ireland. Someone else who told me a bit about it, too, was Edwina Fraser. She was a Burton and they lived down right close by Beechgrove, and she said she could remember this little old lady—Lady Jane Brett—who lived with Uncle Joe Clark, Fred's father, after Tom Clark died. My oldest brother Kenny told me he could vaguely remember old Lady Jane—she would be his great-grandmother—sitting out on the porch, rocking and knitting.

I went to the lumber camps right after my mother died when I was fourteen. I stayed in the office where Dad stayed and I drove a team and I went up to Coulonge and met The Drive one year. And came down.

CARL: I went up when I was fifteen or sixteen. I worked there for quite a few years in the winter and the summer too. I drove on the east branch of the Coulonge River for a fellow named Harry Milks, foreman of the log drive, came from Buckingham, Quebec. I worked there up until about 1934 or '35. Then I left. Gillies weren't operating and there were bad times in lumbering. I went fire ranging up at Grand Lake Victoria, and I fire ranged up there until war broke out in 1939 and I enlisted.

I'd a team of horses in the Gillies camp and I had no stable for the horses, so I made a lean-to out of brush. And they took it well, but it used to be cold in the mornings, of course, and I'd have to get them off to some hay and oats. They could survive at forty

One of the oldest memorials in St. Luke's Anglican Church Graveyard at Beechgrove, Quebec, on N0. 148 is that of Howard and Carl Clark's great-grandfather, Thomas Clark, and Lady Jane Brett, the girl he eloped with to Canada. The cemetery is almost entirely made up of Anglo-Celt pioneers, some of whom, like first settler William Lusk, 1787-1879, proudly engraved on the stone, "Native of County Antrim, Ireland."

below, eh? You'd blanket them and give them lots of hay. As long as horses have something to chew on, they'll keep warm.

G.A. Howard of Shawville[5] used to have the contracts for bringing up the supplies to Gillies when my father was agent there. Him and G.A. were pretty good friends, eh? And so was Alfie Armstrong. One time he was crossing the Ottawa River on the ice taking a load of wheat to Quyon in a straight sleigh and on the back there was a place you could stand. His daughter—she was thirteen—and she was sitting in front of the load of wheat wrapped up in a buffalo robe. The wheat was heavier than the horses, and the wheat went down and pulled the horses and the girl, and they never found any damned one of them. Alfie

had on a fur coat and he said, "If it wasn't for the fur coat, I'd have went down, too." The fur coat probably would balloon out, you see, and hold him up.

I know a boy that drowned in Bobcaygeon and they couldn't find the body. And I don't know who the old guy was but he said, "Take a rooster and put him in the bow of the boat, and when you go over the body, the rooster will crow." It did!

I remember Irvine Armitage. Well, he had a sale and he sold everything off the place, all the livestock. And he came to Duke Roy after and he told Duke, "I want a rooster. By God!" he said, "I've never been so lonesome in my life. I can't hear a rooster crowing in the morning." So Duke gave him a rooster and Irvine was happy again.

*One of the great old Ottawa River steamboats, the **G.B. Greene**, drawn up at the Quyon dock, c. 1910-12. The only remaining ferry on the river above Ottawa still crosses today from Quyon to the Ontario side near Fitzroy Harbour.*

HOWARD: Old Henry Flood, the camp cook, made terrible cookies. I went to the John Bull Depot[6] when I was fifteen years old. My first job was skidding white birch logs down from the mountain, from John Bull to the cook shack. And every time we'd come down old Henry Flood would say, "Come on in and have a cup of tea and a cookie." I'd have a cup of tea but, his cookies, Jesus! They were the size of an ashtray and hard as hell! I'd take them out and give them to the horses and they liked them. Then they got fed up with them, too, and we used to take them and we'd throw them and Jesus! they'd sail right across the lake into the mountain on the far side. So Henry told my father. "You know, Hiram. I caught the young lad throwing my cookies across the lake." And Dad said, "Henry, I'm glad he found some use for them because he sure as hell can't eat them."

When my dad was agent on the Coulonge River, by God, we ate well. He used to send up tubs of sausages and we had butter and I can see Harold Boland's raisin pies yet. Gillies agent had the power to do anything he wanted to do. But my father wasn't like that. He believed in treating the men well and he wouldn't allow liquor in on the limits. If you brought up a bottle, it was passed around, and he never said anything.

CARL: Frank Ahearn—owner of the Ottawa Senators—him and Austin Gillies[7] used to come up to Usborne Depot, to Gillies hunting preserve. Dad was there to welcome them but he said to himself, "I can't nurse those guys," and he went on about his work. He said to me, "Look it, they've got lots of liquor. (They had three cases of Scotch.) Just keep your eye on them. Try and keep them from going out hunting." Well, I mean, what the hell was I going to do, eh? If they wanted to go out and hunt and kill themselves, I couldn't stop them.

Anyway, off they went hunting and none of them killed a damned thing. They were too drunk. So, anyway, they had a case of Scotch left. Twenty-four bottles, in a wooden box, wired round and round. So Austin told me, "Bury the thing." So I buried it in the lake down in the sand—easy digging. And by God, nobody's ever been able to find that case of Scotch at Usborne Depot. Somebody will, some fine day.

HOWARD: I drove a team of horses, one team from Gillies mill at Braeside to the John Bull Depot. I went from Braeside to Portage the first day, and then

*This complex of log buildings at Usborne Depot was built by Henry Usborne, lumberman of Portage-du-Fort, then sold to Gillies Lumber. The smaller building was a sleep camp, the larger an office with stairs going up to an executive lounge and bar. They are now owned by the Upper Ottawa Improvement Company.*

*A landmark in the Ottawa Valley, Labine's Hotel in Fort Coulonge at the turn of the century. Note the hotel taxis.*

it was too far to go from Portage to Otterly, so I stayed over and got into Campbell's Bay in the afternoon. And then at Sandy Creek the next day, and then the Usborne Depot the next day and then the John Bull. It was pretty nearly a week, eh, and this in the summertime. Gillies were building a road from the Usborne Depot on the west side of the east branch at the Coulonge River, and they wanted this team to work on the road. See, in the spring of the year, Gillies used to send their teams to Braeside and pasture them there. If you wanted a team of horses for the summer, they'd lend it to you. The Gillies wouldn't want to have to pay to feed their own horses all summer. And some of those horses used to come up to the camp in the fall and by God! they'd be thin. Because the farmers would work the daylights right out of them, you know. My father used to be agent on the Coulonge River for Gillies and he used to keep his best teams on three hundred acres of pasture land at the Usborne Depot. He was always worried that if he sent them to Braeside he maybe wouldn't get them back alive.

Here's a Jim Doherty[8] story. D.A. Gillies came up to the camp and my dad was driving him around. So they stopped, and got out, and were standing beside Jim Doherty and Jim pulled out a plug of tobacco, took a chew out of it and offered the plug to D.A. Jim said, "Do you chew tobacco, Mr. Gillies?" And D.A. said, "I'd just as soon eat horse shit." And Jim said, "Well, every man to his own taste, but I'd sooner have the tobacco."

CARL: Bartley Bohan[9] was a great-nephew of Paddy Elliott. And he's also related to Jim Doherty, you know. And that's why he was such a great storyteller. There's a guy down here, George Scully, and he was in a car accident a few years ago—oh, quite a few years ago when he was working at the Hilton mine and he lost an eye and smashed his car all to pieces. So they replaced the eye, and it's smaller than his natural eye. And then he turned round and bought a great big car. And Bartley Bohan said, "If he'd got a bigger eye and a smaller car, he'd have been far better off."

I remember one time we came down on The Drive and they used to pay us at La Chute, and then we'd go down to Fort Coulonge by taxis and stop at Labine's Hotel. I went in one day and there was a beer salesman there and he was selling this Maple Leaf beer from Nova Scotia. And in those days they didn't have coolers. They just had tubs full of cold water and they'd put the beer in that. Of course, after the beer was in the tubs for a little while, all the labels came off. Raoul Labine was waiting on the tables and serving us and this salesman was setting up the beer. We didn't want his Maple Leaf. We were drinking, at that time, Black Horse by the quart. Raoul said, "It doesn't matter. He's paying for it. I'll serve you whatever you want." And he (the salesman) thinks it's Maple Leaf. And we would say, "God! That's great beer. Oh, man! Another round here, Raoul. Another

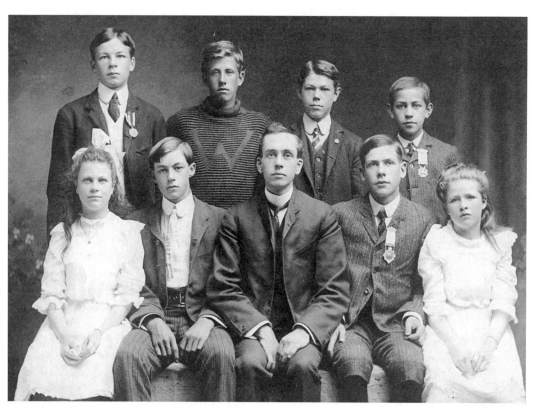

*Like the Clarks, these young students of the Quyon Protestant School, 1904, represent the Anglo-Celt families of first settlers in the Beechgrove-Luskville-Quyon area where some of their descendants remain to this day. Back, L to R: Norman Dowd, Neville Smith, Clifford Pierce, C.B. Mohr. Front, L to R: Mildred Pierce, Stanley MacKechnie, Gordon Churchill (teacher), Milton Pritchard, Linda Lawson.*

round of Maple Leaf." And Raoul would give us the Black Horse or whatever we wanted.

Shanty Jack Gilchrist was a great friend of my father's.

The only story I can remember is him coming to Dad one time when we were living at Campbell's Bay.

"Hiram, how would I go about turning Protestant?" he asked.

Dad said, "I don't know Jack. What's the trouble?"

"Well," he said, "I tried to run a crown and anchor game at the parish picnic over on The Island (Calumet) and the goddamn priest wouldn't let me do it. Priest, pope or parson doesn't do that on me. I'm going to turn Protestant."

HOWARD: Shanty Jack was Donny Gilchrist's[10] father. I can remember when Donny first started to stepdance. He was five years old and his father used to play the mouth organ, and Donny'd stepdance to it. He started early and he died early.

We were talking about Shanty Jack Gilchrist. I'll tell you a good story about him. He got into a good fight with old Dan Payette. You know the Payettes from Campbell's Bay? They had a feud from away back. And they met this day at O'Connor's Hotel and it was the stupidest thing in the world the way it started. One wouldn't get out of the way to let the other fellow pass and finally Jack hauled off and nailed Payette. And they went out in the yard and they fought for an hour. Payette chewed half of Gilchrist's ear right off, but they never stopped fighting. Finally, they got winded. So they stopped for a few minutes, and got their wind, and went back at it again. And it ended up with Gilchrist chasing Payette all through the hotel, upstairs and down. He beat Payette. And when Dan would see Jack Gilchrist coming down the street he'd go away round by the lumberyards in the station rather than meet Gilchrist. Yes, Gilchrist beat Payette. But he'd lost part of his ear.

CARL: One year Shanty Jack Gilchrist wasn't working. It was during the Depression and Dad got him a job as dispatcher at the John Bull Depot. Harold Boland was cooking and, oh God! the food was good! Jack got a boil on the back of his neck and he was talking to George Mcleod on the phone and Mcleod said, "If you get a bottle and fill it full of steam and put it on your neck it'll draw the boil out." Nobody would dare do this to Gilchrist because he'd kill them if it didn't work. And, even if it worked, it could leave a hole you could put a goose egg in. Well, anyway, I came up from the Usborne Depot and Gilchrist told me he had this boil on the back of his neck. He said, "Will you put a kettle of hot water on the stove and let it boil good and get a bottle. Pour the hot water into it, then dump it out, and then crack it on to my neck." So I did that. He hung on to the desk and it started to draw and he said, "By the Jesus, Clark! If I ever get out of this I'll kick your ass right from here to East Branch of the Coulonge!" There was a lump in the bottle about that big. I got frightened because I thought I was going to draw his whole head in. I broke the bottle—I had to—but it took the boil out. Why did I have to break the bottle? To get it off because of the pressure. Anyway, it worked. And I wasn't killed.

Remember I told you about having those horses out and no stable in the winter in the cold? Every Saturday night I used to take a pail of oats in and steam it, put water in it and set it beside the fire, and then I'd put linseed oil in it and give it to them on Saturday night. When they'd come out in the spring, the fur on them was about that long, but when they started to clean off, they were like mice, shiny and really in great shape.

So many old cures. Now you take poison ivy and you get the milk from the milkweed—I'm sure you've heard of that—you've never heard of that? And you rub that on as soon as you can.

HOWARD: Recipe to make blood. You get a bowl of beets. You wash them and cut the tips off them and you dice them, uncooked, and then you put strong De Kuyper gin in. It would do anything for you. That would cure anything for you. Then you drink it. Supposing you have no blood. Or you've lost your blood through a cut on your foot—this replaces it. But, you don't just go and drink a cup of it. An ounce at a time, about three times a day.

CARL: I remember when we joined the army in 1939. My brother Gilbert was married to Marjorie Black from Campbell's Bay—and he was in the same regiment with me. We were in that old Cow Palace at

*Shantymen having lunch in the bush around a fire made to brew a pot of tea. The rest of the lunch would be frozen solid.*

Landsdowne Park there. And Gilbert took this cough and he couldn't get rid of it. So Marjorie mixed him up honey and lemons and rye whisky. She gave him a good big bottle and, of course, he came in to the barracks and treated everybody. And it helped them all. But, then ever after that they called Gilbert, "Rubbie" and he got the name of Rubbie right through his life.

Jim Doherty. We knew him very well, you know. We had a little team of grays and he'd take them up to the camp and he'd drive them all winter with Dad. My father was in the camp at the Swishaw, and Jim Doherty would pick up the mail at the post office and take the mail to the Swishaw Depot. That's all that team and Jim Doherty did. And Dad said, "I was ashamed to own them almost. Coming from Gillies Camp and them so fat."

HOWARD: I remember Jim Doherty calling on somebody to get a bale of hay when he was taking the team up. He phoned and he asked this lady on the telephone and, of course, he couldn't be understood on the telephone because of his harelip impediment. Jim asked the operator, "Does Mrs. So-and-so have a phone?"

The smart-ass operator (who knew who he was) said, "No, but she's got a telephone."

Jim said, "Well, that will do just as well."

He always had an answer!

I don't know whether I should tell you this one or not. He was drawing the mail all through the country and he got this girl pregnant and she sued him. Mick, his brother, had to go and pay the fine. It was a hundred dollars or something. A cheap paternity case. Anyhow, they were coming back and

Jim was sitting thinking away and he said to Mick, "You know, that works out to about five dollars a jump!" He could be crude. But he was a legend.

My God! The stories they tell about Paddy Elliott around here! He used to work in the bush in the wintertime and the mill in the summertime—you know when he'd get the crops in. He used to go to the Catholic church in Sand Point. The priest used to notice him there every Saturday, and one time he came out and Paddy was leaning up agin the church chewing tobacco. And the priest said, "Are you a member of this congregation?" And Paddy said, "Well, I'm leaning that way!"

I remember one time I had a team at the John Bull and I was trying to hitch them on to a towing board, and every time I came back they'd turn around and look at me. I couldn't get them hitched. I took that team back and, without swearing, I put them in the stable.

I'm going to tell a ghost story now. There are three graves on the Crow River. And I was only a kid and I took a load of stuff up for Stewart and Barton, legends in their own time. I left the Fraser Cove, and I wanted to get back to John Bull that night, so Tom Barton said, "Make sure you don't pass those graves just at dusk." And he knew damn well it was going to be dusk just as I got there. He said, "Those fellows buried there come out and they're looking for tobacco." I was nervous I tell you and I looked at the graves going by, but nothing came out.

So I went down to George McLeod and I told him about this. He was an old Scotsman, a great old guy. He was a second father to me, almost. And he said, "Well, lookit, the next time you go up to Fraser Cove, you tell Tommy Barton that the fellows came out, and you had a smoke with them, and they were real nice guys. They talked to you for a while and then they went back into their graves again."

The next time I was up, Tommy said, "How did you get along with the graves the other day?" So I said, "They're damned nice fellows, Tommy. They came out and I gave them makings and each of us had a cigarette and they talked to me and told me about them getting drowned and stuff." And his eyes got bigger and bigger, like saucers. He said, "I know damn well George McLeod put you up to this. But,

you've sure got the shit scared out of Tom Barton!"

CARL: My brother-in-law, Wallace, told this one on Christmas morning when we had a visitor from the West, a young lad about seventeen, name of Jimmy Marshall. My father-in-law had a hunting camp so Wallace was telling us hunting stories and this young Marshall lad was sitting, listening, all ears, you know. Wallace says, "One time back near Holland Lake I seen this smoke coming up. I wondered who the hell or where the hell this smoke was coming from. I went round this corner and here's this old guy making homebrew in a still." He said to me, "Here have a drink." And I said, "No. I don't want a drink." So, the old man pulled a gun on me and he says again, "Take a drink." So I took a drink and he said, "Now take another one." I took another one. Then he hands me the gun and he says, "Now you hold the gun on me 'til I have a drink!" Young Marshall's eyes were just bugged out of his head.

Bill Ramsey used to come down to our place and work. He'd cut wood and we'd give him a load of hay in trade. And going up the mountain, one of his team of horses played out and old Bill unharnessed her, tied her behind, and he got into the harness and helped the colt draw the hay up the mountain. The whole way up!

During the Depression, Dad didn't go up for Gillies. Only two years that I remember he was hired. He was still paid and he had all those Gillies limits to look after. They still had their supplies in camp—flour, hay, oats. And they still had to keep the roads and repair them. So Gillies used some men, but they didn't use the army of men they would have used during the good years.

Now this is where the downfall of Gillies lies. I can remember D.A. Gillies telling my dad, "I think we should go into trucks up here, Hiram." And Dad said, "Look it, the minute you put trucks in here is the minute you start losing money. The country's too rough for trucks." But young Jack Gillies, of course, wanted trucks. Well, the Gillies went broke as far as the company was concerned, but there was lots of money down under the table.

HOWARD: And they ran out of timber like Booth ran out of timber and Bathurst Consolidated—

there's no more timber up there in the Coulonge now. McLaughlin ran out of timber and they quit. But Gillies had some damn fine horses and some good men. I remember Charlie Gauthier from Calumet Island, one of the finest men you'd know. He taught me an awful lot about looking after horses. Charlie would come in after his team had been out all day and the first thing Charlie did was get an old bran sack and he'd wipe their feet and legs off. "Why do you need to keep their legs dry?" I asked. "Well, just like your own legs—you'd get sores on them if you left them wet."

Say, did I ever tell you the story about the time Frank Finnigan and my brother Gilbert fell off the roof? Frank knew my father, Hiram, very, very well. Anyway, one time they had to put a new roof on the Finnigan's Clarendon Hotel in Shawville. And Frank took Gilbert up to see it. Myself, I wouldn't have taken Gilbert as high as this table here but, anyway, they got up and looked over the edge and Gilbert lost his balance. Of course, both of them had had a beer at the time, or two. Frank reached out to grab Gilbert and they both fell off the roof—and you know how high that is?—and they landed on a big pile of pasteboard and cardboard boxes and garbage. And both were saved. They lay there laughing like kids. And Frank was in his fifties.

One time Dad and old Charlie Davis were shingling the henhouse roof, two-storey. They had a scaffold, and then they'd take a board and toenail it into the wooden shingles and use a couple of other shingles for a toehold. So they're shingling away there and then old Charlie says, "Well, Hiram, I'm going to have a smoke." So, they both turned around on the damned board at the same time and away it went. It went zip, zip down and hit the main scaffold and down they went onto the ground. And old Charlie says, "Mercy God! Hiram are you hurt?"

"No," he says, "I'm not. Are you?"

"No," Charlie says, "but I've lost my pipe."

CARL: One time my brother, Arthur, was King Billy and brought home all the regalia, the big King Billy's hat and the red coat, the sword, everything. We'd a white mare, Fly, and I put the saddle on her this night. Davis' bull had jumped over the fence and got in with our cattle. So Harry and I decided we'd

chase the old bull back home to Davises. I put on King Billy's uniform—I was, what?—about ten or twelve years old. I got on this white mare and I got after the bull. I can see him yet. He saw me coming on the white mare, you know, and he just "Oh, to hell, I'm not a bit afraid of you fellows," and he rips up a couple of sods. And I got behind him and gave him a jab in the ass with King Billy's sword, and the bull let out a roar and away over the fence. Old Charlie Davis and young Charlie were sitting on the fence watching us. They said the bull went over that fence just like a deer.

HOWARD: That is true! I'll tell you another thing they did. My brother Arthur had an old McLaughlin touring car, and Carl and Harry got it started and then chased the bull with it. They hit him and he shit on the rad.

CARL: I remember one time—this was up in Eardley the year before we left—we took our white mare Fly decorated in orange and green, to a Twelfth of July celebration up in the Eardley Grove. When she came home she had sweated at the celebrations, and she was pure orange red. God! Mother was mad! She washed her and then took blueing and she got our white mare white again, and she said, "Never again will one of our horses go to the Twelfth of July." Mother wasn't too fussy about Twelfth of July celebrations, anyhow.

Remember, I told you about George McLeod, the old Scot who was like a father to us? Well he used to be at the Usborne Depot and there used to be a Mr. and Mrs. Gagnon there. They kept a stopping-place. They were working for Gillies. And God! they were meticulous! And Felix Gagnon even in the bush came out in a white shirt, and a good pair of pants. And she was a good cook, and my father had his own room, he was the big boss. And his sheets and pillow cases were so white. Well, anyway, they had a Jersey cow at the depot and she stepped on a nail and she got a sore foot. So Felix went to McLeod. (McLeod was the worst man in God's creation Felix could have went to.) Felix said, "The cow's got a sore foot. What am I going to put on it?" McLeod said, "Put a poultice of cow manure on it. That's what they used to use. That would draw it out." So, Felix did. But

*Mother Barnes (1794-1886), also known as the Witch of Plum Hollow, by artist E. Blier, drawn in 1889, just after her 89th birthday. Locals, as well as people from all over North America, travelled to Plum Hollow back of Brockville to have their fortunes told and their predictions made in the little house near Lake Eloida.*

then McLeod punched a whole lot of holes in the poultice, and when Felix was sitting down to milk the cow, George came in and gave the cow a jab and she started to kick. And she saw the poultice on her foot and she plastered meticulous Felix Gagnon with cow manure from head to foot. This is the kind of stuff McLeod used to do, eh?

I can tell you a story about my dad's clairvoyance. I mentioned before that this guy Deschamps was drowned on The Drive and Dad was out on The Drive and Deschamps was drowned two or three days before. Dad was coming up on the far side of the river—he'd crossed over at the bridge that Mike Cobo and I had built, East Branch of the Coulonge River. I seen him coming up and I ran across on the logs. So Dad said to me, "I was talking to Deschamps and he said, 'You've come along good with The Drive.'" I said, "Dad, you weren't talking to Deschamps. Christ! He was drowned about three days ago." Dad said, "I was talking to him just a minute ago." And he looked at me as if I was nuts or something. "Well," I said, "Come on over and talk to Milks. We haven't found his body yet." So, he came across the logs and went in to talk to the foreman, Milks. And Milks said, "Carl's right. Deschamps was drowned at Slide Chute here

about three days ago." And Dad swore he had met Deschamps on the road and was talking to him.

HOWARD: It was the time of the flu, 1918, and Carl and my sister Marion had it. They were pretty sick. And I remember Dr. Dowd came from Quyon and mother said to him, "How is it you never get the flu, Doctor?" "Well," he said, "When I'm outside I take a big chew of tobacco and when I go to go into a house I take a big snort of Scotch."

I can tell you another story about Dad. God! He'd go to any fortuneteller around! Even the Witch of Plum Hollow—Mrs. Barnes. She told him that, when the Twelfth of July celebrations would come around, they'd come to the Clarks to get a white horse for King Billy. She told him to get rid of his white horses. She said, "You've got too many white horses around the place. Bad luck." Dad just said, "Ah, that damned old trollop!" They tell me—I was never there—that she had piled the tea leaves out behind the house like a haystack. Like the tailings from the Hilton mine down here!

The Gillies always tried to have one of their people as a Member of Parliament, for the simple reason that maybe there'd be something like tariffs brought through the House and they'd have a man there to see to it. Bryson was a Member, McLarens, Booths, they all did because it was the way you got things done—immediately.

Austin Gillies was a Member of Parliament. He was Commandant of the Connaught Rangers for years and years and years. He was in the artillery in the First World War. George Mcleod served with him. One of Austin's sons, Sydney, was a captain in the Second World War. Both of Austin's sons were in the army. The Gillies did their share. Another two men I knew very well—we had them with us—were the Rollys. They were connected with the Booths. Mrs. Rolly was a Booth, Fred Booth's daughter. Now there was two men—both millionaires, eh!—and I remember when war broke out, when the invasion of France came along, they were both lieutenant colonels and they both reverted to majors to come back and go into action with our regiment. They didn't have to do that. They had the drag, they could have gone home.

When we were in Iceland at the beginning of the war our paymaster absconded with our payroll—and a blonde. When we got to England, the pay corps in England took all our paybooks into bond and we had no money to go on holidays with. Well, R.B. Bennett—he was a great friend of the Rollys—he used to go with Mrs. Rolly and the Rolly brothers called him Uncle Dick. And they went to him and they borrowed enough money from him to pay the regiment so the regiment could go on their landing leave. We paid them back—by God we payed them back—on payday when we got our pay.

CARL: I remember John Rolly. He was killed in action. He had an Oxford accent, you know. And he'd say, "Claaark, don't you forget you owe me ten shillings."

HOWARD: When I was in Iceland during the war, we used to go down to the public baths. We went into this bath, and of course none of us could read the Icelandic names. The women had a steam shower on one side and the men on the other side, and then the pools were split with a big wall in between. I came out of the shower and was going into the pool for a swim. So Norm Tremblay said to me, "Which is the men's room?" I said, "Back in there, Norm." And about three minutes later he comes running out and there's a bunch of naked women whipping ass with their towels. He'd got into the wrong shower!

I'll tell you another good story about Iceland and then I won't talk anymore about it. We had this cook, Austin, and he had just got married before we went overseas. And he was awful lonely and he'd get drunk and he'd cry—and he'd get drunk every night. Now the Icelandics had built their backhouse on the shore of the Atlantic Ocean. Well, poor, weeping, half-drunk Austin went out and he falls asleep on the toilet and the tide comes in and washes the backhouse out, with him sitting in it. Away the hell out. Slapping in the waves. And the British have what they call a naval bay there with the *Hood*, the *Nautilus*, plus destroyers. They spot this bobbing building and they thought it was the conning tower of a submarine. They lay their guns on it. Then somebody says, "Wait a minute. That can't be a conning tower. That thing's wobbling back and forth." So out comes this horn, "Wheep," "Wheep," "Wheep." They come up, this patrol, and there's Austin sitting on the toilet hole. They get him aboard and they get the toilet back to where it should have been on the shore. And Austin said to me when I visited him recently, "Do you remember the night that I fell asleep in the toilet?" I said, "I wasn't there Austin, but I heard of it." He said, "I came so damned close to getting killed—and not in action!"

CARL: When I first started to work in the government in Ottawa just after the war, I used to see Mackenzie King walking to work. He lived up in Laurier House, and he'd walk to the Parliament Buildings. I was just thinking—like today they have motor cycle escorts and armoured cars, but he used to stroll along Laurier Avenue, up Elgin, you know, and he'd speak to people. And Bob Stanfield when he was in office he used to walk from Stornoway. I used to meet him every morning. I worked in the Connaught Building. And another man who used to walk to work all the time was George Hees.

HOWARD: Well, I remember Les Frost. We lived on Bond Street in Lindsay. I didn't go to work until about eight-thirty, and I'd meet Les Frost and we'd walk down the street together. Some of the lads used to say, "Geez, you must be looking for a promotion." But he was just as ordinary a person as a Frost from Fort Coulonge. Maybe his cousins?

CARL: Yes, the Gillies bought a township around the Usborne, a hunting preserve, somewhere they brought their friends to. Now Austin Gillies was a good guy. There used to be a little half-breed down the road and she had a sort of a crush on me. And George McLeod, he was a great old guy, as I've said before. I came up to him and said, "Margaret Pappa is having a party this Saturday night and I want to go." And he said, "Christ! You can't get there!"

But Austin Gillies was up with his car—a Buick Reno, as long as from here to across the street, and the engine came right down to a point, right into the bumper. I never saw one before. Frank Ahearn had one like it so there was two of them in the city of Ottawa at that time. They were, I suppose, at that time about ten thousand dollars a piece. Anyway, I asked Dad—he was the boss—I said, "Is there any chance of going down to that party?" "No! No way!" he said. "You're here to work for Gillies."

So I told George McLeod. I said to him, "Gee, I'd like to go to the party." And he said, "I'll see what I can do." So McLeod and Austin were talking this morning and Austin said to my dad, "Hiram, I've got a bunch of important mail to get out, and I was wondering if your young lad Carl could throw a saddle on a horse and take it down to Klukes and get my car to Otter Lake?" And Dad looked at me, you know, and, of course, he couldn't argue. So Austin said to me, "Did you ever drive a car?" I said, "Oh, yes, my brother had a McLaughlin Buick and he ran all over the country." So Austin Gillies gives me the key to his Reno and I throw a saddle on Old Dan and I got down as far as Klukes and I got Austin's car, and I think he had a goddamn postcard for me to mail. I had a hell of a time. I damned well nearly ended up marrying this Margaret Pappa. We got into the poteen and the home brew. It was one of the best parties I ever went to. I didn't come back for about two days, but I got the car back to Gillies. I didn't hurt the car any at all.

I'll tell you another thing. When Gillies ceased operation up there they asked me if I'd stay and look after their camps. They had ten camps and they left Henry Flood as the cook. He had a crippled leg and he couldn't get a job anywhere, see? And I doubt like hell if I could at that time—because there was no jobs. So I said, "A dollar a day," that's what they paid me. Now they had a hundred roosters at the John Bull. They had a farm there—Oh God! the garden they used to have! And they had pigs, fresh pork. When my father went away in the fall, he said, "Now kill those roosters." I used to go out in the mornings, and I'd kill a rooster, and Henry, he'd cook it. I ate so much chicken then that I haven't had a hell of a lot of use for chicken since.

But I snowshoed all winter long. Like looking after those ten camps and they were spread out over a hell of an area. Eight, ten miles between each camp. That's a lot of showshoeing. I had my dog and I used to trap. I set traps along the road, eh? I'd bring back the animals and Flood would skin them and dry them. And I made him more money from trapping. I never trapped after Christmas because the snow got too deep, but up to Christmas we'd put in six to eight hundred dollars in fur. And I split that with him. No, Egan was not in that area when I was there. He was gone. It was strictly Gillies.

1  Reference to the Twas appears also in Joan Finnigan's *Tell Me Another Story*, Chapter 18. McGraw-Hill-Ryerson, 1981.

2  In *One Hundred Years A-Fellin'* by Charlotte Whitton, the Clarks and Gauthiers for generations are listed as "Gillies Men." Hiram Clark and Bob Moorehead are listed as foremen, men who, in each camp or drive or raft in any one area, held the whole enterprise as his responsibility as "truly as the captain of a ship."

3  Robert George Brett served two terms as lieutenant-governor of Alberta, 1915-1925. Graduating from University of Toronto medical school in 1874, he practised medicine in Ontario, Winnipeg, Banff, and the Northwest Territories where he established a private hospital in 1886.

4  The Royal Ulster Constabulary, which is Northern Ireland's police force, was not formed until 1922. Clark may be referring to the Royal Irish Constabulary, which policed all of Ireland prior to the annexation of the six counties of Ulster.

5  For more stories from and about G.A. Howard of Shawville, Quebec, master of spoonerisms, see *Laughing All the Way Home*, by Joan Finnigan, Deneau, 1984. Chapter 1.

6  The John Bull Depot and the Usborne Depot were about twenty miles apart on the Coulonge River in the heart of a vast Gillies limit, which was also the Gillies hunting preserve.

7  Austin Gillies, son of David Gillies, grandson of founder John Gillies, lieutenant colonel RCHA, 1914-1919, Officer of the Order of the British Empire, Medaille d'Honneur avec Glaives sen Vermeil, British War Medal, Victory Medal, d. 1938.

8  Jim Doherty of Ragged Chute appears in Joan Finnigan's *Laughing All the Way Home*, Deneau Publishers, 1984.

9  Bartley Bohan's chapter appears in Joan Finnigan's *Tell Me Another Story*. He was a cousin of Jim Doherty, so we might say a storytelling gene ran in the family.

10 For more about Donny Gilchrist see the Griffin interview, Chapter 16.

*Henry Taylor, shown here in his seventies, preserving his memories of his days in the lumber camps through his wood carving.*

# 2

# "During the Depression Men Started Fires to Make Work"

## HENRY TAYLOR – Bancroft, Ontario

*Henry Taylor is the last of a remarkable trio of brothers each outstanding in his chosen field and his community. In 1980 for the first of the oral/social histories of the Ottawa Valley,* Some of the Stories I Told You Were True, *I taped R.J. "Bob" Taylor, the last of the old-time lumber camp cooks, then living in retirement in Arnprior where he died in 1987 just before his hundredth birthday. Jim Taylor worked for many years as foreman on The Drives on the Madawaska River for the Findlay and Ferguson and the J.S.L. McRea[1] lumber companies, becoming a legend in the lumbering saga of the Ottawa Valley. I did not manage to get to him for his life story before he died, but in 1995, I reached Henry, a retired fire ranger and shantyman, then aged ninety-two, living in Bancroft. Through their McCallister grand-mother, the Taylors were related to the McIntyres who came out with the Last Laird Macnab in 1820 and were amongst the chief victims of the Old Chief's various forms of persecution.[2] They fled him to Springtown on the Madawaska and there intermarried with the Stringers.*

**M**Y BROTHER BOB lived to be almost a hundred on his own cooking. When he was in the army I said to him, "Why didn't they make you a cook in the army?" and he said, "Because they didn't need me. They just opened cans of bully-beef."

My mother's people, the Stringers, came from Burnstown on the Madawaska River—and there's still Stringers there. And the river was the highway then. How did they get from Burnstown to Bancroft? Well, Joe Stringer was a real good axe-man. He came to work for the Conroy Lumber Company[3] on the York River. He got a stove for his labour, but the company didn't pay for stove-pipes to go up through the roof. So Joe just cut off four big blocks of wood and put the stove up them so the pipes would go through the roof. And my grandmother had to get up on the bench to use the stove. I remember seeing her.

The Stringers lads came from right near the border of Scotland and England, and there's a good big long story in connection with them. John Stringer and his older brother Bill were on an English ship coming to Canada to trade with the Indians. John Stringer (my ancestor) was a cabin boy on the ship. And he done something that displeased that captain, so the captain decided to give him a beating. Now nobody would have paid any attention to him taking the strap and giving the boy a few strokes. Instead he took a sort of a rope with a knot tied on the end of it. He beat John until he left big dark lumps on him. Bill ordered the captain to quit. But in those days that was mutiny, and the penalty for that was to be hung. There was nothing more said about it and they went

*Henry Taylor's ancestors, the Stringers, were an outstanding Valley family with branches in Carlow Township, as well as around Burnstown and Killaloe. Some Stringer names are written into the history of Algonquin Park as guides and rangers, and Dan Stringer is reputed to have been "the last of the park rangers." Stringer versatility is further demonstrated in this amazing photo of four of them dressed for cricket, a game they must have brought over with them from England. L to R: Robert, 1865-1925; James, 1871-1953; Peter, 1859-1933; George, 1870-1924.*

on up the St. Lawrence River to Montreal to trade with the Indians.

Late in August they were getting ready to go back overseas, so the captain sent a boat crew ashore to get water to provision the ship. Bill Stringer was one of the boat's crew and, when he'd filled his barrels of water for the ship, he didn't bother going back. He wasn't going to take chances on getting his neck stretched. He jumped ship leaving John behind—a fourteen-year-old lad.

The ship started down the St. Lawrence River and it was very hot on the ship so the captain had a small boat towed behind so that he could sleep in the river breeze. Now there was plenty of other men on that ship that didn't like that captain any better than the Stringer lads did. Somebody cut the rope. In the morning when the crew saw the boat was gone, they knew better than go on without him 'coz he'd catch another ship. They'd be charged with the whole works—stealing the ship, mutiny. So they had to go back and pick him up. They picked him up close to the north shore of the St. Lawrence. As soon as he came on board, he blamed the whole thing on young John Stringer, made for him and was going to kill him. John just made a clean dive into the river and swam ashore. Where he went ashore there was a sawmill there, and he hid under a lumber pile. The captain sent boat crews to get him, but they didn't look very hard. They knew if they took him back that the captain would hang him. John stayed there under the lumber pile 'til the ship went away.

He went back up the St. Lawrence to Montreal. When he landed in Montreal, he got in with a gang of men who came from up the Ottawa River. They were involved in the real estate. The head lad was a Sparks[4]—Sparks Street in Ottawa was named after them. They brought their gear along to clear some land and build cabins. John went on with them up the Ottawa River. The Indians there showed him how to set traps, and he got a lot of fur. Soon as old Bob Sparks saw John with all that fur he said he wasn't entitled to it; he said that he was working for him, and he took the fur. John quit Sparks. Sparks told him he hadn't any money to pay him. He offered him one of the cabins and a piece of land that he'd cleared. But John just turned his back on the whole thing and walked away. That cabin and that piece of land that Sparks offered him is right on top of the knoll where the Parliament Buildings sits today. And there was a bunch of McNab's people were going through there—McIntyres and McAllisters—and John joined them and came up to Arnprior.

Bill Stringer had disappeared, yes. But I'll tell you the story. When I retired twenty-six years ago, I went back on the old Taylor homestead in Raglan Township, Renfrew County—that's where they landed on the 13th of April, 1880—I went there when

I retired in 1969 and I built a cabin there using a broad-axe to hew the timber for a square-timber log house. Well, the CBC heard about it and they come and made a film. After they had the film all made— Ken Hale was the lad that made it—I told him the story about my ancestor John Stringer. And Hale found out what happened to Bill Stringer who jumped ship and disappeared.

Bill was an outlaw, you see, according to the white man's law, liable to be hung for beating up that captain and jumping ship. He began trading with the Huron Indians from Manitoulin Island and he just went with them, and he took an Indian woman for a wife. He kept his own name, Bill Stringer. After I had built my cabin there in Raglan Township, a man got me to build a house for him on the Perth Road north of Kingston. And his wife came from Manitoulin Island. So I asked her: "Is there any people there by the name of Stringer?" She said, "Sure. One of my best girlfriends was a Stringer." I said, "Was she dark complexioned?" "Yes, very dark." So I have a bunch of Stringer relations who are half-breeds on Manitoulin Island.

I left school when I was fourteen. I was driving a team of horses with my dad in 1918. They had a little rhyme at that time, "He's the man behind the gun, He's the man behind the plough." I was "the boy behind the man behind the gun." My brother Bob was in France behind a machine-gun and I was behind the plough with a great big team of Clydes. The only way I could get the harness on was to stand on an old chair. They were so well trained I didn't need any reins on them. They just followed the furrows and all I had to do was guide the plough. And them horses, I talked to them and they talked to me. They talked to me because the farm buildings were right at the south end of the hundred-acre lot, overlooking that big Conroy marsh, and when a cold wind would be blowing, I'd have the cap down over my ears, and I wouldn't hear when my sister would ring the bell for dinner. So, if them horses were going north away from the barn, they'd stop right in their tracks and whinny, and I'd take the cap off my ears and hear the bell ringing. And you might as well give up right there 'coz you couldn't drive them any

further. And if they were coming the other way they'd just lengthen their stride until the soil would be rolling like the swell from a motorboat.

I was coming home from school one evening—I was about eight years old—and I seen the lad up the pole there building the phone line. Well, that was the job for me! That was exciting! That was better than ploughing! I went home and my dad had some scrap iron there, and I got some old shredded tires, and an iron spike—just the right things to make climbing irons. I made climbing irons to climb the poles like the telephone man. I can show you an old set I have here yet. And I practised climbing poles. They asked me when I joined the Forestry Department if I could climb. I said, "Sure." I was their head climber. In the wintertime after I got a little older, I got a pair of snowshoes and I snowshoed to school. That was good practice, too. They were the only thing I used in the forestry. I'd put the snowshoes on in the morning and take them off at night. They got so they were my feet, right?

When the first men came into this country part, the pine was thick, it was twilight in under them in the daytime. When they cut that all down, you see, the fire got into it. When I was a boy on my father's farm, you could look out at night and the hills round that big Conroy's marsh looked like a city, lit up with fires. Bush fires. Nobody paid any attention to it until it rained. There was no Forestry looking after that at all.

My older brother Jim joined the Forestry in 1923, and fire ranged until 1927. Then the McRea Lumber Company came and hired him to go back to his old job as foreman on The Drive. He was a foreman all his life. He went with McRea into Algonguin Park and was with them for fifteen years, stationed at Whitney.

When Jim left he recommended me to the Forestry to take his place. So I took a trip up the Mississippi River for an interview with the chief ranger, Harry Legris[5], a Frenchman from Dacre on the Opeongo Line. The Forestry had just started off on a purse string. They only had one truck at each chief ranger's headquarters—that's Ontario government. They said they couldn't afford to have that one truck away too long—it was fifty miles of

*Henry's brother, Jim Taylor, as a forest ranger in the early 1920s. He is driving the 1914 Model T Ford the brothers used in fire-fighting. Note the old-fashioned canvas pack pumps hanging on the front and the canvas water pails on the windshield.*

muddy, dirty road, you see. They asked my brother if he could pay the extra fire-fighters themselves, then call the payroll amount in and they'd bring the money and give it back to him. So he carried his own personal chequebook and paid the men, and they took the money out of the Forestry bank account in Renfrew or Montreal and brought the money back and gave it to him.

Now that didn't do his, Jim's, bank account much good, taking that money in and out, losing the interest. Anyway, that's what Legris told me that I'd have to do. I talked to him straight. I said, "I don't think that's something I want to do." "And you have to have a car," he said. So I told him, "I don't think that I can take that job."

But my brother Jim said, "There's no use for a car up in Algonquin Park where I'm going; I'll leave the car with you." And that's how I come to be a fire ranger. I carried my personal chequebook the same as my brother did, and I kept that up until they started the first tax, putting a three-cent stamp on every cheque. So I kicked about that. I told Legris that I had no way of getting those three cents back.

I wore the Forestry badges for forty-two years. They gave you the authority to conscript anybody to go and fight fire. The only ones that were exempt were the doctors and the millers. Anybody else, if they wouldn't go, you could fine them.

The fire ranger's tower was eighty feet high. You just went up there during the day when there was a fire. You climbed up around about eight in the morning and again at six at night. Sometimes when it was extra dry, you stayed there way on into the night. In the day, when it was real hazy, you couldn't see very far. You could see further at night with the reflection of the fire on the haze. I've sighted fires and it was the reflection of the fire on the haze at night. Our only special equipment was heavy field glasses. You'd look out to the horizon, watching, looking. You could see about twenty miles. There was a fire-ranger's station approximately every twenty miles. All summer long you lived in the cabin at the foot of the tower. In the winter I was a lumberjack.

I remember summer 1923 was crackling dry in the Tweed district, plenty of fires but no lookout

*Henry Taylor climbing the Raglan Fire Ranger's Tower where he watched for fires from 1927 to 1941. The Raglan Tower was taken down in 1974 after fifty years of service.*

towers then and very little telephone communication. In May a lightning fire started at Sunken Lake, Mayo Township. A young lad, a returned soldier from World War I, took four or five men in to fight a fire which was in F. Hamlyn's logging slash. When smoke got thicker the next day, my brother, fire ranger Jim Taylor, was sent in to help. He arrived to find the fire out of control and all the young fire-fighters' men had deserted him. The fire had burned his canvas pail and the handle right out of his shovel! But we had to give the lad his due. He was enough of a soldier to stand by the job until relieved—even although he was dressed in a white Panama hat, a white silk shirt, a pair of light grey flannel pants, silk socks, and black and white patent leather shoes. By the time relief got there, my brother Jim said, "There was nothing very white about that lad. The blood from the black fly bites was running into his shoes!!!"

Deputy Chief Fire Ranger Mick Burns had sent my brother Jim to Hambly's sawmill in Bessemer to get help from the workers there. But all he got from the foreman was a shrug of the shoulders. Jim phoned Hambly's head office in Toronto and in about five minutes the mill was shut down; Jim had a crew of sixty men, all the grub they had on hand and work horses to pack supplies and equipment for the fire.

By that time the fire was reaching east in the slash so we knew the only thing to do was to fall back on nature. We opened a whole series of beaver ponds and in a few hours the fire was under control. People often complain about beaver slashing timber and flooding around with their ponds, but for myself and my brother our hats are off to the beaver. We found, too, that the old-fashioned single-furrow plough and team of horses can come in handy to stop a fire. In those early days we had to use our wits.

In 1927 I took Jim's place as forest ranger on Patrol 32, North Madawaska. That year fire permits were introduced and I drove my Model T hundreds of miles to contact all the settlers in my area and tell them about the new regulations.

Years ago Sundays and holidays were the worst for fires. The roads were awful and there were no ashtrays in those old touring cars. On Sundays and holidays when people did most of their travelling,

they threw their tailor-made cigarettes into the brush on the road and beside the roads. How to start a fire!

One Sunday morning in May 1929, when the hazard was high, I had all my fire-fighting equipment piled into my old Model T. At ten o'clock the phone rang. Raglan Tower and Quadville Tower had sighted smoke. After I got the readings I saw the fire was at a sawmill at the south end of Raglan Township. I cranked up the car and got going. I never tried to pick up crew at the farms along the way for I knew they would all be at church. I never stopped until I was at the little Lutheran church at Schutt. There I raised the alarm and quicker than you could say it, the church was emptied and I had a crew.

When we got to the fire we found it was caused by a camp fire neglected by a fisherman. I was running along the river under a skidway of dry cedar logs at the corner of the sawmill. We grabbed the cant hook from the mill, broke down the skidway, rolling the logs into the water. Then we formed a bucket brigade and saved the mill.

When it was all over the crew didn't look much like churchgoers in their Sunday suits, but they were happy men for they had saved the mill and would all have jobs on Monday morning.

*Photo at the Raglan Tower, c. 1927, just after fire permits were introduced. Henry's job was to educate people about the new fire regulations, travelling his area in the Model T. Henry said, "That year I was administering the fire act with one hand and breaking the traffic act with the other, for I had no driver's licence!"*

You know old Tom Murray[6]? The first lumbering I did was with the Murray and O'Manick Lumbering Company at Cross Lake Bay in from Madawaska. We were all confined at Madawaska. I remember there was a fellow by the name of John Palmer, who would come out there and get the mail, and Guy Rolston, he was the clerk. Sometimes we'd walk the fourteen miles in to camp. I was nineteen. I got forty-five dollars a month for cutting trails.

I was rolling logs in the wintertime. When the sleigh haul started on the 29th of February, 1924, my brother Jim and I was loading logs, and there was a log came out of the poke on the end of the chain, and the logs backed down the skidway and broke his leg. So we gathered him up and took him into the camp. The blacksmith and I made splints for the leg and a board, and when the old doctor in Barry's Bay came to the camp, he said, "That is some of the best first aid I've ever seen." He said, "But for the compensation, I could leave that on your leg and send you home. But, I'm going to send you to the hospital."

And Jim would have been better off if the doctor had sent him home because Jim was forty-two years of age, and he'd travelled the bush from the time he was sixteen, and the muscles in his legs were just like horses' legs. They took our splints and board off in Pembroke and they put a cast on it, but it was too loose and, when they come to take the cast off, the leg was crooked. Jim sent word home for either me or Dad, "Get me out of here." My dad went down and got him out of there, but the mistake was made and they had to correct it in another hospital. They broke the leg over again and, when they took the second cast off, that's the way the foot was going to stay. He couldn't get his heel on the ground.

But Jim just kept right on going. Then in the late 1940s, he was building a dam in Algonquin Park on the river there just below Lake of Two Rivers, to raise the water up to the level of O'Grady's sawmill. He was pulling timber up onto the bridge, onto the dam, and the machine tripped off, and he jumped back onto the riverbank and he came down with his foot on a stone in the loose sand. And he tore the tendons in his heel and, after that, he could amost get his heel on the ground again. He almost cured himself!

I went up for J.S.L. McRae in 1927. I was with them until 1942 when I retired as a lumberjack. My brother retired, too, at that time. In the fall of '42, I went to Deux Riviere as a scaler. I scaled jack pine there—135,000 feet. Then I came home in the spring and went to get my scaler's licence, scaling course, two weeks, at New Mindon, Ontario; I just traded the cross-cut saw for the scaler. The old tally board's still in the cupboard here.

I'll tell you about old Ferdie Conaghan, an awful practical joker. The young lads in the camp on Sundays, when the cook would ring the bell at dinner time, they'd just about tear the door off to dash down to the cookery. If old Conaghan could get one of them sitting with his back up agin a bunk post, he'd tie the braces to the bunk post and when the cook rang the bell, they couldn't get up to run. Another night there was two lads sleeping in the top bunk and they had their feet right close together so their two toes were touching. Ferdie got some cord and he tied them together and he said, "Siamese twins." Well, when the dinner bell went off, they tried to jump up!

This is about the last night that we were in that camp. You had to get up early in the morning, pack up and get out with all the equipment to the train junction. The men set the alarm clock early so they wouldn't miss the train. When the alarm went off in the morning everybody jumped up, got their breakfast, and out to the station at Ralph Lake, packed everything in the waiting box car. But no sign of the train. They decided the train must be late. They were looking at their watches all the time. Old Conaghan couldn't keep from laughing—he had fixed the alarm clock, you see, set them way ahead. Well, we chased Conaghan up and down the railway tracks 'til the train came. We told him we'd make him run behind the train all the way to Eganville if he didn't behave himself.

There was a lad there by the name of Greely, another Irishman. He said he put in one year up around Mattawa. He said it was the coldest country he ever saw in his life. He said that when the teamsters shouted at the horses, the sound never reached the horses; it fell down at their heels. And when the thaw came in the spring, there was an indecent racket when all of the teamsters' shouts thawed out and rang through the bush.

When I was fire ranging in the Depression, men started setting fires to get work. They set so many that the government called it arson. I got fired when the Liberal government came in. When I was gone, those fellows had a free hand—they set even more fires to get work. So they sent a big Irishman—he came in there like a roaring lion, cut a big switch and chased them all through the bush. That only aggravated them and they really went to work—setting fires. So Chief Ranger Legris went to Tom Murray—he was the Member of Parliament for Renfrew—said they wanted me back on. And old Tom said, "Oh, no. Let that Conservative go back across to Hastings where he belongs and we'll put a Renfrew man in there." But old Harry Legris says to Murray, "That's not the case at all. Taylor's got no politics. He's been working for me for eight years and has done a real good job as a ranger. He's the only one that can look after them. He knows the country and he knows who to suspect." So old Tom says, "If that's the case, put him back on."

So that's how I become a fire ranger again. When I came back on I didn't want to see them people going to jail. So I told them, "I'm re-hired with express orders to catch you. Now I don't want to see you people going to jail." They just laughed at me because they thought I couldn't catch them. I was tied to a phone, you see, taking orders from the ranger's tower, and I couldn't do anything in the bush finding them. Even if I did catch them, it would only be my word agin their's in the courts.

So, anyway, the next year, 1935, in the spring, I went back home and they went at the fires again, same people setting fires for getting work. I tracked the

DO YOU REMEMBER 1929?

WALL STREET HAS ANOTHER BAD CRASH; WHEAT TURNS WEAK WITH STOCKS
Montreal Star, Oct. 28.

FRENZIED SCENES IN LOCAL MARKETS AS PRICES CRASH
Montreal Star, Oct. 29.

CANADIAN EXCHANGES HIT IN GENERAL STAMPEDE
Toronto Mail and Empire, Oct. 25.

MILLIONS IN PROFITS SWEPT AWAY AS PRICES CRASH
Manitoba Free Press, Oct. 25.

MARKETS TOTTER AS PANIC GRIPS INVESTORS
Quebec Chronicle-Telegraph, Oct. 29.

HUNDREDS OF MILLIONS LOST IN GREAT MARKET CRASH TODAY
Quebec Chronicle-Telegraph, Oct. 24.

STOCK AND GRAIN CRASH
Winnipeg Tribune, Oct. 24.

HALIFAX TRADERS LOSE HEAVILY IN STOCK MARKET DEBACLE
Halifax Chronicle, Oct. 25.

BIGGEST CRASH SINCE 1914 HITS STOCK MARKET
Montreal Gazette, Oct. 25.

DARKEST DAY IN YEARS ON MARKETS
Edmonton Bulletin, Oct. 24.

SPECULATIVE PANIC SWEEPS STOCK MARKETS; RECORD SLUMP IN LOCAL STOCKS; PANICKY TONE
Montreal Star, Oct. 24, 1929.

*A page of stock market headlines from The Canadian, March 1, 1935. These headlines appeared in numerous newspapers between October 24 and October 28, 1929, sixteen months after R.B. Bennett warned the country on the floor of the House of Commons that the situation was fraught with "possibilities of the gravest disaster." On October 29, 1929, Prime Minister Mackenzie King, in an interview with the Canadian Press, made the amazing statement, "Economic conditions in Canada were never more sound."*

fellow that I suspected. When I got a gang of men working on the fire, I started walking and I hit a trail going towards his house. I followed that trail 'til I come to a little creek that had some mud and I seen the number nine boot tracks both east and west where the fellow had walked and set the fire, and went back home. When I made out the fire report, I drew the picture of the two boots with a cross on the soles.

When the leaves came out on the trees and cut the hazard down and everything greened up, I was building a phone when along came Harry Legris, and Bill Johnston the provincial policeman from Renfrew. They said they would go and interview the fellow. I hung my spurs up on trees there, and got into the car and went with them and tackled the man—I won't bother giving his name—and he denied it. So Johnson started peeking under a couch and the first thing he pulled out was these boots. He said, "Did you ever see them boots?" I said, "No, but I've seen tracks off that tread." So he asked who owned the boots, and it was the old lad's son. Now, I was sorry about that because he had been a comrade with me in McRae's camp where we lumbered together. But I couldn't stop the process. The policeman made him try the boots on. The boots fitted the young lad. The policeman handed the boots to me and he said, "You look after them boots for evidence. I'm going back in to try that old lad again because I'm pretty sure he put the young lad's boots on to throw us off the track." Johnson went back into the house, "If you're a man," he said, "you'll not let your boy go to jail." The old lad clammed up and he wouldn't own up.

So we brought the young lad down and put him in jail and, after he sat in jail there for a few days, he squealed on the old man. He got three months in Burwash, and that young fellow and I was back for McRae's the next winter. And when old John McRae heard about me catching the firebug and putting him in jail, that tickled him. And he said to the young fellow, he said, "I'm kind of surprised about Henry Taylor being able to catch your father. He looks kind of stupid to me." The young lad says, "Don't fool yourself. My father's not as stupid as he looks."

The day that the chief ranger Legris and Johnson the Renfrew policeman came to get the old

lad for jail, I was on the phone line. We had a tent up at the dead end of the line at the camp. I ran a wire in and hung a phone on a post and they'd answer the phone to keep them in connection with headquarters. Now there was another old lad whom I suspected up in Raglan. I knew that, because I had caught one firebug, the others would be out to prove how smart they were. So this other old fellow went right out for half a mile off the ranger tower to the pine along Robinson Creek. The towerman started calling around to the settlements to get help with the fire. He called this house where he knew there was lots of young men. A girl answered the phone. "I need some fire-fighters here," he yelled. "Well," she said, "there's nobody around here today. Even my young brother, Henry, is away." So the towerman said, "Where did he go?" "He went out along Robinson Creek for a walk with Uncle Herman." Well, Uncle Herman was my chief suspect and right along Robinson Creek was where the fire was set. The towerman phoned down to the line camp where I was up a pole tidying wire. I could see down to the cookhouse tent. I seen the cook coming out wiping his apron. I said to McNulty, I said, "There must be a message. The cook is wiping his apron."

So we went down and got the message that the towerman sent about the fire. So Deputy McNulty and I walked out and we found the man and the boy's tracks on that trail. We got in touch with Keith Legris and Johnson the provincial policeman—they had already arrested the other guilty firebug so they handed him over to me to take down to the camp and guard until they went to investigate this new case. Legris and Johnson just went to the house to confront Uncle Herman. Uncle Herman was sitting smoking the pipe and he had just taken his boots off—his old feet were sore from travelling the bush. He was sitting in the rocking chair and, when they tackled him, he denied it. Johnson left Legris in the house with the old fellow, and he went out to get the nephew to witness agin him. Uncle Herman made it to the kitchen, got the boots on and just slipped out the door. When Johnston came in he said to Legris, "Where is he?" Legris said, "He's gone out to the kitchen to get his boots." Legris pulled out the .38

and the flashlight—it was night by that time—and jumped into the kitchen, but it was empty. And that big Irishman, McNulty, did he ever laugh at Legris and Johnson. He said, "A fine pair of hunters you two! Here Taylor and I have wore our feet off to the knees chasing that old buck out of the swamp for you, and you let him pass." Uncle Herman was gone.

The wages for a fire-fighter was twenty cents an hour, two dollars for a ten-hour day. The chief ranger said, "We'll cut that down in half to ten cents an hour." That would be in the Dirty Thirties. I told him, "I don't think that will do any good anyway, because lumber companies hand you a cross-cut saw and an axe and order you to cut a hundred logs for seventy-five cents." And if you couldn't cut the hundred logs they'd give the job over to somebody that could, and that's what caused the unions to be formed, and that's when all the trouble started. The dollar a day was a whole lot better than seventy-five cents.

In the lumber camp up for McRae, sometimes you'd come down at Christmastime and sometimes you didn't. The first year that I was in the camp, Jim and I went in in November and, when Christmas came, we volunteered to look after the camp and let the main gang go out. When the Polish foreman was leaving, he showed us a bunk inside the door and he said, "It's lousy." He ordered us to wash the lousy blankets with hot water. So I hung up a big kettle and put a real fire under it and when I got the water good and hot, I yelled to Jim that I was ready for the blankets. He picked the blankets up off the bunk and held them right out at arm's length. I had a barrel to put the blankets in and throw the boiling water on them. Jim dropped the blankets into the barrel. Then he saw something on his wrist. He pulled his sleeve back and there was a great big louse marching up his sleeve. He pulled it quick off his arm and dropped it into the boiling water. It swelled up about the size of a grain of wheat, and burst, and the eggs spewed out of it all over. Jim said, "That was a close call. That thing would have been a mother and a grandmother twenty-four times over!"

There was another lad by the name of Bill Coffey. He was quite a joke in the camp. His partner was old Ernst Heinke. Now Heinke was a wild man to tell fish stories. The fish kept getting bigger every time he told one. So this evening old Coffey decided to settle Heinke for one evening. Coffey said to the gang, "Did any of you ever have a pet fish?" No

*Left: Henry's brother Jim was described by Henry as a "famous foreman, one of the best river drivers of all times—he was the best man on jumping logs ever seen or heard of." In this 1920s photo, Cecil Sharbot and Richard Bailey of Calabogie are jumping logs on the Madawaska River, but perhaps not as well as the legendary Jim Taylor might have done.*
*Above: Rivermen in pointer boats, c. 1920s, Algonquin Park, striving to move a log jam.*

nobody ever had a pet fish. So Heinke told this story. "One time I had a great big black sucker. That thing was so tame it followed me all over like a dog right at my heels. I was going across country one day, and the sucker was right along behind me. I came to a big creek where an old log was the only way to get across. It had rained and the log was quite slippery. I got halfway across the creek when I heard a splash, and looked around. My great big black sucker had fallen into the creek and got drowned!" That story cured Heinke for a little while.

My brother Jim was foreman for McRae's for fifteen years. He drove the last logs down the Madawaska River in 1922. He was away all across Ontario, driving, in his young days, a famous foreman, one of the best river drivers of all times. I'll just tell you how skilful he was. He was the best man on jumping logs that I ever seen or heard of. And he learned that when he was a small boy. Anything you learn when you're a small boy you never forget. There was a pond on the old homestead right near where I built that log house at Raglan. And Jim practised rolling over on little logs on that pond there with the first pair of boots with leather soles that he ever got. Caulk boots. Nail marks all over the house floors, and mother made him take all the nails out, but that didn't stop him. He could pick up an eight-foot dry cedar log, carry it on his shoulder, throw it into the river, step out onto it and sail away waving back to the shore. Ride the log down river.

When he was a pretty-near old man, just about the time he was retired, away up in his sixties, his eyesight was poor. You've heard tell of people lifting 'til their eyes pop out?

Well, that's what happened to him. He lifted too hard and he burst the blood vessels at the back of his eyes and blood run all over them like a windowpane. He'd go to the Ottawa Civic Hospital and they'd put bloodsuckers—leeches—on his eyes to get the blood out.

The last time it happened to him was that first year that we were up for McRae. Jim was coming down this creek laying out the road when he stepped on moss on a smooth stone. He slipped and fell back and hit his head on a tree. When he got up he was stone blind! The only way he could get out of there was to follow the creek out. He held the axe handle out in front so he wouldn't fall over any old logs and, as long as he could hear the water rattling around his gum rubbers in the creek, he could go down the creek to the gang. When he shouted to them they heard him and came, and away he went to Ottawa, and got the bloodsuckers again. He had to find his way down the creek blind. But as long as he could hear the water, he was alright. . .

1 Begun in 1916 near Madawaska, the J.S.L. McRea Lumber Company continues today at Whitney, Ontario, still run by McRea's descendants. Three generations ago John Duncan McRea, a medical student at McGill University, came to teach school at Eganville, and never left the Valley. Further references in Roy MacGregor's interview.

2 For more on the Last Laird MacNab see *Giants of Canada's Ottawa Valley* by Joan Finnigan, General Store Publishing, 1981.

3 For an interview with one of the descendants of the Conroy lumbering family, see *Tell Me Another Story* by Joan Finnigan, MacGraw-Hill-Ryerson, 1988, Chapter. 17, "Hull to Aylmer; Seven Miles of History." See also *Carlow Township History*, published by the Senior Citizens of Carlow Township, 1977.

4 Nicholas Sparks, 1792-1862, is recognized as the founder of Bytown, later Ottawa. He left Ireland in 1816 with one hundred pounds and immediately began to buy and sell real estate in what became downtown Ottawa.

5 Legris were amongst the first settlers along the Opeongo Line taking up land and building a stopping-place at Dacre, Ontario.

6 References to Tom Murray, lumberman, MPP, appear throughout the oral/social histories. For his interview, see *Some of the Stories I Told You Were True* by Joan Finnigan, Deneau, 1981.

# 3

# "The Stanley Cup was a Centrepiece on Our Dining-Room Table"

## EDWARD "TED" DEVLIN – native of Ottawa, Ontario

*E.W. "Ted" Devlin was born in 1911 in Ottawa, the eldest son of W.F.C. (Ted) Devlin and the former Emily Edith Wade of Winnipeg. The family home was in Sandy Hill. Grandfather Robert James Devlin, "R.J." as he was known for decades on Sparks Street, Ottawa, emigrated from Ireland in the mid-1800s and landed his first job with the* London Free Press, *as copy-boy, reporter, columnist; he was the only Canadian correspondent to cover the American Civil War. In 1869, he moved to Ottawa, the newly-established capital of Canada, where he opened a haberdashery, later expanded to become a highly successful store for men's and women's clothing. His newspaper ads were famous for their originality and humour.*

*When R.J. died in 1918, Ted's father took over the family business, guiding it through the Great Depression and World War II. One of the highlights in the history of Devlin's during that period was the making of a fur hat on very short notice for the Parliamentary Press Gallery to present to Winston Churchill when he came to Ottawa in 1941. Churchill wore his Devlin hat at the Yalta meeting with Roosevelt and Stalin. In 1951, Devlin's was sold to Morgan's of Montreal; the glass towers of the Royal Bank building now stand in its place.*

*Ted attended Lisgar Collegiate and then moved on to spend some years with CBC as news-and-music announcer, along with Ottawa's own Lorne Greene. After World War II he worked as a writer-producer of documentary programmes with Radio Canada International in Montreal. On his return to Ottawa, he did writing, editing and promotion for the Canadian Council for International Co-operation, the Novalis Publishing Company, and the Economics Branch of Agriculture Canada. When he retired in 1976, he and his wife, the former Louise Hudson, moved to her family home in the fishing village of Westport Point, south of Boston, where he says, "they lived happily ever after."*

*Ted Devlin gives us a remarkable memoir of growing up in small-town Ottawa in the 1920s and '30s at a time when if everyone didn't exactly "know everyone," they certainly knew about them.*

IN THE 1920s, my brother and I were too young to go to professional hockey games, but we heard a great deal about the Ottawa Senators and the Stanley Cup they kept winning. They were local and national heroes—world heroes even, world champions no less. When they played in Ottawa, it was a great patriotic event, and Dad, as a leading merchant with large windows on Sparks Street—and knowing many of the Senators personally—went all out for them, with windows full of flags and pictures and streamers and, as centrepiece, the Stanley Cup itself. And overnight, the safest place to keep it was our dinner table. There it stood, Lord Stanley's noble bowl, awe-inspiring, its tall base ringed with silver and bearing the names of all the previous winners (mostly the Senators) bearing up the great bowl, which looked as though it would hold champagne for a whole hockey team.

By the time I was going to hockey games in Montreal, other heroes and other teams were battling for the Cup. Now, a team called the Ottawa Senators is back in the NHL. And most of the original Senators enshrined in Toronto's Hockey Hall of Fame. You must go there now to recall those heroic names: George Boucher . . . Nighbor . . . Gleason . . . Gorman . . . Denneny . . . Finnigan . . . Kilrea . . . Halliday . . . Smith . . . Adams . . . Clancy.

*Ottawa Senators' star defensive wing, Frank Finnigan, in his Devlin hat, perhaps smiling at the thought of his winning goal in the Stanley Cup Playoffs, 1927. The photographer, probably Horsdal of Ottawa, has proudly placed the red, white and black colours of the Ottawa Senators on the left upper corner.*

I remember horses clip-clopping along the early-morning streets of Sandy Hill, bringing us milk and sawdusty ice. You could click your tongue against the roof of your mouth and make a most satisfying imitation of their sound. On hot days, the horses wore straw hats with the ears sticking through, and they ate from canvas bags hooked over their heads. They welcomed an apple or lump of sugar. Their tongues were rough and wet.

In the 1890s, Grandfather Devlin used his journalistic advertisements in *The Citizen* to scold City Hall about the state of the mud on the capital's main business street. He nobly offered to ferry customers across from the north side to his place of business on the south side. By the time I arrived in Ottawa in 1911, Sparks Street was paved, but it was still a pre-motor-age Victorian alleyway that accommodated two sidewalks, two traffic lanes and two car tracks. (I remember the electric sparks and crackles when the trolley came off the wire as the tram turned the corner into Elgin Street.) My father and other Sparks Street merchants made the very advanced proposal of turning Sparks into a pedestrian mall, and finally the city agreed. It was the first of its kind in Canada.

The electric car of the 1920s suggested a sedan chair with a motor. It also suggested an invalid's wheelchair with a superstructure of glass windows. It was steered by a small wheel at the front which was controlled by a sort of joy-stick beneath the front window. The whole front, I seem to remember, opened outward to admit the occupant. It contained a glass vase holding a rose, and its windows were oval. It moved through the quiet streets of Sandy Hill at perhaps three miles an hour. The occupant was the kind of grand lady who wore net collars supported by whalebone strips, and she was probably garbed in black or plum-coloured bombazine, and a Queen Mary hat.

I was only a boy of seven on Armistice Day, November 11, 1918. We sat tensely, waiting for the moment that would tell us the Armistice had been signed and the war was over. Eleven o'clock. The electric light dimmed, then came up again. We yelled and hugged each other. Across the city church bells

*Looking west on Sparks Street, Ottawa, at the turn of the century. Ahearne's electric streetcars are in business, but horse-drawn vehicles and bicycles are still very much in evidence. Note James Hope book store to the right where Ted Devlin remembers shopping.*

rang and factory whistles hooted. We piled into the open-topped McLaughlin Buick and joined the wild parade up Rideau Street to the Plaza. Ottawa and the western world were wild with joy.

I remember the French of 1920s-30s. Leo spoke to the rest of our Rockcliffe gang with an accent. That was the natural way of things. That was the way "the French" talked. It never entered our Anglo-Saxon-Scottish heads that we might, or could, or should, speak to him in *his* language. Oh yes, we had a subject in school called French, with tiresome vocabulary and silly pronunciation; but no one on <u>our</u> side would ever speak the stuff. Leo was the only specimen of "the French" that we knew, and our parents knew hardly more in their circle of friends. "They" lived *over there*—in Eastview or Clarkstown or along St. Patrick Street in, of course, Lowertown. "They" delivered our

mail, drove our taxis, cleaned our houses. We did not expect to know any of "them." Nonetheless, my mother had a close friend who was French (upper level) and who married into one of Ottawa's top-drawer Anglo-Canadian families. A sprinkling of French names appeared in the English-Scottish-Irish enclave of Sandy Hill, some of them preserved in the history books: Panet, Gobeil, Charlebois, Taschereau, Fournier, Quesnel, Perodeau. Some of these my parents met socially, and mother called regularly on the *grande dame* Madame Desbarats. In our clubs and associations, the only French we heard came from diplomats and other personages from abroad. We might muster enough of the language to buy vegetables on the market or negotiate a meal in a Hull restaurant. Normally, we no more thought of speaking French than we thought of speaking Portuguese.

Of course, just as the Boston Irish produced a Kennedy family, so "the French" (in Quebec) produced a prime minister, an army general and—*mirabile dictu*!—a governor general. (Including, thank heaven, Madame Vanier, a woman of enormous charm and distinction.)

When bilingualism became obligatory in government jobs and public services, the French, of course, were ready; they had been doing it for decades, in the shops and offices of Ottawa. It was the only way to survive. And when lack of the required facility with French deprived me of my job in 1971, I understood the economic incentives "the French" had had to learn the other language.

By a pleasant irony, a few months later I was hired by a French-speaking company that published teaching materials in both languages, precisely because I *did* speak English. Thus I spent several happy years, as an anglophone and Protestant minority, writing English-language promotional material with the enthusiastic support and friendship of my "French" colleagues.

C.P. Edwards was one of Dad's best friends and he was a fascinating and amusing uncle to my brother Bob and me. He and his wife Ethel lived in a small cottage at the north end of Cloverdale Road, where the Rockcliffe streetcars turned around. Later we learned that he was a famous and important man, a pioneer—almost *the* pioneer—of radio communications and broadcasting in Canada. In Wales, as a young electrical engineer, he was enlisted and trained by Marconi, when he was setting up the first transatlantic communication by radio. Later, Marconi sent him to Canada to join his Canadian company and to set up wireless transmitters. Then the government employed him as Director of Maritime Radio. In World War II, he won the Order of the British Empire for designing a system for detecting enemy code messages. He represented

*Peace Day celebrations, Basingstoke, England, July 19, 1919.*

Canada at international radio conferences, he headed the committee that allotted radio channels throughout North America, and he initiated the equipping of all large ships with radio safety-devices. In World War II he won a medal for directing the building of one hundred airports for the Commonwealth Air Training Plan. He set up the corporation that controlled all external communications, radio and telegraph in Canada. He wound up as Deputy Minister of Communications. Some uncle!

I remember the first radio (before 1920). A small brown box on the floodlit stage crackled and whistled and roared. A voice came out of it, strange and hoarse, but you could make out actual words. The hall of All Saints Church was full of people curious to hear this invention that brought sounds from far away without wires. That was my introduction to the age of radio. Soon we were buying strange metal gadgets at Woolworth's and pouring over diagrams to make our own radios. Fat round Quaker Oats boxes were just the things to wind your coil on. With the right circuits and a lumpy crystal and a cat's whisker tuner, you could make your black paper loud-speaker squawk out voices and music from KDKA in Pittsburg. In 1938, I joined the Canadian Broadcasting Corporation as staff announcer. I sent words and music from Halifax to Victoria on the national radio network that grew out of the work of my uncle C.P. Edwards (q.v.).

I remember Sis Tomkins who taught at Lisgar Collegiate, 1902-1933. She was really Miss E.A. Tomkins, but you learned that formality after you left the Lisgar Collegiate. My father just managed to

*Fifth Form girls of Ted Devlin's era at Lisgar Collegiate, Ottawa, which celebrated its sesquicentennial in 1993. Standing L to R: Sterling Perret, Eleanor Tett, Ruth Pulling, Ruby Moorhead, Edna Selby, Jean Black, Laura MacDougall, Coral Moorhead, Frances Herron, Eileen McElroy, Winnie Law. Middle Row L to R: Margaret Ness, Myrtle McCourt, Lois White, Jean McJanet, Annetta Landam, Marjorie Adair, Allie McArthur, Jeanine Belanger. Front L to R: Dorothy Wood, Winona Kindle, Margaret McKeever, Mary Monk, Mary Reeve, Dorothy Townsend, May Rogers.*
*Photo courtesy Marion Spence Curie, Lisgar 1918-22. She went on to Queen's for B.A. and M.A., 1926-27, and became one of the first female microbiologists in Canada.*

be taught by her. So did Percy Harris, the coal dealer, whose daughter Betty married my brother Bob. Miss Tomkins induced a succession of mutinous young Ottawans to learn algebra, or at least to pass exams in it. I was one of them. To do this she used an exciting mixture of wit and sarcasm and sheer terror, controlling classrooms full of smart-alecks and hellions with a glare, a word or a hiss. We dreaded being the centre of her attention. She was an Ottawa legend long before she retired. In her post-retirement serenity she visited Dad in his office! "How did you do it?" he asked her, and got the memorable reply: "Always razzle-dazzle the other fella before the other fella razzle-dazzles you."

As a boy I remember the Rideau Canal in the 1920s, '30s. The railway tracks crossed the river, went under the Plaza, through the Union Station and came out on the south side, along the canal. A grimy wasteland of coal-storage bins and junkyards followed the tracks southward. The National Capital Commission, or its predecessor, swept away this remnant of Victorian landscaping, put the new station several miles away and replaced the filthy mess with the handsome flower parkway which can now be gazed at with pride from the National Arts Centre and its canalside restaurant.

When the wind was westerly, Hull spread a pungent chemical smell over Ottawa. "Ah!" we would say, "you can smell Hull today," in our superior down-wind fashion. Especially on hot summer evenings. The Eddy paper mill, the source of the smell, dominated the old Quebec village, with its streets of wooden houses and tall silver church. Between Hull and Gatineau Point, the river bank was a continuous lumber yard, and the river below Hull was always jammed with rafts of logs waiting for the mill. You envied the spacious life enjoyed by the lumberjacks who lounged and cooked their meals in huts perched on the rafts. To the left of the bridge, as you came over from Ottawa (where the Museum of Civilization stands today), raw logs were piled in pyramids, high as houses, waiting to be turned into paper. The paper-making was the cause of the smell and the reason for Hull's existence. Yielding, I believe to public opinion, the Eddy Company finally

removed the water tower, clearly visible from Parliament Hill, which was painted to look like a roll of White Swan toilet paper.

I remember Britannia and Rockcliffe Parks so well. Part of Ottawa now, but then, out in the country, an adventure, an excursion, the goal of a day's outing, requiring picnic baskets, bathing suits for Britannia, and mosquito oil. (I remember citronella.) The Rockcliffe streetcars in summer were made up of rows of open benches, like church pews, with open sides to let in the mosquitos. The ticket-seller shuffled his way along steps that ran the length of the car, rattling his coins in a glass-sided box. The Rockcliffe line ran daringly along the high bank of the river, where the rock gardens are now. The Britannia cars were long brown monsters that thundered along the track as though bound for Toronto. They calmed down enough to deposit you at the pine-covered station, where the pier and the beach stretched out welcoming arms.

Nesrallah's! There it was, as we entered Ottawa from Vanier, on a day in May 1993—windows full of groceries and candies, facing north and west on the southeast corner of Rideau and Charlotte. Under another name, probably it was there before 1920. My brother Bob and I went to it constantly from our house on Besserer Street, a block and a half away, to buy our Charms and licorice chewing-tobacco, and all-sorts, and pink and yellow mints stuck on strips of paper, and Cherry Flips, and blood-orange chewing gum. (Why on earth "blood-orange?") Over fifty years later it was still there to give Louise and me our *New York Sunday Times*. We lived two streets away, on Daly Avenue. Wonder of wonders, the mighty *New York Times*, printed hundreds of miles away in the skyscrapers of Manhattan, managed to arrive on Sunday morning in a small Lebanese grocery store in Sandy Hill, Ottawa.

Oh, the Cliffside Ski Club! I remember the great Saturday expedition of carrying your skis and poles, firmly strapped together, on the streetcar up to the Plaza and hurrying down the dark stairway beside the Château Laurier and catching the big brown Beltline car. We thundered across the Interprovincial Bridge and rattled our way between

Group of "one-pole" skiers who gave skiing its start at the turn of the century. In the early days of sporting life in the Valley only the upper class with leisure and money could indulge themselves in such rarefied activities as evidenced in this photo taken at the foot of Indian Hill on the Quebec side of the Ottawa. Kneeling: Drysdale Holbrook, Capt. T.W. Billy Lawless, William H. Cronk, Frederick Merritt, C. Jackson Booth. Standing: Richard G. McConnell, John A. Armstrong, Henry Y. Complin, Edwin G. Glenney, —, John E. Cox. Lawless was one of the all-round outstanding athletes in Ottawa history, a man who excelled in everything, and C. Jackson Booth was one of the sons of lumber king, J.R. Booth.

the humble cottages of Hull until we came to Wrightsville. It's all suburbs now, but then it was country. At the carstop we inhaled the cold Gatineau air as we strapped on our skis and dug our poles into the snow, adjusted our rucksacks and glided off toward Fairy Lake. The rucksacks, full of sandwiches and thermos bottles, bumped companionably on our backs. On our jacket shoulders we wore the proud badge of the Cliffside Ski Club: winged golden ski sloping from right to left across a purple shield with a gold border.

When the deep hollow of Fairy Lake came in sight, white flat patch of lake with the ski lodge smoking beside it, we shot down the hillside and entered the lodge. It was glorious—smoky and noisy and crowded and full of good food smells. Mother and Dad knew everyone, and we ate our lunch in a friendly roar of voices. The Kirby brothers, Don and Dave, might be there and many other pals. There was hot cocoa and coffee in your thermos, and you could dip into a pot of soup that simmered on the pot-bellied stove. Everyone looked rugged and out-

doorsy and red in the face. Out we went again, joining long lines of skiers striding through the trees toward the next lodge. That as I remember was Birch Valley—magical name, and one of the few I remember. We were all flat skiers then, even long-distance skiers, sometimes up hill and down dale (one of the favourite trails was called the Hill and Dale). The heroic downhill style of skiing, with its obligatory rope-pulls and chairlifts, and the attendant designer ski costumes, came along much later. A long way from the primitive Nordic activity introduced to Ottawa by Sigurd Lockeberg and other Norwegians, sometime early in the century.

I don't remember when the Cliffside club was organized, but I do know that Dad and John Graham and other hardy souls cut the trails through the hills and valleys of what is now the Gatineau Park. Camp Fortune became the biggest and most popular lodge and centre when the Ottawa Ski Club took over. It absorbed the little old Cliffside, and was ultimately able to call itself the world's largest ski club. (I always wondered what Oslo thought of that.) I was proudly conscious that Dad, as well as being a founding member, was also vice president or president for a time. My memories are faint and full of gaps; a visit to the Ski Museum on Sussex Drive would sharpen them and fill the holes, and correct the mistakes.

Now, from the vantage point of about seventy-five years, skiing still has the aura, the glow, of those Saturday morning treks from the Wrightville carstop, up the lonely country road toward Fairy Lake. With that purple and gold patch on my shoulder.

Ottawa celebrated the Golden Jubilee of Confederation in 1927 with the inauguration of the carillon in the Peace Tower and a parade of historical floats. A major event to be represented on a float was the laying of the cornerstone of the old Centre Block of the Parliament Buildings by HRH the Prince of Wales, 1860.[1] HRH was represented standing, golden trowel in hand, before the stone which hung in a sling, surrounded by frock-coated dignitaries and white-coated masons. For some obscure reason I was chosen to be dressed and bearded as HRH. The dressing and bearding were done to all the impersonators in a room at the Exhibition Grounds, and we were then driven about four miles across town to where the floats waited. I was boosted up onto my float, which seemed as large as a tennis court, and there I took my stand, frock-coated and top-hatted,

*Ottawa's tradition of ice carnivals and ice sculpture goes back for more than a century. This is an 1895 artist's depiction of the storming of the Ice Castle by over a thousand snow-shoers from Ottawa Clubs armed with torches, searchlights, roman candles, fireworks, tourbillons. Special lighting from the Ottawa Electric Company achieved spectacular displays for the more than twenty-five thousand people who attended the week-long carnival. Parades, musicales, processions of athletes, tandem drives, reincarnated lumbermen's shanty and Indian encampment, and a fancy dress skating carnival at Rideau Hall rink—all were capped by the crowning event, a gala ball at the Russell House. Many of the capital's renowned either attended or worked as volunteers, including Sir James Grant, W.Y. Soper, Fred Carling, W.T. Lawless, Sir Adolphe Caron, Hon. E.H. Bronson, Hon. T.M. Daly, Lt-Col White and William Borthwick, Mayor of Ottawa.*

before the stone in its sling. Historical figures formed up on the floats before and behind, but I remained in solitary grandeur as my float moved out into the procession. A man in a blue car shouted, "Jump down! I'll drive you back!" I jumped, but the blue car disappeared. So, fully frocked, top-hatted and bewhiskered, I trudged the four miles back to the dressing-room along the hot and crowded streets. It was eighty-five degrees Fahrenheit.

Percival Price, the first Dominion Carillonneur, wore a black beard because the Belgian carillonneurs with whom he learned his trade could only take him seriously with a beard. In the playing-chamber under the bells, he sat on a curved bench and slid back and forth to work the higher bells with both fists, while his feet hit wooden rods under the bench to sound the big bass ones. He had an apartment a storey or two below the bellchamber where he had friends in for parties. In a corner of the room, rods connecting the clock mechanism below with the bells above clanked up and down every hour, and the bells boomed overhead.

When I was growing up and later as a young man, we went to skating parties on the pond in Rideau Hall grounds and glided around to the music of Waldteufel and Strauss, and drank cocoa in the pavilion beside the pond. In our tuxedos and black ties, we took our girls to supper dances in the green-and-white striped tent room. His "Ex" and his lady stood in the entrance hall to greet us, and we felt both at home and very daring in the vast splendours of Government House. In midsummer, all Ottawa—diplomats, generals, admirals, ambassadors, merchants, housewives, children and the little old ladies in tennis shoes— converged on the splendid lawns and promenades for the Governor General's Garden Party. Under huge flapping tents you had tea and lemonade and cakes and ice cream. Along the flower-lined walks you watched the great and the splendid pass by— floating summer dresses, dazzling turbans and saris, medals and swords. From the blue-uniformed Governor General's Footguards Band came the all-pervading sound of Gilbert and Sullivan, von Suppé and Sousa. At any moment you might turn a corner and find yourself delightfully face to face with one or both of their "Exes."

We all read John Buchan, of course, and saw the movies based on his thrillers, some of them by Hitchcock. And then we got him all to ourselves, as governor general, as Lord Tweedsmuir.

Shortly after his installation at Rideau Hall in 1935, one of his aides-de-camp telephoned Dad in his office. "Would Mr. Devlin be free to show His Excellency the ski trails around Camp Fortune?" Dad rushed home, changed into his hiking clothes, and went off to meet the vice regal party. Six hours later he was back, in a state of exhaustion. "That little bird," he told us, "is unbelievably wiry and tough. He led us up and down those hills at top speed. The rest of his party are in a state of collapse." (The reason for the request was that Dad, an early pioneer of skiing in Ottawa, had helped to lay out the Gatineau trails.)

The Ottawa Drama League in the 1930s could not know that the Molnar play, *The Swan*, would become a famous movie, starring the divine Grace Kelly, Alec Guinness, and Louis Jourdan, in the roles played by Jocelyn Chapman, Lawrence Freiman and myself. Ottawa had to make do with us until the real thing came along.

Dorothy White, Gladys and Leslie Chance, Bill Cromarty, Madeleine Charlebois, Jocelyn Chapman, Nancy Barrow, Vals Gilmour, Solange Gauthier, Marian Osborne, Audrey Fellowes, Michael Meiklejohn, Beatrice Whitfield, William Brodie, Dorothy Cruikshank, Nora Hughes, Julia MacBrien, Roger Watkins-Pitchford, Dorothy Yule . . . some of the names are still with me from the ODL's golden age of the 1930s. Above all there was Bill Adkins, the English-born stage manager and set builder, who put it all together and made it happen on the stage. And above all there was Rupert Caplan, who directed us year after year, endlessly encouraging and creative. Many of the actors were English or Scottish, transplanted to Ottawa as teachers or diplomats or civil servants. They lent some artistic verisimilitude to our productions of Drinkwater, Shaw, Pinero, Maugham, Coward, Barrie, Fry, Galsworthy, Rattigan. We native Canadians considered ourselves adaptable enough to blend with them in those plays, and at the same time American enough to bring off the plays of Kaufman, Barry, Behrman, Maxwell Anderson, Odets and Wilder.

For decades before it was swallowed up by The Bay, Freimans Department Store stood four-square between Rideau and George, a block or so east of Sussex. Its only rival as a major department store was Ogilvy's, a few blocks farther east on the other side of Rideau. A.J. Freiman and his wife Lillian were for most of their lives among the most valued benefactors Ottawa had, particularly when refugees from Hitler's Germany needed vast amounts of organization and provisions. I remember that the Freimans were honoured by the Governments of Canada and Israel. But I have personal memories of the family. A.J. and my father were—at least in the field of clothing—business rivals. They were also personal friends. Their son Lawrence and I acted together with the Ottawa Drama League. Lawrence's son, A.J. Junior, and my brother's son, Michael, began a lifelong friendship during summers spent at Kingsmere up in the hills. A happy memory of the Freiman family and their business was their treatment of their biggest rival in the department store business, Ogilvy's. Ogilvy's had a disastrous fire which put them out of business for months. When they rebuilt and reopened, Freiman's welcomed them back with a large box in their full-page advertisement in the *Citizen*.

Yousuf Karsh, a shy young Armenian with a large camera, stood in the wings as members of the Ottawa Drama League rehearsed a play. He was studying the effect of stage lighting on faces. He had come from war-torn Armenia by way of his uncle's photographic studio in Sherbrooke and after studying in Boston. He was courteous and diffident and intense. He opened his studio in 1935. Through the Ottawa Drama League, he met the first of his distinguished sitters, Lord Duncannon, son of the governor general, who sometimes acted with the ODL. The prime minister became his patron, and Karsh was launched. He and Solange were married in 1939. I remember her telling me about his return home after taking the famous portrait of Churchill, which he had prefaced by removing the cigar stump

from the great man's lips. (In that portrait I can see both what Churchill felt toward Hitler and what he was feeling toward Yousuf Karsh.) "When he got home," said Solange, "he was pale green and shaking. He hoarsely confessed what he had done."

Soulange and her mother came from Tours "where the purest French is spoken." In Ottawa, they lived in a dark apartment on one of the glum little streets of Centretown. She worked for a mining company with an office on Wellington Street. There she translated technical journals and letters into English. She was not only French, but very French. She was not beautiful, but in the French way she was vivacious and charming and captivating. She acted with both the French-speaking and English-speaking theatre groups. I was first enchanted by her as "La Belle de Haguenau" in a production by Le Caveau, the French group. Later, with the very Anglo-Canadian Ottawa Drama League, she played an authentically French wife of Samuel Pepys in the London play, *And So To Bed*. To a stolid Anglo-Saxon like myself, Solange seemed to be always performing, with eyes and teeth and hands and elbows and shoulders, modulating in seconds from high drama to glittering comedy. We were devoted friends for many years, and I managed to write a play for her, which the Ottawa Drama League entered in the Dominion Drama Festival. After her marriage to the ascendant Yousuf Karsh, the two of them were among my most entertaining friends.

Paul Horsdal was one of Ottawa's favourite photographers, with a studio on Sparks Street near Elgin. He was Danish-Canadian with a soft and amusing accent and a quirky sense of humour. He and my father were devoted fishing pals. When the peeping and whistling of frogs and tree-toads around the lake kept them awake at night, he roared at them, "Shut up, you demmed weesil-birds! Paul Horsdal is enemy of weesil-birds!"

I also remember . . .

. . . the snowshoe clubs, racquettes on shoulder, wearing their grey and white and red blanket coats, leaving St. Anne's Church after mass and forming a parade along St. Patrick Street.

. . . Will Rogers coming out on the stage of our vast arena and remarking that they seemed to have taken a piece of southern Ontario and put a roof over it.

. . . John Philip Sousa and his massed brasses blasting our happy ears in that same arena.

. . . at the Russell Theatre, Anna Pavlova as the Dying Swan, Sir John Martin-Harvey as "Hamlet" (when he should have been Polonius), DeWolfe Hopper as "Chu Chin Chow," and sundry opera and Shakespeare companies.

. . . the ice palace on the old Plaza, attacked by men in blanket coats carrying torches, defended by men with roman candles, and finally going up in a blaze of red flares and skyrockets.

. . . the handbell in the street that told you the Italian knifegrinder was coming. How he slipped his grinder off his shoulder to the ground and pumped a pedal with one foot to set the grindstone spinning. Watching the spray of sparks as he pressed your scissors and knives to the stone.

. . . favourite bookshops: Thorburn and Abbott on Sparks Street, A.H. Jarvis on Queen, where we bought our John Buchan, Stephen Leacock, Mazo de la Roche, A.A. Milne, Mary Webb, and that wonderful Everyman's Library.

. . . sore-throat lozenges called, mysteriously, Zymole Troches.

. . . Bob Bowman, who lived down our street, whose father was the editor of the Journal, who went to London and became the voice of Canadian hockey on the BBC.

. . . coonskin coats, rumbleseats, hip flasks, the Charleston, and the flapper cartoons of John Held Junior in Life.

Dr. Oliver Martin, dentist and friend of

*One of the great hospitals of Canada, the Ottawa Civic, 1930s, in its pristine architectural glory before massive additions. Note that there are only seven cars parked in front. Perhaps the doctors?*

woodland spirits, was one of the group of my grandfather Devlin's cronies who founded the Echo Beach Fishing Club, some time in the 1880s. Their lodge was on the shore of Echo Lake, a beautiful stretch of water in the Laurentians northeast of Ottawa. They somehow got themselves to Buckingham on the Ottawa River (my family and I used to do it by boat from Hull), and then, probably in a rented carriage, up the rough roads and trails to the river that led to the lake. At the halfway point they dismounted, brought out the glasses, uncorked the whisky bottle, and drank two toasts: southward, to the City Spirits, northward, to the Lake Spirits. (On the way back they did it in reverse.)

Once in camp, Dr. Martin amused his cronies by telling tales of the spirits that haunted the woods and hillsides around them.

This went well with long days on the water and cosy evenings around the poker table in the green light of gas lamps. Outside in the dark woods, his spirits wandered and drifted on the wind—the Ogles, who live in the tops of dead pine trees (rampikes, we called them), the Guppies, Bal Lal, Pargobilio, Briar Vo, Go Bi Or, and the mysterious Willopus Wallopus. Perhaps Dr. Martin (tongue firmly in cheek) was simply doing what the native Americans did more seriously—giving wonderful names to the forces they felt around them in nature. I have never been able to trace any other memories of Dr. Martin beside these in my father's family lore.

My grandfather, R.J. Devlin, put some of Martin's spirits into verse, "Adieu! Adieu! Old Echo Beach," which ends:

Then play your games upon the lea,
Old Pargobilio, play!
A-sailing west-south-west are we,
So Echo Beach, good day!

Our family (R.J.D.'s son Ted, his wife Edith, son Bob and myself) spent many happy summers in the old lodge at Old Echo Beach, which was looked after by the nearest residents, a German-Canadian family named Yank. To get there we had to park the car at a farm and travel a long portage, then row a boat for several miles up rivers and lakes with all our supplies on board.

My father used to tell a story about a family living in the woods near Kingsmere, north of Ottawa, who were so poor that they could not afford a coffin when their father died. So they buried him in the piano.

*This story about Ted Devlin's remarkable grandfather, R.J. Devlin appeared in an* Ottawa Citizen *of the 1930s.*

> Back in the 1880s in Ottawa, the R.J. Devlin store was at 37 Sparks Street, across from the Russell House. The store sold fine furs and imported hats and its very successful owner was known far and wide as a character, a wit, an astute businessman, and an innovative advertiser.
>
> One time when business was slow, Mr. Devlin announced several weeks ahead in the Ottawa papers that he had received private advice that on the twenty-seventh of November, there would come a great blizzard, and that it would be well for the public to prepare for it by being dressed warmly in Devlin hats and furs.
>
> Well, the twenty-seventh of November arrived and the morning broke warm—even sultry. The people of Ottawa were laughing. "Some prediction!" they said. "How will Devlin ever live this one down?"
>
> About eleven-thirty that morning, there came a sharp switch in the weather. A cold wind came out of the northwest and snow began to fall. The storm increased into a blizzard and continued for days. The railways were blocked completely, the city sidewalks and the farm roads were impassable. For three days the storm raged and when it ended, Eastern Canada recorded the greatest storm of its history.
>
> Devlin sold a good number of fur hats and coon coats and thereafter became known as a prophet. But he never revealed the secret source of his weather prediction.

---

1 The future Edward VII makes a chaos-causing appearance in Glengarry County described in Chapter 20, *There's Truth in Every Legend.*

# 4

# "I Worked at Fisher's on Sparks Street until I was Eighty"

## BILL MURRAY – native of Bryson, Quebec

*Bill Murray's ancestors were Anglo-Celt settlers in Western Quebec generations ago. Some of them intermarried with the Pauls, many of whom were Algonquin Indians from Calumet Island, as well as with the Finnigans of Shawville and the Brills of Ottawa. Mr. Murray was born in 1907 at Bryson, Quebec, the "bridge town" over to The Island. His memories of growing up there produce an invaluable record reaching back seventy years into Valley history. But like countless young Valley people, he had to move down to "The Hub" and, for many years, he was almost a landmark on Sparks Street, first with Murphy-Gambles and later with Fisher's. Devlin's clothing store was his neighbour during his career in that commercial centre of Ottawa.*

*Jim Murray, Bill's blacksmith father, died very young, leaving his mother, the former Harriet Wall of Clarendon, Quebec, to raise a family of eight. When I interviewed him, Mr. Murray added to the ancestral story often repeated in the clans that the first Murray was part French, part Scot, came from France and jumped ship in Quebec City. "When we left Bryson in 1921, we were burning books because we couldn't take them all to Ottawa. I had them already in the fire when my mother yelled out,*

*'My God, Bill! You've put your grandfather Murray's books in the fire.' But I had looked at them and they were all in French so I thought, 'There's nothing here we want to keep.' Yes, there were family bibles and everything, but all in French."*

*Wherever he went, Bill was part of the musical and cultural life of the community and he records these aspects in both Bryson, Quebec, and Ottawa, Ontario, over the past century.*

AS A CHILD of five, I remember Bryson as a big village, and then this terrible fire. I can remember mother dressing us. We were brought out beside the courthouse and told to "stay there." I can remember standing there, and Dr. Gaboury lived in the next house to us, and I can remember watching the house across the street burning. All of a sudden, the windows blew out and the curtains went up in flames. That was 1913.

After father died so young, mother sewed constantly for us and for other people, and did all the housework besides. I remember as a child we used to have a man come and plough our great big garden in Bryson. Mother always gave him tea or something. But one time when he came to plough the garden, she wasn't at home. I thought, "My goodness, I've got to give the man something to drink." I went and found a bottle and gave him a glassful. The man drank it down. So Mother came home and looked at the garden and she said, "The man was here to plough the garden?" And I said, "Yes." She said, "My goodness! I never seen anybody plough a garden like that. The furrows are all crooked and uneven." The empty glass was sitting there and she said, "Did you give him something to drink?" I said, "You always give him something to drink." And she said, "What did you give him?" I said, "I got that bottle there and I poured it out." It was a bottle of old liquor kept there for God knows how long! A whole glass!

The house we were living in had about four lots. I can remember picking potato bugs, and hoeing and weeding. And we had the cow, we had hens, and we had the pig which was killed in the fall. Mother put eggs away for the wintertime packed in coarse salt, and the fowl was frozen later, and you'd buy meat and freeze it late in the wintertime and it was put in a barrel packed with snow in the back shed. You could have a January thaw but it wouldn't affect in the shed or in the barrel. I remember Mother putting strawberries in sugar and we had them at Christmastime as if they'd just been picked. And, you know, my cousin Retta Brill told me things about Grandma Murray drying rhubarb. You'd cut it and put it in the sun to dry. Like the Indians. They dried everything.

Mother made dresses for people in the village. People would give her orders—maybe even wedding dresses. I remember her making them long dress skirts with satin lining. She made suits; she would take an old suit of clothes and she'd take it all apart, turn it inside out, and make a suit again. I remember her knitting complete outfits. And I can remember in

*Bryson at the turn of the century as Bill Murray's parents would have known it, pre-fire, when it was a hub of the Pontiac.*

later years she couldn't see to thread needles. I used to thread needles for her. My aunt—that's another one of Dad's sisters—was Mrs. Morin and her husband owned the tailor shop in Bryson and Mother went there to work and learn her trade. At Morin's, the whole top floor was where they sewed and downstairs was where they showed the material and the patterns. Men's suits were their speciality.

That's where my mother trained and that's where Dad met her. After he died so young no matter how hard things were, she never complained, and she always gave the appearance to the village that we had everything. She used to say to me, "Hold your head up, you're a somebody." At thirteen I started to stoop because I was so tall, and they made fun of me, but she'd say, "Straighten up, walk with your shoulders back, you're a somebody."

My dad was a blacksmith. His shop was on what we called The Back Street. There was a hall above it that they rented for dances and concerts. It was a huge building with the stairs on the outside. Apparently he was a very good blacksmith and when they built the courthouse—Mother never told me anything about this—but Mr. Boland, who was the turnkey in the jail, and I were talking one time about

*When I first visited Cadieux's monument on Calumet Island it did, indeed, have Bill Murray's father's ironwork demarcating it. Alas, the site has been moved and all the ironwork taken. For more about Cadieux see* Wintering Over *by Joan Finnigan, Quarry Press, 1994.*

all these terrific doors and locks on the jail and he said, "Your dad made them all. And he did all the ironwork for the courthouse." You've heard the legend of Cadieux? His monument is there on Calumet Island and the chain that went around it—some person told me when I was looking at it, "Your dad made that chain."

Pearl Greer in Bryson opened a little "grog shop," as they called it in those days, and then when they were burnt out in the big Bryson fire, they started a grocery store. When I was about ten years old, I used to work there on Saturdays, and after school 'til eleven o'clock at night. Some of the boys around the village said to me, "You know you're just a damned Protestant and you shouldn't be working there. It should be one of us Roman Catholics." So I went and I said to Pearl, "I shouldn't be working here because I'm only a Protestant and you're a Roman Catholic." She said, "What made you say that?" And I told her about the boys and she said, "You go back and tell them it was Father Murray who suggested you work here. And I'll tell you something else," she said, "your dad was the one who helped us start the grog shop." (Probably because he was her best customer from what I heard later from other people.) Anyway, he had helped her and that was the reason she wanted to help me.

I remember Mrs. Dezouche. She owned half of Bryson. Freddie Dezouche was the only child she had to Dezouche, but she had children to McCoshin, her first husband, a lumberman, who made all the money. We called her Mother Dezouche, and she was a ring-tailed slut if ever there was one. And a Roman Catholic. Of course in Bryson on the Twelfth of July, they had all these Orangemen parading. They even came up from Portage-du-Fort to Bryson on the Twelfth of July. For weeks before, Mrs. Dezouche gathered rotten eggs, cabbages, tomatoes, everything that had gone bad. She had it in boxes on the highway and as soon as the Orangemen appeared in parade, she let them have it, plastered them. But they wouldn't dare touch her, you know, because she owned half of Bryson.

The blacksmith's shop was a thriving business. My dad did wheels for every vehicle; he repaired sleighs and buggies, fireplaces and stoves. I remember Aunt Hannah, Mother's sister, saying to me—they were visiting one time, "Oh, if your dad had only lived, you'd have been the wealthiest people in Bryson."

I remember Dr. Gaboury. He was away a lot of the time in Ottawa. He probably had another practice somewhere because Bryson had a Dr. Hurdman, too. Dr. Gaboury's back yard was next to ours and one time his daughter was in the yard and I talked to her. I went back to Mother and I said, "My, she's a nice person. But why don't you ever see her outside the yard?" So Mother told me she had had an illegitimate child, and she wasn't accepted by anybody, so she stayed in the house or in the backyard all the time.

After the fire, Bryson went down. But before that, it was the capital of Pontiac County. The courthouse was there, the jail, the municipal offices. Lieutenant Colonel de Salaberry[1] was a lawyer in the courthouse. He lived in Bryson—the Salaberry's house is still there. I remember Madame Louise de Salaberry. She made wonderful candy and she passed it out to all the children. And I can remember Colonel de Salaberry so well. He kept pigeons. One time, I went over to their place and climbed the ladder to the loft with a gang of kids to look at the pigeons' nests, and when I went to come back down again, I was too scared and I wouldn't cross this beam and climb down. So they sent for Mother. When Mother came, she said, "Jump and I'll catch you." I was going to do that, and Colonel de Salaberry was there (this was all planned beforehand), and when I jumped he pushed her aside and caught me. I remember being as mad as hell because they had fooled me, and I knew it.

The Armouries in Hull were named the Salaberry Armouries in memory of him. I went there during the war with a friend of mine who was a major in the army and we were looking at a big picture of Colonel de Salaberry. I was telling my friend about the Salaberrys in Bryson when a guy walked up and said, "Bill Murray, I'm Lieutenant Colonel de Salaberry. I'm the son. The one that used to beat you up in Bryson when we were kids." Oh, they were tough kids!

I hated school, but I loved History and Geography. Music was my thing, you know. When I was younger the Marleaus, Ted and Lola, had a big store on the back street. They lived in the back of it and there was a window came out on the corner and some big trees, and I used to stand there and listen to Lola Marleau. She was a music teacher, a very accomplished pianist. I was standing there listening to her one night when it started to rain, but under the trees I wasn't getting wet. Teddy, her brother, came out and he said, "Bill, why are you standing out there in the rain?" I said, "The music." "Oh," he said, "you like music?" So he went away and he talked some French to Lola—they were French of course—and he brought me in to their living-room, and oh, I sat there! And that music! Lola asked me several times, "Why don't you take music lessons?" Music lessons! Where was the money going to come from? So the Marleaus gave me the job of bringing their mail home every night from the post office. I used to get Pearl Greer's mail always then, too.

And so I took piano. I don't know how old I would be when I started, but I was old enough at ten years old to play the organ in the church. I can remember Mrs. Dr. Hurdman was the organist in our little Anglican church. I remember Mrs. Hurdman going away one time. "Somebody's gonna have to play the organ," they said. And Lola Marleau said, "Well, Bill Murray. Of course he can play the organ at the church." So they took me to the church and I did it. I took over and rang the bell—that bell is up at the little church in Chelsea, Quebec, today. And I learnt the mass in Latin. Arthur Marleau was the governor of the jail then. They lived in the courthouse. And Mrs. Marleau treated me like one of the family. She was another big influence in my life; taught me about "the better things" in life, music, the stories of opera, and opera. And Pearl Greer was a great scholar. She became a nun later. She used to give me books to read, that I should read. And I liked reading. She was another influence in my life.

For fun we swam in the Ottawa River. I was almost too fond of swimming—I used to go down and swim alone. I remember my mother shutting me in the bedroom upstairs because I nearly drowned a couple of times. "You mustn't go swim alone. You can't go." But I got out of the window of my bedroom, and got on to the roof of the kitchen and slid down and got over the fence and went down to swim again, alone.

In the 1920s when Hydro built the big power dam in Bryson, all of a sudden we had a whole influx of people, hundreds or more, engineers, and civil engineers, and everything. I would be twelve, thirteen then. Well, when these new people all came in, they came to the Anglican church where I played the organ. Now, Mother had the bearing, you know, of "being somebody." Not that she was ever above people or anything like that. I remember working in the garden this Sunday where we lived on Main Street, and one of the new ladies, a Mrs. Young, came along. Her husband was one of the civil engineers from the Hydro. She stopped and spoke to me and she said, "Who is your mother?" And I said, "We're Murrays, just common people, you know." "Oh," she said, "your mother couldn't have been common."

The next time she talked to me she asked about my father. "Who was my father?" And I said, "I haven't got one." That set her back. The next time I saw her she came over to me and she said, "The next person asks you that question, don't say you haven't got a father." She'd asked questions and found out my father was dead, but no one had ever asked me that question before and, to me, I'd never had a father.

Then we rented a bedroom in our house to a Mrs. Bennett and her husband, a civil engineer. Mrs. Bennett came in, spotted the piano and said, "Can I play?" "Oh please, please." Oh, my God! A concert pianist! "My father loved piano, so I went as far as possible with piano." And they were very wealthy, apparently, in Montreal. And that wasn't the end of it. She started to sing, but she was no ordinary singer. She was opera! In different languages! "My mother loved opera," she said. "So I went as far as possible in singing." And then she showed me, later on, letters from the Berlin Opera Company offering her fabulous sums to go to Germany to sing in the opera and when she'd refused they wrote more letters saying that they'd pay her mother to come with her. But she never went.

Can you imagine our house? Can you imagine Bryson? People used to be standing along the fence listening to the musicians playing and singing. The people from the Hydro used to come and someone would play the violin, and someone sang and, of course, I was in seventh heaven. I can remember one night asking Mrs. Bennett to play Beethoven's Sonata *Pathetique*, which I could play—but nothing like she could do. And she said, "Oh, Bill, it's a hot night and that takes so much energy." I went upstairs to bed—I guess I was a little put out—but I only got as far as the landing when she started, and she played it right to the end, and then she yelled up, "You can go to bed now, Bill."

It was wonderful. The Bennetts were there 'til we moved to Ottawa. About two years. They'd go home to Montreal on the weekends. And she was crazy about children and I remember every time there was a baby, she'd make such a fuss and the baby would start to cry. I said, "You make such a fuss, you frighten the child." She became pregnant in Bryson before she went back to Montreal. Bryson air. The sad story of her life is that after they moved back to Montreal, I got a letter from her husband saying she had died giving birth. The daughter lived, but the mother never came out of the anesthetic. I cried for a whole day.

When I moved to Ottawa, I took singing lessons, piano and singing. Then the Depression came on and I couldn't manage both.

However, when we moved to Ottawa, that's when I went to see Aunt Jenny Finnigan and I met my cousin, Frank Finnigan, and Frank and I always got along well. Isn't that funny? We were two such different people; he was a great athlete and I wasn't. I remember a funny thing that happened. I was at cousin Retta Brill's on McLeod Street and we got a phone call and Frank had run his car over something on Sussex and damaged the four wheels so that it couldn't go. There was a policeman involved, but Frank wouldn't let them touch the car. So the police phoned Retta to see if she'd come down, if she would have influence. And she took me with her. We got out of the streetcar at the corner of Sussex and we walked to where Frank was, holding up all the traffic along the street, and the police were there. I got out of the car and walked towards Frank. And what did he do? He walked right over to me and handed me the keys of the car. "Will you take the goddam thing off the road," he said. He wouldn't give the keys to the police. He wouldn't give them to anybody. Just the right person, a clan member it had to be. Yes, he was drinking.

My dad was the same, you know. He drank. And that was thrown up to me at school when I was quite young, that my father was an old drunk. I came home and I was terribly upset and I told Mother about that. To me an old drunk meant fighting in the village and lying on the street drunk. My mother said, "Oh, no. Your father wasn't like that. He did drink and drank too much, but he was a gentleman. He never raised his voice to me."

Naturally we had friends on Calumet Island and I heard lots about the old Reeder[2] mine. Mrs. Durrell was a great friend of mother's and mother used to take us children often to the Durrell farm for weeks at a time on the holidays. Mrs. Durrell used to come and stay in Bryson and later she used to come and stay in Ottawa with us.

When I used to go down to the Durrell farms, I'd see the Reeders. Then, I had an operation—I guess I must have been nearly twenty—and Mrs. Durrell suggested I go to her farm to convalesce.

And who comes to the farm but the Reeders? Mrs. Reeder had found a gold mine there, and she took a lot of money from investors and then disappeared with all of it. She left two of her nephews behind. Mrs. Durrell and her family were real friends to those boys after their mother disappeared. Somehow, those Reeder boys became very wealthy in the United States. Well, after the operation when I was staying at the Durrell farm convalescing, one morning there was a great confusion. There's a huge car in the yard, and a lot of talking. Three women and one man—Mrs. Reeder's nephew—all got out of a Cadillac, all coming to visit the Durrells, one big tall girl—one of the most beautiful-looking girls I have ever seen—and another one, rather fat and short. Fat and short was Reeder's wife and the other two were her sisters. Well, they came in to the house and I'd come down to breakfast, and we all got talking. As soon as they heard I was Bill Murray, the Reeder man said, "I remember your dad very well. He was always doing things for us. Being a blacksmith, there were things to be done at the mine all the time." So right away they took me under their wing. Everywhere they'd go, I had to go.

One day they said they were going to go to Scobie House at Norway Bay to dance. So away we went in the big Cadillac. Ontario in those days—and I guess Quebec too—was prohibition. We had one

*Scobie House in its very early days. Destroyed by fire.*

dance, and went outside where Reeder announced we would have drinks. Well, I'd had drinks before because mother wasn't quite a teetotaller, you know. She was just dead against liquor. They passed around straight whisky in a little cup as we all sat fitted into the velvet upholstery of the Cadillac. They all took little sips of straight whisky. When I took mine, I remember I ran round the car three times to get my breath. It was boot-legged corn whisky!

We went back in and I tried to dance but, my God! I couldn't manoeuvre. I went to the door but it was the wall—the door had moved. I went to open the door and it wasn't there. So finally some person took pity on me—one of the girls or the Reeder fellow—and took me outside. I was only outside for a while when I felt better and they thought I should have another one. No way was I going to have another one! They insisted I have just a little one. I took it in little sips then and drank it very slowly and went back in to the dance. That night I remember coming home in a Cadillac and I remember the Reeder fellow saying, "Oh, you Murrays got taken, too." And they wouldn't let me pay for anything.

Going back to the mine and Mrs. Reeder—I never heard of a Mr. Reeder—got all these people to invest in that mine, including my father, and the Roman Catholic Church! Mind you, there was gold in it, but there wasn't enough to pay off investors. She built this great big house and furnished it with treasures. Then they built a big wing on the side for the servants and the office, far bigger than the main house. The wing is gone now, but the main house is still there. And when she disappeared, everything was left exactly the way it was. I went through the house later on. In her bedroom, the change was still sitting on the dresser, her clothes were all hanging in the clothes closet, and the bed, and everything just as she'd walked out of it. And it stayed that way for years. For years. In fact, there was another time that I went in and saw that one of the "visitors" had fallen through the hardwood floor where it was rotten in the main hall. The mine would have to go back to 1890 because, if Dad did work for them, it would have to have been prior to his death in 1907.

When I knew the Reeder boys, they were living in New York. By then Victor had gone through World War I and become a flying pilot. After the war he had made a lot of money by taking people up in New York and running a flying school.

When I moved to Ottawa with my mother, I must have been about fourteen. I went to work in a goddam factory. Connor Washing Machines. I'd never been in a factory and wheels were going over my head and belts going past me—I thought I'd go out of my mind. And the noise was just unbelievable. My brother, Jim, got me in there. He was a mechanic and he loved it. I hated machinery. I worked in Connors with Jim for ten or twelve dollars a week. From six till six—Saturdays, too. Oh, that was a terrible place! It wasn't heated—imagine! The toilets froze. They had to put a blow torch beside them to keep the water running. The water in the machines used to freeze and you were freezing, your whole body was freezing, your hands would get numb. You weren't allowed to wear gloves because they'd get caught in the machinery. So that's probably one of my big reasons I took ill. I was completely out of my element there. Because, you see, I'd lived with mother and was very fond of music and was quite a good singer and I'd made all these friends in Bryson... That's when I was so glad to meet my cousin Retta Brill who lived on McLeod Street in Ottawa. I met her and **she played the piano**. Oh, how wonderful! My first relatives that had anything in common with me.

At Connors factory when I took sick, I went in to hospital and had an operation for a gastric ulcer. I was supposed to die, but I didn't. No penicillin, you know. I remember they gave me castor oil to drink and they told me, "If this goes through, you'll live, and if it doesn't, you won't." Uncle Joe Wall had died when I was in the hospital, and he had the same bloody thing.

I was in Dr. Cavan's private hospital on Elgin Street. I still don't know how the bills were paid. Mother wouldn't allow me to go to the Civic. Every person we knew who went to the Civic Hospital died. Everybody thought I was giving birth because Dr. Cavan's was mostly maternity cases there. The bill must have been fantastic. I have an idea my Aunt Hannah paid for it, Mrs. Clark, mother's sister. They lived in Ottawa. They had dough. They came from Bryson to Ottawa. They owned a grist mill at one time. Aunt Hannah and I got along very well. She was different from Mother and she was very careful around money too, I can tell you. She was crazy about me because they'd had five girls who nearly all died of tuberculosis, and one son my age. When I came to Ottawa, Elwood had just died, her only son. So she took me over. They were building a cottage out on the Mountain Road there and I took to Aunt Hannah like a duck takes to water. Her husband, he was one of the ones building the filtration plant in Ottawa and he worked overseeing it until he died.

Back then I think the city ended at Somerset Street bridge and then it was Hintonburg, that was really the city limits there. I remember I took up singing lessons on Sunnyside Avenue where the streetcar turned. That was the end of Ottawa. Sparks Street—that was something. The old Russell Hotel was closed, but there were still stores in the lower part of it. The Château had just been built. I was in seventh heaven when I found the Russell Theatre and people came and played—it wasn't all pictures then—live on the stage. I heard people play the piano, I heard people singing. Opera. I heard Caruso at the old Russell Theatre. I heard a good many times—what was the fellow after him that was so well-known? He was a Canadian, a great opera singer.[3] I know he was salesman for Godferson Trucks before he took lessons. He lived in Kingston. We used to go to the "gods" for twenty-five cents. And The Dumb-bells[4], and dancing. You could go to the pictures for ten cents, but I had to spend twenty-five cents to go to the Russell Theatre because the things I was interested in I'd see there. I can remember when that great Canadian singer was there. And I went to go to the gods and they were sold out. I had to pay a dollar to sit on the stage, and he turned and sang to us on the stage. Seventh heaven.

The old Russell was burnt, I think, so badly that they tore it down. They had to keep the old Russell Hotel going because the old Russell Theatre was

*Skating party at Rideau Hall, Ottawa.*

heated from it. When the Russell Theatre disappeared, there was really nothing took its place. The Capital Theatre was being built then. They would have "live" nights. It wasn't all movies. They had vaudeville part of the time. I heard some good things in the old vaudeville. Karina Thompson. She was gorgeous. She was one of the first people I heard in the Capital Theatre. She was a singer. But the old Russell was wonderful. And for sound the gods couldn't be beaten; you could hear everything, but you couldn't see what they looked like—little dots on the stage—it was five storeys up. The next person's shoes were in your back. There was no comfort at all. You could rent a cushion and take it with you. You went up a separate staircase. You didn't go in with the others. The boxes and first balconies were separate. They were all red plush. Every person there went in evening clothes.

The Russell was right across from the old station. Another street, Canal Street, ran down and another street went up and the old jail and the courthouse were in there. The Russell Hotel was right on the front and the Russell Theatre was like the continuation of the Russell Hotel. From the lobby of the Russell Hotel you could walk a catwalk over the yard and into the main lobby of the Russell Theatre. The police station was down from that and there was a wharf along the canal and a street ran along the canal, Canal Street. Boats went up and down the canal. The mail was delivered by boat when I first came to Ottawa. The post office was where the war monument is now. The boats brought the mail in and, if you walk through the tunnel there, you'll see the old entrances to the post office. Still there.

After I got out of Connor Washing Machines, I went to Murphy-Gambles. I thought I'd try the best. My mother had always said you should. My sister Mina came to Ottawa from Cache Bay with her husband, who was supposed to be worth all kinds of money, an older man. So we went to live on Carling Avenue with them and we were right up with the Joneses. And through my music, I seemed to fall in with all kinds of people all the time. One of the people who thought the world of me was Mrs.

Stothers; Perley Robertson was her brother.[5] They were titled, you know.

She influenced me to open a hot dog stand. She said, "Bill, why don't we open a hot dog stand?" So I had a hot dog stand at Hog's Back and I'd make some money on that because things were bad then, you know. Mrs. Stothers put me in touch with Edgar Knoskey. She said, "Now, he's an artist; he knows all about building hot dog stands." Knoskey was a builder in Ottawa. Highfalutin people. I met Edgar and I met his fiancée, Miss Sylvester—she was the Sylvester Flour people. We went out to Hog's Back and we started business. He designed it. A crooked house, all crooked doors and different colours and strange windows in this hot dog stand. It was really a scream because I was running a hot dog stand and, at the same time, I was going to Rideau Hall for events. Bessboroughs[6] were there then. I met the Bessboroughs—he was interested in music. I went to Rideau Hall with friends like Mrs. Stothers. I was invited to skating parties at Rideau Hall.

Business at the hot dog stand was terrible because all my friends coming out to Hog's Back took it as a joke. I couldn't possibly be doing this for money, you know. And you know what used to happen? There'd be a big party at Rideau Hall or the theatre and they'd drive out in evening clothes. Well, when they'd get to my hot dog stand, all the other people who were there left, of course. People that were really paying disappeared.

Ogilvies was good, but Murphy-Gambles was the most prestigious. I remember Walter Murray, owner of Murphy-Gambles, came to me when he knew I was there and said, "You know we must be related." He had just come from Scotland.

When I came to Ottawa there was no big rink. There was a small rink off Laurier—Dey's Arena. I remember. My brother, Jim, took me. We stood in the cold and nearly froze. Standing room only. The only reason I was interested in going was just to see cousin Frank Finnigan play. We seemed to be kindred spirits. We were also clan—very important.

During the Depression time, I went to Toronto because my sister Margaret was living there. She was married to Clinton Martin, well-off lumber people

Ottawa's Team 1926.

July    SUNDAY 15    1917
The Stars.

Alex Connell
Goal

George Boucher
Defense and Captain

Reginald "Hooley" Smith
Right Wing

Ed.F. Gorman
Defense

Frank "King" Clancy
Defense

Frank Nighbor
"Centre"

Alex Smith
Sub

Frank Finnigan
Forward

Gy. Denneny
Right wing

Subs. "Hec Kilrea    Hagan

*One of the Ottawa Senator teams Bill Murray might have seen when he went to see his cousin, Frank Finnigan, play.*

from Cache Bay and Sturgeon Falls. When he retired, they went to Toronto. They had one son the same age as I was. Now Judge Reimer had been the judge in the courthouse in Bryson. And I knew his daughter, Mrs. Smith. She had one son who was my age, Walter Smith—but we always called him Walter Reimer because she and her husband were separated—they were very wealthy people. Walter and I went to school together back in Bryson and we were always great pals. When I moved to Toronto, I got in touch with them. Well! They made the biggest fuss over me! They were living with the big shots in Rosedale, so I

was there a lot of the time. And nothing would do but they thought I should go to Upper Canada College because Walter was starting at Upper Canada College and I was his pal. They insisted. So I went and was interviewed **and** accepted. Can you imagine? I should never have allowed myself to go that far. Walter's family invited me back for games and social events. So I'm invited to afternoon lunch at Upper Canada College and who do I sit next to? Lady Bailie![7] She started talking to me about things she thought I should know about, assuming I was in the same social class as they were, and I could see Mrs. Smith, Walter's mother, jumping in to save my hide.

Of course I couldn't go to Upper Canada College. My sister Margaret's husband lost everything in the Depression, but I got myself a job, assistant to the manager at Hart House Theatre. I was in my glory, but there was a lot of all-night work. We went to different homes to rehearse sometimes because the people who were in the theatre were all connected. Lady Bailie's two sons were in a Hart House play so we were invited to their house for an evening to rehearse. I had forgotten about meeting her at Upper Canada College. I didn't want to go to Lady Bailie's. "You have to come," they said, "and take notes." (I'd gone through business college and I could take shorthand.) Well, we're all standing in the lobby of Casa Loma and Lady Bailie comes down the stairs dressed in evening clothes. Oh, she was gorgeous! And she sees me, recognizes me, comes over and talks to me. My excuse for not going was that "I wouldn't know anybody." And they all said, "So you *didn't* know anybody!"

I went back to Ottawa. First I worked on Bank Street at Collier's Candy Store, right beside the Alexander Hotel. What a job that was! I did everything. Candy and soft drinks. Like a Laura Secord's. Mrs. Collier made the soft drinks and I packed them in ice. In the basement she had these big tanks filled with water, and then you added ginger and stuff, and you put the sugar in and all the essence for ginger ale. And you brought it up in the top, and you packed those tanks in ice—there was no refrigeration.

And do you know who one of my best customers

used to be? She came and talked to me every day. Their big homes were on Metcalfe Street. She used to come in there to buy ginger ale. So one day another woman said to me, "Do you know who you're so chummy with? That's Mrs. Jackson Booth."

My mother's mother knew the Booths when they came to Ottawa years before and they peddled around Ottawa—they didn't have any money at the beginning. One of them courted my mother when she was a widow. He sent her roses, he wanted to marry her. With all her kids! My mother used to say, "I wouldn't marry again if every hair on his head was pure gold."

When I was with the Colonial Coach Lines, the Ahearns[8] used to come in there all the time. The Ahearn boys came to talk, talk, talk. Their father, Frank Ahearn, owned the Ottawa Senators. One of them flew an airplane. He was a pure ass. At Colonial Coach Lines, R.G. Perry was manager when I was

there. He came from Kingston. And R.G. Perry was a friend of that great opera singer that died, the Canadian one. He lived in Kingston, you know, and he worked for the Colonial Coach Lines before he went to study in New York.

Charles Lindbergh came to Ottawa and landed at Uplands. Everyone wanted to see Lindbergh. R.G. Perry, my boss, was a flyer and he was going to take me up, but then he couldn't. He said, "I've arranged for you to go with Booth." I wouldn't go with him. He was nuts. Do you know that he flew under the bridge going over to Hull one time? That was a favourite trick.

I went straight from Murphy-Gambles to Fisher's on Sparks Street. When I was working at Murphy's, the Fishers used to all come in there to eat, and Spud Fisher was interested in music and I used to meet him at different musical events. So when Murphy-Gambles was sold to the fellow who

*Left: Mrs. T. Frank Ahearn (the former Laura Lewis), left, and Miss Margot Fleming (later Viscountess Hardinge of Montreal) were among the Ottawa socialites who attended the Historical Ball at Quebec City, December, 1927. Mrs. Ahearn appeared as Lady Hamilton wearing blush rose chiffon with blue, and Lady Hardinge as Madame Drucour (1760) in chartreuse green taffeta. Sitting on a raised dais in the Red Room of the Legislative Council, Governor General and Lady Willingdon (as Charles the First and Henrietta) received guests, including: Sir Charles and Lady Fitzpatrick, the R.L. Blackburns, the August Tessiers, the C.G. Powers, the John Bassets, the Alexandre Tachereaus, the Donald Atkinsons, the Lemoynes and the Austin Gillies.*

*Right: J.R. Booth's daughter, Ella, married J.B. Bessey and lived in one of the many mansions along the Aylmer Road. She made the news when her visit to a Montreal oculist cost her father, The King of the Timber Barons, a thousand dollars. Photo c. turn of the century.*

married the daughter, the new owner wouldn't take me because of my age—I was closing in on seventy. I went to Fisher's and I was there until I was eighty.

Fisher's had asked me several times to come to them, but I don't like moving or doing new things. A friend of mine that I liked very much was Errol Schrim. He came over and he said, "Bill, I hear that the new people at Murphy-Gambles think you are too old—they won't take people your age." And he said, "We'd like to have you at Fisher's in the worst way." So I said, "Okay," and I just walked across Sparks Street. I never missed a beat. They tripled my salary. But no pension. I was too old for pension. I went back and worked part-time and they would have had me still. But I finally quit at eighty.

1  de Salaberry, a distinguished Quebec family going back to the eighteenth century, predominantly military but also involved in civil service and legislature.

2  For more about the Reeder (Rideau) mine on The Island, see Jerry Griffin's interview. The mine was known by both names.

3  Edward Johnson. For further details, see Greg Guthrie's interview.

4  Dumb-bells, a vaudeville group of servicemen from the Third Division of the Canadian Army, formed during the First World War. After the war's end in 1918, they toured England and North America.

5  A wealthy Ottawa family, given to philanthropy.

6  Sir Vere Brabazon Ponsonby, ninth Earl of Bessborough, Governor General of Canada, 1931-'35. R.B. Bennett was Prime Minister during Bessborough's term.

7  According to Murray, Lady Bailie was a member of a wealthy Toronto family, major supporters of Hart House Theatre.

8  The Ahearns were one of the exceptional families of Ottawa at the time. Thomas Ahearn (1855-1938) was a genius inventor and a wealthy industrialist who founded the Ottawa Electric Street Railway in 1891. His daughter married H.S. Southam. His son, Frank Ahearn, owned the Ottawa Senators in their early glory days in the 1920s.

*Bearded J.R. Booth, with his son C. Jackson Booth (left), inspects one of the last loads of white pine from Booth's Madawaska limits. C. Jackson Booth was a renowned playboy with funds to travel the continent as a "professional fan" of hockey, lacrosse, baseball, soccer, horse racing and social events. J.R. Booth died shortly after this photo was taken in 1925, age 100.*

# 5

# "For Some Obscure Reason I Always Wanted to be a Newspaperman"

## GREG GUTHRIE – Ottawa, Ontario

*When the* Ottawa Journal *was closed down in 1980, I went to Jack McClelland of McClelland and Stewart and said, "I'd like to do a book on a great newspaper's history, tape some of the journalists who gave the* Journal *its quality of excellence. If not me then somebody should." McClelland's reply was, "Nobody ever makes any money out of books about newspapers." By the time I had started to organize for this book and decided that I was going to tape people in "The Hub" as well as "The Spokes" of the Ottawa Valley, many of those great* Journal *people were gone. However, I did manage to interview Greg Guthrie.*

*Guthrie was born in Ottawa in 1914. His ancestry is Scottish and many of his ancestral ties are to the Maritimes where he often visited his mother's family, who came out from Scotland in 1814, to St. John, N.B., and Picton, N.S. His paternal ancestors also came out from Scotland generations ago.*

*Except for those periods when he went to sea as a young man and again overseas as a major in the Ontario Regiment, First Armoured Brigade, 1940-45, in the Second World War, the greatest part of Guthrie's life story unfolds in Ottawa. His interview enhances the social history of the*

*capital through layers of intertwining themes,* Journal *people, politics, hockey, with specific and sometimes hilarious stories of great characters, like the inimitable Joe Finn of the* Citizen; *first lady mayor in Canada, Charlotte Whitton; Ottawa Senators' star Frank Finnigan; politically canny George McIlraith; silver-tongued Grattan O'Leary of the* Journal; *the renowned Minnie Gordon of Queen's University; Judge Willie MacGregor of Pembroke; and, finally, Dief the Chief.*

FIRST OF ALL, I went to an Ottawa school for kindergarten children on Wilbrod next to St. Joseph's Church and, after that, I went Elmwood which was then known as Mrs. Philpotts. Then they took small boys as well as girls—I think the authorities thought the boys were a threat to the chastity of the young ladies so they re-opened it as Elmwood with a formidable principal called Mrs. Buck. She finally terminated the boys, turned it into an all-girls' school, and I went from there to Ashbury, a boys' school entirely. Dr. George Penrose Woolcome was a wonderful old fellow, founder and principal. An Anglican minister, closely resembling the bald-headed eagle, a spare man with very little hair, he always wore a clerical collar, which was about three sizes too big for him. His passion was teaching

Latin and I struggled with amo, amas, amat, but apparently I wasn't a very good student. He beat on me many times with his cane. Finally he gave up and sent a letter to my father—a very diplomatic letter—saying that he thought it was in everybody's best interests if Gregor "pursued his studies elsewhere."

Dad had played cricket with Reddy Griffith, who was the headmaster at Ridley in St. Catharines. Reddy had a reputation of "straightening out" difficult boys, so I was dispatched to Ridley. 1928. I'd be about fourteen. I followed in the footsteps of my brother George—the oldest in the family. I spent some time at Ridley quite happily, but I didn't care much for Reddy Griffith.

I wasn't a great student. I got by in History and English, things like that, but Latin and French were a lost cause, and Mathematics was hopeless. Anyway, in those days you had to have, I think, thirteen subjects in Senior Matric to get into any of the good universities. And I failed on a couple of subjects. I decided that the time had come to pursue other things. Besides, my father had died in 1929 and so it was quite a financial struggle at home being the onset of the Depression.

I came back to Ottawa and, for some obscure reason, I wanted to be a newspaperman. I went to see Harry Southam at the *Citizen*, a family friend. He was very kind to me, taking pains to point out that he was reducing the salaries of old-time employees rather than letting them go, so he could hardly hire any new hands. My father had represented the Canada Steamship Line as a lawyer. Through that connection I got a job as a deckhand on a Lake ship on an old veteran called *The Midland King*, which I joined in Toronto.

I'd always wanted to go deep sea because my mother's family had always been associated with the sea in St. John. My grandfather Smith had operated clipper ships; he was a ship chandler and a ship owner. They were United Empire Loyalists. Our common ancestor was Dr. Nathan Smith who had been the surgeon-major of Delancy's Brigade in the Loyalist Forces and they were thrown on the beach at St. John. I had an affinity for the sea. I left school at seventeen and was off to sea. I lasted about five years. I was in pretty bad shape with malaria and various other things so I came back to Ottawa.

At first I wasn't doing much and a friend of mine, Jack Gleason, started a thing called the Mayfair Film Society. Son of old John Gleason—they used to live on Delaware in The Driveway area there—and every Sunday evening we'd assemble in his apartment in the Mayfair and he would show these silent movies. Billy Baldwin—who later was a Pathfinder during World War II and got shot down—he was working at Dr. Gelder's radio station CKOY, so he had access to sound effect records and Cyril Davis set up turntables so he and Billy used to supply the sound effects to these silent movies, which were sometimes quite hilarious.

The main excuse really of the Mayfair Film Society was to get together and have a few drinks. Then Jack decided he'd start a weekly newspaper. It was just written for in-house gags, you know. He got me to write editorials for the paper attacking the "demon rum," which I wrote with great vigour and venom. I never thought anybody outside the gathering would read it. But it turned out that Walter Gilhooley of the *Journal* did. Meantime, I was despairing; I was about to go and work for Lever Brothers out in West Africa on a palm oil estate when Walter Gilhooley phoned one day and he said, "How would you like to be a reporter?" So I said, "Why not?" He said, "Come down and see Mr. Lowry at the *Journal*, he's looking for someone."

So I went down and saw Tom Lowry and the first thing I knew—I was a little staggered—I was hired as a reporter. That was in late 1938. Bill Westwick was in the sports department with Walter Gilhooley, the sports' editor. On the desk there was a chap called Boudray whose chief hobby was repairing watches and lighters. On the desk was Larry Jones—this was in the daytime—and Scotty Scott was the telegraph man and old Wilber Manchester was the district editor. George Casey, a wonderful guy, was the police reporter. Kay Dillon was there and Leslie Johnston, social page. Gratton O'Leary was an editor. And E. Norman Smith and P.D. Ross used to appear periodically—they'd come out of their hole there. And Sally Sadler was

*For close to half a century, these men were the major influences and guardians of excellence on the old* **Ottawa Journal**: *P.D. Ross, president of the* **Journal**; *E. Norman Smith, his partner and successor as Editor and President; and Tom Lowrey, Managing Editor. In 1886 P.D. Ross bought for $4,000, "mostly borrowed," a half interest in the* **Ottawa Evening Journal** *from Alexander Smith Woodburn, the original owner. In his memoir,* **Retrospects**, *Ross reported that when he joined in, the circulation of the paper was about 1,700, of which 600 were "dead-heads— namely, free papers to somebody."*

secretary; she was the watchdog who sat up in the so-called library, which nobody ever consulted. Charlie Lynch was on The Hill for the term. George Carroll Green covered City Hall. Brian White ran the *Farm Journal*, two floors down, with Mr. Henry. Alf Sykes covered Hull. Bill Ketchum was very much there, and George Prudhomme. Monty Tachereau was the photographer and Monty had an assistant called Marian Townsbury. Monty still used that powdered magnesium in a flashpan. (Instead of strobe light.) Gerry Flynn was one of the office boys, a wonderful lad who got killed in the war. A later arrival was Dave Ghent. Will McLaughlin was the theatrical editor. He was a hangover from the days when the old Russell Theatre was something to write about. He had a little cubbyhole office and he used to wear floppy felt hats and a cloak and he'd sweep into his office. He paid little attention to anybody else.

Vernon Kipp was very much there. I do remember Vernon because he was always writing spirited editorials about bad drivers, inconsiderate drivers, drinking and driving and all that. He looked

after civic stuff—City Hall and so forth. Mayor Stanley Lewis always used to drop in and consult Vernon. But Vernon had had an operation for cataracts on both eyes and he lost peripheral vision, and, fresh from writing an editorial and braying bitterly against bad drivers, he'd go down to the *Journal* parking lot, leap into his car and shoot out onto Sparks Street without looking right or left. You'd hear squealing of brakes and Vernon would drive off oblivious of the whole thing.

Well, when I went to work there I ran across an old acquaintance who was then in bad odour at the *Journal*, Joe Finn.[1] His father, D'Arcy Finn, was managing editor of the *Citizen* and he had just finished firing his son Joe for multitudinous sins. I don't know, but I'm sure he phoned Tom Lowrey and asked would he give Joe a job. So Joe came on, worked days, made himself insufferable so they moved him to nights. That didn't work out so he ended up as an assistant in the sports department. Of course, that was fatal because it gave him all sorts of spare time to think up all the tricks for which he was famous.

I was one of his first victims. I was switched to nights—Frank Williams was day city editor, Wilber Boudray was night city editor. Sunday night was a mad house because Wilber was always getting into rewriting all his district correspondence, which were all hand-written things. They paid by the inch so they were overwritten and I had to condense them. You had to rewrite these damn things for Wilber and you had to make all your calls to the district and do all sorts of rewrites and heaven knows what. Sunday night was awful.

Well, right in the middle of this chaos I got a phone call. I went into the phone booth. A man demanded the curling scores. In those days we didn't run the curling scores. He identified himself as Rochester Murgatroyd, said he was a friend of P.D. Ross's. So I happened to be sitting in the phone booth looking out and I looked over towards Westwick's desk and I saw him laughing with his hand clapped over his mouth, and a great light came on. I said, "Just a minute Mr. Murgatroyd." I left the booth and went around to the sports department. There was Joe Finn with the phone cradled in his hands. So I said something unprintable to him.

Finn perfected poor Rochester Morgatroyd into a real character that went on and on, and tormented many many people, including Wally Ward at the Canadian Press, and later Roual Mercier, Crown Attorney. Down at the courthouse, Finn would get in a wrangle with poor old Charlie Bray, in charge of wills for Carleton County, about Joe's brother's will. Charlie would try and tell Joe it was in Pembroke because he died in Renfrew County. And Joe would immediately get irate and charge Charlie Bray with drinking in the Albion Hotel. Oh, he tormented everybody—including me.

For a while I was on the police beat at night and I'd be coming back to the *Journal* about three-thirty in the morning and I'd have to duck into all the rows of exit doors in the old Capital Theatre and look up at the window of the sports department because Joe would have a whole series of water bombs waiting for me. So when I went into the *Journal*, I'd have to dash from the front door and these bombs would rain on the sidewalk. Well that was fine, no repercussions

because that early in the morning someone would clean up the mess on the sidewalk and the front steps of the *Journal*. Well, one morning E. Norman Smith arrived before the cleaners and the place was covered with Finn's water bombs—it looked like toilet paper all over the sidewalk. So that put an end to the water bombing. Joe made squares out of paper, quite ingenious, and when they came down they made quite a drencher—he was a terror.

We had a tennis correspondent called Ferd Lothian who worked at one of the government departments. He used to come in late at night with tennis scores. And Ferd was a very deliberate character, you know; put on his gloves one at a time very carefully. He had a car and he'd park it in front of the *Journal*. One time while he was in the newsroom, Joe Finn went down and put one of those torpedoes (an explosive device) on his motor. Everybody crowded to the *Journal* windows and waited to see poor Ferd Lothian leave. Ferd came down, opened his door, sat down, pressed the starter and there was a great bang and a cloud of smoke! Ferd shot out of his car like a rabbit across the street. Then he came back in and phoned a tow-truck and had the car towed away. The next time Ferd was in, Joe asked him what happened. "Well," Ferd said, "it cost me thirty-six dollars for repairs." Of course, the torpedo did no damage at all so we all knew he got taken at the garage. Joe was delighted, of course. (The torpedo was an explosive device that you attached to the top of a spark plug, and when you started the motor, it exploded. But it's just like a firecracker. It doesn't do any damage to the motor.) Joe was always going to the joke shop on Bank Street and buying all these things like itching powder. Yes, there was a joke shop on Bank Street and Joe was a patron.

*In Toronto I spoke to Helen Gougeon, a contemporary of Greg Guthrie on the* Journal *in the days when the social page was very important, and to Doug How, another journalist and author who had spent considerable time "on the Hill" with* Time *magazine and* Canadian Press. *They both added to the repertoire of Joe Finn stories.*

GOUGEON: In those days the social pages were very competitive—between the *Journal* and the *Citizen*. The editors checked every single social note in the *Citizen* and, if you didn't have it in the *Journal*, you were scooped. Well, one time the *Citizen* ran a social note which read, "Lord and Lady Taboma are resident at the Château Laurier Hotel." There was a great kafuffle in the *Journal* social department because they did not have this very important information. I was covering the hotel beat and I was supposed to pick up social items and pass them on to Kay Dillon and Leslie Johnson of the *Journal's* social pages. But I had not been told about Lord and Lady Taboma. I telephoned the Château immediately and they confirmed there was no Lord and Lady Taboma staying there.

On further investigation, it turned out that it was another Joe Finn trick. Taboma stood for "Take a bite of my ass."

That was some of his low-level humour. He was a wild man then. His son is now head of CSIS, ironies of ironies. Anyway the social pages were very very important then; people read them.

GUTHRIE: Doug How, author, journalist, and my colleague in Ottawa journalistic circles, spent time "on the Hill" as Executive Assistant to Hon. Robert Winters, then Minister of Public Works, with *Time* magazine and more extensively with *Canadian Press* in the press gallery, 1945-53. He tells some Joe Finn stories garnered from those years in Ottawa.

HOW: This was long after I was in the Press Gallery. I was back in Ottawa and Dick Jackson of the *Journal* and I found ourselves leaning up against the bar in the Press Club together, and we got talking. We'd known each other for years, and it was common knowledge that Joe Finn was a tremendous practical joker, and that Jackson had been one of his favourite targets. So that time Jackson told me this story:

1980. They had just opened the last of Mackenzie King's diaries, year by year, for thirty years. Somebody called up from *Front Page Challenge* and asked "Is there anybody around the press gallery who would have known Mackenzie King?" And

somebody said, "I think Dick Jackson must have known him, he's the veteran around here." So I said, "Sure," and they flew me to Toronto. They didn't guess who I was on TV and afterwards they all got talking to me. And Pierre Berton jumps in, of course, and says to me, "You people in the Press Gallery, why didn't you know that Mackenzie King was a nut?" And I said to Berton, "How much do we know of the private life of Pierre Elliott Trudeau? I hear stories but I have no real idea." Berton pressed on, "Did you know Mackenzie King?" "Well," I said, "I knew him the way the press does. And I used to walk my dog on Laurier Avenue and so did Mr. King and we'd meet, and we'd talk about our dogs. And that was it." So Berton said, "Were you ever in his house?" "Well— once," I said. "When was that?" Berton asked me.

So I told them this story. One Christmastime, I got this call from Mr. King's valet or butler and the voice said, "Mr. King is entertaining and he'd like you to come in for a sherry." So I said to myself, "What the heck," and I went. He couldn't have been more gracious as a host. We talked about our dogs and all around the thing without ever really saying anything much. We looked at the picture of his mother under the light. I had a sherry and left.

Until that night on *Front Page Challenge* when I had just told that story to Berton I never twigged. I got on the plane to Ottawa and was putting my seatbelt on when, all of a sudden like, like a bolt of lightning, it hit. Why had I been the only guest at Mackenzie King's that night for sherry? That bastard Finn! Finn called me up and invited me and I'd fallen for it like a . . .

King died in 1950, so over thirty years would have elapsed. I sat in that seat putting my buckle on and saying to myself, "Oh my God! That bastard Finn!"

GUTHRIE: Oh! The Belle Claire. Everybody went in there to drink. It was owned by Harry McMillan at the time, and everybody used to repair there, and some of the bachelor reporters even lived there. After the war, I remember, Danny Odette lived there. It was a fatal mistake for poor Danny because, if anybody wanted a reporter in a hurry, they'd just go next door and rush him out. But we had some great times in the old Belle Claire. Lorne Manchester was there, George Blackburn was the Pembroke correspondent.

Speaking of drink, Scotty Scott was a great friend of mine. He was a great big man, a barrel, and Scotty and I would get together, and he drank Teams Plate Rye, and Scotty'd pour a slug and open his mouth and go glug, and at this he always said, "I have to swallow it fast. I was gassed in the First War."

I remember one morning ending up with Scotty in the Belle Claire, and we were both hungover, and started drinking again, and we decided we should have a shave. So I said, "Alright Scotty, I'll shave you and you shave me." So we went into the john and shaved each other and, oh god! we both turned up in the *Journal* office with nicks all over us!

Scotty was a great one. He went to Pittsburgh, set up as a mining stock consultant and did very well for himself. One day he came back to Ottawa and he phoned me and I went down to lunch with him at the Château. I always remember, he pulled out a roll of American bills that was hard to get his hand around, of big coarse American bills. So he was doing alright for himself. I liked Larry Jones, too. He went up to Toronto and became a big wheel in the advertising business.

After my stint on the night shift, I got sent up to Pembroke, 1939, about the time of the outbreak of World War II. I applied to join the navy and I was told I could be nothing but a writer. I said, "What's a writer?" And they said, "Well, you'd write." In other words you were a clerk. So I said to hell with that. I didn't want any part of the air force because I wanted to be able to swim or run. So the next thing was the army. I consulted Bill Ketchum. And Bill knew many military people, including Colonel Topp. So I went down to see Topp and he said, "Well, we're not taking anybody now but it's bound to expand. The best thing for you to do is to join the militia." "Well," I said, "I'm up in Pembroke." "Oh," he said, "my old friend John McLaren Beattie is the colonel of the Lanark and Renfrew Scottish. No problem." So the next thing I know is I'm a second lieutenant in the Lanark and Renfrew Scottish.

John McLaren Beattie was an amazing character. He had been badly wounded in the First World War in his right arm and it was pretty well shattered. Poor John McLaren Beattie told me that he was convalescing and he got a permit to go to Ireland in 1916. He was in Dublin, coincidental with the Easter Uprising, and John McLaren Beattie had gone down to the post office to mail a letter when the Easter Rebellion broke out and John McLaren Beattie was caught in the post office. He'd pretty well shattered his arm there and he could barely raise it. He could raise it just by willpower enough to salute. When the second war broke out, he tried to get back in the forces. He had to have a medical exam and, of course, they turned him down. One night in the mess we were having a drink and he showed me the X-rays—the original ones from the war—and all you could see between the elbow and the shoulder was a mass of fragments and the modern ones showed just a thin line of bone where it had re-knitted.

Willie McGregor[2] was the magistrate in Pembroke, a character of the first order. He would deal very leniently with the ordinary people who came up, but, if anyone broke the game laws, he'd throw the book at them. One very amusing incident occurred involving Deavitt, the embalmer for Malcolm, the Protestant undertaker in Pembroke. Deavitt was an inveterate poacher. He loved to fish

*Greg Guthrie's tank crew, Italian campaign, 1944, World War II. Padre Smith, Pete Jamieson, Jake Slinger, Tank-Commander Guthrie.*

and hunt, but he would never do it in season. One time he went up to Chalk River to pick up a body. Coming back at night through the Petawawa area it was dark, and nobody was around, and he thought this was a great time to jacklight a deer. He always carried his equipment. So he drove off the road in among the pine trees. He came to a glade, set up the spotlight and sure enough he nailed a deer and shot it. He was just loading the deer into the hearse with the body when he was surrounded by game wardens. What he hadn't realized was that the area game wardens had been holding a meeting at a lodge just a few trees away, and when they heard the shot, they ran to it.

Well! poor Deavitt! Deavitt was the president of the Fish and Game Club. The next day he was to have one of the biggest funerals ever held in Pembroke—Senator White, descendant of the founder of Pembroke. What was poor Deavitt to do? He's under arrest. They've impounded his hearse—with the body! They brought him up on charges before Willie McGregor but, to handle the White funeral, he had to go and beg the loan of a hearse from the Catholic undertaker, Neville. Poor Deavitt, he never lived that down. Years after the war when I wasn't in the newspaper business anymore, I was up in Pembroke and I went to see Deavitt, my old friend. He has this magnificent new establishment up on the back street and he said, "Would you like to see my new hearse?" So I said, "Sure." We went out to a very big garage, and the beautiful new Cadillac hearse was there. And I looked over in the corner and there was a tarpaulin hanging up covering something. I said, "That wouldn't be a deer would it?" Deavitt went and pulled the tarpaulin aside and sure enough there was a deer carcass hanging there. So I said, "You're up to your old tricks." "Nothing's changed" he said.

Johnny Johnston was the *Citizen* correspondent in Pembroke at the time. He was the son of the Crown Attorney. We got on very well together. I lived in the Copeland House in the bachelor wing with various Hydro workers and RCMP. Mrs. Roy ran it, and it was wonderful. Another bachelor was old Jack Campbell. He was in charge of vehicle

licences. A war veteran, he'd lost an eye and he was pretty well shot up—the hip, the stomach and the leg. He was in very bad shape. And he used to pretty well live on gin. He was a wonderful guy and most helpful to everybody—sort of "the father" of the bachelor wing. The Copeland was a great experience.

Then, as Colonel Topp had predicted, things livened up in the spring when the Germans invaded France. They called up the established 4th Infantry Division and, of course, everyone was clammering to be part of it. The Footguards were mobilized in Ottawa, but the Lanark and Renfrew were told to send a company. So, lo and behold, I found myself as part of the Lanark and Renfrew Company that went to the Footguards. That's how I got in the army. After the war I came back to the *Journal*.

I came back in October and went to see Tom Lowry. I was talking to Tom when a girl called Betty Fraser from the social department came in—almost in tears—and she said, "Mr. Lowry, there's a man in the library who says he's going to commit suicide." So Lowry—he's accustomed to these weirdos who came in—he said, "Well, you go and tell Leslie Johnston to talk to him." Leslie went out and talked to him. Subsequently the guy left. I'd passed him on the way in. Didn't pay very much attention to him. It turned out it was Igor Gouzenko on his first visit to the *Journal*!

Gouzenko came back that night and met Chester Froud, "the man in the green eye-shade." And who else . . . oh, God! there were several others I should remember. Sydney Checkland. Sydney had come from Britain and Sydney was rather strange. He always wore high, starched, stiff collars and tie and a bowler hat that was so old it was sort of greenish, and he was a master of Pitman shorthand and he took everything down at great length and transcribed. Well, most of what he transcribed was consigned to the waste paper basket—he was doing a real-estate column.

After the war things had changed quite a bit. I also remember the night editor before the war was Dave Adamson. The presses then were in the basement. Later they built that extension that took

*Under the arch and to the left, the overhead sign for the old Copeland Hotel where Greg Guthrie and Joe Finn stayed on assignment in Pembroke, and where Judge Willie MacGregor once drank. Destroyed by fire in the 1980s.*

part of the parking lot and it ran out to Queen Street, but before the war they were in the basement. The ground floor—you went up steps and there was a great glass thing and that was the business office—the classified, I think, was on the right side. On the second or third floor, Joe Phillips was head of advertising—they had a floor to themselves. The business manager at the time was Colonel Parkinson and he had an office that overlooked Queen Street. And the switchboard was just inside of that. The British Pension Committee was on one of the floors. The *Farm Journal* was on one floor and then the editorial on the sixth floor. The composing room was on the seventh floor. The building inspectors were always after the *Journal* you know, because of the weight on the seventh floor. It should logically have been in the basement. Old Phil Maloney was the stereotype I remember—they were a great bunch in the composing room. They were a breed apart. Gratton O'Leary used to come in late at night and hob-nob with Leslie and Kay. He usually brought a bottle with him. He was in the sports department then and he was always betting with the sports department and he would always choose the underdog. Particularly if he had an Irish name, he'd bet on it. And he usually lost. Of course, Bill Westwick, head of the sports department, knew what was going on.

One of the most harrowing experiences I ever had at the *Journal* was the Judge Madden case. The papers never covered divorces in those days. Judge Madden was a county judge whose wife was going to divorce him and, against all judicial and legal advice, he decided to contest it. E. Norman Smith called me in—I was doing the courthouse then. Opposite Joe Finn—Joe had gone back to the *Citizen* by then; he'd been reinstated. E. Norman said, "I want you to cover this, write running copy, and send it to me by office boy, and I'll edit it." I thought, "Oh, God! Even my mother can't read my handwriting," and writing running copy is no picnic. Anyway, I'd scratch off the court proceedings, send it out and they'd splash it all over the front page of the *Journal*. Somebody told me that it sold a thousand extra copies in Pembroke alone. I never did find out why

they decided to cover Judge Madden's divorce—it was quite unprincipled in that day. They ran the results of a court case every month or so, but a divorce!

The only other time I had to write running copy was in Belleville in a police inquiry—which was quite funny. There was a disgruntled provincial policeman who'd left the force and brought charges against an inspector. Judge Peter McKay was named to head the inquiry, which was held in Belleville. I went down and had to do running copy for the *Journal* and Joe Finn was there writing running copy for the *Citizen*. I ended up having to write both for the *Citizen* and for the *Journal* because Joe took off chasing a girl. He'd say, "Cover for me." This happened again on a murder up in Pembroke when Joe was overtaken with booze . . . it was a wonderful opportunity because all the things I wanted to write for the *Journal* and knew they wouldn't print, I wrote for the *Citizen*.

The *Journal* was a better paper by far. They had better staff, better people at the top in the sense of editors. Gratton and E. Norman were unsurpassed as editors and they demanded the highest standard and they got it. You had to be very careful with addresses, names, initials. A correction was a major event in those days. The wrath came down from the top.

After the war, the *Journal* had really exceptional people. Helen Gougeon was another character. They called her Millie Slop Cabbage. Tommy Little gave her the name—I don't know why—but it stuck. My first encounter with Millie was when I came back from overseas and we came in on the Catherine Street line—there used to be a station right at the Bank Street subway there. I got off the train and went to Lansdowne Park. There was a reception and who turned up but Helen "Millie Slop Cabbage" Gougeon and Tom Van Dusen. So, Millie interviewed me. That was the first time I saw her. Oh God, she was a wonderful girl!

I remember we'd come back from covering something with maybe a little too much to drink and Millie would type our story for us. I always remember, too, Tommy Little had a boat called the *Undine*. One night, we were cruising down the

Ottawa River and everybody went swimming. Little got hold of Helen's panties and when we came back up the river her black silk panties were flying as a flag from the masthead. This was on the Ottawa River. Tommy brought the *Undine* into Ottawa on the Rideau Canal, and he used to dock it at the foot of Fifth Avenue. I remember Bill Walsh leapt off the *Undine* with a line one night and went into the water beside this dock. Danny Odette was there and reached down and pulled him up. So we teased Danny. We were going to put him in for the Dow Award[3] for heroism.

The *Undine* was named after a water sprite in Greek mythology. It had been built originally for the Coristine lumber people down on the lower St. Lawrence. It was a great boat but, by the time Little got it, it looked like a rundown slaver.

It was quite an undertaking coming through the Rideau Canal locks. One time when we were on the Ottawa, Bill Walsh, Tom Little and I decided to go on a holiday. Little went down by car and he was going to meet us at Ile Perrôt. And Bill Walsh and I went down on the *Undine*. When you come through the locks, there's a cement buttress that forms a channel and the *Undine* was coming down to make the turn into the channel, and Little threw it into reverse, and the clutch slipped, and it didn't go into reverse, and it kept ploughing on, and we hit the cement. That was fine, no damage apparent. The next day we were out in the middle of Lake St. Louis just lying in the sun and, all of a sudden, Bill Walsh said, "I hear water." So we went down and God! the water was floating the floorboards! So we got back to Ile Perrôt and pulled into a dock and a fellow said, "Well, the best I can do is put pumps in her." So he pumped it all night, and there had been a lot of damage, and all the marinas and dock yards were filled. This fellow couldn't handle it, so he said, "Go on down towards Lachine and see if someone there can help." We're merrily going down the St. Lawrence when we see the Royal St. Lawrence Yacht Club. Little said, "We'll pull in here." So we pulled in, and the *Undine*—well, it looked as I said like a slaver, dirty and unkempt—when we pulled in, this man says, "You can't dock here." Bill said, "Let's

speak to somebody in charge." We put a line out and we're bobbing alongside the dock when this very dignified man in a blue blazer and a Panama hat comes down. He looks at the *Undine* and says, "I know that boat. I used to own that, but it wasn't in that condition." And he turfed us out. Apparently he'd built it as a beautiful yacht. He was the commodore of the Yacht Club or some such.

So we pushed off and went further down till we came to a boatyard and the man there said, "The best I can do for you is pull it out and put a temporary patch on." When he pulled it we could see the great hole at the bow. The best he could do was put heavy canvas over it and seal it with tar. We set off to go back up the Ottawa. Going up across the Lake of Two Mountains there was a strong wind blowing and the waves were battering on the bow right where the patch was. I thought, "Oh, God! I just want to get home," and I turned around and there was Little lifting the floorboards and trying to tie them together! Anyway, we survived and got the *Undine* back. I don't know whatever happened to her.

But I often think of that *Journal* staff after the war: Tommy Van Dusen, Steve Franklin— "Gentleman Steve"—Bob Blackburn, Dick Jackson on the desk. John Dalyrimple and Ainsley Kerr—oh, God! there were so many good, good newspapermen! They gave the *Journal* its status. But they were underpaid. I find it ironic that the *Journal* would demise and the *Citizen* would survive. A sad commentary. I can't remember the salaries. It wasn't very much. I always remember when the guild came in and set the target at two hundred a week, and it seemed astronomical then.

Hockey was major in those days. A goalkeeper I remember was Alec Connell. He was a wonderful man, secretary of the fire department. I used to go in and pass the time of day with him. He was always full of fun and oh, there were a lot of them, like old King Clancy. He used to come back in the summer and work for an Ottawa paving company, and I remember one day with Joe Finn talking to Clancy when he was overseeing a job down in front of the courthouse. He was as happy there making pavement as he was in Maple Leaf Gardens.

*A kitchen party with "Journal talk," c. 1950s. L to R: Tony Cyr, Greg Guthrie, Tony Wright, Dick Jackson, Tom Van Dusen.*

*Journalists gathered for a press conference in the Press Gallery, c. 1950. L to R: Paul Paradis,* **Le Soleil;** *Tom Van Dusen,* **Ottawa Journal;** *Norman Dowd, —Mosher, —Hall, John Leblanc, Canadian Press; Bob Neilsen,* **Toronto Star.**

Senator star Frank Finnigan moved from the Ottawa Senators to the Toronto Maple Leafs to be on the first Leaf team to win the Stanley Cup. Here are the 1931-32 champions: Charlie Conacher, Frank Finnigan, Hap Day, Conn Smythe, Dick Irvin (coach), Frank Selke (business manager), Ace Bailey, Bob Gracie. (Back) Tom Daly (trainer), King Clancy, Andy Blair, Red Horner, Lorne Chabot, Alex Levinsky, Joe Primeau, Busher Jackson, Harold Darragh and Baldy Cotton.

This is a story that I attribute to Bill Westwick. Clint Benedict, a great goalie for the old Ottawa Senators, was known to take a drink now and then. Before the game. After the game. And sometimes even during the game. One night at the Auditorium, he was leaning with his elbows on the net, as he used to do, and the play was at the far end of the ice and Clint's standing there watching the play lackadaisically. Well! That happened to be the very night that a real earthquake hit Ottawa! The Auditorium was built half on one type of soil and half on clay. Only half of the building was affected. Clint's end of the rink wasn't affected. But, as he was looking down the ice, the far end of the ice and all the players started to ripple. Bill said that Clint swore off drink then and there—forever.

I remember Dey's Arena. Actually you went in off Laurier and you walked across a kind of bridge into the top of the arena and then you went down into the seats from there.

I remember Hec Kilrea and Cy Denenney and I have a great Frank Finnigan story. One day I was sent down to Hulse and Playfair to cover the funeral service of Bishop R.C. Horner's wife. R.C. had established the Standard Church, The Holy Rollers. So, the room was very crowded, and it got quite agitated. It became quite fervent with yelling hallelujahs! rolling and jumping, and various other things. The whole thing got a little much, so I went out into the hall to have a smoke and who did I meet there but another refugee—Frank Finnigan. His wife was a Horner from Shawville, a descendant of R.C. Horner, and Frank had attended through a strict sense of duty, but he obviously didn't want any part of what was going on in the funeral parlour. So we hid out and chatted in the hall for quite a while, while the hallelujahs rang out. I never forgot that.

Well, my next encounter with the Horners was, of course, when I was up at Parliament Hill and ran into the Horners from Alberta, the "Western

Horners." But they all had a strong attachment for the people in the Valley. Out West there was Jack, and the good doctor and then the father, Senator Horner. But then they elected from North Battleford, I think, Albert Horner, and he was a wonderful soul. He was a huge man and Jack Horner told me Albert's proudest boast was that he could lift the rear of a loaded hay wagon. And looking at Albert I could well believe it. Albert was a very gentle soul—compared to the other Horners.

I'd known George McIlraith for years and we always used to kid about "Captain George." He was the Captain of the 2nd Battalion of the Foot Guards during the Second World War and he did a great many favours for the regiment because he was a very influential politician, behind the scenes. He never was in the limelight. But he was a very competent

*Greg Guthrie as Commander of Escort to the Colours, Trooping the Colour, Coronation Day, June 2, 1954.*

man. He appeared to be very dry and sort of staid, but he wasn't. He had a great sense of humour, very keen insight about his fellow yeomen.

McIlwraith story. George was running Liberal in his usual constituency of Ottawa West and the Tories put up a doctor, very prominent and very popular and given quite a good chance to beat George. The day before the election, Gratton O'Leary, a great supporter on the *Journal*, and naturally for the Tory candidate, engineered a picture of the doctor and his wife going to the polls to vote. Now the doctor happened to live out of the riding in a rather magnificent mansion. The picture showed the doctor and his wife swathed in a mink coat coming down the front steps of the mansion to vote. And of course, this cost the doctor dearly. George triumphed by a substantial margin. Ottawa West in those days was largely a working-class place. This just reinforced the fact that the doctor was prosperous and lived out of the riding in Rockcliffe.

I was covering City Hall when Charlotte Whitton arrived with Greg Connelly of the *Citizen*. We used to have great sport with Charlotte because Charlotte was a master at innuendo. I remember she was running against George Nelms and she came in one morning, and Greg and I went in to see her, and she said, "Isn't it awful?" I said, "What?" And she said, "What people are saying is just terrible." I said, "What?" She said, "They're saying that George Nelms can't have children. That's why he adopted them." Of course, it was obvious it wasn't the others—it was Charlotte who had planted the rumour to begin with. She was the greatest little alley fighter that you ever saw, but she was a very peculiar woman in that, if she wasn't fighting with someone, she was dull and listless. If she was fighting two or three people, she was at the top of her form. She just loved contesting things.

I always remember when the Queen was going to open the new bridge down on Sussex. There was a contractor, Harvey McFarland, a very celebrated character, and Harvey was about the same height as Charlotte, about the same build. Anyway they arrived down on the site and Charlotte was in her robes, and she's bustling around arranging this and that, and Harvey's there beaming in his best suit, and all of a sudden Charlotte looks up and she sees a great big sign "Built by McFarland Construction," which was sure to catch the camera's eye. She strode over and said, "Harvey McFarland, you son-of-a-bitch! Get rid of that sign!" Harvey had to have the sign taken down.

Paul Tardiff told me that, when he was first elected comptroller and she was elected mayor, they had a sort of preparatory meeting before they took office. Nobody knew anybody else, and they all walked in and he said Charlotte started the proceedings by telling them one of the most obscene jokes he'd ever heard. They were left gasping.

She and Paul carried on a feud very publicly, but behind the scenes, whenever they wanted anything done, they agreed on it, and it went through because the rest of the council were negligible quantities—Paul and Charlotte ran the whole damn thing.

Charlotte had a phenomenal memory—one of those photographic memories—and we were talking to her one day about that case in Alberta when she was tried for criminal libel because of something or other she'd said about child care. And she started to recite this passage from the Criminal Code, and we looked at her sort of sceptically and she said, "If you don't believe me," and she called into the lawyers' office next door and had Tremeear's Criminal Code

*The head table for the annual Press Club Ball, Ottawa, 1952: John G. Diefenbaker, MP; Charlotte Whitton, Mayor of Ottawa; Hon. Ross MacDonald, Speaker of the House; Norma Guthrie, Mrs. MacDonald, Greg Guthrie, President of the Ottawa Press Club.*

brought in, and turned to the passage, and we read it. And it was word for word what she'd said!

I remember listening to her addressing, of all people, the Engineering Society. It was in the ballroom of the Château and she spoke about the history of the Outaouais. That was the first time I heard her popularize the name Outaouais. She spoke for about an hour-and-a-half and you could have heard a pin drop. She was fascinating.

One more about Charlotte. At the old Exhibition Grounds—Herb McIlroy was running it—and there was a lady there Violet—I've forgotten her last name—an elderly lady who worked in the office and she was chatting with me one day and she said, "Oh I remember Charlotte Whitton. I'll never forget her." I said, "Why?" "Well," she said, "we were playing hockey, I was playing for Pembroke and she was playing for Renfrew and she boarded me and fractured my skull." That's our Charlotte. And she boarded many other people afterwards.

Another time was when I was president of the Press Club and we were having the Press Club Ball, Charlotte was invited and she didn't have an escort. So she asked a bachelor—John Diefenbaker—to be her escort. She got John, poor unsuspecting John, and she said to him, "I'll pick you up. I have the car." Dick Jackson of the *Journal* got hold of this story and he ran a story on the front page, "You send the flowers, I'll bring the Caddie," or something like that. But old John sat through it. I have a picture of the head table.

Following my experiences attempting to unionize the newspapers, I decided I wanted a new job. There was a vacancy on the Diefenbaker staff for an Economist Class Five—that's the top economist, so I went through the Gazette as an Economist Class Five. I got letters from people all over that said, "I can't believe it. You can't add two and two and get four, and you're posing as an economist." Yes, I went to work for Dief and on my way up to the Parliament Buildings I met Jim McCook coming down. So I told him I was going to work for Dief. Jim said, "Oh, God! he's impossible to work for." Well, it turned out to be the smartest thing I ever did. I had a ball.

One day Dief and I were talking about conventions and other things. I said, "Well, I must tell you, Mr. Diefenbaker, if I'd been a delegate at that convention, I wouldn't have voted for you." Well, of course, the Chief never let a thing like that rest. He had to retaliate. He said, "Oh! Did I ever tell you about the Winnipeg convention when your Uncle Hugh Guthrie ran for the leadership?" I said, "No." He said, "Well, he was the odds on favourite. He drew first place as speaker."

Of course, the party in those days was named what it had been when Sir John A. named it—the Liberal Conservative Party. My uncle, of course, had started life as a Liberal and went over to the Union with Sir Robert Borden on the conscription issue, and he stayed. So the Conservatives always looked askance at Uncle Hugh because he'd once been a Liberal.

"Guthrie got up at the leadership convention," the Chief said, "and he started off with that magnificent voice of his. `This is the greatest convention of the great Liberal party.' "Of course," Dief said, "that was his death knell." So I said, "I get the message, Chief." Oh, God! he was funny! But he would never let something pass without retaliating.

Dief had an encyclopedic knowledge of sport. And he was like Gratton O'Leary. He always picked the underdogs. Marjorie Mulvihill, who's now a senator was then a secretary there, and he always called her "The Irish Girl." He came from Saskatchewan and she, of course, was an Ottawa Rough Rider supporter. Whenever Saskatchewan played Ottawa they'd have a bet.

I remember one time in Winnipeg we arrived and got in the suite, and the Chief went into the bedroom to change his shirt and he said, "Turn on the set and get the baseball game." I turned on the set but I hadn't a clue about baseball. The Chief said, "Who's playing?" I said, "I don't know." So he came to the door and listened and heard some names and he said, "Oh, that's so-and-so, and that's so-and-so pitcher, and his run average is so-and-so." He knew the whole damn thing. Amazing. And he knew boxers. They'd invite him out to the Civic Centre to watch on the big screen the big prize fights. He always bet on Mohammed Ali. He liked him. Dief could have made a fortune as an actor. If he was telling a story he would play the parts, and he had some hilarious legal stories.

I remember one he told me. Before Alberta was a province, the magistrates were chosen more for their local standing than for their legal knowledge. A Hudson Bay man called Magistrate Squirrel was presiding at the court when apparently some local had taken a boat and hadn't bothered to ask the owner's permission. So the Northwest Mounted Policeman looked up in his book the charge for taking a ship without the owner's consent—piracy. So the police charged the thief with piracy and Magistrate Squirrel said, "How do you plead?" The fellow said, "Yeah, I took it, sure. Guilty." So Magistrate Squirrel said to the officer, "What does the Criminal Code say the penalty is?" "Death," the officer replied. Magistrate Squirrel said, "You're hereby sentenced to death, and sentence is suspended." And Dief said that the first act of the Alberta legislature when it was formed as a province was to rescind that law.

He also had a very wide knowledge of human nature! Nothing ever staggered him about what humans could do, one to the other. This myth that he was so straight-laced was pure nonsense. In his legal practice, he'd run across every form of perversion. Any ex-service man could do no wrong as far as he was concerned. He'd protect them as best he could.

I often think of my father now. He was a lawyer. He went to McGill and Osgoode Hall and he was at the University of Toronto, too. He came from Guelph and his brother, Hugh, was the politician— he became minister of this and that. But Dad decided to set up practice in Ottawa. He came about 1902, I believe, and settled here. He met my mother when he was at Osgoode Hall. My mother went to school at Miss Neill's in Toronto and that was where they met. My father was an avid gardener and I can remember as a small boy being taken with him. He'd hire a taxi and we'd set off and go out in the country and tramp in the woods and he'd dig up jack-in-the-pulpits and God knows what—things I never knew of, and bring them back, and plant them. But he also had a huge garden down in St. Andrews and took great care of that. Loved it. Strangely enough, he was also a poet; he wrote five or six books of poetry. He published originally under the name John Creighton—I guess he thought it was unseemly for a lawyer to be a poet. He was a great friend of Duncan Campbell Scott.[4] They used to bowl together out at the country club on the Aylmer Road. He wrote a small book about that other Canadian poet, Archibald Lampman.[5] But I remember Duncan Campbell Scott coming to our house. He was a great authority on the Indians.

Also one of Dad's great friends was—they'd gone to school together in Guelph—was Edward Johnson[6], the Metropolitan tenor. When he used to sing at the old Russell Theatre, he'd come up for dinner. Not long before he died, when George Drew was in Stornaway, Edward Johnstone came to stay there and we were invited down to see him. We had a very nice time discussing old times. But George Drew had articled in my grandfather's law office in Guelph. George had commanded a battery of artillery in the First War and he was pursuing my cousin Cissie with intent to marry, but he was beaten out by Eric Irwin who was an officer in his battery. She married him, but there was a sort of connection there. I always knew George and I liked him.

Strangely enough, I recently received a letter from a man, a retired professor at the University of Toronto, called McGregor and he wrote and asked did I have any connection to Norman Gregor Guthrie? I said I was his son, and he wrote back, sent me a copy of my grandfather Guthrie's account of his ancestors arrival in Canada, from Edinburgh.

My great-grandfather and his wife set off for America with their three daughters and two boys. On the voyage, the mother and father, one girl and one boy died of typhus or cholera. So the two girls and my grandfather were taken in by their mother's brother, a McGregor, a lawyer in Toronto. He was raised by the McGregors and studied law and became a lawyer and settled in Guelph and that part of my story I hadn't known anything about. I knew Mother's side from way back, but I'd always puzzled about the Gregor and McGregor in the family because my sister's name was Katherine Gregor

Guthrie and my oldest brother was George Gordon McGregor Guthrie.

Mother's family were Gordons from Pictou, and my other brother's name was John Leslie Cameron. Mother's Gordon connection's gone now from Pictou. But they used to drop by in at St. Andrew's, Minnie Gordon[7] from Queen's University and her brother Alec—Alec was a Presbyterian minister in Quebec City of all places, he had the old garrison church—he'd been in the First War as a padre, he got the MC, too. Alec was funny and Min was a professor of English. Well, she'd pick up Alec and they'd drive down to St. Andrew's. I remember one day they arrived in this blue roadster, and the rumble seat was up, and they had two strings from the windshield to the back of the rumble seat and the laundry was hanging on it. It looked like a gypsy caravan!

I always remember one time we sat down—the whole family for a meal—and my brother George

*For over seventy years the Journal was delivered to mailboxes in the remote corners of the Ottawa Valley, in this case the Swisha (Des Joachims.) These Journal boxes are now collectors' items.*

had put a whoopee cushion under Min. Well, she struggled, and she couldn't get off it, and the more she struggled, the more it went off. I thought she was going to die laughing. There were tears streaming down her face. She thought it was the greatest thing that ever happened, in fact, I think she took the whoopee cushion with her. But, God! she was a character! I loved Min.

Minnie Gordon was something else. Of course, her father, Black Dan Gordon, was first president of Queen's. That's when it was a Presbyterian college and he had St. Andrew's church when Sir John A. was prime minister. But Black Dan was a character because he went through the famous Pictou Academy, graduated at thirteen. They put him on a stagecoach to Halifax. He got on a ship and went to Edinburgh and he didn't come back until he was an ordained minister, something like seven years later. I thought, how many thirteen-year-olds nowadays would take off like that? They might take off, but not with intent.

On one side of my family there was quite a religious tendency—one was a Presbyterian minister and he had a Presbyterian church on Elgin. He liked the ladies, but he ended up with a big church in Baltimore. John Gordon and his wife were killed in some kind of an accident, and Cissie, their daughter, came to live with us in Ottawa. She was married from our house—I remember that 'coz I was the page— about eight I was—and I was done up in a Scottish outfit—the whole kit and caboodle. The old church they were married in was taken over by the Little Theatre. It stood on the corner of Besserer and something, and then it burned. Anyway, I always remember cousin Cassie's groom, Eric Irwin. He'd just come back from the war, and he was in uniform and he had these magnificent riding boots and britches and the Sam Browne and all. He had a great moustache; he smelt of Scotch whisky and leather and tobacco. Wonderful.

Another reporter at the *Journal* before the war was Charles Ivors Lynch and he wrote a column from Parliament Hill. After the war, he became city editor. He was given to roaring and ranting. And I remember old Wilbur Manchester—grouchy old guy but I got on all right with him on the *Journal* before the war—Wilbur had been a railway telegraphist in the southern States and he came to the *Journal* as a telegraphist when the news used to come in by key. There was a little room behind the city desk where he still had his key, and then he got into that from the teletype room where the teletypes were. Of course, teletypes put him out of business but he still had his key and every Saturday he used to come in to run a wire from the bookies. He used to get the race results from all over the States, and everywhere, and pass them on. He was a funny old guy. He had stomach trouble and he had some wild green mixture that he used to drink and he had an old coffee mug which he got from the Uwanta Luncheon (it was a *Journal* hang-out, corner Bank and Queen, across from the Capital Theatre). One of those solid china things and it was just coated with this green mixture—he never rinsed it out—and he'd pour this dollop and mutter to himself. But he was absolutely amazing. I watched him at the key one day and the messages were coming in on the key and he was rolling a cigarette for himself as he'd finish—put it in his mouth, light it, and then he'd catch up. He was quite incredible. And sending—he was just lightning! Then he'd come out and sit down with the District Editor who had the weirdest assortment of correspondents from all over the Ottawa Valley, from Merrickville to Mattawa, oh, some of them were wild. They were paid by the line, so they would pad everything. The annual Strawberry Festival in Richmond would run to about three columns, and Wilbur would be muttering away to himself. . .

1 For more Joe Finn stories, see the Joe Gorman interview.

2 Judge Willie MacGregor of Pembroke, a renowned Ottawa Valley character. He appears also in the interviews with Roy Wilston and Roy MacGregor, nephew of the memorable judiciary.

3 A newspaperman's joke, referring to Dow's Lake.

4 Duncan Campbell Scott, 1862-1947, along with Charles G.D. Roberts, Bliss Carman and Archibald Lampman, was one of the major figures in "The Confederation Era" of Canadian poetry. An administrator in the Department of Indian Affairs for over fifty years, he was known for his wisdom and humanity. The house where he lived and worked on Lisgar Street in Ottawa has been torn down, but there is a memorial plaque on the edifice erected at the site.

5 Archibald Lampman, 1861-1899. After his premature death, Duncan Campbell Scott published The Memorial Edition of Lampman's poems.

6 Edward Johnson, internationally renowned Canadian tenor, born at Guelph, 1878, died there in 1959. He made his operatic debut in Padua, Italy, in 1912. After three years at the Chicago Opera, in 1922, he went to the New York Metropolitan Opera where he remained for thirteen years. Bill Murray heard Johnson at the Russell Theatre in Ottawa when he was on a Canadian tour.

7 Wilhemina "Minnie" Gordon, daughter of first principal of Queen's University, Daniel Miner Gordon. She taught in the English Department at Queen's for forty years and, long after her retirement, was one of the colourful characters on the streets of Kingston driving her vintage roadster according to her own traffic rules.

# 6

# "We Should Have Separate Roads for the Transport Trucks"

### ROY WILSTON – Pembroke, Ontario

*In the process of recording the history of the Ottawa Valley through its lumbering saga, I had very specifically sought out the people or the descendants of those who had been involved in that major industry: shantymen, river bosses, river drivers, tallymen, lumber camp cooks, timber barons, camp clerks, teamsters. But I was missing one of the people with one of the most dangerous jobs of all—driving the huge lumber trucks loaded with tons of logs down the narrow lumber roads out of the bush to the next part of their journey to market. Then someone told me about Roy Wilston of Pembroke. However, when I went to tape him, as so often happens, not only did he tell me marvellous stories of his days as a lumber truck driver, but he went on to regale me with tales of his later days as an OPP officer in Renfrew County, of the unforgettable Judge Willie McGregor, local magistrate (who also turns up in Greg Guthrie's life story and Roy McGregor's interview), of poaching in Algonquin Park, of bootlegging back of Killaloe. Although Roy Wilston was born in the Muskoka area in 1918, his life story was embedded in the Ottawa Valley where he died in 1994, a few years after I had taped him in Pembroke where he was living with his wife, the former Margaret Sewell, originally from the Temiskaming area.*

MY GRANDFATHER TOM MURPHY—I know he was Irish with a name like Murphy—he was a coal miner and he came over here and worked as a timekeeper in the Ottawa Valley lumber camps. I remember him vaguely; a nice old gentleman. But I was so very young. I remember more of my father's father, Joseph Wilston, a postman in England, a justice of the peace there and, by trade, a wheelwright and a carpenter. But he always had the hankering to be a pioneer. That's why he came to Canada. With three jobs on the go, he couldn't make enough money to raise his family back in England.

Back in England, they were advertising Canada was this, that, and the other, getting the people to come over and go out West. I think my grandfather chose Muskoka from reading brochures and papers. He settled in Hamilton when he first came over and, as I said, he was a carpenter, but the wages were so low he couldn't see any life there at all. Another thing that decided him was the free land in Muskoka. He cleared so many acres of ground and built a log house, twenty by forty, and was on that for five or six years and then he got his deed to a hundred acres. He also did work for one of the lumber companies, keeping their dams in repair. All the logs then came out of Algonquin Park down the Big East River. Later, the hemlock was taken out; they took the pine out first. I was born and raised on a farm just north of

Shaw trucks. The Maclachlins, Gillies, Gilmores, Barnetts, and other major players in the lumbering trade have disappeared from the Valley scene, but minor companies like the J.S.L. McRae Lumber Company of Whitney and the Shaw Lumber Company of Pembroke have survived. The first John Shaw arrived at Lake Doré in Renfrew County in 1847 and last year his descendants, Herb Shaw and Sons Limited, celebrated a one-hundred-and-fiftieth anniversary.

Huntsville and when I was about eighteen I left there. I worked with my dad on the farm and in the bush and in the lumber camp. It was the Muskoka Lumber Company and they had limits in Algonquin Park. I couldn't see any future in that for me, so I got into driving log trucks. I logged out of Algonquin Park and they used to run three trucks a night into Huntsville. A rough life, but very interesting.

Almost every section of bush they logged out would have one terrific hill, eh? A long, long sand hill. And they used to have a young lad, or an old fellow, whose job it was to build a huge fire and they put an iron plate over it; then they put earth on top of that and that burned all the moisture out of that sand so that there was absolutely no moisture in that sand at all. And that's what they spread on the hill to hold you with these terrific loads because they were big, eh? Oh, monsters! Tons and tons! And I remember coming onto this one hill—I can still see it—and it had a curve at the bottom. I started over the thing, and it had been raining, and I could see the whole hill just going out—like that! I kept it going slow for a little while and then it started to slide, so I threw the thing out of gear and let her roll. But the bottom of the slope had banks about four or five feet high and it was a solid wall of ice, eh? I came into that curve, and holy boy! I just hit that wall of ice and the next thing I knew I was straightened out and away!

Once I had to jump when the truck rolled over into the swamp, about 20 miles out of Huntsville. Jump to save my life. What scared me more than anything—and I'm not ashamed to admit it—I was terrified of going across the lakes. You see, we had a hundred-and-twenty-five to a hundred-and-thirty tons on the trucks, and the lakes would be lit up at night. They'd make ice roads.

They put water on and the ice would normally be about three feet thick, but with that terrific load on ice like that—the only way you could go across it safely was just creep, creep. Sometimes a fellow would lose his nerve and speed up and the first thing you know—bang—and down she'd go. With hardwood on, the truck goes right to the bottom like a stone. You'd always drive with the right foot in the truck and the left foot on the runningboard just waiting for a crack. I seen the ice ahead of me undulating just like a snake's back. That's where you had to hold your cool, eh? That would be over Big Joel Lake, Little Joel Lake, New Lake—those were the three big ones that I logged over. Probably two miles of terror. When you'd go in empty there was no problem, but coming out, you had to take it cool and easy. You'd maybe have to cross two lakes. I never went through myself, but I saw my buddies go down. They made it out and the reason was they had their foot on the runningboard and were just tensed like a coiled spring ready to go. They'd be forty feet from the truck by the time the thing was halfway down. See, if you had pine on or any kind of soft wood, the back end of the truck would float, but, with hardwood, it just goes straight down.

Then I got on the transport and I went driving transports and I made fifteen hundred trips into North Bay in the ten-year period. I had some hairy experiences on transport, but I was lucky. I was coming north out of Toronto down that long haul at Landing Hill. I got about halfway down and everything was under control and all of a sudden there was this terrific bang right underneath me. What had happened was the drive shaft—right under the seat about eighteen inches in length—had broken right off on the one end and it was flailing around. The first thing it did was strip all the brake linings off, so I had no brakes. Then I'd hear this thing rattling right under my seat and I thought something terrible was going to happen. I rode it right out. I coasted pretty near to Bradford Marsh, and I got out and I was shaking so bad, I couldn't even have told you my own name, Eh? It was rather funny, but it could have been rather tragic.

Another time I lost my brakes and had a runaway on a big hill—I coasted for seven miles that time. The truck was showing over a hundred mile an hour on the speedometer! The last time I looked, she was lying on the hundred mark and I had a third of the hill to go. I had a helper with me, and he says, "It's all right to let her go, Slim, but for Christ's sake keep her between those posts." He was down on the floor, and he was praying.

He was an apprentice—he was helping unload in North Bay and I let him drive the machine back empty when he was just starting. He became a top driver. He drove on the trans-Canada run.

Another time when I was going down the same hill and I'm ripping along really good and I came around one bend in the hill and there was two cows on the road. One had its tail end to the white line and the other had its head. I thought, "What am I gonna do? If I hit them dead-on, they'll come over onto the windshield. I'll hit the one in the rear end and the other in the head and that will separate them." When I got just about up to them, one took about three steps ahead and I just shot in between them.

It was really a tough job in those days. The Department of Highways didn't have a night crew on and there was no sanding done on the hills. We had to do it ourselves. If we came to a hill and it was ice-covered, we'd get out with the shovel and do it ourselves.

From 1941 to 1948, I drove the highways. I was into North Bay nearly all the time. I was on a schedule and I had to drive hard and make time. I couldn't fool around. In those days you didn't make a lot of money. You were paid by the week. Now they make huge money. You're paid for every little thing you do. When I first started, there was not even hospitalization. They were getting that the last year I was there and they were beginning to make good money, eh?

I was extremely lucky that I was never hurt on the transport except for small things; I had two head-ons in that ten-year period and in both cases I was cleared. The other vehicle was on the wrong side of the road. After a bad accident you've got to get right back in the vehicle again. My first head-on, it shook me up. No, I didn't have nightmares. I knew you couldn't stop something that weighed twenty-four tons loaded. I was very fortunate. I won three driving awards in that time put out by the Zurich Insurance Company. In order to qualify, we had to have five years of highway driving without a chargeable accident! And if you had as much as five dollars for a first offence, you lost your driving for that year.

We should have separate roads for the transport trucks. Unfortunately, nowadays we're getting too many cowboys on the transports. The reason for it is the big money. They're paid by the ton/mile. I hire out for some outfit that's drawing gravel and I get so much a ton, so much a mile. The faster I roll, the more I make. In my time, we weren't in that big of a hurry because we were paid by the week. If we saw a couple with a flat tire, we'd stop and help them, have a chat. Now you wouldn't do that. You'd lose money. It's a shame, you know, because we were known as the Knights of the Road at one time.

Putting salt has made it possible to operate day and night on the highways, except for very bad ice storms when the salt won't work. But it's terrible how it rots the machines. It rots everything, eh? The tractor alone, which is the truck part, will run you from seventy-five to a hundred-and-fifty thousand dollars—without the trailer. Most of those truck drivers say their rig is worth a hundred grand. They wash it after every trip. It's the only way to counteract the salt and they keep it waxed underneath—you could see your face in the nickel.

I had a great time in the transport while I was on it, but it was getting a little bit much for me. I was in charge of that area, the Huntsville and surrounding area for fifty miles. And if some of them got in trouble on the highway at night, they'd phone me because I used to be a highway driver. That's anyone who drives from point A to point B. There's the highway drivers and there's the pickup men that work in the cities and towns. So they phone me and I'd be getting up at all hours of the night to put on a spare tire or something. And I thought to myself that, ten years down the road, I didn't know whether I was going to be able to do this or not. So we talked it over and the wife Marg suggested I try for the OPP. I joined and was assigned to Killaloe.

There was one thing I liked about being in the OPP station at Whitney. It was a one-man detachment and I was it. But, first, I had three-and-a-half years' experience in Killaloe, a good place to learn. I went there in the fall of '51 and I stayed there till the spring of '54, and then I went to Whitney and in Whitney, as I said, you were everything. If you were in trouble up there, only two people would get called—one was the priest and the other was the police officer. So, as well as ordinary policework, you had to sit and listen to somebody talking about his line fence, or what he feeds his rose bush.

You had to drive eighty-five miles from Killaloe station to Pembroke if you wanted to lock somebody up or go to court, a hundred-and-seventy-mile round

trip and nobody left in Killaloe while I was gone to Pembroke. One time I took this fellow in for being drunk, falling down in a store and knocking over all the canned goods. I took him into Pembroke from Whitney, locked him up and went to our office to get some stuff I needed. I was there maybe half an hour and then I drove back to Whitney. I got there and there's that son-of-a-gun standing in front of the same store, tipping a bottle. What happened? Well, he had a relative here in Pembroke who came down, paid his fine and took him home. A real little prankster, you know, always in trouble. I said to myself, "That's the last guy I'd take in as a common drunk. But if it's an impaired driver, I'll have to."

Anyway, about two weeks later, same guy pulled the same trick—he's drinking and driving. I said, "Come here, Nick. Get in the car." "Ha-ha-ha," he

*Two heritage landmarks now gone from the Pembroke scene: the old Windsor Hotel, destroyed by fire in 1983 only days after this photo was taken; and the Pembroke Railway Station, one of the rare lovely old stones of the city destroyed in 1982 by the railway company. The building was distinguished by stained glass windows and was one of the few stone stations in the Valley.*

*Victoria Hall, here decorated for Christmas, c. 1935, remains as a heritage site in the heart of Pembroke.*

goes. So I get in the car and I drive him up Murray Brothers lumber road at Barry's Bay for about twenty-five miles. I hit him three or four kicks in the ass and I said, "You walk home!" He came staggering into Pembroke the next morning at daylight! I was there two-and-a-half years and I never had to touch him again. Roadside justice!

Magistrate William. K. McGregor[1] told my chum and I when I worked in Killaloe, "I have no respect for police officers that are charged with assault, but, by the same token, I'll back you men when you stick up for yourselves."

I'll tell you how well that worked. When I was in Killaloe, there used to be a chap there whose father had a store and he'd get on a bender every once in a while. A lad, I'd say, would be in his early twenties. He would steal from the father and mother at the store and buy wine from the bootlegger and stuff like that. Ted and I were getting a bit fed up so we decided we'd take him in. Now this fellow I'm talking about, if you had him in the car, he'd be just fine for a little ways and then he'd just jump up and grab you by the neck, you see? When you're doing fifty or sixty miles an hour, it's rather a risk to security, to say the least. Darned if he didn't do that when Ted and I were together and Ted says, "That's enough." We put him out in front of the car, and we batted him back and forth three or four times, and put him back in the car and drove to the Pembroke lock-up. And just as we got to the lock-up, who should come walking out but Magistrate Willie McGregor? He took a look at him and he said, "Put that one in the county jail for eight days before you bring him to trial." And walked on and never said another word. So he backed us up, as promised.

Another time we were in court at Killaloe and there was two old Irish ladies there—we used to be in court once every two weeks—and we had these two old Irish ladies, and one old Irish lady had charged the other one with creating a distrubance by cursing and swearing—that's a section in the Criminal Code. And Judge McGregor was there and he said to this old lady who had laid the charges, "Mrs. O'Hara, you claim that Mrs. O'Reilly cursed and swore at you and used bad language. Before I can decide what I'm going to do about this, I have to know what she said

to you." She said, "Your Honour, you never heard such god-damned son-of-a-bitch language in your blue Jesus life!" And there's three policemen jammed in the door trying to get out, and the old magistrate, he put his hand over his mouth and his face went red. Right in Killaloe!

Willie McGregor died some years ago. I used to pick him up and take him partridge hunting in the fall, but it was more that he just liked to go and drive around the country, eh? And I'd pick him up, and he'd buy six bottles of beer and we'd have that, and we'd go round the back roads, and he'd be telling me his stories. He was a very interesting man.

I had this amusing little incident happen when I was two-and-a-half-years in Whitney. One of my girls had finished public school and we had to move someplace where there was a high school. So, I asked the "powers-that-be" to move me. And so they said they'd move me into Pembroke, which was fine. The day before I was to leave, the old lady Mrs. Parks, the local bootlegger—"the Queen of the Bootleggers" we called her in Whitney—she had several boys and two daughters that were the worst hellhounds in the whole area. Well, she came to the house on the afternoon before I was to leave Whitney for Pembroke and she said, "I want you to come down to my place tonight. I'm having a corn roast for you!" "Holy Geez!" I said to the wife, "I'll never come out alive." Every one of those guests at the party I'd arrested or beat up—if it wasn't one thing it was the other. But she invited me down there and there was going to be about fifteen of them. I said to my wife, "If I don't go I'll be a coward for life, eh?"

So the Parks lived in a place that was called Death Valley—that's what it was known as in those days. No policeman was ever supposed to go there. So I went down to this little log cabin just outside of Whitney and I got there about eight-thirty at night when it was just getting dark. There was three or four cars there and I knocked on the door and Mrs. Parks says, "Come in." And, I go in and there was about a dozen or fifteen of these characters sitting in this big, huge kitchen, chairs around the wall. And each with a bottle of wine or a bottle of beer in their hand, eh? I'd arrested all of them for one thing and another in the few weeks before. So I entered into the party and I had a great time. They didn't think I'd come, eh? And they were just so pleased I went to the bootleggers' party in Death Valley!

That same old lady Parks, about two years after I came to Pembroke, was brought into the hospital there. My wife was a nurse; she was working at the Civic Hospital, and Mrs. Parks was brought in. I always kind of liked the old lady. I know she was a bootlegger but I had a kind of respect for her. She was a terminal case. She recognized Marg, eh, and she said, "Do you think your husband would come and see me?" Marg said, "I'm sure he would." Mrs. Parks said, "I'd like that. You know, he arrested every one of my boys, but they were asking for it. I'd like to see him again." And I went up and took her some flowers, but the poor old lady died about a month later.

If there was a Whitney girl who had got in trouble and was going to have a baby and the parents would kick her out—they'd do that up there, no place to go—old Mrs. Parks would take her in. And her only source of income was bootlegging. I can't remember her first name; we always just called her "Ma Parks." Death Valley was just outside of Whitney. The road in joined onto one of the main roads that came into Whitney. It was where the Parks and the Bowers and Majinskies and lots more of them lived—a real bunch of outlaws. My chum Ted that was OPP in Whitney before me, he got beat up by one of the Parks women.

Women! Oh, vicious! You wouldn't believe it! Anyway, Ted was down from Barry's Bay with the cruiser this day and he noticed this car ahead of him all over the road, so he pulled it over and it was Carl Soleby and Myrtle Soleby, who was Mrs. Parks' daughter. So Ted informed Carl he was arresting him for impaired driving. Carl was a big guy, eh, and there was no way he was going to be part of that. Ted attempted to arrest him and quite a fight ensued. Ted was a pretty good man and so was Carl and they were slugging it out on the highway and there was a great big pool of water on the other side of the road, like a frog hole, eh? And Ted would drive Carl into this frog wallow and he'd come up all slime and come right at old Ted again. He was wearing him right down, but he forgot Myrtle sitting in the car. She walked up behind him and hit him with one of her high-heeled shoes, with the spike heel on it, and just opened him from here down to here. The officer from Killaloe went up and arrested the two of them, her and Carl. You wouldn't want to go to Death Valley too often on a domestic charge.

*The invention of the pontoon airplane was a boon to game wardens and park rangers who could then manoeuvre from lake to lake tracking down poachers and illegal trappers. Light planes equipped with skis for landing would be used by park rangers like George Phillips of Whitney.*

*Renowned park guides, Steve and Jack Ryan, at Whitney, 1927. In his book* **Along the Trail,** *park ranger Ralph Bice lists many of the early great rangers, including Bob Balgour, Eli Fonjini, Jack Stringer, Jack Culhane, Bud Calaghan, Jim Shields, and Pete and Telesphore Ranger. Chief rangers included Tom McCormick, Jerry Kennedy, Bill Lewis and Dan Ross. Ross was the first park ranger and was the same great river driver who appeared in Ralph Connor's Glengarry Schooldays.*

I did quite a bit of liquor work when I was in Killaloe. Not so much in Whitney, although I did a certain amount. Old Mrs. Parks we used to raid on a periodic basis, like once a year or something. The neighbours would start complaining or something . . .

I have a funny incident to tell you. Mrs. Parks had been hit for bootlegging and appeared before Magistrate Willie McGregor in court in Barry's Bay. She pleaded guilty. The judge said, "Mrs. Parks, that

will be a fine of a hundred dollars and fifteen dollars and fifteen cents for court costs. Would you like time to pay for it, or do you want to pay for it now?" "I'll pay for it now," she said.

Now she'd gone to school with Willie McGregor, the magistrate, and she was a great big woman, huge, eh? And she waddles up to the table—and Bill's sitting there watching and wondering what next—and she looks him right in the eye and she pulls her dress way out at the neckline and she puts her hand down her front and she has "Northern Equipment," eh? And she pulls out a huge roll of money and she says, "Ha, ha! Willie, I bet you thought there was nothing down there but tits!"

In Whitney I lived next door to the game warden. There was one game warden and one police officer up there, eh? Bruce Turner[2] was the game warden and a fantastic man out in the bush. Bruce lived next to me and sometimes he would ask me to go with him because in those days, if he was going to stop a vehicle on what was known as the King's Highway, he didn't have the authority. They do now. They also knew that the game warden was more or less handicapped and didn't have the same powers that we did. We had the same powers as the game warden, but the game warden didn't have the same powers as the police officer. So I'd go and help him and, if I was up against it, he would help me. I also got help from a couple of fellows up there who belonged to the Ministry of Natural Resources.

One case that I got involved with was when Bruce Turner came to me and he said, "I'm going to disappear for anything up to a week and only my wife and your wife and you will know where I've gone. I'm going after that bunch of poachers that's operating out of Whitney and I'm going to be in the park" (Algonquin). And he told me what lake he'd be on in case he didn't reappear. And he said, "I'm taking a sleeping bag and just enough food to get by and don't be surprised if I don't come out until I get them." He stayed in that sleeping bag for six nights and five days, stayed right in it day and night, and he finally got them. They had traps set all through the park. They'd take a run through the park, maybe twenty miles, and set traps here and there. Once a week they'd go and pick them up. He was waiting for them. Can you imagine anybody being that dedicated?

There was snow on the ground, December. He brought them to Whitney and held them in Whitney and then he took them in and locked them up in Pembroke, and they got out on bail, and appeared in court on a certain date, and were fined X number of dollars and the traps were confiscated. Under the *Game and Fish Act*, anything that you are in possession of as a poacher is confiscated right down to the vehicle. They usually get them back.

In Killaloe, Ted and I were watching a bootlegger one night—it was at Round Lake Centre, which is in the Killaloe area—and I was about two miles out on a road and my chum was in behind the house with a walkie-talkie and he said, "There's a car just left. They bought liquor, so stop them and hold them." So I stopped the car and asked them to get out and the two fellows got out and I noticed a rifle in the back seat. I reached in to get the rifle and the fellow was quicker than I was and he said, "You're not getting this goddam rifle," and he took a swing at me and took the hat right off my head. But my chum was on his way, and he came roaring in there, and we took them and locked them up, and went back and raided the bootlegger. But these two guys we stopped were two guys the game warden had been trying to get for two years and we, just by accident, ran into them. We seized everything. Their truck, their rifle . . .

George Phillips[3], a real character in Whitney, I met right after going up there. He was the park superintendent and he was also the flier. He flew the Forestry aircraft. He was a flier in both world wars— in the Second World War he was an instructor at Camp Borden teaching a group of young lads. He'd get them together and he'd say, "Look, I'll teach you everything I know. You're going to learn how to fly a plane level, upside down, every which way there is. But if I bring you back from a flight and you've thrown up in that plane, you'll clean it out with a toothbrush." And, he held them to it. "And," he said, "on top of that, you'll give me a bottle of liquor every time you get sick in an aircraft." His liquor cabinet was full at all times.

He was a fantastic guy. One time he scared the pants right off me. He took me into the lake one time—in those days you had to, supposing somebody set fire to the brush in the park. Well, the Forestry men got paid for it, but I had to go in and investigate how much was burned and all that. And there was this little lake up near Aylen Lake and part of it is in Algonquin Park and part of it is out of the park. But this little lake from a thousand feet up, it looked about like a teacup and old George flips the plane like this and I said, "It's pretty small, isn't it, George?" "Oh," he says, "we'll make her." There was pine trees all around the perimeter of this lake, see? He slips the thing in like this into that lake—oh, it was a beautiful landing. I go in there. He waits for me and I do what I have to do.

And he'd been sizing the thing up and he says, "Roy, I've got news for you." I said, "Geez what is it? News from you is never good." He laughed and he said, "Do you see that mountain there?" I said, "Yes." He said, "On the other side is a big lake." I said, "Is that right?" He said, "Well, you're going to walk up that." I said, "You go to hell." He said, "I can't lift off the lake with the two of us in the plane. You're going to have to walk out over the mountain, and I'll get out of here somehow, and I'll meet you with the plane over on the other side, on the big lake."

The plane was sitting at the shore and George says, "Here's a piece of rope. Put it in that ring at the back of the plane and tie the other end to the tree, and I'm going to start her up, and I'm going to run her right up to the rope and, when I signal with my hand, you cut that rope with your knife." He took off— he got off the lake—and he was about thirty feet from the tops of the pine trees heading straight for them and I thought he'd had it. But at the last minute he pulled back on the stick and just skimmed over the tops of them.

Well, it was a hot day in the summer and I had my gun belt on and handcuffs, and everything. The gun belt alone weighed about ten pounds. I was supposed to walk through the bush and up the mountain for about two miles, no trail or anything. And I did. George Phillips was then about sixty-five and he lived at park headquarters on Cache Lake, and from Cache Lake to Smoke Lake where the plane used to be kept was five miles and, right up to the day he left the Forestry, he ran that five miles every morning. A fantastic man!

He used to swear in the plane all the time, with the radio going all over the province. He was grounded two or three times for swearing, but it was just his natural way of talking, eh? He was used to being with men.

He hated poachers with a vengeance. I lived in Whitney right on the Madawaska River and they used to come in with the plane sometimes and land on the river right by my house. This one time he called me and he was really mad and he was swearing and he said, "Roy, can you meet me at the back of your place in five minutes? I've located some poachers in the park and I want you to help me." I went down and there was a little wharf. He said, "I won't even stop. You jump on the pontoon as soon as I go by." He comes roaring in and touches her down there at the end of the dock, and I jump and land on the thing, and before I'd got into the plane, he'd thrown her wide open and took the thing off and me trying to get in the door. I yelled, "Damn you! Wait 'til I get in!" He said, "We haven't any time, boy."

So we get up to this lake, Joel Lake in the park, and he said, "They're on that island." And that's where they were. Somebody had gone in with a four-wheel jeep. I said, "Where do I come into this picture?" (I figured he'd got something horrible planned for me.) He said, "If they're still there, I'll drop down and you get out and you hold them, and I'll send a bunch of rangers in and we'll confiscate everything they've got: boat, jeep, the whole works."

I wasn't too happy. There were four of them when we spotted them from the air. He said, "You put them under arrest." I said, "Okay, but don't you be long getting back here. In another two hours it will be dark and I can't guarantee I can keep them corralled that long." He said, "I'll have men here in about an hour." And he sent in three or four rangers in about an hour, and I had them all rounded up, and we seized everything. They really didn't give me a hard time. I was armed and they weren't.

They were fishing, but that lake was closed to fishing. Certain lakes were closed one year and then open next year. They wanted them to have a year to breed. But George was death on poachers. He was always calling me for something like that. That was treetop hairy flying, just clearing the treetops. He flew fighter planes in the First World War. They were just like little flies. There's one in the War Museum and I just stood there. I couldn't believe it.

Here's something that happened at the Cross Lake area, which is out from Madawaska in the Whitney Detachment area. It was during deer season and the father had come home at dinnertime and leaned his rifle up against the wall in the summer kitchen. At that time, the little boy aged six and his five-year-old sister were playing around. The boy picked up the father's rifle and pointed it at his sister and the rifle went off and got the little girl between the eyes, killing her instantly. One of my superior officers wanted me to lay a charge of criminal negligence at this time, which I refused to do because I didn't think the father did it intentionally and he was going to live with that for the rest of his life. As a result, there were no charges laid in this incident.

A few days later, this same officer and I were hunting deer and he was behind me carrying a loaded rifle and he had one in the chamber, which is a no-no. He stumbled and the rifle discharged and it blew the side of my boot out—just grazed my ankle bone. And I turned to him and I said, "You see, accidents do happen." And he never had anything more to say about laying charges against the father.

For the first fifteen years I enjoyed the OPP, but for the last five I was thinking of getting out and, finally, I got out. I'll tell you why.

The OPP was a good outfit at one time, but like everything else, it started going down hill. I didn't like the "powers that be," the top echelons—they didn't seem to be the same as they were when I started out. It was a matter of statistics. It got to be paperwork. That, I could have lived with, but on that paper they wanted to show where each man was producing X number of fines or arrests per house. Yes, they say they don't have a quota. They're liars, because I used to make out the sheet. I was detachment commander before I resigned. If you don't keep up to your quota you're called into headquarters to see The Boss.

There was the time when we were still in Huntsville, before I went into the OPP and I was driving transport. I used to leave very early at four o'clock in the morning and Margaret, my wife, would go back to bed afterwards. This one time she sat bolt upright in bed, absolutely terrified. Scared to death! She didn't know why. And then, all of a sudden, she started to laugh and lay down again and went back to sleep. So when I came home she was telling me about it and I said, "Did you happen to look at the clock and see what time it was?" And she had. The clock was on the dresser. "Five o'clock," she said. And I said, "You did exactly what I did at exactly the same time."

You see, I was coming down a big hill fully loaded at five o'clock when I lost the brakes. I was absolutely full of terror, scared to death. But I ended up with the front end of the transport on the church steps, and that's when I laughed. That little church saved my life. I laughed because I felt I was half blessed. And I lit a cigarette and relaxed right there on the steps of the little white church at South River.

---

1 Judge Willie MacGregor appears in interviews also with Greg Guthrie and Roy MacGregor.

2 Park rangers, in a somewhat later period, were also referred to as game wardens. In his history of Algonquin Park, Ralph Bice lists many of the rangers, chief rangers, and superintendents, but Bruce Turner is not amongst them. Again, he may belong to a later period. Today park rangers and game wardens have become conservation officers.

3 George Phillips, Park Superintendent, 1943-58. According to author Ralph Bice, Phillips' "whole life was spent flying." It was during his term that most of the summer hotels in the park were torn down, ending an era in Algonquin Park. Phillips was a champion heavyweight boxer during World War I.

*The White Church at South River which saved Roy Wilston's life.*

# 7

# "It Ain't Braggin' if You've Done It"

## ROY MacGREGOR – Ottawa, Ontario

*Writer Roy MacGregor had always urged me to "get to his father, one of the great old storytellers of the Ottawa Valley." And I really did try two or three times. But Duncan Fisher MacGregor was then living in Huntsville. To interview him would have required a long journey and a stopover. In 1995, I tried again. Mr. MacGregor, because of illness, had been moved to a seniors' home in the Valley, but Roy assured me his "mind was as sharp as ever." I phoned Roy's home in Ottawa to say I was on my way to see his father, only to be informed he had died a few days before. I was shocked and disappointed, but it was happening all the time; the old-timers were dying off and taking with them all that precious life story, legend and social history. But all was not lost. Because Roy has inherited his father's genius for storytelling, I was overjoyed when he said that he could pass on some of his father's stories that he remembered.*

*Roy MacGregor was born in the Red Cross outlet in Whitney in 1948. He went to school in Huntsville, but the family maintained close ties with Whitney. In 1970, he graduated from Laurentian University and in 1986, joined the Ottawa Citizen. He has written twelve books, including* Home Team, Last Season, Home

Game. *In 1972, he married Ellen Griffith from Huntsville and they have four children.*

*Roy's father, Duncan Fisher MacGregor, was born in Eganville in 1907, his mother, Helen Geraldine McCormick, at Brulé Lake in 1915. They met when Mr. MacGregor was working for lumberman J.S.L. McRae[1] at a mill on Lake of Two Rivers. Mrs. MacGregor's father, Thomas McCormick, was a park ranger and a bookkeeper, working in the latter capacity at one time in Barry's Bay, probably with Murray and O'Manick Lumber Company. He married Beatrice Dowd, also from an Eganville family.*

*Through his father, Roy MacGregor reaches back into turn of the century Valley history—hockey, baseball, humour, and characters. Roy tells a few of his own, including some about his remarkable uncle Judge Willie MacGregor[2].*

**S**OMEWHERE in those MacGregor ancestors there is a dropping of the Roman Catholic faith and a taking up of the Protestant faith, and in the Ottawa Valley that was a serious business. My father's father was Grandfather Daniel MacGregor from White Lake—there's all kinds of MacGregors still throughout the area. Grandfather Daniel MacGregor married Annie Keenan from the Eganville area. I don't know about her background except that her

*The first Duncan MacGregor, Roy MacGregor's grandfather. Photo by Pittaway of Ottawa.*

father was one of the Nile Expedition[3]. All the history books encourage that they were Indians and voyageurs who went on that trip. Not true at all. They were the Celts; the Irish and the Scots of the Upper Ottawa Valley made up the bulk of that force and they've largely been forgotten.

My feeling is that genealogy tends to belong to the educated, people who can take themselves back to the *Mayflower* and all that. So many of us in the Ottawa Valley would have to accept the fact that somewhere down the line the people who came were probably illiterate, probably came in steerage, had no records, weren't even able to keep any records of the ships they came out in. Basically, I think that's one of the reasons why there's such a strong sense of

"home" in the Ottawa Valley because that's where education and awareness began. In all the travels I've done, political and otherwise, the only place I ever felt like I was back in the Ottawa Valley was in Newfoundland. I remember the feeling just washed over me the second I landed there. Everybody had said, "You're going to love the people of Newfoundland—they're so funny" and all that. Well, I'd met them all before, the humour, the music, the hospitality—I have to be careful how I say this—and the absolute love of lying.

My father, Duncan Fisher MacGregor, would, I think, probably qualify as one of the great characters of the Ottawa Valley, but he had no sense of his own, shall we say, "underground fame." He had a wicked sense of humour. He was an intriguing observer of life who came from a highly educated family yet had no formal education himself. He had a brother who became a lawyer and then a judge, another brother who became an engineer, his sisters became teachers, and much was always expected of them. But my father was only four when his father died. His father had been a very prosperous lumberman who went around buying lumber and selling it, jobbing. He was jobbing in the middle of the bush when he had a stroke and they couldn't get him help quickly enough and when he came back he deteriorated and died in 1912.

His wife really held things together and, with the help of Bill—my father's brother, later the renowned Judge MacGregor—got the rest of the kids educated. It was there for my father but, when he got to Grade Eleven, he would get one hundred in things like Mathematics and Geography and, in particular, History, but he'd get zero in things he wasn't interested in. So he just quit. He opened up an ice cream stand in the middle of the Eganville bridge. He was always one of the world's worst businessman and, even though he had been brought up in Eganville, he seemed to fail to realize that the Catholics lived on one side and the Protestants lived on the other. He opened up an ice cream stand in the middle of the bridge and nobody would come. An ice cream stand with palm trees, if you'll believe that!

Father'd be seventeen, eighteen, in 1925. Then, like all the men who were about to be dealing with the Depression he boarded a train and went west. To do the farm thing. When he came back—things were getting tight because the Depression was coming on—and J.S.L McRae offered him a job that would pay fifty cents an hour. He stayed with McRae for about fifty-five years. He started young and then he took the courses that would allow him to become the tallyman, the scaler. He took the scaler's exams, and he got all marks in the nineties. Hardwood was his speciality and, of course, because of market demand, they were cutting almost exclusively hardwood throughout those years. Then he became the foreman, and he lived at the mills at Lake of Two Rivers, Hay Lake, Lake St. Peter which was much more toward the Bancroft area, then back to White Lake, and a long time at Whitefish Lake right in Algonquin Park.

My memories with my father are very, very happy. He was a responsible adult, but he could be very childlike. He sang us stupid songs and did silly things, and he had his weaknesses, including the usual weakness of the Ottawa Valley—drinking. Of course, he came from a situation where you weren't to have booze in the house or even around the house. So in the park there was always plenty. He would have booze hidden everywhere. When I'd be with him he'd stop his car, get out and climb into the bush, come back with his trousers rolled up or soaking wet, but he would have three beers in his hand. Three stubby beer that had been in a creek for a month, or there'd be a mickey he'd hidden under a log somewhere.

Our family has all kinds of funny stories about that. My brother Jim tells a really funny one about going back in the park with Lornie Pigeon from Madawaska—he's our uncle, married to Mary McCormick. The Pigeons were great Cache Lake people. One time they were away back in the park and they had portaged across three different lakes. One of the guys goes to sit down for a smoke and sees something glinting in the grass. It's a mickey of brandy. And he says, "You can't believe what I found over here." And Lornie, who's nearly eighty at this time, jumps up and says, "God darn it! What the hell! I put that there nearly three years ago. I forgot all about it!"

For me, my memories of the Ottawa Valley are all filled with funerals because they were always such an exotic affair and a bit scary. I remember going to one up the Traymor Road. Aunt Minnie of the MacGregors, married to a McGilligan. Anyway, Aunt Minnie had died and I guess my parents had no choice but to take me. First of all, she's laid out in the parlour and there's keening going on and I guess it had been going on for some time, and I remember— I guess it's my most vivid memory—I was maybe four years old and I remember the smells, and I remember the feeling of being in there, and I remember a woman picking me up and taking me to the casket and making me touch Aunt Minnie. I even remember her words. She said, "If you touch the dead you'll never be afraid of them."

And the women were in the kitchen and the teacups were going and all the chatter and everything was smooth and that kind of bustle that takes place where people know things are going on that you shouldn't overhear. Out in the woodshed the men were hammering back the mickeys and the alcohol. I do believe they had to take the window jambs out to remove the casket. They had to take Aunt Minnie out the window. There was no hearse or anything. They actually carried the casket down the road with us trailing behind, into the little cemetery there. And there the hole had been dug and there's the service, and the turf was shovelled in. Everybody stayed until all the shovelling was done. It's just so vivid.

My father had no sense of the value of money, apart from giving it away or just spending it. He never was without work, but he never had any money nor do I think was he ever paid. He showed me once—he had a slip of paper signed by J.S.L. McRae, which gave him six per cent of the profits when he joined the company. He was part of the McRae family, but he never took that issue up with J.S.L. McRae. He had no sense of what his value was, what he should be worth. I remember one time he got offered a job out in British Columbia because he stood at the top of the scaler's test, and he turned it down to stay with his brother-in-law, J.S.L. McRae. He might have fared better out West.

Most of the time we never had a car. One time away back in the fifties, he lost about five thousand dollars gambling on stupid stocks. You see what used to happen, people would come around these lumber mills selling penny mining stocks. And my father and a bunch of the other guys would line up like the fools they were and buy these penny mining stocks. We've got all kinds of these documents for companies that no longer exist. He was always thinking he was going to get rich and that would solve all his money problems which, of course, became marriage problems. He drove my mother absolutely batty because she never knew what was going to happen, and then they would have to turn around and go "hat in hand" and beg to Janet McRae, who was J.S.L.'s wife—and my father's older sister—an absolutely wonderful person—who would always bail them out. J.S.L. was Dad's brother-in-law, which was why he was supposed to get six per cent of the company profit. McRaes ran the operation—it certainly wasn't our family. But Dad didn't collect. He never even asked for it. But he wanted us to know about the arrangement so he showed the papers to us.

To me, growing up there—Whitney—was such an odd place. It was like the McRaes were a royal family, and Marjorie McRae approached sainthood,

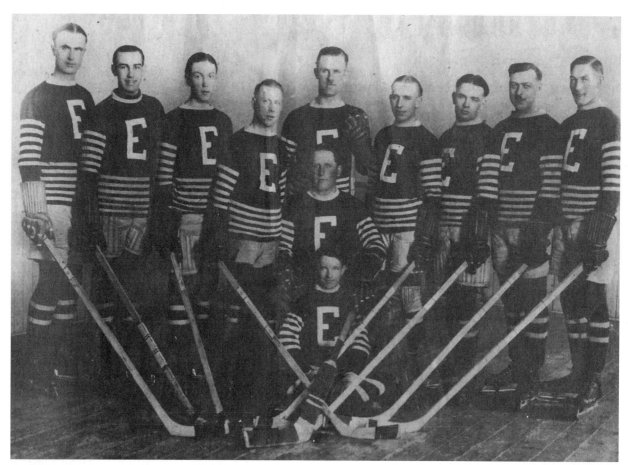

*The Eganville Senior Hockey team, 1927-28. L to R: H. "Tiny" McKibbon, Howard Valliquette, Harold Costello, Dick Zadow, George Shane, Ed Freitag, Duncan MacGregor, Mickey Freitag, Bob Patterson. Seated: Albert Middlestadt and mascot James Reeves.*

still does. She was always doing such good work and good things for people. She was a daughter of J.S.L. McRae. She's still there, but Marjorie MacGregor now—she married a cousin. The McRaes were always very well off—and very well thought of, I think. Everybody else in Whitney was lower on the scale. But I always felt—because we were related to them—we were sort of middle ground. I was quite young when we lived there, but we had no electricity, no telephone, nothing. Nor did anyone else. Except the McRaes. They were the first to get electricity, and indoor toilet.

The McRaes had a huge house and the McRaes lived on the top of the hill and then, right beside it, they rented us a little home for a dollar a month, and then right on the other side they rented my mother's parents, the ranger and his wife, a home for a dollar a month. It was really a clan thing. When we were children, we'd Grandmother McCormick on one side and then the McRaes on the other, and of course, because my father's father had died so young and then his mother died in 1948, and Mrs. McRae was older, we very much regarded her as a grandmother. It was really quite clannish. I don't

know whether it's true in other parts of the Valley or not, but parents never seemed to have friends other than family and you never seemed to visit anyone other than family. And the family could go on forever; you were forever being told how someone was related to you.

## FOSTER HEWITT

*Director of Radio*

### Maple Leaf Gardens

The broadcasting of all events in Maple Leaf Gardens is under the supervision of Foster Hewitt, Canada's Premier Sports Announcer.

*For information as to appointment and Radio Advertising rates*

*Phone* FOSTER HEWITT

MAPLE LEAF GARDENS          WAverley 1641

*A very young Foster Hewitt, broadcaster for NHL games on Saturday nights for half a century. Taken from a Toronto Maple Leaf programme, c. 1930s.*

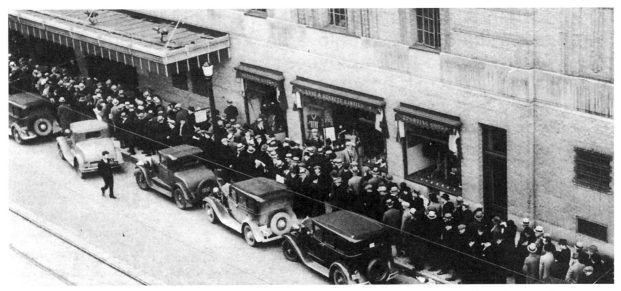

*Lining up for tickets outside Maple Leaf Gardens in the early 1930s. Note the cars and the formal attire of everyone in the line.*

Both my father and mother said that hockey was the great winter event. My mother told stories of when she was a teenager, how Dr. Brooks in Eganville always had a cutter and the horses "at the ready" because he would always have to go out on house calls for miles around. And Mother said that on the winter weekends Mary Brooks and her brothers would get Dr. Brooks' horse and cutter and other young people would get other cutters, and they'd all wrap up in huge blankets and robes and travel up the Barr Line to Douglas, watch the hockey game and come back. It was very clean fun. There wasn't drinking. People presume that there were things going on—but there wasn't. A lot of those young men didn't become bad drinkers until much later in their lives. My Uncle Bill who, I guess, was killed by drink, he was a complete tee-totaller right up until his late twenties or thirties. When they turned to it, they sure turned to it.

My father followed hockey passionately and baseball passionately. He remembered way back when somebody bought the first radio. They had to put earphones on and they were trying to get the first hockey game—Foster Hewitt. And this great howling would come over the air and just about deafen you and they'd pick up a little bit here and there, and they got so excited about it, just the idea . . . and then it all would fade out.

Then, of course, Dad took us to games in Toronto. Mr. Snyder, a lumber salesman, would give him four tickets a year so he could take us down to the NHL games. Going to the city was just so frightening. I remember my brother and I were afraid to go to the Maple Leaf Gardens—for one thing the washrooms had great troughs for urinals—huge! My brother and I were just petrified, the biggest we'd ever seen and we were afraid to go in. And Gordie Howe was playing and my father would say, "There's the greatest hockey player you'll ever see." I hated the Leafs. Detroit was my team.

Oh, my father had so many stories! Unbelievable half the time. He told about one time he and one of his buddies were out fighting a forest fire and they became convinced that the fire was cornering the fish—all my father ever really was interested in was fishing. So they tied little cords to their paddles and they had hooks—he maintains—baited with bacon, and Dad and his friend caught one hundred and thirty speckled trout during the forest fire that they were supposed to be fighting.

He told great stories about playing baseball. He was a good athlete, played for the Eganville hockey and baseball teams.

"Strange Happenings" is the title of another favourite baseball story.

I remember one game in 1922 in Eganville. Arnprior was playing Eganville and in those days baseball was serious business. Dick Zadow—"Hat's Off" we called him because of his bad temper—was playing second base and the Arnprior player took off from first for second. The Eganville catcher threw the ball to Dick to catch the player stealing the base and the umpire called him safe on second. Dick just threw the ball at the umpire and hit him on the head. The umpire, enraged, chased Dick all around the bases in an effort to avenge himself. The umpire was a big fellow and very aggressive looking. Anyway, Dick escaped into the crowd and, of course, the pro-Eganville crowd protected him. But he did not dare return to play the game and a substitute took his place. I thought it was really funny and the fans had a great laugh over this incident.

Father used to play hockey on the Bonnechere River and one of his favourite stories there was that there was a great game going on—I think they were playing Douglas—it was a big crowd, and the crowd came and stood always to one side of the rink so that their backs would be to the wind. Also they would give the players protection from the ice and the wind. He said the game was going on full force and the whistle blows. Nobody could figure out why. So they all stopped the play and they're all looking around trying to figure out the call, and the referee skates to the other side of the rink where no one's standing, and he turns his back to the crowd and has a pee. And the whole game has to wait while the referee relieves himself. Then he finishes, blows his whistle, and off they go again.

He talked about hockey all the time. At their home they got the *Journal* and he would memorize the sports pages. And he also delivered the *Citizen*, and one of the old guys down the road, Mr. McClintock near the Bonnechere River, always gave him the *Citizen* sports section after he delivered it. So he'd have both sports sections and he'd read them all and he knew everything. He once came down to Ottawa to meet some pals in Hull where the Yankees were barnstorming and he saw Babe Ruth play. Yes, in Hull. It was one of the great events of his life. He loved to talk about the Renfrew Millionaires, and Frank Nighbor, and Cyclone Taylor, and Frank Finnigan, and all those people. They were the gods back then. He saw them live. But he often would say—and I picked this up from him and I believe it certainly—that for every person that made it in the NHL there was always another person who didn't—who stayed in the little towns, yet were great players.

Dizzy Dean, of course, was one of the all-time baseball greats. After Dizzy Dean and his brother had won fifty-one games for the Cardinals, Dizzy was quoted as saying, "It ain't braggin' if you've done it," and my father always used to quote it.

And here are two true baseball stories from my father.

The first time I came up to Whitney was in 1929, August 30th. There was a picnic at Madawaska that day and Whitney was playing ball and of course they wanted to know if I played ball. I played in Eganville and, loving the game, I was quite happy to play for Whitney. The ball park faced the Catholic church, centre field. Anyway, the first time I came up to bat, I hit a line drive centre field. The church door was open and the ball hit in front of the church, bounced up the steps right into the church. Result— home run. The opposition team complained and railed and ranted that it should have been a double. Anyway, the umpire ruled it a home run and the fans from Whitney were quite happy. I must say that the umpire was James Costello, a friend of mine. James was a good friend of John Barleycorn as well, and he was in some shape to decide on this incident. He used to take a two-ounce drink every inning and by the end of the game, he was in great shape and the ball was just a blur to James. Anyway, Whitney won and everybody was happy.

One time at Barry's Bay, Killaloe was playing the home team and Jim Costello was the umpire. At that time the umpire stood behind the pitcher. Of course Jim, as usual, was well oiled up to do his duty calling strikes and balls. Anyway, Cuddy the Killaloe pitcher got fed up with the calls so he just wound up and, instead of throwing the ball, he just hung onto it. Jim took a second look and called it a ball. Cuddy protested. "I didn't throw the ball." he yelled. "Well," Jim said, "In that case I'll just call it a balk[4]." And he moved the base runner from first to second.

Jim continued as though nothing out of the ordinary had happened, and it was so funny. As you know, in baseball the umpire is always right whether he's wrong or not. We had a great laugh over this incident and Barry's Bay won the game.

Another one from Dad:

The big mill at Erie had burnt down and J.L.S. McRae decided to move to Two Rivers. This was in 1933 when the Depression was at its worst. Wages were twenty dollars a month for a top hand and fifteen dollars for trail cards. Well, the mill started producing in 1934 and I went up to grade hardwood at the mill. I worked ten hours a day, six days a week. There was no road through the park at the time, only the railroad to Parry Sound. Most of the employees lived in Whitney and Barry's Bay and Wilno. The ones living in Whitney went home on Saturday evening on the railroad that the company had for transportation. We had good meals and Tom Cannon from Whitney was the cook. At that time you could buy a one hundred and fifty-pound pig all dressed for five dollars and a quarter of beef for three dollars. Eggs were fifteen cents a dozen, and milk was ten cents a quart.

The only good price was beaver or mink fur, and a large beaver skin would get you sixty dollars—at least two months' wages. Some fellows were trapping and doing quite well at

*J.S.L. McRae, 1891-1970, with the station master at Whitney. When he died at age seventy-nine, his son Donald took over the mills.*

it. Of course it was illegal to trap in the park and if you were caught, you paid a large fine and you'd be banned from the park. Then Mackenzie King, the prime minister started building airports around the country to give employment to the unemployed. They picked out Two Rivers right beside the mill. Across the creek the army ran the project army style and suited the men with army issue. We had to build a bridge across the creek and they started building the airport. It was a godsend to the McRae Lumber Company as they supplied all the lumber for its buildings and teams of horses to do the work.

Well, it wasn't too long until the army lads at the airport started selling clothes to McRae's men and, really, in a month's time we were all decked out in army clothes. You could buy the following: army boots, two dollars a pair; shirts, twenty-five cents; pants, two dollars; underwear, fifteen cents; and socks, twenty-five cents, sometimes cheaper. They sure ripped off the government. The army bosses at the airport project used to sell the beef and pork at Barry's Bay and pad the supply inventory, and

*In the 1950s the lumber company abandoned horses and decking line to load the huge timbers onto sleighs and trucks, using tractors.*

Hotel Algonquin was an early rustic structure situated back from the grand Trunk Railway Station overlooking Joel Lake. It was believed to have been built about 1908 and was operated for a number of years by Ed. Colson, his sister Annie running the outfitting store nearby. Unlike most wooden hotels in the Valley, Algonquin did not burn, but was eventually taken down.

sometimes the gang were very hungry. Also they would put anyone's name on the payroll as dragging a team, and then pocket the pay cheques. There were all types of humanity, former convicts, ex-RCMP officers, real down-and-out characters, a few war veterans, World War I, down on their luck. Most of them came from Montreal, Quebec, but very few French. At our McRae camp, we had one hundred men and on the airport project there was about the same number. Just to give you an example of how they padded the payroll. For example, in our camp we had one bull cook for all the men. The bull cook's job is to carry all the water, clean the camp, keep the fires going, bring in all the wood for the fires. On the airport project, they had fifty bull cooks for the same number of men. They'd raid the supplies and make home brew, and they used to get pretty high at times.

We'd spend our summers in Algonguin Park. Once every summer the most important person that we knew would come to visit—Uncle Bill MacGregor. He looked like my father, but an older version, very stately, and he seemed very colourful. And we knew

that he was a judge and we knew that was really important but, more than anything else, he would show us kids where he'd been shot right through the neck in World War I. As a little kid I remember climbing on the back of the chair to look at his war wound. He had been shot right in the back of his neck and out the front, and he had a scar on both sides and he would let us look at it. Then I would imagine what the war must have been like. He was highly decorated—he had gone with the Black Watch, to fight for England, and in the Black Watch at the same time had been Edward the Prince. You know, the famous abdicator. So he had marched with him. He was so far from being a bragger. I didn't hear any of those stories from him, and he only indulged us to let us look at his war wound. He'd show us where he'd got shot and we'd try to imagine the bullet going through, and this was very romantic to us.

But the later stories my brother picked up when he moved to Killaloe to work for the bank and realized just what a legend Judge MacGregor really was. I can tell you the story of his most famous quote. One that got in every newspaper in Canada. This local guy's up in front of MacGregor on some charge so serious he has hired a fancy expensive

Toronto lawyer to defend him. The big Toronto lawyer has pleaded his case brilliantly and, of course, had won by any other definition. And Uncle Bill's sitting on the bench in Killaloe simply staring at this brilliant orator and finally he issues an edict. He says, "That may be the law in Toronto. But that is NOT the law in Killaloe."

I heard all these stories about how when he was driving from Killaloe to sit at the assizes in Pembroke, he would consume a bottle of whisky. I was sitting with his wife one time, my Aunt Mary, and I told her that I'd heard that story and she snapped, "That's absolutely not true." I thought, "God! I've overstepped my boundaries here." And she said, "He only drank a mickey on the way."

1  See Henry Taylor's interview.

2  Judge Willie MacGregor, a legend of the Ottawa Valley, appears in Greg Guthrie's and Roy Wilston's interviews.

3  So capable were the rivermen of the Ottawa at using these small wooden boats (pointer boats) in heavy currents that, when the British army determined to rescue besieged General Gordon at Khartoum, deep in the continent of Africa on the Nile River in Anglo-Egyptian Sudan, it was to Canada and Canadian boatmen, primarily from the Ottawa Valley, that the task fell. In September, 1884, a contingent of about three hundred and seventy Canadians set out for the Nile to undertake relief of Khartoum. Dispatches from London commented on the ability of the rivermen to accomplish what British sailors could not. Charlotte Whitton, *A Hundred Years A-fellin'*, 1943.

4  In baseball, a balk is an uncompleted pitch, entitling the base runners to advance one base.

*The old Highland Inn at Algonquin Station. It also had an outfitting store and was the base for some famous park guides, like Tom Salmon, Angus McClennan, the Mays brothers, and the Bice Brothers.*

# 8

# "Believe Me, the Ball Players were Just as Good in the 1920s as Today"

## LARRY MORIARITY – Douglas, Ontario

*Larry "Mr. Baseball" Moriarity was born in Douglas, Ontario, in 1908 and has lived there all his life. He spent twenty-seven years doing roadwork for the County of Renfrew and seven years after that as caretaker of the Douglas school. In 1941, he married Esther Enright from Douglas where they raised their children. About the 1850s the Moriarities came from County Cork to settle near Quadville just off the Opeongo Line. When I asked him, "How did they find their way into the bush around Quadville?" he replied in his inimitable style, "Well, they just kept on coming and coming. They'd meet somebody else walking up who'd tell them about greener fields further on, and they just kept on coming until they landed in a few miles from Quadville." His mother was Elizabeth Enright whose family had pioneered at Yankeetown on the Opeongo Line. Both Mr. Moriarity's grandmothers were Conways from the Opeongo Line.*

*Before I went to interview Larry Moriarity, I was told to ask him for baseball stories. It did turn out that his abiding passion in life was baseball, although he was also a hockey enthusiast.*

I REMEMBER my Grandfather Moriarity in Douglas. A cook in the shanties in the wintertime,

then he'd work at the McNab sawmill in the summertime. There used to be two mills in Douglas: the Alan McNab sawmill with forty men on the job and, right beside it, the flour mill with twenty men on the job. A busy town! Campbell was in with McNab for a time at the flour mill. They produced brans and shorts and three grades of flour—Rosebud, Carleton, Empire. It was Alan McNab, the sawmill owner, grandfather cooked for in the shanty. The second year, McNab said to him. "Why don't you come to Douglas and bring your family and I'll get you a house to rent." He just went home to Quadville, picked up the family and left, about 1932.

I went up to Quadville one time before they moved to Douglas and I listened to Bill Cuddy and Grandfather Moriarity tell stories. A pack of lies, you know. I dare not laugh. One story he told, he said, "Bill, didn't we get up early to the shanty in those days?" And Bill said, "Yes." Grandfather went on, "I mind one time going up to McRea's around Whitney in August. We had to walk forty miles into the camp. When we started out there was ripe blueberries everywhere. You could pick a nine-quart pail in ten minutes. We kept on walking and walking until finally one day we were up to our knees in snow."

Father J.J. Quilty would have the big picnics up here at Douglas called the Monster Picnic. Grandfather Moriarity cooked the beans at Douglas. They'd picnic all day and play baseball all day. Four thousand people came to the Monster Picnics. Grandfather would start on Monday and get his camboose all ready and get his beans in the ground and covered. He buried the beans in huge iron pots with covers on them, and then he'd put the sand on them. He'd leave them there from Monday to Wednesday. He wouldn't let them do it. He had to. Because they might let sand in. They built the fire in the middle. That sand was hot two nights before the picnic, and he put all those pots in a row, and they were boarded up on each side and then he poured that sand over the top of the pots. The Monster Picnic always was a Wednesday. Tuesday evening he had the beans all cooked in iron pots, covered. He really knew how to handle them.

Father Quilty and Grandfather Moriarity were great friends all their lives. Before one of the Monster Picnics, Father Quilty came to my grandfather and said, "How much beans do you want me to buy?" Grandfather said, "Oh, we've got to get one of them long cotton bagsful, one hundred pounds." Father Quilty said, "I'm going out to Bolger's Corner. I'll get the beans there." "Oh, no," Grandfather said, "If you get them there you can cook them yourself. I'll only buy them at McBreen's. They're the only beans I trust." That's the store on the Main Street still here in Douglas. So he got his way. Father Quilty bought them at McBreen's.

At the Monster Picnics they'd have boxing matches. I remember one time two fellows all the way up from Ottawa boxed. And I remember one fellow that never was at a picnic and never was at nothing before in his life, and when he heard that a boxing match was going to be on, he arrived at the Monster

*Douglas baseball team in Eganville, c. 1907. Back row, L to R: Walter MacDonald, Stan Livingstone, Neil Cochrane, Hugh Devine, Tom Johnston, Joseph Beach. Front row, L to R: George McNab, Hugh Livingstone, Tom Neville, Les Livingstone, Arthur Forsythe and Archie MacDonald. The mascot is Dudley Moore, killed in action World War I.*

Picnic at six o'clock in the morning so he wouldn't miss it.

There used to be about three baseball games. In the morning the Douglas team would play against a team from the cheese factory down on the Fifth Line. Then the Renfrew and Eganville and Calabogie and Cormac teams would all play. And the winners played all. I think it was a sixty dollar prize. Every cent went to the church—they had two great big men—must have been near four hundred pounds—they weren't much good to do anything else—they had them taking the tickets. It was twenty-five cents, and they counted the money that night and it was one thousand dollars.

The Monster Picnics petered out when Father Quilty died. He came to Douglas in 1905, died in '44. A long time, eh? I went up to the graveyard one night and Father Quilty was sitting outside. He said, "Come sit with me and have a chat." I sat down with him and along came the Bishop of Pembroke and another priest. They were trying to build a church in Renfrew, a second Catholic church. The Bishop of Pembroke said, "Father Quilty, I want you to leave Douglas and go to Renfrew to build that new church." And Father Quilty said, "How do you think me and eighty-five Renfrew bootleggers would get along?" And the bishop just jumped in his car and left Father Quilty and me sitting in the graveyard at Douglas.

This is about the Dirty Thirties. Hard times. We had nothing. And I got up early this morning, no breakfast, but I was walking out to see my uncle, Yankee Paddy Enright at Quadville. I was about half way when I came upon Gerry Sheehan cutting grain in the field with the binder right next to the road.

"Where are you going this early?" he asked.

"I don't know," I said.

"You're out on the road and you don't know where you're going?"

"Well, I thought I'd head for Yankee Paddy's."

"Do you want to work?"

"Well, yes."

"Jump the fence."

So I started stooking the grain with slings. Yep, and then he said he'd a couple of loads of hay to get

*Larry Moriarity's ancestor, the magnificent Yankee Paddy Enright from Yankeetown on the Opeongo Line, c. 1875.*

in. "We'll change jobs," he said. He brought the horses out to run the hay fork. The first load was all right, got all the hay up into the mow in the barn. The second load of hay on the fork he shot up. But I wasn't stirring in the mow. "What's wrong up there?" he shouted. I didn't answer so he come up and there I was out, white as a sheet on the ground. "Are you sick?" he asked. "Well, I don't know if you'd say I was sick, but a little bite to eat would help," I said. "Do you mean to tell me you had nothing to eat for breakfast?" I said no. "Well, no wonder," he said. "It's eleven o'clock now. You go and lie down under the shade of that elm and rest there. As soon as she calls for dinner, I'll shout at you." Once I had the dinner into me away I went. I worked there for about three or four weeks and then Gerry asked me how much I wanted. I said, "Whatever you feel is right." He gave me eighty-seven dollars, a dollar and seventy-five cents a day, a fortune. I said, "You've done really good by me." "Well," he said, "we got two jobs done here together. I could get the ploughing done while you did the rest. And if you hadn't been here, I might never have got the ploughing done before the frost had come. I'm satisfied if you are." "Well, I guess so." I said.

What did I do to make a living and raise my family? Anything I could get. I had a hard time on fifty cents a day. I was telling one of my sons that I used to leave here in the morning at seven o'clock on the bicycle and drive out three miles in the country, work all week on the farm, and I got three dollars. That's fifty cents a day. My son said, "I couldn't do it." I said, "You had to."

We were playing hockey up in Pembroke when a long distance call came for Father O'Brien. He called back to see what was wrong and when he come back we asked him if he would be staying for the rest of the game. He said, "Not likely. The two Fitzmaurice lads were shot by Tommy Gibbons. It's not likely I'll be back at all."

It seems the Fitzmaurices had a bush back behind Gibbons' land and in order to get up to their bush they had to go about a mile around. So they decided to go through Tommy Gibbons' property. Tommy was in the Douglas Hotel down here and he overheard what they planned to do. So that night the Fitzmaurices were crossing through and Tommy was waiting on the hill. He said later he didn't mean to shoot Joe, but he just got behind a tree and yelled at the Fitzmaurices, but they paid no attention to him. He shot poor Joe first, and Ed took off and he was a

*Hockey lost many a championship player like Cecil Code in hard times when skates were too expensive even at the prices listed in this CCM ad taken from an old Ottawa Senators' programme, c. 1935.*

good piece away from Tommy when he shot him on the sleigh. They found Joe easily but they didn't know where Ed was. Father O'Brien said, "We'd better go and look around the buildings." There Ed was, dead on the sleigh. Tommy was tried and put away. That happened the night I was playing in the Upper Bonnechere Valley Hockey Championships 1945/46.

Tommy Neville, a great lad, owned the general store here for a long time. Now, we could beat Cobden any night of the week, there or at home. They had a good hockey team—big buggers. But we couldn't beat Bromley. I remember Tommy used to say, "Too many cornflakes. Them fellows eat corn in the morning." Anyway, Tom had this playoff game

this night and after the first period Cobden was 2 - 0. I went to sit in the player's bench behind Neville and Jordon, the manager of the Cobden team. I heard Jordon say, "We have you now, Neville." Tommy put his hand in his pocket and pulled out a roll of bills. "A hundred dollars. Put up or shut up." Jordon never said another word and we beat them 4 - 3.

Barry's Bay was in the South Renfrew League. Cecil Code was a young farm lad I loaned a pair of skates. Cecil said to me, "If only I had a pair of skates I could skate." Well, he was about the same size as I was so I loaned him my skates. Holy God! He went around that Douglas rink! He was a great skater and about three times as fast as me. After that he told me he used to skate from his farm to Renfrew on the

*No less than renowned Renfrew photographer, R.L. Handford, was engaged to take this Douglas hockey team, winners of the 1930-31 George Cup. Larry Moriarity and his lifelong friend Alan McNab were teammates for this event. Back row, L to R: Tommy Shirley, Bob Byers, Alan McNab, Harold Breen, Larry Moriarity, Billy Barr. Front row, L to R: Arnold Ritchie, Wilbur Neville, Malcolm McNab, Tommy Neville (coach), Jack Barr, Jack Stitt.*

Bonnechere River. It's fifteen miles from Douglas to Renfrew and three miles from his place to Douglas. Eighteen miles. He never played hockey. He had to farm. But skate! When he told me he skated to Renfrew, I said, "What did you do with the skates when you got there?" "Hide them at the bridge," he said. "Go up to town, come back and put them on again. About an hour. Bring groceries back home on my back."

We went on sleighs to the hockey games in Eganville, Cobden, Bromley, Northcote. People volunteered—Mildred Barr, Alan Neville, Irvin Andrews. Leave here at five o'clock in the evening and got home at two or three o'clock at night. Snowdrifts up and down, up and down. We'd try to get there to play at eight and it would be twelve o'clock before we'd be leaving there. Young Andrews was driving the team one night coming home to Douglas and we were all half asleep and we were coming down the Fifth Line. Somebody had left a load of hay on the shoulder to the side of the road and the team—the horses were probably half asleep too—didn't pull out far enough and the corner of the sleigh hit the hay, threw us all out into the snow. Young Andrews got home that morning at five o'clock.

R.M. Warren, MP, put up a cup for junior hockey. He thought Eganville had the best team of all. There was Cobden and Eganville, Douglas, Bromley and Northcote in the league and we won that 1938 championship. Played it off in Renfrew. Mac O'Neil played goal, fourteen years old and he was good at it. And, you know, there was a pile of them lads on that team went to war and never came back. Harold Sheehan, Donald Watson, Lloyd Stuart, Pat Serson.

Tom Murray, a great baseball man, was MP for Renfrew. After a big storm one time, they came to Eganville to plough, but that's as far as they went. Johnny Briscoe called Tom Murray to get the plough to come down to the Highway 60 to 17, to open the road to Douglas. But, they didn't get to first base. Now I had worked for Briscoe on the roads so I went in to Briscoe's Store in Douglas, and J.M. said, "I was talking to a friend of yours." I said, "Who?" "George McNab," he said, "He called me this morning and wondered if I could help him to get the road ploughed from Eganville down to the highway." I said, "George, we're all right. We have the road ploughed ourselves from here to the highway. We can get out." "You're president of the North Renfrew Liberal Association," he said, "You should have no trouble," he said. "Can't get to first base," McNab said. So he said, "I just wrote a little note and put it in the mail bag to Barry's Bay for Tom Murray."

Now, there was an old gentleman, Jim Gorman here, who was about eighty years old and when he got his pay cheque, he'd say to me, "Larry, you couldn't take a trip today?" He wanted me to go on the train to Eganville and get him a bottle of brandy and a bottle of rum. So I went up on the train. The Eganville liquor store was right across from McGillicott's Hotel. I went in and who is sitting in the window but Tom Murray? So over I go. My train wasn't leaving for an hour and we talked away and all at once the snow plough landed in Eganville. Up jumped Murray and opened the cab door of the plough. Murray told the ploughman that he had to go to 17 to Douglas, and the ploughman said he wasn't going. He had been told up in Renfrew just to go to Eganville and that was as far as he was going. So Tom said, "Alright, get out and we'll get some other driver to drive it." That changed his mind. At five o'clock we saw the plough coming round the corner in Douglas. Of course, J.M. Briscoe and Tom were great friends. Great Liberals.

One time I was passing the post office and there was Tom sitting there. I said, "What the hell are you doing sitting out in the street?" "Oh," he said, "you have to have somebody to talk to. They pass me here and they stop and they talk." I said, "What are you doing for a living now? Do you go up very often to the lumber camp?" "Oh, an odd time," he says. "Mostly I'm picking blueberries now. I was out all day yesterday and I was too tired to go today, but I might go tomorrow." Tom was eighty then. He was a great man. Never got fussed up or mad. He was even.

Stuart McNab, one of our ball players, was a terrible lad for swearing. Something went wrong in one of the games and Stuart said, "Holy Jesus Christ!" Father Quilty said to him, "Hey! Hey!" right

*Bands like this one would no doubt take part in Old Home Week Celebrations in Pembroke.*

at the ball game, at the ball field. "Any more of that McNab and you'll have to go home." It must have been over fifty years or sixty years later when his sister-in-law died—he came back for the wake, he had a business in Quebec, something to do with wool—and he came over to me at the wake and he said, "Do you remember the night that I was swearing and Father Quilty was there? I think of that a thousand times and I'd like to apologize to Father Quilty." "Oh, it won't do any good now," I said. "He's gone."

Alan McNab was a great friend of mine. His aunt was Lieutenant-Governor of Saskatchewan, Lizzie McNab, his father's sister. She lived in Ottawa for part of the year because she had to, but she had a fine residence in Pembroke, too; the McNab home on Main Street. Alan used to take me to Pembroke to visit Aunt Lizzie, to collect the money or the Christmas presents. One Christmas we went to Pembroke with a load of flour from the McNab mill in Douglas. Alan knew that she was at home in Pembroke, so that's where he went to collect. She gave him twenty bucks and he was supposed to share it, five dollars each, for Bob, Malcolm, Margaret, his brothers and sister. But Alan kept the twenty dollars.

He spent it all in Pembroke. Clothes at Freiman's Five-and-Ten store and that's a good few years ago, just before he went to college, University of Toronto. At the time Eganville had a ball team with players from Ottawa and around and the McNab lads played with them, too. All-Star Eganville Team, 1934.

One morning Alan came rolling into the upstairs of our house in Douglas. "Get up. Get up. Come on to Pembroke—it's Old Home Week." (There was baseball teams from the States and all, and the Perth team, there was a whole bunch of them. Eganville had picked a bunch. Eganville finally won the play-off. It took days to win; they played all week.) Alan said, "Malcolm and Bob are going to play ball with Eganville and Pembroke today. We should go up with them." I said, "How the hell will we go? The best I can do is fifty cents." "Oh," he says, "I have seventy-five. Come on. Let's go." So we went over to the McNab house and out comes Malcolm, his older brother. He said, "What are you fellows doing?" Alan said, "We're going to Pembroke." "Oh," he said, "You're not. I'm driving the car and you're not coming. You're not coming to bum off me all day." Then Bob, another brother, came out and he said,

"What's up, lads?" Alan said, "Well, we thought we'd go to Pembroke but I guess our minds have been changed." "Why?" Bob said. "Malcolm won't take us. He said he's driving the car and we're not going up there to bum off him all day." Bob said, "The back seat of the car is empty. Jump in if you want to come." So into the back seat of the Chrysler we jumped and away we all went to Pembroke—Malcolm, Alan, Bob, Larry.

Anyway, when we got there there was a lad at the gate and it was twenty-five cents to get in. That meant that I had a quarter and Alan had fifty cents left. There was a wheel of fortune there and Alan said, "I think I'll try the wheel of fortune." He got three paddles for a quarter and if you won you got a dollar. Thank God that he won two straight times! He lost the third time. So we went away with three dollars and a half. Dinner was fifty cents.

Alan went off some place and I was by myself, walking up and down, when Shorty Mills, the manager of the Eganville baseball team, came along and he said, "Just who I'm looking for." I said, "What do you want?" He said, "I want you to play ball. Two farmers left after the first game this morning and they were supposed to be back. One came back and the other one isn't coming back. I want you to come and take his place." I said, "Where do you want me to play?" "In the outfield." "No," I said, "but I'll get you a guy that can play the outfield." "Who?" "Alan McNab." "Good," he said. And we march into the dressing-room at the grounds and Malcolm said, "Where are you lads going?" Finally Shorty came and handed Alan the baseball. "What are you going to do with that?" Malcolm asked. "Play ball," Alan said. I stayed watching the ball game and in the ninth inning with two men out and a Douglas lad batting last, one man on first, Alan came up to bat. By God! He put the ball in the river, made a home run and won the game 4 - 3! So we had a great time there laughing and celebrating. We went into the dressing room and Alan dressed, and when he went to take back the uniform to Shorty Mills, Shorty shook hands with him, and when he took his hand away there was a ten-dollar bill in it! There was a taxi out at the gate of the park and we took the taxi for thirty-five cents and off

to the centre of Pembroke. Malcolm and Bob started looking for Alan and couldn't find him. Finally they heard about the street dance and finally about nine o'clock at night they run into me. They said, "Where the hell did you fellows go?" "We're up here listening to the music." "Where the hell are you getting all the money?" And Alan said, "Well, Malcolm, we didn't have to bum it, anyway."

My grandfather's brother lived across in Chapeau. Dan Moriarity from The Island. I said to Grandpa Moriarity, "Would you come to Chapeau with me? I'll rent a car and somebody to drive us and we'll go to Chapeau." "No. No. If Dan wants to come over here, let him come." I was going to give him a little special trip because for twenty-five years the brothers had never seen each other. Grandpa said, "He comes to Pembroke. It wouldn't hurt him to come on down to Douglas."

My mother heard us and she had a way with her father, so she talked to him and in about fifteen or twenty minutes she called me and she said, "I think Grandpa will go with you." So I went up the street and hired a fellow to take us. We had to cross on the ferry from Pembroke to Chapeau at Desjardinville, and landed in Chapeau about nine o'clock. When we arrived Dan was in bed, but his wife was there, and a couple of the girls, Ida and Freida Moriarity, nurses-in-training at Renfrew Hospital. Aunt Mary, Dan's wife, went up and said to him, "Come down. You've visitors here." He said, "Tell the goddamn fools to go home. No time to go visiting at night after nine o'clock." She came down and the two girls said, "We'll go up and see him." "No. I don't want visitors at that time of the night," he says. So down they come. Aunt Mary said to me, "Let's you and me go up and see what we can do." So up we went. "Who the hell are you?" he said, "Out at this time of the night. I don't know who you are." I said, "I guess you don't because I never saw you before." He said, "Who are you anyway?" I said, "I'm Lawrence Moriarity." "From where? Who's your father?" I said, "Michael." "My brother?" "No, his son. Michael's also my grandfather. What about you coming down and having a little chat?" He said, "Maybe I will." So Dan came down the stairs and into the kitchen and he saw him, and I'd say that Dan stood there for ten minutes and never opened his mouth. Finally they got around to saying something to one another. About twelve o'clock we all decided we'd go to bed and leave them. When we came down at seven o'clock in the morning, Dan and Mike were still there talking. All night long after twenty-five years!

Dr. O'Reilly was the doctor in Douglas and he used to go round the country giving needles to the kids and making calls. So this day I decided to go with him. After he had one school done, somebody came rushing along and said, "Holy God, doctor! You're wanted up at Mount St. Patrick." He named someone who was awful sick, and he said, "We'll have a fellow take you up and bring you back." "What are you going to do while I'm up there?" Dr. O'Reilly said to me. I said, "I'll go to the priest's house"—it was Father Francis Kennedy then—"and talk to him and that's where I'll be when you come back." Dr. O'Reilly must have been three hours away so Father Kennedy had a long time to talk to me. So he was telling me about Moriarities and Poupores and Kennedys who all lived on Allumette Island, just across from Chapeau.

And this is what he told me: "When we were children, we used to have to pass Dan Moriarity's in the evening when we were coming home from school. He wasn't around when we'd be going to school in the morning, but he'd be there in the evening, sitting on the porch. One evening Dan said to the kids, `Tell Kennedy that goddamn old father of yours, he's no damn good, never was good for anything. Him and the goddamn Poupores.' All Catholics. And then I remember he said, `I'm going to stop Kennedy's funeral when it passes here.'" Father Francis said, "When we got home we told Dad what Dan had said. He said, `Don't mind that old lad. He's crazy.'" Father Kennedy said, "But you know what? My father died and the funeral had to pass Moriarity's to go into Chapeau to church, and wasn't Dan Moriarity's house on fire and everybody stopped to help put out the fire. Yes, all the Poupores and the Kennedys whom Dan had cursed so roundly."

Teresita, my daughter the nurse, trained in Renfrew Hospital. And she told me this story. There was an old lad from Mount St. Patrick, away up at the top of the mountain on the Opeongo Line. Johnny Kiley he was. He never was down from Mount St. Patrick in his whole life and when he was seventy-seven years old they took him down to see the doctor, and the doctor put him in the hospital in Renfrew. He wasn't long in hospital before the nurse came along with a needle and he chased her to hell out of the room. Then the matron came in and he said, "To hell with you." Chased her the hell out. The head nurse came in and he damn well put her out, too. Teresita wasn't on his floor but they went and got her, thought she could deal with an Irishman from Mount St. Patrick. So she went in to Johnny Kiley and she said, "God damn all Irishmen, can you sing?" "Damn right I can sing," he said. "You've got a nice room here, lovely view," she said. "There's no goddamn nice rooms in a hospital," he said. "But," she said, "if you look out there you can see all the cars going up the road." And he turned round to look and—bingo! She needled him. Afterwards she said, "Sing me a song." So he sang her, *In the Garden where the Praties Grow*. She said the old bugger could really sing, too. After that he wouldn't let anybody else near him, only Teresita.

My dad was in the Ottawa hospital, and there was just Mary and I at home, and Mother was down there. We were sitting out on the porch at about half-past-seven in the evening when down come the lady from the telephone office and she said, "There's a call from the Ottawa hospital that your dad is dying down there." We had no money or nothing. We didn't know what the hell to do. All at once George McNab went up the far side of the street to the store, going for his cigars. He stopped and asked, "How's your father doing down there?" "Well," I said, "They're just after sending a message that he's dying." "What?" he said. "Have you got some way to go to Ottawa?" I said, "Not yet." "Well, Alan will be over with the car in a few minutes."

So my uncle, Yankee Paddy Enright, and my Aunt Annie, mother's sister, and her brother came with us. We went down to the old General Hospital. We hit for Aunt Annie's where my mother was staying. There wasn't a light there at all. This would

*Larry's friend, Alan McNab, might have had an early automobile like the one shown here.*

be about eleven o'clock. I said, "That's a funny thing." So we went to the General. Oh, God! it was quiet in there! You wouldn't hear a mouse stirring. I knew where Dad was. I went up on the floor and I met a nurse and I asked her about my dad. "Who is that?" "Mick Moriarity." "Well, the last time I seen him he was sleeping like a doll," she said. "Holy God!" I said, "We got a message in Douglas that he was dying." She said, "I've been on the shift since four o'clock and I never seen him dying or heard tell of him dying and I've been in dozens of times." Away we went, back to Annie's. Alan said he'd like to have a little sleep so I took him upstairs and he threw himself on the bed and slept 'til morning. In the morning he said, "I want to take a little drive." He was away a couple of hours and he came back laughing and happy as hell. He had got a *Toronto Globe* and read in it where he had passed his lawyer's exams. So he said, "I don't give a damn whether I go home or not." But that's a friend—George McNab saying, "Alan will be over in a few minutes to take you to Ottawa."

Dad had an Uncle Dan Moriarity who was in World War I for four or five years. He enlisted in August at the Ottawa Fair in 1914 and he came back in April 1919. Of course, he was an awful man to drink. So one night Dan happened to come along and my dad and I were sitting on the sidewalk in Douglas. He was pretty tight, and my dad said to him, "Should be ashamed of yourself going on like that all the time. What the hell good does drink do you. Half the time you're hitting telephone posts right in front of you because you can't see." Dan said, "Well, just shut up for a minute. You'll be pushing up daisies a goddamn long time before me." Holy God! My dad died in '38 and Dan didn't die until '74.

No, not the Dan Moriarity in Sheenboro and Chapeau. This was my dad's brother who lived in Douglas. He left in 1908 and when his mother died, they didn't know where the hell he was. They couldn't find him for the funeral. Then, holy God! who walked into our summer kitchen one day but Dan. My mother asked him where he had been and he said, "All over the goddamn world!" He got wounded in World War I about nine hours before peace was signed. A couple of blocks of cement fell on his leg and broke it. I remember he was down here one fall and he hadn't a nickel to his name, but he went down to Paddy Conway, his uncle in Douglas, and Paddy was living alone, and Paddy said to him, "Dan, if you'd like to stay with me 'til you get some work, it will be all right." One day I was passing down by the telephone office and Mrs. McKeon came out and she said, "A telegram came for Dan. Do you know where he is? It's from Sutton, above Sudbury. Try and look him up." The telegram said, "If you're short of money and can't come, we'll wire the money." So I went over to Conway's and told Dan and he said, "God! they're after me. They want me to work in the shanty as a teamster. That's the J.L.S. McRea Lumber Company in Whitney."

Dan disappeared up north. Some years later I got a ride up to Sutton, found Dan all alone and tried to get him to come home with me to Douglas. He was getting old. He told me his old age pension and his army pension came to the post office in Sudbury and he had told them on no account were they to give them out to anyone else. "But," he told me, "as soon as they come, I will come home." But he never did come and I never saw him again. Never heard anything again until they sent me word he had died up there. His wife was buried here in Douglas and I wanted to bring him home to be here with the clan. And all the relatives were pressuring to bring Dan home. So I went to Father Tom Hunt. I told Tom and he said, "You just stay at home. You're about to get yourself into a lot of trouble." "Why?" I asked. "Well, you'd have to pay for the train ride and the burial and everything. The army is going to take real good care of him up there." So Dan Moriarity is buried up north there somewhere.

One time I had a really big gang of lads working on the Douglas rink flooding it for a hockey game that night. It was a January thaw and Father Quilty came along and he said, "You'll never make it for the game tonight. Send the lads home. Cancel the game." "Well," I thought to myself, "That's not very smart. They're working like beavers and, even if we don't

make the game, we'll have layers of ice down. Not very smart to send them all home." So I said to Father Quilty, "I think we'll just keep on trying." We did. And we almost made the game, but in the end we had to cancel.

Oh, yes, I remember Wyman Townes. I was only a young lad eight or nine years old when I seen him going around Douglas with the horse and the little wagon. Wyman told a lot of stories and a lot of people have told stories about him. He was a kind of a cook too, Wyman. I remember a neighbour of ours, August Freibig, was going round Douglas one day. George McNab stopped him on the street—at that time he had a lumber camp away up around Balaclava—and he asked August, "You wouldn't know anybody who could come cook for me in the camp?" August said,

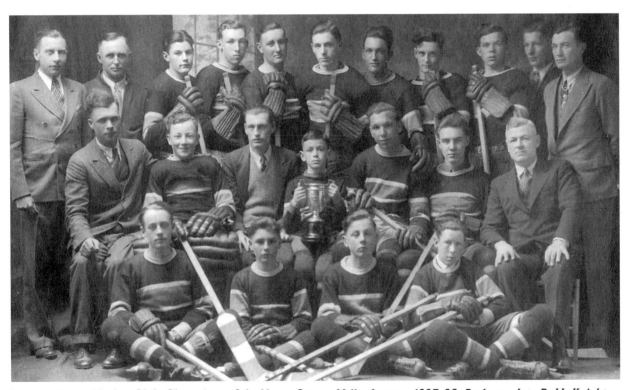

*Douglas Junior Hockey Club, Champions of the Upper Ottawa Valley League, 1937-38. Back row, L to R: H. Knight, vice pres; James Walsh, coach; Joe Neville, Joe Shirley, Gerald Welsh, Orville Lynch, Tom Sheehan, Jack Gilmour, Harold Sheahan, Lloyd Stewart, Harold McEachen, secretary. Middle row: Ed Gallagher, pres; Mack O'Neill, Larry Moriarity, manager; Tommy Neville, mascot; Edmund Valiquette, captain; Donald Watson, Tom Neville, hon. pres. Front row: Donald MacDonald, Joe Moriarity, Anselm O'Neill, Pat Searson.*

"Wyman Townes can cook. But . . ." "But what?" said McNab. "He is now dead," August replied.

I worked at the Douglas school for seven years as a janitor, and I used to help the kids play baseball or coach them at noon hours. And the nun came along to the baseball diamond and she said, "You can't play hardball here. There's somebody going to get hurt." I said to her, "You just take off back up to the school and when somebody gets hurt I'll quit helping and coaching. Kids get hurt more doing nothing than playing baseball." After I left my job as janitor at the school, if they didn't put a whole lot of play equipment, slides, teeter-totters, logs, what-nots right in the back end of the ball park. And didn't three or four people get hurt. One kid broke a leg sliding down the log.

Hugh Livingstone had a farm out of town, across from us. 'Course I was a young lad watching him all the time. I was walking out to my Uncle Yankee Paddy's one day at noontime and saw Hugh out in the yard pitching ball at the building. Yes, he had a hole cut in the wall of the barn and he was pitching through the hole, and he had a young lad in behind throwing him the ball back. He went up to Coppercliff and played for a couple of summers up there. He was one of the greats, Hugh Devine, another great, a catcher from Osceola. I remember one day he was playing for Douglas in Pembroke — we knocked the hell out of Pembroke—and the next day he got caught in his farm machinery out in Osceola and got killed.

Pat and Mike came over from Ireland and bought a farm in the Valley. They were two great baseball pitchers—they didn't know which one was the best. But anyway, the two of them were having a pint and they were talking this night and Pat said to Mike, "I wonder if they play baseball in Heaven?" Mike said, "I don't know, but whoever dies first be sure and come back and tell the other one whether there's baseball there or not." So anyway, in a while, Mike died and went to heaven. So this day Pat was in the field and along come Mike from heaven. Pat said, "What about the baseball in heaven?" "Well," Mike said, "there's a good thing about it and there's a bad thing about it." "Well, tell me the good thing," said Pat. Mike said, "They play baseball there. And the bad thing is that it's your turn to pitch on Saturday."

I don't care what anybody says, Larry Moriarity says the ball players in those days were every bit as good as today, as good back in 1909 as in 1996.

*In 1994, the new Douglas ball park was dedicated to Larry Moriarity. Once again, the lifelong friends, Al McNab and Larry, pose together as they did as young men years before. L to R: Alan McNab, Tommy Gallagher, Larry Moriarity, Donny Sheehan, Sil Donahue, John McEchen, Mike Gallagher.*

# 9

# "For Every North American Indian Who Disappears, I Disappear"

## WILF PELLTIER – Member of the Ottawa Tribe, Ottawa, Ontario

*Most of the history books I have read recorded that the Odawa, or Ottawa, tribe to which Wilf Pelltier belongs had been wiped out in the seventeenth century during the tribal wars between the Iroquois and the Algonquin. Yet, when I first met Pelltier at a writers' gala in Ottawa he told me he was a member of the Odawa clan. "Indeed," he said, "there are numbers of us in Ottawa and many more around Detroit." Prior to our meeting, I had already resolved to include in this book some of the original settlers in the Valley. I was delighted to discover when I visited to tape him, that not only was he an aboriginal survivor but, also a wise teacher and great storyteller.*

*Raised around Wikwomiking on Manitoulin Island, Wilf Pelltier later gained a reputation across Canada as a native peoples' rights leader and as a guest storyteller and singer at Carleton University where he was quoted as saying, "I love to be amongst the students because they are more open to ideas, imagination and humour." Pelltier's favourite comedians are oldtimers like Jack Benny, Myron Cohen, and George Burns. He says that today's comedians on television "don't have enough character in their faces to be funny." Certainly Pelltier has enough character in his face*

*to be reminiscent of that other great Indian comedian, Cherokee Will Rogers. Pelltier has written five books including* No Foreign Land, For Every North American Indian Who Begins to Disappear, I Disappear, *and* A Wise Man Speaks.

*I am truly privileged to be able to include this rarest of rare interviews, wisdom-layered, laughter-filled, with a surviving member of the Odawa tribe of the Ottawa Valley. To the best of my ability I have adhered to his Native mode of storytelling.*

INDIANS DON'T need any relief from whites. All they need is relief from white assumptions, white attitudes, and white good intentions. Some of us seem to have found the relief we need in laughter. Laughter is a great teacher. You learn from it with your gut more than your head.

All our humour is mostly in our own language and it's very difficult to come out with stories and legends in English that have anything to do with our own language. Call it Indian if you like, but I don't do that. I generally give a tribal background, whether it's an Odawa (Ottawa), Ojibway, or Cree. It really can't be translated. I think that's why, when it's translated, white people don't think it is funny. Our whole view is entirely different. You can't argue in our language; it just turns into laughter. Well, there's

101

*Wilf Pelltier, a distinguished member of the Ottawa tribe.*

no words that can be bad, you see, or even forbidden words. So when somebody goes to use one, somebody else will turn that word into something else and then everybody just breaks up. You can scold a child in our language, but even in scolding it's *how* you do it. It's not to put a child down. Leave him his dignity, but let him know that he did wrong.

I find that white people are always consciously aware, as opposed to an unconsciousness that the Native People have. Now, I can't speak for all the tribes, but pretty near all the tribes I know are like this. And where there's any native people gathering, you'll find nothing but laughter—and it's continuous laughter—so long as they're talking in their own language, even if there's other people around who don't understand them. Like some of their own children don't speak the language now, but so long as they speak in their own language, you'd find it very funny, very humorous. It's the usage of the words, and how they use the words, too, is very important. Very humorous people.

We were told a long time ago by old people and some of our own elders that we originated around Ottawa. Our name was Odawa, which means "traders," and then it got changed into Ottawa. That was an anglicization. And it's like that all throughout the country. No matter where you go, they've taken our tribalism and changed it into something else. We were then taken from Ottawa and we moved up along the Ottawa River, maybe close to Timiskaming, but certainly up as far as across from Mattawa. Then we moved over there into Lake Nipissing and we travelled through Lake Nipissing down. Now there was another group of us around Detroit and all that area up through there, and they moved north from there and settled around Mount Clements, and then all through Michigan. One group of Odawa went as far as northeastern Oklahoma.

The tribe that disappeared mostly was the Hurons. It was the Hurons that the Odawas got in a tussle with—well, the Hurons were the first native people that became Christian, but they were also a renegade group and they claimed to belong to the Algonquin nation, which is what we belong to as a nation. I don't know how many Odawas there are left in this country, in the Americas, but there's five or six thousand of them up on my reserve at Manitoulin Island. And there's a lot of them in the States. The city of Ottawa is full of them.

My grandfather didn't really pass me stories. He used to sing songs. And through them you hear bits and pieces of history from a lot of other people, you know. Like the elimination of the Hurons; there's only that tribe north of Quebec City. It's a Huron village, I guess they'd call it. There's Hurons there and they're mixed now, you know. It's like a lot of Odawas are mixed with Ojibway.

What happened was, you see, when the Europeans came here they brought clergy with them and these clergy kept saying that we were honouring false gods. So they went around and they destroyed all the symbols that we had, from community to community, and they went through from here in Ottawa down to as far as Detroit, and then they swung north and went up through Michigan doing this. And then when they got to Mackinac Island, they crossed over to the island—to Manitoulin—and destroyed all our symbols all through Manitoulin, and then they crossed from Manitoulin down to west of the Bruce Peninsula and then they came down and they settled some place there where they build this Fort Saint Marie.

Well, all the Iroquois were after them and we were after them. It was just the old ladies and the old men who couldn't get out and were still in camp when the Hurons destroyed everything. So when the young people got back from hunting—all the men got back and the boys—they decided they were going to "get them" for this. So they chased the Hurons all the way up through Michigan across over to Manitoulin, and they joined the other tribes and there was what they called a Potawattame. The Iroquois caught the Hurons and the clergy at Fort Saint Marie and they destroyed them. That's before our people got there. We were after them, too, and, if we'd have got to them, we'd have done the same thing, but we didn't reach there in time. Oh yes, we would have done them all in because the Hurons were with the clergy, you see. They were converted. That's the story and all our people know that story. It's been passed down and that's how it happened.

One of the great chiefs we had was Chief Pontiac and he took all the forts except Fort Detroit; that was the only one he never took. Eventually he got killed in Missouri—in St. Louis, I think. He's buried in Kansas. I'm not sure, but I think it was a Miami Indian that killed him because they couldn't recognize him with all those head men sitting around. I guess by that time they were calling them "chiefs." That would be the designated spokesman for the tribe. And they used to change that, too, you know. One might be a designated spokesman one day and next day he'd be a different person.

We had clans. Like my name never was Pelltier, but that's what the clergy came in and called us. They took all our Indian names away from us and they called us all Pelltier. We had the clan, the one clan.

I don't know how long ago my great-grandfather moved in to Manitoulin Island, but it was out of the way and the people were content there. There was plenty around there to keep them alive. Of course, there isn't now, but at that time there was fish and game of all kinds, and now that has been mostly run out of there. In fact, there's still a lot of deer and we don't have as many bears as they used to have. The wolf population has been cut down quite a bit too. We could trap on the island. The only thing we didn't have was there was no blueberries grew on that island. We had to go off the island to get them, and bears would have to go off the island to get them, too, so they swam back and forth, you see. There was a constant swimming back and forth of the bear population. And because there were a lot of wolves along the north shore, they used to chase a lot of deer over onto the island and there was a lot of slash on that island, so deer could hide amongst the slash and get away from the wolves. As far back as I can remember, it was nothing to have deer walk right up to you. Standing out in your yard or, when we got cattle in there, being amongst the cattle. When I was young, you used to see them all the time. You'd wake up early in the morning and they'd be feeding right at your back step, you know.

Living on the island as a young boy, to me, it was just like heaven. It was home, I guess, and it was very exciting because of the kind of lifestyle we had. We lived for the day and we weren't thinking about tomorrow. Lived for now, right now, while we're alive. So all the stories and all the various information that you get, it was handed down and a lot of this was handed down through legends and stories, but they were always very funny—but in my own language you see—it does make a difference when you try to tell it in English.

What I can tell you about stories and legends has really got to do with similarities all across the Algonquin Nation and that runs from the East Coast to the mountains in Alberta and then past that.

I don't know too much about the history of the mountain people and the coast people, although I've been there lots of times. There's a lot of history on the western tribes and they say there were certain things going on over there. I have no idea—I just laughed most things off. Knowing the native people from across the country, I don't believe any of that stuff that's been written because it's somebody else's eyes who sees it, and it's all through their values and their culture.

It reminds me of a story. Once I was on a mountain a few years back, oh, up on top, out in British Columbia and there was another fellow with me and we were standing barefoot on some green grass—there was no green grass anywhere else; everything else was burned out and they used to let cattle loose up on that grass—and he said to me, "Wilf, if you were in charge of everything, what changes would you make?" I figured that was a pretty loaded question, so I looked up and I looked around and I looked at a nice big white fluffy cloud and I said, "You know, I think I'd put more clouds up there in the air. No, I've changed my mind, everything is just right." Then I heard these meadowlarks singing all through there and boy, it was beautiful, and I thought, "Gee, if I could just put a few more meadowlarks out and different birds singing, what songs we could get." Then I changed my mind about that and I again thought that everything was just right—just leave it alone. Then I thought about some bear and deer. I'd have them walk up here. Then I changed my mind about that and again thought everything is fine.

And then I looked down at my feet and I seen a board lying there and it was weatherbeaten, but it had been moved—maybe a cow had stepped on it or something and one end of it started very narrow and got wider until it was about two inches wide, and then you could see the bare ground and at the other side the grass was all bent coming from under that board. "Ah," I thought, "I'll move that bent board back to where it was and let this bent grass grow up." I don't know what made me pick that board up. I didn't pick the whole board up, just the one end, and when I did, I looked there and about three or four spiders rushed at me and came right up to the top where my finger was. And, God, I could see them really plain, you know, and they were mad. And underneath that board it was full of insects; they were just going every which way. And there was deep holes dug down in there and on top of that board, there had been some kind of insects that had made grooves in the top and the place had thousand of insects under it.

The reason for that piece of grass being green, there was an old well used to sit there and it was filled with stones and I guess there was water underneath there and that kept that grass green. Well, I put that board right back down where I got it—or tried to. I don't think I did the right thing, but I was shocked. The guy spoke to me and he said, "What's wrong, Wilf?" I said, "You know, I lost my sight. My vision narrowed to that one thing, that grass, coming out from that board in my attempt to improve this place, to make change." And I said, "I lifted the cap off their world."

So, you see, that's what happens when people go and they look at an Indian community and they think that there is no action in there, that there isn't recreation, that there's no education, no lawyers, no this, no that. They should have churches and they should have all these other things from an outside world that lives a different lifestyle than we do. They, too, lift the cap off our world and they destroy it.

The cap was lifted off our world on Manitoulin Island. We had all the recreation we wanted; yet, one time they brought in a recreation director and he tried to learn us to play games. We didn't have games. We had play. And there's a big difference because games is the stuff of war. It means there has to be a winner and a loser, and one person becomes better than another, and competition begins. But we only had play. Everything we did was play and if you want to call it recreation, we had it. It's a learning situation you're in all the time, every moment, every day. It's the same down here; people say they are going to universities to learn. They're not going there to learn, they're going there to get information. Education is all the time, all your life. An Odawa father teaches his son how to trap. Well, he doesn't even teach; you just watch him. You just go along with him and you go along with other people and you learn by that—if they allow you to learn.

One time when I was a young boy, I was out hunting with two fellows, so I said, "I'm going up through here and I'll meet you down at one of those big piles of rocks down there." They said, "Okay." Those two guys never said anything. It was all swamp up there; there was no way I could get through there. But they never told me that. They just let me go. But the possibility is always that I could have gotten through and that was not robbed from me; it was not taken from me. I had to come all the way back down . . . But the white people, they would have told you, "You can't get through over there; it's all swamp," and you'd never even have the opportunity to try to get through. And that is the difference. And that is the learning process.

The other thing we learned about, animals, we learned through stories in the wintertime. We'd do what we had to do to sustain ourselves from spring through to fall and when the snow came and animals and birds and insects, some of them went to sleep and they'd sleep for the winter, then we would gather round the big fires and the stoves and the old men would tell stories, and sometimes you'd just fall asleep right there on the floor. They'd just cover you up and that's where you'd spend the night. It was very different and some of those things took years—even now there's some stories that I've been told and I don't know the meaning of them. Someday maybe it'll come across to me.

I'll tell you one story first, about a turtle. It was swimming across the lake and two guys were in a canoe and this was a bay. And on the other side of the bay there were lots of deer and they all came down at night to the water. So they thought, "Well, we'll just camp over there and then we'll go around there early in the morning." It was just a short cut across. And there were a lot of rocks along the shore, so they'd hear the deer stepping on these rocks.

Anyway, they were paddling across and they saw this turtle swimming in the water, a big turtle, and right in the centre of its back moss grew, and they had never seen a turtle like that before. So one guy said, "Boy, did you see that?" And the guy in the back of the canoe said, "Yes. I want to get him." And the fellow up front, there was nothing he could do. "Don't touch him," he said. "Leave him alone," he said, "you don't know what that is." The other fellow, he says, "Oh, that's just a turtle." So he had control in the back of the canoe and so they went back and they went up beside the turtle and he grabbed that moss right in the centre of its back and threw it in the canoe. And the other fellow told him again, "You'd better let that animal go." He said, "Leave it alone, don't touch it. That's very strange. I've never saw one like that before." "Oh, no," he says, "I'm going to have this for our food tonight. We'll make some soup."

So when they got across to the other side, they set up camp, found a nice mossy ground to lay down on for the night, and built a fire that wasn't too far from the water's edge. So the guy got out this big pot and he started to boil this turtle and the other guy, he just ate the food he had brought. The first guy said, "Wait for the turtle to cook." But the other fellow went ahead and ate, and he said, "You should have let that thing go and leave it alone." So the guy took the soup and he drank the soup and he tried to offer it to the fellow who was sitting in the head of the canoe, but he wouldn't drink it. He said, "What you did was wrong. It wasn't the right thing to do."

So, pretty soon after that, they sit back to have a smoke and this guy got up and picked up a pail and he went and got a pail of water and he drank some of the water and pretty soon he'd drank the whole pailful. This guy looked at him and he said, "Boy, you must have been thirsty." And he was thinking, "Gee, that's strange that he'd drink all that water." So pretty soon the guy got up and he went and got another pail of water and with one gulp he drank that whole pail down and he still wasn't satisfied. He got up again and he went down to the water's edge and he started drinking right from the lake—lying on shore and drinking.

The other fellow had finished his smoke and everything and he hollered to him, "How come you're not back? What are you doing drinking so much water?" And there was no answer. Well, he couldn't see the beach because of the fire, so he got up and he went towards the beach and when he got there the fellow's head was stuck right down in the water. He kicked his feet and he said, "Get out of there; you're drinking too much water." By that time his shoulders were in the water. So he grabbed his feet and he tried to pull him, but he couldn't, and he kept going further and further into the water. Finally, he grabbed a hold of both his feet and stuck them under his arms and dug his heels in and he tried to hold that guy and pull him back out of the water, and that guy just kept going further and further into the water. Finally, he was right up to the water's edge with his shoes in the gravel and he was being pulled in, too, so he let go and slowly, little by little, that guy disappeared down into the water. That was the last he ever seen of him.

Now I was told that when I was maybe ten or eleven years old by an old fellow I used to go out hunting with, and we were out hunting at the time when he told me this story, and to this day I don't know exactly all the messages in there. But it gave me something to think about all my life. Every once in a while, I think of that story. I just don't know what it means. But some day I will. Some day it will be revealed. I think it meant, if you don't know what something is, leave it alone. Don't destroy it. But there must be something else in there.

The legends we used to tell centred around a mythological figure we had and our people called him Nanabush or Nanabush-O. I don't know how to spell it. We never had it written. The Crees call him Ne-sock-eye-shock and the Woodland Cree call him Whisky Jack, and I know that Blackfoot call him Napi.

These stories just start. They have no beginning and no end. You can add on if you want to put an extra story in because these stories just go and go and go, and you can stop wherever you like and take it up the next night and start talking about that guy from another experience or something. We'll use Nanabush in this story.

Nanabush was coming up through the woods, up a little bit of a hill, and there was a lot of small trees where he was and the odd big one. He could hear all this laughter and he said, "I'm so tired. If I could only laugh, I'd feel much better." So he went over where all this laughter was, and here it was chickadees all sitting in the trees and they were taking their eyes out of their heads, and they would throw them up in the air and wait and they'd fall back in their sockets, and they'd start to laugh. And they laughed and laughed.

So Nanabush wanted to get in on this laughter and, of course, all the animals knew Nanabush and knew what he was like. He had a lot of powers, this Nanabush. He could turn himself into a snake or a wolf or a moose—anything he wanted. But if there was any of those animals around, he couldn't do it without their permission, so he couldn't play this game with them. He begged them. He said, "Can I play this eye game with you?" They said, "No, Nanabush, we know what you're like. You can't play." And they kept throwing their eyes up in the air and they'd fall back in the sockets and they'd laugh and laugh and they were having such a good time and he got down and he begged them: "Please, brothers, sisters, I'm so tired and I've come from such a long way. Can I play the game with you?" So finally the head chickadee spoke up and he said, "Well, alright, but there's a rule you have to keep. One rule." Nanabush said, "I'll do whatever you say. Just let me play."

The head chickadee said, "We only have one rule and that is when we say 'stop' everybody has to

stop." "Oh," he said, "I'll agree to do that." So Nanabush threw his eyes up in the air and they landed in his sockets and he started to laugh with all the chickadees and he was having a great time.

Finally the head chickadee said, "All right, that's it. Stop!" And they all stopped. Nanabush said, "Just one more time, just once more. I promise you I'll stop, but just let me throw them up just once more." And they said, "No. We said 'stop,' you stop."

So, with that Nanabush threw his eyes up in the air and he waited and waited and waited and his eyes didn't come down. Then he hollered to them: "Brothers, sisters, where are you?" But they had all gone. Gone to roost, I guess. So there he was, no eyes and he was wondering, "How am I going to get my eyes? How am I going to be able to see? I know, a spruce tree has gum on it and I'll just blow that gum up one side and blow up another one and put in my eyes and I'll have eyes again."

So he started out to look for a spruce tree. Well, I shouldn't say look—he set out to find one. But he kept falling over logs and the ground was not level and he'd fall down and he'd get up and he'd start again. Finally, he came to a tree and he put his hands around the tree and he said, "Brother, tell me what kind of a tree are you?" And he said, "Nanabush, what's wrong with you? Can't you tell by my low branches that I'm a cedar tree?" "Oh," he said, "brother, I've lost my eyes and I cannot see. I'm looking for a spruce tree. Could you please send me on my way?" So the cedar branches pushed him on his way and he walked, tumbling and falling again, and he came up to another tree and he put his hands around the tree and he said, "Brother, can you tell me what kind of a tree are you?" He said, "Nanabush, what's wrong with you? Can't you tell by my bark I'm a birch tree?" "Oh," he said, "brother, I've lost my eyes and I'm trying to find a spruce tree. Could you send me on my way?"

So he went on and pretty soon he came to another tree and put his hands around it and he said, "Brother, tell me what kind of a tree are you?" "Nanabush, can't you tell by my needles I'm a pine tree? What's wrong with you anyway?" "Oh," he said, "brother I've lost my eyes and I'm trying to find a spruce tree, would you please send me on my way?" So the pine branches pushed him on his way. He fell and tumbled and got up to a tree and put his hands around the tree and he said, "Brother, tell me what kind of a tree are you?" He said, "Nanabush, what's wrong with you? Can't you tell by my gum I'm a spruce tree?"

And that's where the story ends. You see in those legends what it does, it teaches you—that's where our learning came in. It teaches you all about trees and the barks on them, about how they bend down. See, when he came to that birch tree he had to bend way down to touch it because birch grows to the branches away on top. I forgot to add that in. But that's part of the learning.

The vulture was, at one time, the most beautiful bird in the world. It had beautiful coloured feathers; it had everything. Of course, Nanabush used to ride on its back. He'd call that bird and the bird came and he'd get on its back, and the bird was getting so tired of carting him every place, you see. So one day just after he had passed a lake, he just tipped his back like that, you know, and Nanabush fell off and he fell all the way down and there was a great big hollow cedar tree—it was really hollow inside—and he fell in there. He was down amongst the roots and he couldn't get out.

So animals came by, the wolf came along, and Nanabush was hollering for help, and they said, "Ah, that's just you, Nanabush. We're not giving you no hand." None of the animals that came by would stop to help him. Finally a rabbit came through and the rabbit said, "Well, I'll give you a hand, but I'm just a rabbit and I'm not very strong, so I don't know what I can do." Nanabush hollered up, "You dig up there on top and I'll keep digging down here and try and get between these roots to get out." They both started digging away until they got a little hole between, but Nanabush could hardly squeeze up between these roots and then the rabbit said, "Well, I've got a long tail. I'll drop that down and you just hang onto the tail and I'll try to pull you and get you past those roots and then you can crawl out."

So Nanabush hung onto the tail and the rabbit was trying to get away and pulling on top and slowly

Nanabush was able to make his way through those roots and then all of a sudden, just as he was getting through, the rabbit's tail broke off! And Nanabush climbed out on top and he looked at the rabbit and he had no more tail and that's how the rabbit got a short tail.

"Now," Nanabush said, "I'm going to give you some gifts for getting me out of there." He said, "You'll be able to turn three colours. In winter you'll be white, so you'll blend in and they can't see you. In the spring you'll be grey, so you'll blend in with the forests. In the summer you'll be brown so you'll be like all the grasses and leaves and everything and you'll be able to blend in with the forest." You see, when you tell these stories in Indian the usages of the words are very different from what I'm telling you now in English. There's laughter all the way through this, you know.

The white man sometimes says that native people are the only people who had any real freedom. Well, we didn't call it freedom. It was a way of life where we were in complete harmony with all life.

That's what freedom is, of course. I guess we've got a word for freedom all right, but I just don't know which word to use. I don't know if it's even a single word. You might have to use three or four. We were not a talking people, not like here in this white society. We were very silent and we visited in silence except at story times when we'd tell stories; but at other times we didn't use very many words.

If we went to visit somebody we could sit with them quietly and nobody would talk. We just sat down. I'd just get inside the kitchen and I'd see a box and I'd sit on that box and somebody would bring me over a cup of tea or meat or biscuits—whatever they happened to have. I'd have that and they'd just nod at me and somebody else comes in and they just nod. You didn't say nothing. But you're in total harmony with everyone in that house. You're visiting, actually; that's what you're doing. If there's anyone sick that you know, or not feeling well, you knew that, too, and maybe you'd go in and see them. Nobody had to tell you anything and you don't ask. So it was like that with the animals. It was like that with the fish and all the insects, with the leaves on the trees, with the rocks. You just knew.

You knew you were a part of it. That's the way it used to be when things were clean. The old people often talk about that. The old men talk about how it used to be and they'll say, "It used to be that way." That's what they'll say to you, very much unaware that it's still like that. I've sat in a tepee with old men—I've been working with old men for over thirty years now—they were from all over and we met in Alberta on the Morely Reserve; that's between Calgary and Banff.

What I wanted to do that time was try to bring wisdom and energy together, but there was no rules, no regulations of any kind. People just came. All ages came and we had lots of tepees put up and we had tents of all kinds. There was even trailers and those big buses they call Winnebagos, people from all over, from the East Coast right down to New Mexico, Arizona, Florida, Oklahoma, Utah, and from the Northwest Territories. Two or three big bus loads had come of all ages and they come and camped there and we had this thing on seven days, at the end of July and the beginning of August.

I used to sit in because I was running the whole thing. There was a chief on the reserve but he was pretty busy, Chief John Snow. He'd have all the kitchens set up for me, and first of all when we started we didn't have electricity or water up there. Eventually we pumped water down from the Beaufort River and the Beaufort runs into the Bow River just right there. So we put pumps on there and put water taps and finally got electricity in there and we used to build our campfires at night.

We'd go in and we'd do a ceremony in there and I'd sit down and the old man who was going to do the pipe ceremony would sit on my right, and then next to him would be the Fire Keeper, and all the other old men would be sitting over to the left. And all the other people who came in, we'd have the water boy I guess you'd call them now, and he had a pail of water that he passed around and gave everybody a drink. There was certain things you had to do, like you don't know where you're going to sit when you go in. They had a Keeper of the Door and he'd bring the person in and bring them all around that fire. You had to circle that fire and then he'd point down. And all this time not a word is being spoken.

When I'm sitting there I never start off in any way. I just sit down there on the ground and look around and just wait for somebody to speak. The only time there was any words was when they prayed. They'd have the sweet grass and that would be passed around, and then the pipe. I'd fill the pipe for him and then he'd light it and then he'd start to speak in his own language and do the pipe ceremony, and then that pipe would go all the way around 'til all the tobacco was burned in it, and then it went back to the Fire Keeper and he'd clean it all out and fix it and lay it down and then we'd just sit there. Sometimes we'd sit for half an hour and not a word is said. Nobody spoke.

Then I'd start to get up and then everybody would get up and we'd all leave. And people would ask me, "Well, did you have a good meeting, Wilf?" I'd say, "Yes. One of the best." "Well, what did you talk about?" "Oh, lots of things. We talked about everything."

You know what happens in there; it's almost unbelievable the silence. You knew what everybody was thinking, what was happening with every single person in that room, and you'd just look around and all those feelings would just flow out, and what we didn't need went into smoke and out the tepee at the top. The messages we wanted for the community would go up through there and they went out all over that community, so all the people would know. They would know, too, automatically.

I did have a rough time a few times with young people—young Indians from Chicago University—they wanted to know where the agenda was and what was on next, "How come you don't have an agenda?" "What kind of a meeting is this we're coming to?" They just didn't know and sometimes they spoke and when they spoke they never spoke directly at the subject particularly. They'd speak around it, but you knew what they were talking about.

See, one time they were talking about keeping white people out of there. They said, "Oh, they're always coming around in here." And these were guys maybe fifty years old. There was two or three of them in there, and this guy was bringing it up and he said, "I think we should keep them out of there. They've got the rest of that park over on the other side, they can stay over there. This of ours is sacred ground and I don't think we should let them in here. They treat us just like animals in a zoo. Always taking pictures and they never get our permission."

After this discussion had gone on, I never said nothing. They just nod at me when they're ready to speak and I just nod and they'd go ahead. So there was no dialogue back and forth, eh? That didn't happen. A man spoke and said what he wanted. The next one spoke and said what he wanted. And then there was silence. Always in between all these things.

But, after this happened, you know—finally, quite a while later—an old man got up, old Joe Mackinaw—he was from a reserve in Alberta, but he

was now living in the mountains—and then his son got up beside him and the old man spoke in Cree and his son interpreted because there was all different tribes there who didn't understand. And those who didn't understand their interpreters would interpret for them, whether into Navaho or something what it was the old man was saying. So he said, "As the pine grows beside the spruce and the spruce with the cedar and the cedar with the hemlock, so all are welcome in my lodge." And he sat down. He was saying: if trees don't discriminate, how can I?

And that's what I got all these years sitting with those old men.

Among us, the native people, women were maybe more than equal. The woman had a place even above the men. It was man's duty to walk in front of a woman, always. And that was strictly for protection so that whatever he came up against at least she'd have an opportunity to get away. He

Grand Lac Victoria E. Racicot Photo 1909

walked like that always, in front. But the women are the ones who kept the home and raised the children and the men were always away hunting in order to provide. And the women had a place of honour everywhere, no matter where—in fact, a double place if she was carrying a child. She was very honoured. That's the way I've always known and that's the way I've always seen it.

And you know, Indians have always had trouble understanding the white man's concept of justice. I can tell you a story about that. A middle-aged Indian trapper kept getting these court warnings to appear and he kept ignoring them. His former wife wanted half of what he had under the new property division law. Well, the Indian trapper had no use for such kind of new white man's laws. But finally a police officer trekked into his bush camp and said, "Joe, you have to answer the summons or they might put you in jail."

Well, Joe didn't want to go to Toronto. He didn't understand English too well and he was hopping angry because his former wife was living with another man and Joe figured the new man should damn well keep her. But finally he made the long trip to Toronto and, for the first time in his life, sat in the white man's courtroom. When his name was called, he stood up, smiled, and bowed to the judge and all the people. The judge deliberated and said, "Two hundred dollars or thirty days."

Joe thought about that for only a minute or so. His smile was big this time. He stood up and said, "Your Honour, I'll take the two hundred dollars."

*Phar Lap, the "red racetrack riot from the Antipodes," in a moment of repose. A huge gelding, the big bay measured sixteen hands, three and three-quarter inches high. Born in 1926, Phar Lap was five at the time this photograph was taken. He was being trained for the Agua Caliente Handicap and a summer campaign on other American tracks.*

# 10

## "My Father Brought Phar Lap from Australia"

### JOE GORMAN – Ottawa, Ontario

*Joe Gorman was born in Ottawa in 1923, attended Glebe Collegiate, and served in the Royal Canadian Air Force. On his discharge he entered the family business with his famous father, Thomas Patrick Gorman who, in his youth, was an outstanding athlete before becoming owner of the Ottawa Senators, the Chicago Blackhawks, and the Connaught Race Track in Aylmer, Quebec. Joe's grandfather came to Canada from Galway, Ireland, and shortly afterwards married Mary McDonald of Charlottetown, P.E.I. In the Maritimes, he edited a newspaper and was president of the Press Gallery. They had six children, Joe's father, "T.P." being the fourth. The family moved to Ottawa where "T.P." married, in 1911, Mary Elizabeth Westwick, an aunt of the illustrious Journal sports editor, Bill Westwick, and sister of "Rat" Westwick, outstanding athlete in the early annals of The Sporting Valley.*

*T.P. Gorman died at Ottawa in 1961, but long before that, in 1936, his sons, Joe and Frank, had taken over control of the Connaught Race Track. While he was running the track, Joe's abiding interest in history prompted him to buy from the CNR Olive and John Diefenbaker's private car and move it onto the Connaught site*

*at the Aylmer Road entrance. Doug Harvey lived in it for three years while he scouted for the Montreal Canadiens.*

MY FATHER, Thomas Patrick Gorman, was a page in Sir Wilfred Laurier's parliament in the 1890s. He told me his mother took him up to the Parliament Buildings by the hand. He had his old shoes on and he had his good shoes in a paper bag and his mother left him there—at nine years of age. His father, my grandfather, also T.P. Gorman, had died at an early age. As a page in the House of Commons, my father told me he used to sit there with his legs crossed in front of Laurier and wait to take messages. He was the youngest page, and they used to play terrible tricks on him. One trick they pulled on him in the House of Commons—he fell asleep in the cloakroom where the page-boys used to wait until the bells would ring, and he woke up and he rushed into the House of Commons and sat down before Sir Wilfred Laurier, and the whole House of Commons burst out laughing. While he was sleeping the other boys had blackened his face with boot black.

You see, in those days people played pranks on everybody. It was a form of entertainment. There was nothing malicious, there was nothing mean about it. It was just part of the scene. Like, my dad told stories of some of the tricks the hockey players played on

113

*Baseball team composed of House of Commons pages, 1905. They played against pages of the Senate, students in public schools and at Ottawa University. Following shirt numbers they are 1. E. Hudon, 2. J. Lavaseur, 3. Paul Barbeau, 4. J. Boulay, 5. Ernie Healey, 6. E. Delerme, 7. G. Arbique, 8. Joe Gorman, 9. E. Lefebvre, 10. E. Choquette. A 1937 Citizen writer described the House of Commons pages as follows: "they did look class in their Eton suits, silk socks, patent leather shoes, white cuffs and stand-up collars—and they grew up to fill such positions as senators, assistant deputy ministers, reps of the Canadian Pacific in London—and not forgetting Tommy Gorman of hockey and horseracing fame who was a page at the age of nine."*

each other. Greg Guthrie told how Joe Finn[1] used to make water bombs and hang them outside over the entrance to the *Journal* and, when you went in, you got absolutely deluged. And Finn would use contraceptives to make the water bombs!

After my father worked as a page, D'Arcy Finn took him to the *Ottawa Citizen*. And then he became sort of the office boy. Finn took a liking to my father and taught him how to write and edit, and that's how he became sports editor there. One of his first big breaks or scoops occurred in 1912. The *Titanic* sank when Father was in New York. D'Arcy Finn—it was all by telegram at that time—got the passenger list

from England to my father in New York and he spent the next three or four days on the docks of New York. As the boats would arrive with the survivors, he would check the names. So all you do is reverse the list and you've got the list of the people that are dead. That was sent back to Ottawa and, at that time newspapers used stringers, and the Southams who owned the *Citizen* sold this scoop of my father's all the way across Canada. I wasn't born, but I remember him telling me that. He had a world scoop. But a reporter on the *Citizen* didn't make very much money.

My father was working in the sports department at the Ottawa *Citizen* when the Halifax explosion occurred in 1917. D'Arcy Finn was the editor and he grabbed my father out of the sports department and he said, "Gorman, get yourself down to Halifax!" My father went by plane to Montreal and Montreal to Boston. When he got there, a train was pulling out of the Boston station. He yelled to the conductor,

*When T.P. Gorman filed his* Titanic *report from New York for the* Citizen, *Grattan O'Leary,* Ottawa Journal *editor and reporter, also filed a story on the disaster. The* Citizen *accused the* Journal *of simply doing a rehash of* New York Herald *reports, claiming that O'Leary was never on the scene. The* Journal *and O'Leary immediately took action for libel. Photo of O'Leary in his* Journal *office, c. 1922.*

"What is that?" and he said, "It's a hospital train going to Halifax." And my father jumped on. He said the train was moving when he jumped on, and that the conductor yelled, "You can't come on this train." And he said, "You can't put me off!" He was on the first train into Halifax. He told me about walking along the main street in Halifax and he said that all the glass and all the windows were blown out. He said he walked into a store and took a typewriter out of the store, and found some paper, and he started copy and then he found the telegraph office which was, again, a shambles, but the operator was there. And the operator told him the lines were down, that they weren't getting anything out, and my father said, "I don't care. Just start sending." And he wrote the first-person copy of the Halifax explosion with no idea whether or not it was getting through. Strangely enough, it was. It got through to the Ottawa *Citizen* and, again, it became a world scoop. Imagine! One of the first reporters on the scene of the Halifax explosion! I guess we've learned that it was almost as bad as an atomic explosion.

I have never heard my father talk about Harry McLean and his part in the Halifax explosion. But they were good friends. Harry McLean used to come in from Merrickville to the Auditorium to the hockey games all the time. He loved hockey. And he had a beautiful cocker spaniel dog which he used to bring to the games. We used to lock it in the office, and the darned dog got out one day. Now you've got six or seven thousand people watching a hockey game and the dog got out of the office, ran down the halls, ran through the crowds, found Harry McLean and jumped right into his arms. Somehow or other, I was called and I went and carried the dog back to the office and put a note, "Do not let the dog out."

I grew up in an interesting family of Gormans. Uncle Joe was killed in Italy in 1917, but Uncle Louis Gorman was the original "Environment Canada." He was with the Department of Fisheries, I guess. At 38 Euclid—the family home was in the Glebe—he had all these strange instruments that nobody understood, but he measured the dew point and the rainfall and the wind and all that stuff. He was the original Dominion Meteorologist. I can remember in 1933, my brother Frank and Uncle Louis—they were each up twenty-four hours a day because Bell had run in a special telephone line and they were phoning this information wherever they could because the Italian government flew thirty-three flying boats across the Atlantic and they needed the weather from here so they could predict what the weather was going to be. He fed them the information and they flew them over to the World's Fair in Chicago in 1933. I remember that. And I remember all the early meteorological charts.

My grandfather, Thomas Patrick Gorman, had a brother who went from Ireland to Boston and from Boston right through to California. He did very well out there and he had one child and his wife's maiden name was Keiley and the one child was Thomas Keiley Gorman, Thomas K. Gorman, who joined the priesthood at the age of thirteen or fourteen. He had an amazing career. The apostolic delegate was crossing the United States and they realized that there wasn't a Catholic bishop for the State of Nevada, and so Thomas Keiley Gorman, at the age of thirty-eight, was the youngest bishop appointed and he was consecrated as the Bishop of the State of Nevada.

The United States is quite different from Canada; the schools and the hospitals and the institutions are funded privately. If you wanted to get a licence to open a gambling joint in Nevada you had to see Bishop Gorman. Reno and Las Vegas. And I've been to the high school in Las Vegas—it's the Thomas Keiley Gorman High School. And Tom, as I say, was very close to the Governor of Nevada. He ended up in Dallas, Fort Worth, as the bishop there, died in 1981. I went to his funeral in Dallas.

Bishop Tom and I used to sit in his library at night—he had a beautiful home which he bought and paid for himself—the church didn't pay for it. His family left him very well off, and again that's very different from up here. There a priest could retain his own real estate. Wherever he went, Tom lived very well. I used to kid him, "You're more of a financial man than you are a priest." He'd come back with a very quick remark having to do with the financing of institutions—like the casinos.

My father and Bishop Tom always kept in touch. I remember he used to drive his Packard cars up here from Nevada and stay at the Château Laurier. Totally unpriestly, don't you think?

My father was the secretary of the Connaught Park Jockey Club in Aylmer, Quebec. It was started in 1912 and all the Siftons from Calgary and the Richardsons and the Southams[2]—all the prominent people invested in it. And some promoters out of Buffalo, New York. With the march of time my father became the secretary of the company and as these older people, or families, lost interest, their stock would come up for sale and so my father would buy a few shares here and a few shares there. Being the secretary of the company, he knew where all the shares were; he could gradually accumulate them and it gradually became his business.

Father was in New York when he sold his interest in the Ottawa Senators here. He then bought the Hamilton Tigers from Percy Thompson for $75,000. They went on strike that year and they didn't play in the Stanley Cup so, he bought the

*First meeting of the National Hockey League, New York, 1926. Note each delegate has been provided with promotional Lucky Strike cigarettes. Amongst the men of power and money gathered for this historic event were L to R: —- (rep. from Pittsburg); —- (rep. from Toronto); Charlie Quarrie (Toronto St. Pats); Dave Gill (Ottawa Senators); Redmond Quain (Ottawa Senators); Sam Rosenstein (Montreal Maroons); Jimmy Strand (Montreal Maroons); Eddie Gerard (coach, Montreal Maroons); T.P. Gorman (New York Americans); —-; —-; —-; Frank Calder (President, National Hockey League); Bill Foran (trustee, Stanley Cup); —-; Leo Letourneau (Montreal Canadiens); Joe Pattraneck (Montreal Canadiens); Cecil Hartt (Montreal Canadiens); Bill Dwyer (coach, New York Americans); Col. Fitzpatrick (Madison Square Gardens); —-; —-; Art Ross (Boston Bruins); Tom Duggen (Boston Bruins); Benny Leonard (Pittsburg).*

whole team and the franchise, moved it all to New York and formed the New York Americans. The whole kit and caboodle became the New York Americans.

Madison Square Gardens was owned by the bootlegging money of Tex Ricard and Bill Dwyer. They brought my father to New York to run the hockey operation for them. It was the new Madison Square Gardens at that time. Just opened and that was where I saw my first hockey game. The New York Americans and Montreal Canadiens, 1926. I must have been about three years old, for at that time we were living in the Forest Hotel in New York and they didn't have babysitters. So what do you do with a three-year-old? You take him with you.

Bill Dwyer had the greatest of all delivery systems in the city of New York for liquor during prohibition. He owned the New York Americans hockey team, but he had the greatest—listen, this is where the money came from—he had the greatest of all delivery systems. He used the New York Sanitation Department! The department used to haul all its garbage out to the garbage scows and they were towed fifty miles out into the ocean, and dumped. But, at the same time, the boats with the liquor which was being imported into the United States was delivered to the garbage scows and brought into the city of New York. And then he had a delivery service that took it out to all the speakeasies. Bill Dwyer must have been a bigger bootlegger than Joseph Kennedy.

Let me explain how my father got to California. He went to Mexico first. You see, they only raced two months a year here at Connaught and then all of a sudden they were opening up a new racetrack in Tijuana, and they had no people that had any racing knowledge or would know how to run a horse-racing track. And there was prohibition in California at that time and no gambling in California. So they built this beautiful racetrack and casino and everything at Tijuana, Mexico, which was right across the border from California.

They brought all Canadians down there. They brought Canadian stewards to run the jockeys' room, my father as general manager. We all went. We lived in Mexico. My father used to go on ahead of us to the racetrack, and it was all winter long the racetrack ran. We lived right on the racetrack and he would buy the car of the year after the race meet was over, and drive it back from California to Ottawa. And it would take us twelve days, fourteen days to drive home because the roads weren't paved at that time. We'd have our luggage on the running board. And you'd put the canvas over it. But living in Tijuana, Mexico, was like the Riviera. Rita Hayworth, fifteen years old, danced in the casino there, she and her father. I remember Little Caesar, the great guy that played all the gangster movies, he used to come down there. Clark Gable and Carole Lombard, all those Hollywood people came down there on the weekends.

Now this racetrack was phenomenally successful, but they had no refrigeration, no way of keeping food. So everything would come down from San Diego. But it all had to be fresh because they couldn't keep it for the next day. So they used to over order all the time. My father used to do this, and then they'd give it away to the Mexicans. There'd be a line-up about two or three blocks long of Mexicans waiting at the racetrack at night to be given all this food. My father was a god to the Mexicans and we could go anywhere in Tijuana at that time. It was only a small city then and at the border we would never have to get in line—they'd just wave us through. Both the American and the Canadian customs.

Somewhere there's a picture of me and my father arriving in Mexico off the train with my mother and my brother and my sister from Canada into something like ninety-degree heat, and I had on a Charles Lindberg helmet and goggles, the leather coat, the breeks, the big boots. I got off the train and he said they took pictures of me. Getting off the train in Los Angeles into this ninety-degree heat and I'm dressed like Charles Lindberg.

We were there four years and then the Mexican government took the race track over in 1931. The *big* success in father's life in Tijuana was he brought Phar Lap from Australia. Anytime you ever talk to an Australian . . . Phar Lap, he's the national hero. He brought this wonderful horse to race and he won the hundred-thousand-dollar race at Caliente. He'd won everything in Australia and he could have swept

North America. If you're ever talking to an Australian, they have the carcass of Phar Lap stuffed in the museum. If you ever want to open the door with an Australian, just say "Phar Lap." That's all you need. He was a wonder horse. His heart was twice the size of a normal horse's heart.

My father heard about Phar Lap of Australia. From California my father wired the trainer and offered to bring the horse to America. The trainer-manager wired back, "Yes, I'll come. But I need four thousand dollars." So my father, for Caliente, the race track, went to Jim Crofton and said, "Look, we can get this great horse from Australia, but the man wants four thousand dollars." And Crofton said, "Gorman, the guy's probably a con artist and you'll never see the horse." Father said, "Well, I think it's worth the gamble." So they wired the trainer four thousand dollars in American money. Telephone communications at that time were non-existent so everything was by telegraph. "Please send us details about arrival," they wired. And the trainer wired back that they were loading Phar Lap on such-and-such a ship and the horse would be arriving in Los Angeles on such-and-such a date. Los Angeles was about a hundred-and-twenty miles up the coast from Tijuana, so my father and a group, they went up with a horse van truck. They're waiting for the wonder horse and, by God! if the trainer doesn't walk off the freighter from Australia with this huge, gorgeous-looking animal, Phar Lap. And they loaded him in the truck and the photographers were there and the newsreel cameras. They did the whole Hollywood promo thing on it. They shipped the horse down across the Mexican line to Caliente, the great racetrack. And the horse was entered in the hundred-thousand-dollar Caliente Handicap—which he won easily.

That's the only race Phar Lap ever ran in America. They shipped him up near to near San Francisco to rest. They were going to bring him east and race him in all the major races in the East and that's when the bookmakers got to him, poisoned the horse and killed him. My father had an exclusive contract to manage the horse in America. The manager of the horse never went back to Australia; he stayed in the San Francisco area. Then the carcass and the bones were shipped back to Australia to preserve in a museum. But my father never owned Phar Lap.

In California, my father would deal with the owners and trainers. He'd contact these people who would have stables of race horses because the industry was just beginning on the west coast at that time. They would basically buy the horses and own the horses, but they'd be signed and registered in somebody else's name, but the racetrack would put up the money. If you've got a good stable of horses, but you haven't got money to ship and you need money to come to California and get established, the racetrack would say, "Pete Wilson, he's okay. If he needs ten thousand dollars, send it to him and he'll bring his horses here and he'll race them and we'll profit from it." You can't run a racetrack without race horses.

The same thing would happen when my father was running the racetracks in Montreal. He'd get hold of Joe Binstock or Harry Hoffman and say, "Harry, we need fifty extra horses." Harry'd say, "Fine. Send me some money." And Harry'd go and get fifty horses and ship them into Montreal, but they'd all be in other people's name. They never put them in the name of the racetrack. 'Coz the public wouldn't like that. So they'd give them names of other people so they'd never lose any money on that. Then my dad came back to Canada and he took the Aylmer Connaught Track and made it into a landmark.

As I said, the Mexicans had taken over their racetrack, but again they're stuck with the problem of how to run it, and make money. My father was on his way back to California to help them when Joe Cathanridge and Leo Danjaron basically shanghaied him off the train at Chicago. They said, "Gorman, we want you to run this hockey team and get us our money back because McLaughlin doesn't know what the hell he's doing." So that's how my father ended up in Chicago for two years and won the Stanley Cup, and Cathranidge and Danjaron got their money back.

Jim Norris and Arthur Wurtz, the father of Bill Wurtz that has the Chicago Blackhawks, they owned the stadium but they didn't own the hockey team and they were squeezing McLaughlin. Major

McLaughlin who owned the Chicago Blackhawks was married to Irene Cassell. McLaughlin was high society in Chicago. His family business was importing coffee. He was living very high. The Chicago Black Hawks hockey team was named after his regiment that fought in the First World War. They were the Black Hawks. That was the name of the regiment and that was the name of the hockey team and they played in the big stadium in Chicago, which is just now being torn down. There's a new one going up. But that's how my father got to Chicago.

And at that time Chicago was Al Capone's town. My father lived in the Sherman Hotel, which was the hangout for the Capone boys and he knew Al and got along with him quite well. But Cathranidge and Danjaron had the racetrack and one of Capone's guys wanted it and my father got a note from Capone one day . . . I'm not sure if I still have it or not . . .

If you like the birds and the flowers
Get out of Chicago in twenty-four hours. —Al.
Father got out of Chicago. He came back and took over the Montreal Maroons and they won the Stanley Cup there. Again. With Alec Connell and Lionel Conacher, the Big Train, who has just gone into the Hall of Fame. It's impossible that he wasn't in earlier. And that Frank Finnigan isn't in yet. That's impossible to believe, too.

Father was born in 1886 and from an early age was a great lacrosse player. At twenty-two, he was the youngest member of the Canadian Lacrosse Team when they won the gold medal in the London Olympics of 1908. We had the gold medal, but, again, our home in the Glebe was vandalized and it was stolen—this was back thirty or forty years ago.

I remember a wonderful story about Frank Finnigan. There was a scout for the Toronto Maple

*A 1908 photo of the Capital Lacrosse team and fans taken in holiday attire in front of the Russell Hotel, New Westminster, B.C. upon their arrival to play for the World Championship with the New Westminster Royals. The line-up was illustrious and included: Peter McGregor, ardent Caps supporter who had travelled across the continent to cheer the team; Whiteley (Shiner) Eastwood; Frank Cummings, a star Cornwall player; George Bryson of the Bryson lumbering dynasty; Jack Shea, Bobby Pringle, and Cyclone Taylor of the Renfrew Millionaires; Angus (Bones) Allen; Don Cameron, another brilliant Cornwall player; Art Warwick, who was borrowed from the Torontos; Ernie Butterworth; Gordon (Bunny) Carling, who joined the team at Calgary as a fan; Jack Ashfield; Dave Mulligan, former owner with his brother George of the Ottawa Russell Hotel; Charlie Scott, borrowed from the Montreal Athletic Association team; Bill Fagan. The off-field antics included fist fights, gun shots, two attempted lynchings and barrages with rotten eggs. The Caps lost.*

Leafs, Squib Walker. Squib was Connie Smythe's scout and he did very well for the Maple Leafs over the years. But Squib didn't know the era that your dad came from and somebody, I think Alex Connell, told Squib he'd just heard of a hell of a hockey player up in Shawville, "You'd better go and see him, 'coz if you miss him Smythe will be mad," they said.

"What's his name?" Squib asked.

"Frankie Finnigan."

Squib didn't make the connection. He took the bus or the train up into Shawville and started looking for this young flash who was going to be the next superstar, and he finds Frank running the Clarendon Hotel—with white hair! Poor Squib.

My father introduced professional baseball to Ottawa, amongst other things. We'd bought the

Auditorium here, and we had the Ottawa Senators, and the Quebec Hockey League, and we had the racetrack going and he just loved baseball, and so we got a Class C franchise in what was then the Border Baseball League. Kingston, Ottawa, Odgensburg, Watertown, Geneva. It was a sixteen-team league, a Class C league. And some good ballplayers—Doug Harvey, Pete Karpuckley, Johnny Russian—and this was Class C ball. They were professional.

And then the International League ran out of places to play and they brought the New York Giants to Ottawa. They leased the rights to baseball here because we owned the lights and the lease on Lansdowne Park. Willy Mays played here in Lansdowne Park. The great Willy Mays. When I mention that people say, "Oh no." I say, "Look, Willy Mays played in the outfield at Lansdowne Park with the New York Giants in the International Baseball League and I was there. I saw

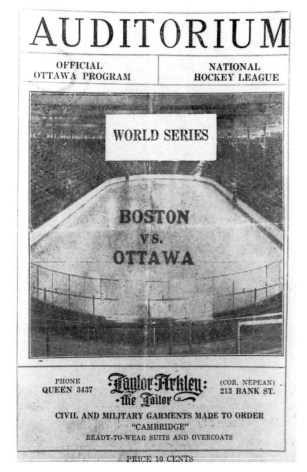

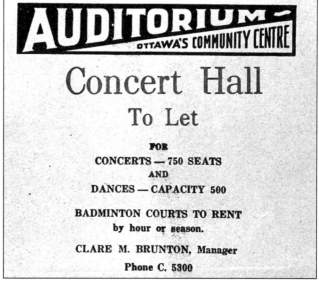

*Rideau Hall, the Russell Hotel, the Ottawa Little Theatre, the Château Laurier, the old Auditorium were all centres for Ottawa's cultural and sporting life in the 1920s and '30s. When the Auditorium closed in 1967 after forty-four years at the heart of the city, Guy Lombardo and his Royal Canadians were featured at the dinner. Present to honour its history were King Clancy, Punch Broadbent, Cy Denneny, Bill Cowley, Frank Finnigan, Syd Howe, Aurel Joliat—all NHL players and stars from the early days of hockey.*

*A world and several careers away from his House of Commons page-boy duties, T.P. Gorman sits rinkside in Chicago with Major Frederick McLachlin (right). From the looks on their faces it would seem the Black Hawks are winning, c. 1940s.*

him." And they say, "Well, how come he didn't stay here?" I say, "The Giants at that time owned Minneapolis, the franchise in Minneapolis is triple A, and they were trying to sell that franchise so they took their good ball players out of here and moved them back to Minneapolis and Willy Mays went." But he did really play in Ottawa here.

I can tell you about the time the Duke of Windsor tried to buy the Montreal Canadiens. My father and I often spoke later of this affair, but it never became public.

In 1945, when I was about twenty, I chauffeured my father, then owner of the Montreal Canadiens, to several meetings with famed Montreal industrialist, Izaak Walton Killam, then considered the wealthiest Canadian of the era, thanks to holdings in financial institutions, pulp and paper, minerals, media.

The Canadian industrialist and the Duke of Windsor, former King of England, were neighbours in the Bahamas. His connection with the Nazis and his abdication to marry American divorcée Wallis Simpson made him a liability at home so, after his abdication the Duke spent the war years as the Governor of the Bahamas. (He was there when Sir Harry Oakes[3] was murdered, of course.)

The Duke of Windsor and Wallis Simpson would live in New York or Paris, but they would often be back and forth to Montreal and what Killam wanted (whatever his private reasons) was to widen the Duke of Windsor's contacts and influence in North America. He proposed to Gorman in meetings that he would buy the Montreal Canadiens for the Duke of Windsor.

A noted North American promoter and showman, impresario, wonderful athlete and dedicated sportsman, my father undoubtedly saw

*Opening ceremonies of the Ace Bailey benefit game, played at Maple Leaf Gardens, February 14, 1934, and won by the Leafs over the NHL All-Stars, 7 - 3. This was the first NHL All-Star team ever assembled.*

greater vistas for himself in this plot. He was always working to expand the NHL from the six-team "box," which Connie Smythe had managed to keep it in.

But my father told me that when Killam approached Canadian Arena Company owner, Senator Donat Raymond, about buying the club and the Forum, he was rebuffed, and my father was forced to quit as Canadiens manager.

One of the founding fathers of the NHL, my father had assembled a powerful Canadian team that had just won the Stanley Cup for the second time in three years. After Killam made his offer and was rejected, my father abruptly left Montreal to manage the Ottawa Auditorium. That was July 1946. All this happened over a period of about ten days, as I recall, and then came the blowup with Senator Raymond.

Any idea of selling the team died with the Gorman dismissal. Senator Raymond sold the Canadiens to the Molson family in 1957, two years after Killam's death. But can you imagine the Canadiens being owned by the Duke of Windsor?

When I came out of the Air Force in 1945, I should have gone back to school, but I didn't. I went to work for the family. My father and I took Barbara Ann Scott on a skating tour of Canada after she won the Olympics. She had all these expensive advisers and yet nobody was doing anything for her. Father said, "Let's put together an all-Canadian ice show." And then drew up a contract. She made two hundred thousand in thirty-nine weeks. She lived in a trailer. Her mother was "Mary Queen of Scots." I called her . . . difficult, and Barbara was difficult. But, it's the only real money she made in the skating game as a professional skater. They took her to New York and then out to Hollywood but—how can I put this?— she was not photogenic. They couldn't do anything with her. They put her into acting school, but nothing came of it. Nothing worked. And she wasn't tough enough to be in the business.

The gal that I got to know was Sonja Henie. She was the toughest, roughest, son-of-a-gun-of-a-gal I ever met in my life. But she survived in that business and she made a lot of money. How did I get to know her? Again, through my father. She was having trouble with her ice show and she needed places to play, so she came to Canada. She played all through the Maritimes, in Ottawa, in Montreal. Father set up her tour and I travelled with the show and that's how I got to know her. People say, "How did you know Sonja?" I say, "Well, I wasn't her skating partner. I was her drinking partner." She's buried in Norway. She had the largest private collection of Riopelles now in Oslo, Norway, in the Sonja Henie museum.

What was her other wonderful expression? Oh yes, she was number three in the box office in the United States at one time. And somebody asked her what was she going to do with all her money, and I remember her wonderful quote, "Oh, I'm thinking of buying California." She just loved it so much. Again, that's part of my father's story. He knew all these people—knew how Henie ended up in Canada. She had the ice show—The Sonja Henie Ice Review— and then the stands fell down in Philadelphia, and, all of a sudden, they're getting hit with law suits. So they loaded everything up on the train and brought it to Ottawa and we kept her going for about three months to get all the legal things straightened around. The sheriff was showing up with warrants and papers. Whenever we saw anybody who looked like a sheriff, we ran.

Joe Finn did some terrible things to me. Finn had a completely different sense of humour . . . well, when D'Arcy Finn, his father, fired him from the Ottawa Citizen and he went to work for the Journal. His own father fired him! He did a fish and game column in the Ottawa Citizen, which was quite popular, but the editors at that time weren't very bright and Joe would slip things in—say, if I'd been travelling somewhere and I'd come home, he'd run a section, "Joe Gorman has just been up North on a fishing trip and he caught 'this fish' and he caught 'that fish.'" But we all knew he wasn't referring to fish. He was referring to young women.

Joe Finn and Greg Guthrie were overseas together and they ended up in Pembroke together as stringers for the Journal and Citizen. And Greg said constantly Finn would say to him, "Do my column or cover for me because I've just seen a girl down the street," and he was gone. Greg said he spent half his time in Pembroke covering for Joe Finn.

*As well as being renowned for its recreational facilities and events, Aylmer, Quebec, was known far and wide as a great hockey town. Photographed here is its 1890s team: Back row, L to R: Jack Allen, Mr. Ogilvy, Charlie Symmes, Archie Martin. Centre: Joe Morgan and an elegantly dressed gentleman who would have been the coach or manager. Front Row, L to R: Arthur Moore, Harry Symmes, Joe Garton. Arthur Moore would have been a member of the David Moore lumbering family of the Aylmer Road, and the Symmes brothers of the Wright-Symmes connection who, amongst many other things, built Symmes Inn on the Ottawa River in 1825.*

One story I can tell you. Chester Froude was on the *Journal*, a young fellow, and his father owned the *Calgary Herald*. He was working down here with Finn on the police beat and, you know, in those days you helped each other out. Well, this young fellow, Chet, was waiting till Finn went to the washroom and then he was reading his copy, and filling his own story in. Well, one time, Finn made up a whole story about a rape. Chet read it, went back, re-wrote it, sent it to the *Journal* and the *Journal* ran it. Even though his father owned the *Calgary Herald*, he was immediately fired.

Joe Finn's immortal creation was Zotique Laframboise. This was a purely fictional character, well remembered by anyone from Ottawa and the Ottawa Valley in the 1940s. On the police beat, Finn covered accidents, fires, murders and in all his news stories Zotique Laframboise would be the first on the scene, quoted as a witness, and usually saying something like, "I never seen (in broken English), I never seen nothing like that before, myself, never—"

It was ten years before an editor on the *Journal* caught on to Joe Finn's greatest practical joke, his creation of the ubiquitous, fictitious Zotique Laframboise.

Goalie Clint Benedict was playing for the Montreal Maroons. I was at the game and you could hear the crack all the way through the Forum in Montreal. Benedict was never right after that. The mask he had covered the face but it didn't cover the forehead. It was Howie Morenz who raised the puck and hit Clint Benedict in the Montreal Forum.

A ski jumping story here. Bill Westwick wrote it, and it was wonderful. They had built the ski jump out at Rockcliffe; You took off and landed out in the Ottawa River. Olaf the Great, a Norwegian ski jumper, came over to demonstrate the art of ski jumping. Beforehand they told him what the slope was, and the takeoff, but he misunderstood them. Olaf the Great goes down and pushes off and gives a great jump and he sails out over the Ottawa River and lands on the ice and breaks both his ankles. And that is a true story. Bill Westwick, as sports editor, wrote that story about how Olaf the Great landed somewhere out in the middle of the Ottawa River.

Johnny Quilty won the Calder Trophy. He was playing between Toe Blake and Joe Benoit. And he won at eighteen years of age—the Calder Trophy as best rookie of the year. Howard Riopelle has told me that he also was a great natural boxer. He was a natural all-round athlete. He could play anything, but Quilty was, again, one of these boys that went overseas and came back really burned out either from war or from drink or from living. He came back and tried to fit back into society, and never quite made it. Johnny died an alcoholic.

Ice races at Aylmer. They attracted enormous crowds. It was a great winter sport and you could, you know, stand around and freeze yourself and watch these horses running. And have a drink at the bar. Flasks. Everybody had a flask. I can remember back in our home—before it broke up—as a kid you'd go through things and find a silver flask, and you'd ask "What are these for?" People used to carry them in their breast pocket. It was a normal thing to do. There was a pocket made for it, in the coat.

And gambling. They used to have the roulette wheels and the casino-type gambling in a separate tent. And book-making. There was no separate tent to keep the horses warm. The way you do it today (it must have been the same then, too), you shave the hair off so the horse never gets wet, and you put a blanket on him and, if the blanket gets wet, you take the wet blanket off and put on a dry one. There was a bar so you could have a drink. Don O'Dwyer died a few years ago. He was around eighty and he was the big horse trader in the Aylmer area. He would remember all that.

We'll call this story "Saving Hockey." Ralston was the Minister of National Defence and nobody could get an appointment at all, not Red Dutton who had served in the First World War (who lost two sons in the Second World War), not B.P. Bickle, Vice President of the Toronto Maple Leafs, not Bill Tobin in Chicago, not even my father. Nobody could get to Ralston so my father called Mrs. D.C. Coleman.

Now at that time there were three beautiful Lynch girls here in Ottawa. One married Hugh Labatt of Labatt Brewery of the famous kidnapping—if you remember the Labatt kidnapping? It was one of the most famous kidnappings—I think it was seventy-five-thousand dollars. The other girl married D.C. Coleman of the Canadian Pacific Railway—she had her choice of two men; she could have either married MacKenzie King or D.C. Coleman. King was crazy about her. She was the love of King's life. And there was a third girl. She never married. But they were from Sandy Hill here in Ottawa. So my father called Mrs. Coleman. He knew the inside story and told her that he needed an appointment with King and nobody could get to him. She called King—she could call at any time—and he said, "Certainly." She arranged for the delegation from the National Hockey League to come to Ottawa here to save hockey because it was going to be shut down. Because Ralston was insisting that everybody be conscripted. No exemptions. Ralston was a very unfair man because he didn't realize that Canadian Pacific were turning out tanks, they were turning out airplanes, the war effort was going on here at home. It was a wonderful effort by a small country; we were only about eleven million people at that time. We weren't a big country. We weren't a wealthy country.

Anyhow, the NHL delegation came to Ottawa here and at the appointed time they went to Mr. King's office. He received them. He listened to them, and they agreed to using Red Dutton as the prime example. Red lost two boys in the Second World War and he had served in the First World War. King said, "Fine." He picked up the phone and he called Mr. Ralston and he said, "I'm bringing some gentlemen down to see you. I want you to listen to them." And he took them, personally, down to Mr. Ralston's office in the Parliament Buildings. He took them in, he introduced them to Mr. Ralston. He said, "I'd like you to listen to these people and I'd like you to consider their request, and, gentlemen, after you're finished I want you to come back to my office. I will be waiting to hear from you." And that is what saved the National Hockey League. It was a lady that saved the league. I've never seen that recorded anywhere.

1 Joe Finn stories are told by Greg Guthrie.

2 Canadian dynasties of wealth and influence, the Siftons and Southams were synonymous with newspaper enterprises and the Richardsons with grain and gold.

3 Sir Harry Oakes, discoverer of gold at Kirkland Lake. He was made a baronet in 1939 and retired to Nassau, Bermuda. His murder there in 1943 has never been solved.

*Wherever there were horses there was excitement, as in this colourful and chaotic scene at an unidentified railway station where horses are being loaded for transport and sale.*

# 11

# "Horses, Horses, Horses—And a Horse Railway"

**BENNY DUKE – Pembroke, Ontario**
**GERVASE O'REILLY – Quyon, Quebec**
**GILBERT ARNOLD – Grenville, Quebec**

*Whenever and wherever in the Ottawa Valley I went to interview people associated with the lumbering saga, the name of Benny Duke came up as one of the great teamsters of the era. Some years ago I tracked him down at Marionhill in Pembroke, where he was then living. Although Mr. Duke was born at Fort Coulonge, his father, Dick Duke, kept a stopping-place on the Black River eighteen miles from the Fort. It was there that Benny Duke spent his earlier years. He also remembered the second stopping-place on the Black, Sammy Deneau's, about a mile or two further up river. His mother Maddie (Martha) Bennett was born and raised "up on what they called The Ridge going to Waltham." The care and feeding of horses from Benny Duke should be of interest, even value, to modern day horse lovers.*

**M**Y MOTHER'S father came from Belfast. And my dad said his mother was a McClelland and he was born up at Petawawa. And then he was running the mail with a horse and cart to Waltham at that time, and he met my mother who was working for the Brysons[1]. And they got married and there you are.

The timber barons stayed at our stopping-place: the McLachlin brothers from Arnprior, J.R. Booth from Ottawa. Oh, I remember them! I remember

Alex Taylor, a wonderful man. He run the company for the McLachlin brothers. We used to call him "The Agent" and he had a lot to say because Dan McLachlin left everything up to him.

We had one, two, three, four, five stables. There used to be a hundred teams going up and a hundred coming down. They were portaging hay, oats, and provisions. They had to take it up to the depots and there they put it into a keepover. They'd build a keepover and put a man there all summer to look after it. He had to turn all the oats. He'd start at this end of the bin, and he'd turn it, and then he'd take the flour and turn it upside down, all like you'd turn cheese. There was enough hay and oats there for maybe fifty camps in one keepover. When I first started, they were company camps and then they started putting in jobbers instead, you know.

I didn't go to school very much. In those days you didn't have to; you could go out and get a job pretty fast. You went up to the lumber camps and they gave you what you call a time sheet—and so much a day at that time—and they'd take whatever you had bought at the van out of that, so there was nothing much left. When I first went up to the camp, my father was running the Swishaw post office for J.R. Booth, so I asked him one day, I said, "Dad, when you see (Alex) Taylor, ask him if he would give me a job." He used to take older people that summer and put them on the road. "Old Man's Home" they used to call it. And they had horses and wagons, and when I went up I was sixteen. I went up when the fair was on in Fort Coulonge. I went up to Deneau's that night—taxi took me there—and this man who was working for McLachlin had three teams of horses: two teams on the wagon, the other team behind. So we went up to McLachlin's halfway. The foreman there took me on to a man who was building the pheasant house. Timber Baron Dan McLachlin had all the fancy fowl that you could name up there. He had a man looking after them. When Renfrew Fair was on, he'd take all these prize birds down to Renfrew. On the road when time come to feed all the birds, he'd make the teamster stop so that they could eat. They were his pride and joy.

Then Mr. Taylor came to me and said, "I'm going to take you up on the improvements with Ernie McMillan, a good fellow who is building dams, eh?" So he took me up and I did well there. I stayed 'til Christmas and I could have either drove teams for Mr. Taylor or went scaling as an assistant scaler. Instead I got a job in Fort Coulonge. I wanted to play hockey, and I got a job with Mr. Tom Jewitt that run the general store, so I didn't go back. The next year, I think, or the year after, they pulled up and closed everything. The McLachlins. I don't know what happened. It was a family affair. It was just that they all wanted their share . . . well, they were all big spenders.

I heard all the pheasants and prize birds—Dan McLachlin let them all go. Into the bush. They said they'd survive. I don't know. But he had peacocks and everything. And, you know, the farmers portaging in the winter when they'd go into the halfways and these stopping-places, they wouldn't pay for their meals. Booth would charge them, but not McLachlins. They fed the men with chicken and everything. Oh, they were some company! I don't think you could get anybody to say anything bad about McLachlin Brothers. It's too bad they folded.

So I stayed with Mr. Jewitt for a year and then I went into the Hurdman Lumbering Company. That was 1930. And I seen Lloyd Neville, one of Booth's head men, and I said, "I'd like to go into the Hurdman, I'd like to get a team." He said, "Sure, you can go in and swing timber." I said, "If I can do it." "Oh, the foreman there will show you how," he said.

I was pretty lucky with getting good teams. Mr. Neville thought a lot of me and he could depend on me and he'd give me a good team of horses. They were big heavy horses—Percherons and Clydes. Not too many Belgians. The time they drew the square timber, there was a whole bunch of horses sent up from Ottawa and they were pretty, like the black horses. Remember the beer with the black horse on it? There were greys and blacks. I had a good team in there that year, too. I brought them out in fair shape. I never had a team that I was ashamed of when I brought them out. On the skidding, we didn't go out until just coming daylight. There was three trail cutters, two log makers and two rollers. Well, one of the rollers would take one of my horses. I'd take the other on the trail, eh? Because you could only take one at a time. One ahead of the other. And we'd go out and I'd put them in the whippletrees and I'd start to pull logs into the skidway, and they'd roll them. Big logs. They'd put the line around them and pile them up. Just about getting dusk, we'd start back to camp. We'd do that 'til Christmas. After Christmas, the sleigh haul was going to start, eh? So I'd haul logs then with two sleighs, one behind the other. With cross jibs. But on the sleigh haul, that was a different tune. I used to feed the horses more oats and everything because they had to run down big hills. On hills like that they'd put sand. But on the runaways, they'd put hay just to check them, so they wouldn't run away and break their legs. But if you got stuck on the hay, then they had to put on sand. So maybe three trips a day or so. I enjoyed it.

Every morning I'd get up, get my lantern, go out and get two pails of water from the river, lake, whatever, and give each horse each a pail of water. Then I'd go and get two gallons of oats, one for each horse. I'd get a flake of hay and shake it up for them, and then I'd put the harness on both of them and then go in and wait for my breakfast. During the day to take care of them, I went into the skidway and they loaded me and the first place I'd come where they were tanking—they used to tank the roads to freeze them for the sleigh runners—and there was a hole

*An array of twenty-five horse and carriage stalls still standing in a remarkable state of preservation at Grace United Church, McDougal, back of Renfrew, Ontario.*

there and a pail and I'd go and I'd water my horses. At noon, I fed them the same amount of oats and hay as I did in the morning.

At night we'd go out and curry them—we had such pride in them—and maybe sit on the manger, and have a chew of tobacco, and start talking "horse." Everybody had to go to bed at ten to nine, so we'd slick them down, and feel them all over to see if they had any lumps or sores where the harness was hurting them, eh? That's where I came in good. I could fix the collar with pieces of blanket. If the horse was sore some place, I'd take the weight off it, and put something under here and above that, and then there'd be no weight on it, and in a few days it was gone. It never happened too often. We took care of our horses and, if one had a sore leg, we wouldn't press it or push it because it would just get worse, eh? The foremen were all pretty good. You'd leave that horse in and they'd have what they called the barn boss—he used to clean out the stables—and he'd get the oats ready and hay and he'd look after them. There was the odd time, sure, they'd be lame and I'd take them into the blacksmith's shop, and specially on

the skidding they'd get a stub in, eh? They cut the trail, eh? And if there was something sticking up, maybe it would go into the horse's heel or some place. They'd go in and they'd cut that out, eh? And then you'd get a piece of leather and okam and tar, and put that inside of the shoe.

Before my time, they say there was a lot of teamsters that abused their horses. Those Gaspés! I heard a lot about them, but, thank God! I wasn't with them because I wouldn't have stayed with them. But where I was, most of the time, they were all pretty fair teamsters. My teamster pals—they're all dead. Well, I'll tell you some good teamsters. Sam McLean, Tom McLean, and Abraham Desjardins, all from Fort Coulonge. They could take the team into the camp, and skid, and bring them out in the spring in good shape. And they could fix their harness. I was lucky I never had a sick horse, but they had something they used to put in a quart bottle. Not Dr. Bell's Wonder Medicine. I used that sometimes. But this, they'd make the horse swallow it—I forget what they called it. They'd get the horse's head pulled up and then they'd put the quart in there and then they'd have to hit him sometime to make him swallow. They were breathing heavy, too. 'Coz they were running all day. They were working hard. Well—them hills! They had to go, eh, because that big load was behind them. And on a lot of runaways—but I never saw any horses killed where I was, but other places they . . . Well you've heard the stories.

I was a horse lover and there was a lot like me. The foremen were all satisfied with us 'coz the next year they wanted us to go back again. Night feed was the same thing again. Water, hay and oats. I used to give them a little pinch of coarse salt in their box— each one of them—and I had a little soda I used to give them every Wednesday night. I didn't give them much else. If you give them too much salt, it would stiffen up in their kidneys, eh? But, if you'd just take a little pinch, it would keep their hair nice and smooth, and it was good for their water and everything.

A lot of teamsters fed saltpetre on Saturday night; I never fed them that. I found out that you had to be careful with it. Soda seemed to help them, like it does with a person, eh? Once a week. I found out from old teamsters. I used to watch them pretty close, you know, to see what they were doing, and I learned from them. I used to go and find out what they were doing, watch the hitching of the horses in the winter. They used to shave them, eh, in the cold weather. And Abraham Desjardins, I asked him one time when we were through driving horses, "Abraham," I said, "I saw you had nice horses and I never saw them with any hair on them. What did you use?" "I'll tell you," he said. "Vaseline. Vaseline's good for everything."

Well, it stood to reason—anywhere the harness touched the horses, he put Vaseline on and it would soften it, but he never told anybody. As I said before, Tom McLean was a good teamster. He said, "I could have told him what to do, but I wouldn't tell him." He kept everything to himself.

When the horses went out of the lumber camp, I went out too. The machinery came in, and it was no fun anymore; no more horses. All the horses went out; even all the axes went out. After fifteen years with Booth, I got on with the road survey in Pontiac, and I was fifteen years with them. At the end, they gave us two thousand two hundred dollars. They gave us two thousand each with J.R. Booth on it—his picture—and we needed two hundred to come home. We were sub-jobbing. Subcontracted and cut our own roads and we hired our own lads. That was at Kippewa. We didn't take our own horses. They had horses right there. We used to go up the lake. They had a boat called *The Fleck*. Mr. Fleck used to be one of the big men for Booth, so they christened that boat *The Fleck*. It would run to Christmas. You'd hear that boat coming for miles, every day. It would break the channel, eh? We came down one year at Christmas and we got off on the ice, see, and got back on the boat. We could hear that whistle blowing for miles.

*When I went to tape Gervase O'Reilly in 1990 at his home in Quyon, Quebec, I was really looking for hockey stories for my book, Old Scores, New Goals, History of the Ottawa Senators, 1891-1992, and he did have a few of these in his capacity as a lifelong fan of Valley hockey. Because of his long association with the Quyon Fair as president, and because of his valley-wide reputation as a lover of great horses, I also wanted him to tell me about horse racing on the ice of the Ottawa River in the early days. This he did. Gervase O'Reilly's mother was a Rowan from Fitzroy Harbour. His father, John James O'Reilly, was killed by a runaway horse on Cole Street, right at his own gate by his own horse. He raised Clydesdales and Standardbreds. Gervase died in 1998 at the age of ninety-one, one of the last of the old unaccompanied singers in the Valley.*

*In the days before the automobile and mechanization, men were sometimes accused of taking better care of their horses than their families. Indeed the buying and selling of good horses often made the news as in this item from the Shawville Equity, April 30, 1891:*

> *On Friday last, Mr. John Horner purchased from Mr. P. Mullin, of Bristol, the well-known stallion, Black Prince.*

*As well as being occasions for pride and status, horses were essential for survival, for making a livelihood, for all forms of transportation and commerce.*

*Again in the 1890s the Shawville Equity records:*

> *Mr. John Horner of Clarendon leaves for the Mattawa with ten teams on Thursday. He will be engaged drawing supplies to the lumber concerns, and will make Mattawa his base of operations. A number of loaded teams belonging to Mr. John Thomson (Mountain Jack) of Litchfield, passed through Shawville on Monday.*

Sure, my father would have known Big John Horner of Radford. They were both into Clydesdales, Percherons. Horner was well known all over Canada, I guess, for inputting and buying the best of stallions that he could get.

I knew about the Gilbert Arnold farm at Hawkesbury where everybody used to go to buy their prize horses. Gilbert Arnold had about five thousand horses there at one time. I didn't go down to buy from him, but I was secretary for the Quyon Fair and, at that time, the government loaned us breeding stallions. I'd say a good horse got three hundred dollars a year, provided there were so many mares in foal by that horse. Wilsons, George Frazers, and there were others, too, had horses promised and used to go down to Gilbert Arnold's. There they exchanged horses and Gilbert would take in the horses they had for a certain period of time until he had worn out his—there were too many young mares in—so they would change horses and get new ones.

**Horsepower provided by a ten-horse hitch for haying and harvesting.**

Arnold had about four huge farms. There were some at Grenville. I think his big fire was at Grenville, a disastrous fire there at one time. Horses burnt. Valuable horses. We were there shortly after the fire and I remember one horse was standing in a stall—why he was kept I don't know, but he must have been a very valuable horse. He had his head against the wall and he was pressing—he was burnt so badly and that was one way he had of relieving the pain—he was standing there pressing against the wall. Gilbert wasn't there that day. The fields would be full of horses, a sight to behold. All kinds of horses. He had a buyer that time working with him, Tom McNeilly, whom I knew, too. He used to go to the States and buy truckloads of Percheron stallions and Arnold wouldn't have seen them or know what he paid for them until they were unloaded at his farm. He imported horses from France. He was known all over Canada. He was the biggest dealer in Canada. Maybe North America.

In 1920, the Quyon Fall Fair really started. Shawville and Chapeau are the only ones in the Pontiac that are older than that. As kids we felt lucky if we got a half day off from school to go to the Quyon Fair. I have dates back to 1910 with the horse races at Quyon—on the ice. They came from the Ontario side—Arnprior, Carleton Place, Renfrew—to the races at Quyon. We had two days racing, about the 16th and 17th of February on the ice. You had to have it late enough to get deep safe ice and then you had to have it early enough before the thaw came. The last races were in 1926. It snowed the night of the first day, so they cancelled the races for the next day because they couldn't clean the ice. That time it was cleaned with an old road grader and four teams of horses. The grader cleaned it right down to the ice.

Now, some people think that the drivers were at that time in a kind of a sled but, no, they were on bikes, like the ones they use today with wheels.

There was a mare came from New York state to race, name of Romalla. She won three heats and, after the races were finished, the owner went to the stand and asked if he could drive her against time. He wanted to beat the ice record, half mile on this course. And she went and she beat the half mile record. That's 1922.

I remember the Quinns from Aylmer—they still live there. Quinn had a stallion, Mick Sweeney sired by Joe Sweeney. A handsome big horse. Dark brown. Shiny. And Bill Sharpe, the blacksmith at Fort Coloungue, had Darkey Hal. Another one that he had that I remember well was Daisy McKenzie. A mare, Daisy McKenzie. Billy Sharpe's father was also a blacksmith.

There was no starting gate so they had to score them on their time. If somebody was ahead of them they were sent back. Ring the bell and start again. And the horses would all slow down when they heard the bell and go back and score again. I remember one time there was a horse ran away and they were wondering how they would get him stopped and everything. The starter said, "Leave him to me and I'll stop him when he comes round again." And he got up on the grandstand and, when the horse came up the stretch, he rang the bell and that horse slowed right down. And they caught him. Horses are smarter than we think they are. They haven't been given enough credit at all. They opened this country. Transportation, labour, bush work—there was nothing better in the bush than the horses. They've slaughtered so much bush with these skidders, clear cutting. I remember one time I was talking to Wyman MacKechnie[2] and I said, "You know horses don't get enough credit at all." He said, "We'll get together some time and we'll write a book on it." Well, we just didn't.

The starter was a special person. Oh, yes, he had to be qualified to know the rules of the races and he was the boss there, really, on the ice. If I'm not mistaken, Cochrane from Carleton Place always started the races because there weren't that many people who could do it. And not just that, but there weren't very many ice races. They used to have ice races down at Ottawa. I think they did at Alymer, too. But Quyon, at that time, had the BIG race meet on ice.

Back then, Quyon was a thriving town. I remember when we had three county offices, two funeral directors. And we had three shoemakers, two blacksmiths' shops, two saw mills, and all kinds of general stores. A sash and door factory. I can remember myself, as a child, there were all kinds of stores along the main street. There was a little five-and-ten-cent store. And there was even a millinery store in Quyon—Mrs. O'Connor.

At the ice races, they would have a blacksmith there in case a horse pulled a shoe racing. Of course, without shoes on that bare ice, they couldn't race. They did the shoes a certain way for racing on the ice. It was like a kind of a side cork that kept them from sliding sideways. But all the shoes were sharp. That was the dangerous part of it. They'd cut themselves if they overreached. That's what horses have often done. Catch the heel of the front hoof, it would cut them badly with sharp shoes. So the blacksmith from town would go to the ice races. He'd take all his equipment with him. They had tents on the ice, you know, for the horses between heats. And the blacksmith would set up in a tent. And there would be steam coming out of that tent as though you had a fire on in there. They would blanket them up, put on their coolers. Oh yes, everything was very well taken care of. And you could get hot dogs and coffee. They had stands there, you know. A shot of whisky? Well, you took that with you. In your hip pocket. That kept you warm. I'm talking again about the twenties. At that time it wasn't a sin to have a little flask and sip it. I was a young gaffer when these ice races were going on. We couldn't leave school unless they gave us permission. It was painful that first day to stay in school. We wondered how they'd get along without us.

Horses were in my blood. My father, it was in his blood, too. He'd raised Clyde horses and Standards. I didn't know him at all because I was only fifteen months old when he was killed. I worked with my Uncle William, my father's brother. He was just the next farm to us and I went there quite a lot. They had Percheron horses. And yet, when I bought one for myself, when I saw this young three-year-old mare, I had to have her. And she was a Clyde mare. That was my first Clyde mare.

*Horsepower moving hay loads across an ice bridge probably on the Ottawa River.*

I think back then if you won one race you went into first position at the pole. Now, I'm not too well up on the regulations and the rules of racing. The track would accommodate about six or seven horses. And if there would be more than that, they would trail. Since they were timed, they could trail. Entrance was fifty cents. Bets were under the table.

I remember Toots Cecile from Pembroke. Paddy McDermid had Captain Hal here from Arnprior. The Dolans from Portage-du-Fort. From Fort Coulonge, we had the Sharpes and Eddie Davis. Chapeau is a long piece away in the wintertime. Lloyd Horner of Radford had a famous mare named Dot. She was hard to beat. But she was never on the ice. Just fairs.

We had one of the best dirt tracks in Western Quebec. But I'd go a little further than that. We had a secretary and a president from the Metcalfe Fair, Dr. Gamble and—I can't remember the other name—anyway he asked me one time when I was involved in the Quyon Fair, "Who keeps your track?" I said, "Fred Fraser?" "Oh," he said, "you've got the best track in the east." That's the way he put it. A good track? Keep it level, keep it solid, and Fraser was using at that time, stone dust. It wouldn't have been stone dust at first—it was only in later years they used stone dust. That's ground rock. After Fred Fraser, it was under the supervision of Jim Menary who was a great horseman in Quyon, too. I know he had one great horse called Banquet Rex.

There were no purses for these races on the ice. No winnings. I suppose they got their expenses. They weren't doing it for money; they were doing it for love, for sport. They were amateurs. At that time in the Pontiac, the horsemen drove their horses down here to Quyon and any that came a distance came by train. They had lots of hotel stables here at that time. Fairbanks and Kennedys—Gavan was later. The horses were well covered in these big tents between heats. Then they'd take them to the hotel stables for the night. I think they could accommodate twenty horses at each stable. You see, at that time there were stables in Quyon. Billy Boland had a stable; Jim Menary had a stable.

Billy Boland's last mare that I remember was Lady Boland. I had her for a couple of winters just for her feed. She was a dandy. I had an experience with her one night going home in the wintertime. At that time the road went alongside of the station and it was a moonlight night. And I knew how she worked; she'd start out walking, and then she'd trot a bit, and then she'd open up. Driving along there and the moon was shining and her shadow was right alongside of her. Well, she was bound that shadow wasn't going to pass her and I was bound that I was going to try and stay in the cutter because I had another sharp turn coming up and I knew I couldn't control her. So, anyway, I sat down on the side of the cutter and I held her and she went round that bad curve, and I let her go then. Oh, I had such rides with Lady Boland!

Quyon hockey teams, they played on the ice out here on the river; they never had a covered arena like Shawville. Quyon was a hockey town. They also played a lot of lacrosse here. No, we didn't drive a horse to the Auditorium! We drove a horse to Fitzroy Harbour or to Arnprior, and went on to Ottawa on the train. I went to hockey matches in Dey's Arena even before the Auditorium was built for the Senators. I couldn't say I remember how we got there, but I saw our "Shawville Express"—Frankie Finnigan—play. I saw the Rangers play in the Auditorium and Boston. At that time, there was only six hockey teams in the National Hockey League. When I went down from Quyon to hockey games, a whole gang of people would go, whatever the train would take. I had some aunts living in Ottawa and I would stay there. In those days you couldn't afford to go to the Château Laurier and stay over!

As a young lad, I played bush hockey. I knew I'd never make the big time. But I loved skating and playing hockey. A good skater? Well, I thought I was. We used to wear out the rink here every Saturday night. Open air, of course. Skating with the girls. Not this two-hand thing. She just put her hand in here and you had a free hand and she had a free hand. I loved it. We didn't have music. But I saw them skating to music. In Dey's Arena, the Governor General's Foot Guard Band used to play between periods. If the Ottawa Senators were winning, they'd play *There are Smiles That Make Us Happy*. And if they were losing, the band would play *Pack Up Your Troubles in Your Old Kit Bag*.

I remember more of the great horses! Dick Sweeney had Night Rider. Lady Cecil was owned by George Moffat from Quyon. Norma was the other mare of Menary's. The familiar names in the racing were Dr. Laframboise, Tracy, Butler, Sharp, Davis, Proudfoot, Menary, McNulty, McKay—that was a Shawville man—the Horners and the Quinns and Andy Lascelles. And, of course, the Proudfoots. Hughie Proudfoot told me that they owned Darkie Hal. But they were always in horses.

And I remember when the Cornwall Colts played against Fort Coulonge in Shawville. The Cornwall Colts! Can you imagine that? They got to Shawville! In the early thirties! The Cornwall Colts were really a good hockey team. They had speed and they had a little bit of everything. They won. They beat Fort Coulonge in Shawville. Fort Coulonge came down to Shawville to save the Colts a little travel. Also remember Shawville had a covered rink so that was the other reason.

In 1987 while working on *Tell Me Another Story*, my fourth oral/social history of the Ottawa Valley, at the suggestion of Hugh MacMillan, then fieldman for the Ontario Archives, I travelled to interview Gilbert Arnold at his home near Grenville, Quebec. I didn't need much urging really because I was already familiar with the name Arnold in association with the history of purebred horses in Canada. The Arnolds were also among the first Anglo-Celt settlers in that part of Quebec.

I was warmly welcomed by Mr. Arnold and his wife, the former Doreen Beland of Fort Coulonge, Quebec, and spent some hours taping him. I think it is safe to say that, although he was a descendant and part owner of what had been one of the largest horse farms in North America, he was, by the time I arrived, much more interested in the genealogy of his fascinating and often prestigious

ancestors than he was in the pedigreed stock his family had bred for four generations. A few weeks later, and before I could get the transcript back to him to be verified, Mr. Arnold died.

The Arnold Farm at Grenville was a landmark for half a century and familiar to hundreds of buyers, sellers, horse lovers, breeders who visited there over the years. As a young child I had often heard my grandfather Big John Horner of Radford, Quebec, talk about going to Grenville. And after I had taped Gilbert Arnold, I went to visit my father and mother in Shawville, Quebec. "Do you know anything about Gilbert Arnold and that farm at Grenville?" I asked. "Know anything!" my father exclaimed. "I remember taking your Grandfather Horner down there to buy a horse."

My great-grandfather, the senior and first Irish who came to this area, his name was Thomas Arnold and his wife's name was Sarah Gawley and they came from near Ballybay in County Monaghan, Ireland. In the year 1840. They had several sons, but one of their sons, Isaiah, came to this farm and he didn't have too much education. He was a cobbler, shoemaker, harnessmaker, wheelwright and a sort of a little bit of a carpenter. We still have his old, old tools and various equipment that he had which were out in what we called our previous harness shop. When Isaiah came here, he signed a petition which is in the Public Archives in Ottawa. In 1840, in Grenville, he was one of a group of early settlers who wanted a lot of land for the Methodist Church to be established in Grenville, Quebec. Which petition was granted and the United Church is still located on that lot and there's a plaque up there about Isaiah's son, my grandfather James Arnold, being a member of the church.

When Arnolds first came to this farm, it was not a crown land grant. They leased it for a nine-year lease from the Taylor estate, absentee landlords who owned a lot of land around here then. We own most of Taylor's original two hundred acres, but at that time we're talking about forty-five acres. That farm was eventually split between two brothers, my great-grandfather, Thomas, and his brother, James, both school teachers, both registered in the old schoolteachers' book here for this district. They had a fairly good handwriting but their brother, Isaiah, the shoemaker, didn't have nice handwriting. Instead of going to school, he went to work for some cobbler, you see. But his father, Thomas Arnold, my great-grandfather, the first one who came, he had beautiful handwriting—he was a schoolteacher. Sarah Gawley, his wife, could hardly write her name.

It appears the Arnolds came out with the Gawleys who were also living at Ballybay. I visited there in 1983 and I spent a while around that district. I saw the original Gawley farm. Well, a farm in those days over there was a field—what I mean was I saw the Arnold field next to the Gawley field. And the field was leased. The land didn't belong to them. It was leased from a landlord and in their case the landlord was an absentee Anglican minister.

On my mother's side, the Bigelows were very famous in the United States for horses. It was in the family and, if you know Ireland, it's in their blood—horses. And it was in the American Bigelow side, too. That's the reason why my grandfather specialized in horses. When he was a young boy, they didn't have any good stallions around here. So he, with his mother and another brother, Frank (who has no descendants), they arranged to buy this purebred Percheron stallion called Claudius. We have his papers here. And this Claudius was imported from France to Montreal and, since the Arnold family then

*Horsepower providing transportation of supplies, unloading for ships in harbour; probably at Montreal.*

had just a little farm, they were a poor family and they couldn't pay for the horse in cash. They had to pay for it over a period of time.

Oh, it cost a lot this horse! I don't remember how much. Don't forget there were no tractors in those days. He had to improve the horses, but no people had purebred mares, so there's no registered descendants of Claudius. He was bought from the French government stables in France in the Percheron district. A man named Walker was sort of the guarantor, financier. My family had to pay him. Walker didn't want to be bothered with the horse, so he put it in the name of another fellow called Dalby. But, anyway, the Arnolds just got Claudius paid for and then he died. Then they started to buy other horses, especially from the United States. So, my grandfather was going to the States to buy horses. Then he went over to France to buy them directly. He made trips to France before the First War to buy purebred horses.

Claudius was born in 1887. He was bred by this fellow in France, imported in 1890 by the Nationale Company, Montreal. Now, the Nationale Company is the French Government Stables in France and the third owner, Dalby, he had a mortgage for his owner James Arnold, my grandfather. In the stud book, Claudius is number twenty-three, with his registered pedigree from France. Claudius was the first one of many prize horses. Rosco was here with my grandfather, too. He's another one in the first stud book, but he came from Nova Scotia. Another one, Vagarie—he was from France. Anyway, my grandfather was involved in horses from the time of 1890, when that document came over here from France to him. At that time, Arnolds' was a general farm. It had horses of many breeds, purebred Holstein cattle, Yorkshire hogs, Shropshire sheep, poultry. He had those nice white poultry—Silkies. My grandfather was a very good farmer.

My father had been to McDonald College, 1914-18, and had graduated in agriculture. He was in the Canadian Officers Training Corps but, because of his bad eye, he wasn't fit to serve so he stayed there. At McDonald College my father's professor of Animal Husbandry and Farm Management was Dr.

Barton, who was later deputy minister in Ottawa, and they were great friends right up to the time of Dr. Barton's death.

Then here's what happened. My grandfather died. He went to the Canadian National Exhibition in Toronto and he was getting out of a streetcar with a Methodist lay preacher—he was a very religious man so there was no question of him being drunk or anything—he didn't watch out because he was in a rush to catch a train and a car hit him. So, in the hospital he died from pneumonia. This was in 1926.

After my grandfather died, my father was so anxious to get rid of the cattle, the pigs, so he had a big auction sale and he sold all the registered Holstein cattle. Most of them were bought by T.V. McAuley who started a very famous herd, the most famous in the world at the time for Holsteins, down at Hudson Heights. My father was so anxious to get rid of his stock to turn everything into horses. He was a horse man. He kept enough cows for us for our milk, the odd pig for our pork, and that's how the Arnolds went from general farmers to stud farm, horse farm.

At its peak, there were over five thousand horses on this farm. We had a hundred farms scattered around Eastern Ontario and Quebec and we owned farms as far down as Nova Scotia and we still own land up to Muskoka. In 1939 and '40, my father began selling horses to the Government of France. War had started and France had a French Purchasing Commission here in Canada, including people in charge: a Count de Rousse de Salle, Commandant Maurice Quedrue, a Captain Panisset, who later became Dean of the College of Veterinary Surgery at St. Hyacinthe's. Those men were all part of a group buying horses and they were what you call artillery horses to pull the French 75 cannon, which was the best little field piece at that time. We were not breeding horses for them! We were simply supplying them with horses—breeding some, buying some and dealing in them. We had big farms here. My father, and his father, and his grandmother before him had been dealing with France importing horses. We had very good relationships with the French. Three generations at that time and then it went to four generations with us, my brother especially. My brother at one point had had bad experiences with his businesses in France and with certain friends of his there and he had lost a lot of accounts. But despite that, our relationship with France remained good. Remember my grandfather had been France's main supplier of horses in the First World War, supplying them with cavalry and artillery horses. This was recorded in the newspapers at the time. And before that, he'd been an importer of breeding horses from France. Our relationships with France are indeed long-standing.

I had an experience in France with de Gaulle. We were afraid to talk to him. He was a huge big man, and he was cross looking with a big nose and one of those square hats, you know. Anyway, he was watching the French government horses go by, horses to pull French 75 cannon, sold by Father to

them. Then France fell and my father had to buy back thousands of horses from France. Orders to liquidate them from the collaboration government in France—Petain, Laval, some of that bunch.

As I said before, the Arnold farms at the peak had thousands of horses, rows of exceptional barns, and thousands of acres across Canada. Then we went into the urine business—I was one of the first to catch on to the importance of the urine business. Our foreman at the time chased the Frost Pharmaceutical manager away when he talked about mares' urine. The Frost man approached our manager who was a Gawley and who thought the whole idea was ridiculous. But the Frost rep got to my father and my father was interested. This Gawley didn't have any education and my father was a graduate and he listened to this man, an Irishman called Sheen who was the plant manager at Charles E. Frost. So, we agreed to collect some

*Horsepower moved the old Horse Railway that once ran passengers going up the Ottawa River around the Chats Falls Dam and Chats Rapids. The railway ran from Pontiac Village to Union Village, both settlements now gone without leaving a trace. The single horse walked without protection on a boardwalk twenty to thirty feet above ground.*

urine and I was the one who was delegated to do it. And I worked on it for years. Because of this huge urine business, we had up to five thousand horses, plus another five thousand on loan and used in our production. A tremendous herd at that time.

My father had got rid of *everything* and later on he regretted that his cattle were gone because they became terribly valuable and he had had a very good herd. His father, James Arnold, had built it up. He was the son of Bigelow and he was the founder of the Montreal Mill Shippers Association, one of the founders of the Canadian Co-operative Wool Growers and the founder of the Grenville Farmer's Club. My father had got rid of it all except the horses.

Then, when my father died, I wasn't too interested in horses but I had a brother, Jeff, who was. I want to tell you what happened then. After my father died, my brother was more interested in a meat slaughtering plant we had, so he slaughtered and got rid of, very quickly, all of the purebred horses that my father had built up. My brother's wife was interested in riding horses so he got rid of everything else and that put us as purebred horse breeders down to zero. In 1988, the Arnolds have got to the stage where the only horses in the stables belong to one of my sons or their wives. They're just riding horses.

1  The Brysons were timber barons based at Fort Coulonge, Quebec. They employed many servants on their estate situated at the covered bridge on Highway 148 where the magnificent white frame mansion, stone accountant's office, and some barns remain today.

2  References to and stories from Wyman MacKechnie appear throughout the oral histories. His descendants at Wyman, Quebec, continue his traditions of excellence in Quebec agricultural circles.

*Below: Throughout the Valley, family pride was heightened by having members who went surveying. For not only was such a career envied as a "cash paying job," it was also a life of adventure and danger. Surveyors returned home full of story. From Wilf McAra's life as a surveyor comes this magnificent photo of some of his contemporaries proudly holding their transits. McAra is in inset, left. First settlers in the Beechgrove-Eardley-Quyon area, McAras still live there. They once ran the Quyon ferry.*

# 12

# "We Grew Up Surrounded by Surveyors and Surveying Talk"

## STEVE BRABAZON – Ottawa, Ontario

*When I was attending Lisgar Collegiate, Ottawa, during the war years, it became trendy for the young people who ordinarily would have attended private schools in Rockcliffe, Elmwood and Ashbury, to cross over to Lisgar and blend with the less privileged. Amongst these teenagers were descendants of the Ottawa Valley timber barons—Gillies, Edwards, Gilmores, Brysons, Davidsons—and others with special lineages— Crerars, Carlings, Woods, Sopers, Bishops, and Brabazons.*

*In 1978 when I began my oral/social histories of the Ottawa Valley, it was often my father with his acute sense of awareness of the stories of the lumbering dynasties and all the monied interconnections who sent me off in important directions: "You must get to Big Jim McCuaig," he'd say. "You must get to the Owen Tollers (Brysons)." "You must get to the Brabazons of Portage." I am indebted to my father for many important leads.*

*During our interview Steve Brabazon recreated the village of Portage-du-Fort, a riverside depot for the passage of supplies and lumber in the days when it was a grand centre of Anglo-Celt activity bustling with the comings and goings of leading citizens, like the Usbornes, Rattrays, Reids, Thomsons, and Brabazons.*

*Steve Brabazon was born in the Renfrew Hospital in 1924 and lived in the ancestral Brabazon home at Portage-du-Fort until his parents moved to Ottawa to further the education of their children: Dorothy, Gerald, Eleanor, Russell, Jack, Claude and Steve. Steve graduated from Lisgar in 1945, went into business in Ottawa, married Constance Jarvis of Chesterville. They now live in retirement in Ottawa.*

I GREW UP in both Portage-du-Fort and Ottawa surrounded by surveyors and surveying talk. My grandfather, father and Uncle Jack were all in the business; my grandfather and father working on surveys throughout the Pontiac—Thorne, Shawville, Sheenboro, Fort Coulonge, Norway Bay, Bristol— and for the Upper Ottawa Improvement Company; my Uncle Jack on the Yukon boundary survey.

When my father or Uncle Jack arrived home from surveys across the country and into Alaska, there was such storytelling went on at the dinner table that the servants waiting to clear the table would become impatient and annoyed!

Surveying even goes back to my great-grandfather, Samuel Levinge Brabazon, who was born at Levington Park, County Westmeath, Ireland, in 1829. When he came to Canada he already had his surveying papers from Dublin University and had already married in Ireland, Margaret Clark. He settled at Lachute and taught in Montreal at McGill. He moved to Portage-du-Fort to follow the development of the country and to be closer to sites which needed to be surveyed. In Portage-du-Fort, he bought the big brick house from General Merchant Reid and generations were to be raised there, the later ones to remember and revere it as the site of joyous summers. The big brick was just up the hill on the Shawville Road past Mountain Jack Thomson's[1] house, a classic frame which survives well preserved to this day. The big Brabazon brick survived the Portage fire of 1913, ironically only to burn down in 1954 when the family had left and it was being rented. Of his four children, three were born at Montreal and Lachute, only Mary Ann, the youngest, being born at Portage-du-Fort. All are buried in the cemetery there.

Samuel Levinge Brabazon died at Portage-du-Fort in 1906, but not before he had initiated his eldest son Gerald Hugh Brabazon into his chosen profession. Gerald was tutored at home by his father through high school while he also served an informal apprenticeship with his father as a draughtsman and surveyor. One year he worked with a government survey party under his father, which travelled by train to Fort William and then by wagon train to Fort Garry to survey the land that was later to become what we know as the Prairie Provinces. It was reported that many times they encountered friendly Indians or had to contend with hostile Indians. He worked at first as an assistant to his father, but later and following his father's death, he branched out on his own, surveying the towns and townships of the Pontiac.

From his earliest years, Grandfather proved to be a remarkable man, excelling in swimming, boxing, canoeing, hunting, horseback riding. He went to live with the Indians to learn the ways of the forest and was versed in river and Indian lore. At the tender age of twenty-three, he was elected Mayor of Portage-du-Fort, serving for eighteen years in that capacity, and as

*The patriarch of the Brabazon surveying family, Samuel Levinge Brabazon of Portage-du-Fort and Ottawa, immigrant from Ireland, died July 12, 1906.*

Warden of Pontiac County for thirty years. The dates are not known, but somewhere in his early life he was appointed slidemaster of the timber slide on the Ottawa River built to circumnavigate Bryson Chute. During his tenure of that position, he lived with his family in the residence provided for the slidemaster opposite Bryson, Quebec, on Calumet Island.

My grandfather had gone to McGill for his civil engineering degree. This automatically gave him his surveying papers, but he would have to write his Dominion Land Surveying exams after that. In 1885, he went off to serve in the Northwest Rebellion as a lieutenant in the Dominion Land Surveyors Intelligence Corps under General Middleton[2]. On his return from the Northwest Rebellion, he was given a gold watch fob by the village of Portage-du-Fort and presented with a silver knife, fork and

*Left: Second generation Brabazons at their house, Portage-du-Fort, Quebec, c. 1900. Seated in the carriage is Mrs. Claude (Jessie) Brabazon and young daughter Dorothy. The lady in the apron is Pat Cross, the family cook.*

spoon by Princess Louise[3] in recognition of services rendered.

His federal political career began in 1904 when he was elected Conservative member for Pontiac County. He was defeated in the 1908 election but re-elected in 1911 and sat until the dissolution of the Twelfth Parliament in 1917.

While he was an MP, 1904 to 1917, there was great concern amongst the towns and villages of Pontiac County that the proposed CPR railway extension should serve each and every one of them. There were no professional lobbyists, of course, in those days, so each person had to do his own lobbying. In the family papers are some historically fascinating pleas to my grandfather in the House of Commons in Ottawa.

J.W. Hennessy, entrepreneur of the well-known Hennessy clan of Fort Coulonge, hired no less than the renowned Mountain Jack Thomson of Portage-du-Fort—scaler, tallyman, bush ranger—to assess the amount of timber which would be made available

for sale if the CPR extension went up from Waltham into the Pontiac. In a letter to Hennessy from Portage-du-Fort, dated January 20, 1913, Mountain Jack gave his report:

Recently as requested by you I have made an examination of the Townships of Waltham, Allumette Isld., Chichester and Sheen in Pontiac, Que. As far as it was possible to do within the short time at my disposal with a view of getting something reliable in the way of information as to the quantities of timber which would be within easy reach of the Railway Line if the C.P.R. branch was extended for a few miles further say eighteen westward from Waltham to Sheenboro.

From personal observations during the present trip as well as from information obtained through the most reliable sources and also from the knowledge gained in going over the district many times during my twenty years in the Government Service as Forest Ranger.

I have prepared from the date collected in this way an estimate of the quantities in each of the Townships which I have no hesitation in saying may be taken as approximately correct and which show in all a total of

| White Pine | 16,625,000 ft. B.M. |
| Hard Wood1 | 1,471,000 ft. " " |
| Railway Ties | 18,500 cords |
| Pulpwood | 335,000 cords. |

The attached statement showing quantities in each Township and concessions. In no case should the haul to the Railway exceed five miles.

I need not remind one who is so familiar with the Upper Ottawa Country and its natural resources especially in its timber wealth what tremendous advantages a railway through this section would mean not only by providing easy and rapid transportation to the mills and to the markets for the timber of all sorts, but it would also be a great incentive to the farmers in the vicinity to go more extensively into dairying and mixed farming for which the country is admirably adopted.

And I feel sure you will agree with me when I say that the traffic on the C.P.R. would be increased to a very great extent if the line was pushed on to Sheenboro.

The statement of quantities I enclose herewith which I trust may answer your purpose.

Yours respectfully,
John Thomson,
Bush Ranger.

Hennessy forwarded Mountain Jack Thomson's report to Brabazon as an enclosure to another interesting letter revealing the social history of the times dated January 20, 1913, only a few days after he had received Thomson's report:

I enclose herewith report made by John Thomson at my request, of the quantity of Pulpwood and lumber available at the present time in the Townships of Waltham, Allumette Island, Chichester and Sheen, that would no doubt be manufactured and shipped to market if the Pontiac Branch of the C.P. Railway was built from Waltham Station to some point in Sheen Township.

I have been doing business with most of the farmers in the above named Townships for over twenty years, and know the country well, and I consider the quantities of Pulpwood and lumber as given by Mr. Thomson a safe estimate: in fact, I do not know of any section of country during my travels for J.R. Booth where there are such quantities of the very best quality of Poplar, Balsam and Spruce Pulpwood. And in addition to timber and wood owned by farmers as given in Mr. Thomson's report, Mr. Booth owns the Timber Berths just north of Waltham, Chichester and Sheen with immense quantities of all kinds of timber, a great portion of which can only be marketed by rail, and providing the line was built to Sheen Township it would bring these limits within hauling distance of the railroad, for all timber that will not float by water to market.

There are a large number of prosperous farmers living in those Townships who would also undoubtedly ship large quantities of hay, grain and stock.

I am of the opinion that if this matter was placed before the proper officials of the Canadian Pacific Railway Company, that they would look into it, and see for themselves the facts of the case that they would build the line from Waltham Station, say fifteen to eighteen miles further on and by so doing increase their revenue on the Pontiac line very greatly.

Yours very truly,
J.W. Hennessy.

T.E. Barry, Chapeau dealer in "stoves and tinware," lobbied Grandfather Brabazon in a letter dated July 5, 1913, in which he states, "under present conditions I do about Five Thousand Dollars Business. With the railroad without a doubt my trade would easily double as it would open up so many different branches in the lumber trade."

From Chapeau, General Merchants Poupore and McDonald on February 5, 1913, came a five-page letter outlining their "humble arguments in favor of the project which we have in view," and "wishing Brabazon every success in his forthcoming meeting with the president of the CPR railway." It is not quite clear how, but Poupore and McDonald were also organizing other merchants in the Pontiac to lobby for the extension. Poupore and McDonald talk about a decline in the lumber trade, which would be counterbalanced by the railway extension into new stands of timber. William McDonald added a little P.S. to the effect that, "needless to remind you the figures in regard to our business are confidential except for the purpose we stated in the other letter."

> In answer to your recent favor asking us for an expression of opinion as to the benefit to our business to be derived from the extension of the P.P.J. Railway to Chapeau, we respectfully submit to you our opinion on the matter based upon twelve years of experience.
>
> Our business established in 1901 with a turnover of $9,000 has steadily increased until this year it has attained a total of $45,000. You may say after reaching this statement "you are not much in need of a Railroad."
>
> One fact, however, must be borne in mind that we would never have been able to build up this business if we did not make contracts each year with the lumbermen for their Hay, Oats, Etc., enabling us to market the produce of our farmers who in return favoured us with their patronage. This market meant seventy five per cent of our trade.
>
> This year the first in the history of our business, we have not been able to make a contract owing to lumber operations being on a smaller scale than usual. As a consequence we must seek a market elsewhere. Here our difficulty begins.
>
> Situated ten miles distant from Waltham and eight miles from Pembroke, we are not in a position to pay the same price for produce as our competitors, hence we are obliged to calmly view the trade pass our door. Remember that is due, not to indifference or lack of energy on our part, but entirely to lack of Railway facilities. To-day the greater part of the produce of this section is marketed in Pembroke. That it is all shipped via C.P.R. we would not care to vouch. With one competing road already there and another under construction, the C.P.R. by extending their Pontiac line to this point would retain the business of this entire section. Chapeau, so centrally located, would become a large shipping point. Picture in your mind what this would mean to the business of this village. We are firmly convinced that we would double our business within the next five years.
>
> One more point before we finish. A representative of the C.P.R. who called upon us about two years ago remarked they were under the impression that they handle the traffic of this Country at Waltham Station. We tried to put him right by stating that their share of the trade at that point was not more than ten per cent, a statement which we are in a position to prove. Take our case as an example, you would naturally suppose that we received all our freight via Waltham. Such however, is not the case. Heretofore, we have favoured the C.P.R. at Pembroke, but like many others we feel that if this Company will not build their line here, to which we consider we are justly entitled, our little bit of business will go to the G.T.R. (Grand Trunk Railway).

Despite all the lobbying and meetings, the railway was never extended beyond the roundhouse at Waltham. But after my grandfather finished with politics in 1917, some of his influential friends whom he had tried to help with the railway extension gathered together to lobby for his appointment as a senator. The signatures are so blurred as to be unreadable, but the letter dated from Ottawa, June 25, 1917, to the "Right Honourable Sir Robert L. Borden, P.C., G.C.M.G., Prime Minister" makes clear the intent:

The undersigned representatives of the leading commercial and industrial business establishments in the Valley of the Ottawa, beg to draw your attention to the fact that there is a strong feeling throughout the Western portion of the Senatorial division of Inkerman, that Mr. Gerald H. Brabazon, M.P. for Pontiac, should be appointed to the seat in the Upper House for this division, now vacant through the death of the late Senator Owens.

No doubt J.W. Hennessy was one of the obliterated-by-time "undersigned." The very next day, June 26, 1917, he wrote from Fort Coulonge to my grandfather in Ottawa:

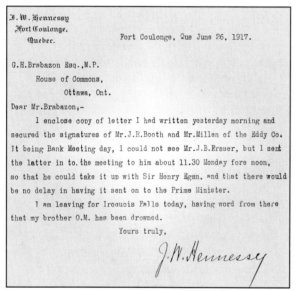

J. W. Hennessy
Fort Coulonge.
Quebec.                        Fort Coulonge, Que June 26, 1917.

G.H.Brabazon Esq.,M.P.
        House of Commons,
                Ottawa, Ont.

Dear Mr.Brabazon,-
        I enclose copy of letter I had written yesterday morning and secured the signatures of Mr.J.R.Booth and Mr.Millen of the Eddy Co. It being Bank Meeting day, I could not see Mr.J.B.Fraser, but I sent the latter in to the meeting to him about 11.30 Monday fore noon, so that he could take it up with Sir Henry Egan, and that there would be no delay in having it sent on to the Prime Minister.
        I am leaving for Iroquois Falls today, having word from there that my brother O.M. has been drowned.
                                Yours truly,
                                J. W. Hennessy

*Hennessy letter reproduced in full.*

Talk about name dropping! In eight lines Hennessy managed to mention three timber barons: Booth of Ottawa and Hull, J.B. Fraser of Pembroke and Sir Henry Egan of Hawkesbury and Ottawa. However, all that influence and heaven only knows how much from other directions failed to make my grandfather Senator Brabazon. Instead he was appointed Superintendent of Government Reservoirs on the Upper Ottawa, October 3, 1917. When he retired in 1933, for the six years before his death in 1938, he raised prize fowl and improved the Brabazon gardens at Portage-du-Fort.

Growing up in Portage-du-Fort and then in Ottawa, I always remember my father, Claude, being away on surveys for six months of the year and then home for six months, often doing reports. He had not attended university but had gone right into the field with Grandfather. From them and from my Uncle Jack, who was then working on the survey of the International Boundary between Alaska and the Yukon, we were constantly regaled with adventures and imbued with a sense of geography. Even when we went to Ottawa to live, Portage-du-Fort was our second home to which we went every holiday and for the entire summer holidays off school.

In 1879, my grandfather married Nellie Murphy from Cobden, the daughter of the village harnessmaker. Their big brick—Shawville fired bricks again?—still stands in the town core there today. There must have been something about those

*Brabazon grandchildren at Cobden frolic around the old Peerless which Aunt Blanche and her husband Jack Moxam drove from Calgary home to Cobden by way of Cleveland, New York City, Old Orchard Beach, c. 1912.*

*A Boyle-Murphy-Brabazon clan croquet game on the lawn of the Boyle house at Cobden, Ontario, c. 1900. L to R: Grandpa R.D. Boyle, Uncle Russell (R.S. Stewart); Uncle Atwell (Robert Atwell); Aunt Blanche (Mrs. J.A. Moxam); Uncle Edward, Aunt Mary E. (seated together); Aunt Margaret (Mrs J.M. Thomson); Aunt Norma (Mrs. George Colton); Jessie Winnifred (Mrs. C.H. Brabazon); Grandma Boyle (nee Mary Alice Murphy). The inscriptionist adds: "I think Jessie Winnifred is wearing her graduation dress (Stanstead)."*

Cobden girls because my father in 1912 married Jessie Winnifred Boyle, the eighth child of R.D. Boyle and Mary Alice (nee Murphy) of Cobden.

I so well remember huge clan gatherings at the Brabazon house in Portage-du-Fort: the Doctor Murphys from Renfrew, the Coltons from Fort Coulonge—Aunt Norma had married one of the Coltons—the Boyles and Murphys from Cobden. Even in those early days, most of the relatives had

cars and they travelled to my mother's events on those bad roads from every direction.

One of my mother's sisters, Blanche, had married a man from the West in lumber out there, J.A. Moxam. There are family pictures of the Peerless in which they drove from Calgary to Cobden. In the year 1912! The story is related that my mother and father met them first in Cleveland, Ohio. The four of them then took the train to New York City and Old

Abbitibi L.E. Racicot Photo 1901

*The Brabazons brought home many fascinating mementos of their surveying expeditions in far-flung places. Examples here show a postcard of canoes on the Abitibi, probably from Uncle Jack Brabazon who worked on the Alaska survey. The second one shows a more permanent surveyors' camp and one even boasting a steam tractor.*

Orchard Beach where they holidayed together, then returned to Cleveland—presumably to pick up the Peerless—and drove home to Cobden. There must have been great excitement in the clan welcoming committee after that landmark journey.

Of course in the house at Portage-du-Fort there were servants, cook, maids, gardener, but entertaining all the relatives was a large undertaking and I often wonder how my mother managed it all.

Well, not only did she manage it all but, on occasion, she packed up and went to visit my father in the wilderness on his survey work where he lived in tents, travelled by canoe, fought the mosquitoes and black flies—he hated them the most. I think my mother enjoyed these forays into the forests of the Upper Pontiac and, as my brother Jack can tell you, she even took him along one time to visit Father. After all, he was away six months of the year so his family got lonely for him.

The summers of my youth at Portage-du-Fort were happy ones, indeed. We swam in the Ottawa on the lovely clean beach in front of St. Luke's Church—that was before it became clogged with logs. We fished below the falls—you can imagine how great it was—we had our own tennis courts. The river was restricted in those days—you couldn't go above Portage on the river and you couldn't go below Chenaux Falls so there was no such thing as a motor launch—we went by canoe and rowboat. I had so many brothers and sisters and cousins that we didn't do very much playing with the children of the other residents of Portage-du-Fort in those days, but I do remember Frank Toner, Kenny Fraser, the Toys, the Reids—they lived in Montreal, but they came for the summers.

The river was always full of logs. At Bryson there was a chute, but not at Portage. They sailed through the main channel and on down in high water, and also through a smaller channel next to the village. There was no assembling and disassembling of cribs so we really didn't see the riverdrivers, but periodically the rivermen from the ICO[4] would come in their pointer boats and collect the loose logs, shuffle them off again on their way down the Ottawa to market, to market.

Both my father and his brother, A.J. (Jack) Brabazon, worked in Alaska. One of them sent a postcard home of "the Indians encountered on the International Boundary Survey of Alaska." According to their report, "the Indian chief offered to swap one of his wives for C.H.B.'s (Claude Hugh Brabazon) high boots. On returning to camp one day the survey party found the squaws feasting on canned tomatoes, generously reinforced with tobacco."

*The Indians encountered on the International Boundary Survey of Alaska by Steve Brabazon's father, Claude, and Uncle Jack.*

*The Perth Choral Society in the Town Hall, 1930s. Perth wasn't entirely a sporting town.*

# 13

# "I Played all the Warrior Sports"

## RUSTY WHITE – Perth, Ontario

*I taped the inimitable Rusty White at his home in November 1994. Born and raised in Perth, Rusty was eighty-three at the time of this interview and could still talk "all day long about sport." He turned out to be one of the last living and most knowledgeable spokesmen for the foment of small-town amateur sports in the 1920s, '30s and '40s. His interview is full of interconnections, including both amateur and professional sports. In his day, he played all the "warrior sports" on teams in Perth and throughout the Ottawa Valley, on both sides of the river. As might have been expected, he had a collection of rare archival sporting photos.*

*A veritable Renaissance Man, Rusty could and did excel at every sport he ever played, always "for the love of it." "All through my teens and early twenties," he told me, "I was far more interested in sport than girls."*

*His grandfather, railroader William White, came from Scotland as a Home Boy in 1885. "He was lucky," Rusty said. "He got nice people who brought him up as a son. The Flemings of Perth. George Fleming was one of their sons and I was told that he and my grandfather were just like brothers." Rusty White's mother, Bella Kirkham of*

*the Kirkham Road off Highway 7 near Perth, died of typhoid fever when Rusty was only a year-and-a-half. In his later years, when he could no longer play what he called the "warrior sports," he took up golf and proceeded to win the Links O'Tay championship four times. He was recently awarded a life membership there.*

I CAN REMEMBER every game I ever played. Certainly. I can still remember that I scored goals in a certain way and how I scored it. I have total recall of what happened. When I was playing junior hockey, the guys would get a paper with the scoring averages—and I'd read the scoring averages over, give them the paper back, and I could tell them how many goals and assists the guys got by just reading it over once. I had a photographic memory. For sport. I had a good memory, but I had a great memory for sport. That game when we played football in Dundas and then went on to the NHL game with Chicago in Toronto, even today—fifty years later—I can nearly remember that whole game.

I never became professional because, in those days the amateurs were making more money than the professionals. Trevor Higginbottom played for the Ottawa Senators in goal in the early thirties and he got a hundred-and-fifty dollars a game. That's three hundred dollars a week, which is twelve hundred dollars a month—say for six months—seven thousand dollars. The pros were only getting four and five!

I had a chance to go to Pittsburgh. It wasn't pro then; I was league amateur—Lionel Conacher played there the year before. I'd just started work for The Perth Shoe Company and my boss advised me not to go. He said, "You can go if you want and your job's here when you come back." So I didn't go and the team folded the next year. They had big name players there. I was a good senior hockey player. I could score goals like mad.

I don't think many players really were motivated to turn pro. Carl Liscombe went pro here in the early thirties. He was born in Perth and lived here for a little while, but he wasn't really a Perth boy. Les Douglas was the first one who went pro from Perth, and I coached him. He went to Windsor Bulldogs. I played hockey until I was about forty-three. But along with playing, I coached, too. There was a bunch of guys talking and they asked me what sport I liked best. Football. And what sport second? Hockey, basketball and then baseball. And this guy

*Perth Senior Champions 1922-23.*

## TOURNAMENT CHAMPIONS 1935.

## LANARK COUNTY INTER-TOWN SNOOKER.

*Pure proof that Rusty (Ronald) White excelled at every sport he touched. Here he is with his fellow champions: Front L to R: Arnold McFarlane, Gordon Brown, Fred McMannus, Francis Vallely. Back L to R: Harold Somerville, Squirt Atkins, Syl O'Donnell, Rusty White, Evan Pownall.*

says, "What the hell's wrong with you, Rusty? The game you liked the best you played the least." But any sport. It didn't matter. We didn't get ice 'til Christmas, you know, in those days. We were training in the Perth Armouries and they had badminton there, too. And they picked up a badminton team for a tournament, and I won it. I'd never played badminton in my life before. But I'd played tennis.

I didn't play lacrosse. Lacrosse was gone. Lallies in Cornwall made lacrosse sticks and they sent them out all over the country—for nothing. To get the game going again. I was up at the fairground one night and I thought I'd take a dab at lacrosse. Holy Geez! There was an old guy there, Hod Richardson, and he was a wrestler and everything. I went by him and he turned round and he cut me across the back of the legs and I looked to see if my legs were going down the field. I wanted to play

hockey. That was it. But lacrosse killed itself through real killers.

At first they played hockey in the drill hall in Perth. The first organized game of hockey was in 1894; Perth beat Smiths Falls and Smiths Falls beat Perth. And then they had no place to play because the government wouldn't let them play in the drill hall anymore. So they used to play hockey on the rivers. Perth rink was opened on New Year's Day, 1900, and then they had a place to play, with Brockville, Smiths Falls, Carleton Place and Almonte. (They were into the lacrosse, too.) Then they brought Ottawa teams in— like Ottawa Victorias. We played Pembroke juniors when I was playing junior in 1930 and we went to Carleton Place by car. We got the train from there to Pembroke and back to Carleton Place and then home by car. That was the only way you could do it then.

Back then skates cost two dollars or so, but I don't know about the uniforms. There was a lot of rich guys in Perth and I think they supported all our

*Perth team that played in the Stanley Cup semi-finals against the Marlboroughs (amateur), 1904. Senior Eastern Ontario Champions. Back L to R: F.L. Hall, secretary; George S. James, manager; J.A. Meighen, coach. Middle L to R: James Rooney, left wing; Norm Elliott, point; John Wilson, captain and rover (also renowned in lacrosse and bicycling); John Rutherford, goal (all his sons played hockey); Wm. Lannon, right wing. Front: William McLaren, centre; Robert McLaren, centre point (both McLaren lumbering). Note bowler hats and seven wine glasses.*

*Perth hockey team, 1934, lost championship of Rideau group to Brockville. Front L to R: John Howie, coach; Doug Howie, centre; Ken Richardson, defence; Wilf Rutherford, goal; Bert Rogers (wino but great athlete, baseball outstanding, from Peterborough); George White, forward; Vince McQuiggan, treasurer; J.C. Murphy, trainer. Back L to R: John Munroe, defence (working on construction of No. 7 highway, came to Perth to play hockey, went to Queen's for football, all-Canadian, ended up refereeing in Big Four, used to say, "I'm just a fair hockey player, but I sure can play football."); Earl Spalding, defence; James Healey (great skater) forward; Rusty White, defence and goal; Bill Cooper, forward; George Dickson, sub-goal; Mervin Hicks, committee.*

teams. I think every town the size of Perth had rich guys—they owned the whole of Perth. And bicycling—don't forget bicycling. There was a guy by the name of Johnny Wilson, lived right here, was a really great bicyclist. I've got pictures of him on bicycles in Toronto and all over. There were cycle clubs all over the place in those days.

But, Johnny Wilson was also a great lacrosse player and hockey stick-handler, really smart. He played hockey for Perth, along with his brother, Tug Wilson and Kelly Douglas. We had a couple of imports, I think, on the 1904 Perth team. Perth played Marlboroughs for the Stanley Cup. Paid the imports to come here. In a way they ruined sport for everybody. In the twenties, they were bringing them to Perth for baseball and hockey and they'd give them part-time jobs in the Jergen's or Wampole plants here in town. The imports would come in to work late, or maybe wouldn't come at all. So then the plants just quit giving them jobs. That spoiled the imports.

In the early days players from Perth who went to the professional teams were Carl Liscombe in the early '30s to Detroit, and Les Douglas in the late '30s. Billy Smith ended up with the New York Islanders. He was really dirty. I think he was he called "Dirty Billy." He didn't get along with us at all in minor hockey. His brother, Gordie, played a bit of pro—not much. Some guys played good amateur which was, you know, just a step down.

Yes, a lot of players would go from junior to senior, or they'd go out of town to go up. But I didn't do that. I had a pretty good job at the shoe plant. By that time I was in charge of warehousing. So I just went on playing amateur hockey. Got a little bit of money but not that much—under the table. But the rules were a lot more strict in those days. If you lived in Perth, you played for Perth—you didn't jump all over. But, we didn't have a senior team so we could go anywhere we wanted. We were free agents, but not worth millions though, like today.

In 1942, March, Perth had to play-off with Fort Colounge. I was no dummy. I knew the rules well like, "You don't have to play a play off game on an open-air rink." Fort Colounge only had an open-air rink, so I refused to play. So we took the game to Shawville. We went up in station-wagons to Pembroke, went across the river—ice bridge—and the water on top was about a foot deep. Our goaltender wouldn't get into the station-wagon. He was hanging on the outside. He wasn't going to get in, he was so scared. So we got to Fort Colounge and had a flat tire. They put on a special train to take us to Shawville and the guys were coming on the train and throwing beer bottles up into the old passenger coaches. Oh! It was wild!

So we beat them. Fort Colounge was no opposition at all. The station-wagon had had a flat tire, so we left it in the garage at Fort Colounge. We

*Perth Junior Hockey Team, Lanark County Champions 1936. Back Lto R: W. Burke, G. Palmer, J. White, B. Headrick, J. O'Gorman, C. Ferguson, R. White, G. Pownall, G. Beatty, Dr. Blair. Centre L to R: J. Palmer, M. Lee, T. Harper, L. Douglas (capt.), W. McManus, J. Rutherford, R. White (coach). Front L to R: N. Ready, O. Troy, G. Tysick.*

went by train back to Fort Coulonge. The garage had fixed the flat tire. But we had no spare tire, and about three miles out from Perth—bingo! A tire went and we had no spare. Seven o'clock in the morning we're all walking into town. With our hockey gear over our shoulders. I went straight to work. They wouldn't do that today. People were tough then. Things were different.

In that junior team in 1930, we were going up by train to Pembroke and Happy Hoover, he played in the city league and refereed. Jesus! He told us some great stories. I was sitting with him and God! My eyes were about this big the stories he was telling. He told us about a couple of times after Pembroke games he had to go out through the window at the back of the rink because the local fans were going to get him and string him up.

We played in Pembroke. We'd a pretty good team – all Perth guys. And one player his skate broke—Ed Code—one of our best players, and then another,

Doug Howie, his skate broke, too. So we played without our two best men and they only beat us 2 - 0. Griesbrechts and all those famous guys. And they came back to Perth and we beat them in Perth—we had our full team and we beat them. It was home on home total goals. They beat us by one goal in the total goals.

In those days it was different, eh? I remember playing goal at one end and all my back was covered with tobacco juice—the fans were spitting tobacco juice on me. It was wild. But it was fair. If I got hit playing hockey, I didn't jump up and start swinging like today. I just remembered, that's all. Maybe I'd go down and shove the puck between the guys legs, laugh at him or something.

We'd a fellow played forward—Slim Haley. In one burst I think he was the fastest of anybody I ever saw. Just in a burst. Zoom! Zoom! We'd a pretty good line and, if he got knocked down, he'd jump up and fight right away. So when we went to play in Smiths Falls—myself, Haley, and George White, no

*A handsome young Windsor Bulldog, photographed with symbols of his pride and joy—his leather team jacket, his late 1920s convertible and his hockey stick. Gervase O'Reilly (in "Horses" chapter) comments on the surprising fact that the Cornwall Colts got to Shawville, Quebec, and it is just as possible the Windsor Bulldogs got to Perth.*

relation—I told the coach, "If I signal you, get Haley the hell off the ice." I'd see Slim Haley get all red and I'd know damn well he was going to fight so I'd signal coach to take him off. Otherwise the whole place would be in a brouhaha. I remember one night, Haley got a penalty and you had to go into the Smiths Falls players' box to serve your penalty; they had no penalty box. I don't know how but I could tell something was going on. I turned around and here a spectator had reached over the boards of the box and was holding him up in the air by his hair! There was a great big fight then. Everybody got in on it.

In those days when you got hurt, if there was a doctor around, he was usually a spectator. I was over in Carleton Place and I think it was midgets were playing and this kid went down. And they rolled him over on the ice and Holy Geez! Blood! It was awful. And the doctor lived right across the street. He came in and he fixed the kid up. And I was talking to him afterwards and I said, "It was a pretty bad one?" "Rusty," he said, "If I hadn't been there, he'd have died." Cut an artery. The doctor said, "I can't ever remember it happening before."

Carleton Place loved to fight. You'd get a penalty and you'd have to go into their players' box, eh? Which was suicide. Why? Because you'd be in there with all the Carleton Place players. So this night I get a penalty and, of course, I knew the ropes, and I wouldn't go in. The Ottawa referees knew I was right, so they didn't make me go in. Next year Carleton Place got a real penalty box across the rink. But that night they'd have killed me and I knew it.

I played junior hockey in 1930 when we went to the Eastern Ontario junior finals, eh? Not Ottawa and district, just Eastern Ontario. The little towns. Every town had a team and every town had a senior team. Perth would have seven hundred people at a senior hockey game. It was wicked the amount of amateur hockey that was played in those days. That year we were on the championship team, but there was no organized league then. We just picked up an all-star team out of the town league, and we just kept on going, and beating them, and beating them. We beat Smiths Falls, we beat Carleton Place, we beat Chesterville—they were supposed to be good—we

beat them and then Pembroke put us out in the series. The same thing in 1942. A guy said to me, "Why don't you pick a team up and play exhibition games?" So I did. A couple of us old guys—all the rest were young guys, eighteen, nineteen and twenty—so when the time came I put the team in for the play down and we just kept going, just kept going and we won the intermediate championship. Beat everybody. Cornwall beat us out in the finals, got the senior championship and we got the intermediate. But the Cornwall team had I don't know how many players that had played on the cup winners the year before. We just kept going. Pembroke was supposed to beat the hell out of us, but we beat them.

Sometimes we played play offs in March when the rink was just slop. Lots of times, we'd be wringing wet. I remember playing in Carleton Place one night and a guy by the name of Dave Morrison—he could have named his price with the Canadiens—a good goalie—but he drank. The ice was so slushy you couldn't carry the puck so we just played "shoot." He'd shoot it down, I'd stop it and raise the puck back. In the old days, if you were a good raiser of the puck, you were a good hockey player. One time the McLaren family here challenged anybody in seven-man hockey. Yes, a whole family of McLarens, seven of them. One of them was a kind of a sissy, but they were going to use him in goal. Nobody would take up their challenge. Bob, Bill, Merv, Lloyd, etc. Frank McLaren played hockey for Marlboroughs, lacrosse for Toronto. He played in England in front of the Queen. There were a couple of other seven-brother teams out West, but they never challenged the McLarens.

Perth had that good junior hockey team in 1930. In 1931, Norman White—no relation—broke his shoulder early in the year and he came and asked me if I'd play defence. I said, "Sure." I could play everywhere. I used to play centre on the first line and defence on the second line. Play sixty minutes. It was a little different then. They just skate now whether they've got the puck or not and they go like hell. In those days, you only went like hell when you got the puck. I knew hockey players that looked like old men until they hit the blue line and then, Holy Geez! They were gone.

In 1936, I was coaching the Perth juniors. Pembroke beat us 11 - 0 in Perth the first game. They had all the Griesbrechts. The Perth team didn't play that badly, but they were awestruck, eh? They'd read about the Griesbrechts and they were terrified of them. Wilfred McManus ended up a big-time goalminder. He played for the Oshawa juniors when they won the Memorial Cup. He never made a good save; like, he never let in an easy one, but he never made a good save. We went back up into Pembroke and we beat them 3 - 2. Right in Pembroke. The first loss they had all year.

I was playing all the sports at school. I got quite a few upper school subjects, not all, but I got some. They liked me there for football and I was a good track man, too. I held the pole vault record for years at Perth Collegiate. My favourite sport was football. I played that at high school and we had a town team. We had an Olympic Club here. It was a boys' club. We formed it. The bunch that I went to school with they stuck with athletics long after. I don't know why. I wasn't going to play football—my favourite sport— because of hockey. I didn't want to get hurt so I couldn't play hockey. I was always protecting myself for hockey. In the Perth rink, they had a hardwood floor—they put the ice on top of that—and we used

*Perth Collegiate Track Team, 1924, Lanark County Champions.*
*Rear L to R: Dr. J.H. Hardy (principal), Vince Cameron, Ford Dickson (great runner), Bill Clement, Earl Spalding, Hub Wilson, Joe Gould, E.B. Code (coach). Middle L to R: Charlie McDonald, George Dickson (great), Jack Lapointe (great runner, went to Regina Rough Riders), Jim Patterson, Mike Steacy (a tough guy, to the States). Front L to R: Ron Hughes, Jim Duncan, Jack King, Lloyd Strong.*

to practise football there. And this Bob Code, he ended up at Queen's, he was running the team I guess and there was a guy came in to Jergen's to work—Don McAlpine—never played football. Code put him at quarterback. Never played football. So the guys came to me then—everybody used to come to me—and told me about it. So I thought, "Well, geez, I'd better go out for football." So as soon as I went out for football I was the quarterback and I was the coach right away. We played Smiths Falls and Carleton Place and New Edinburgh of Ottawa. We'd a pretty good team, all local boys. So about 1939, we put our names in for the Intermediate Eastern Ontario play downs. There wasn't that many teams

then. So they asked us if we would consider a hundred-and-fifty dollars' expense money, and play in Dundas, near Hamilton. We said sure and we got four cars and took the hundred-and-fifty dollars and away we went on Friday night. We played up there Saturday afternoon. They only beat us 15 - 0 and they had four guys that had played for the Hamilton Tigercats the year before. Were we ever proud of ourselves! We gave them a hell of a battle; it was only 5 - 0 at the half. The days of amateur sport, eh? How wonderful!

Before the game a leather salesman came down from Oshawa (Oshawa was in the league with Dundas and Dundas had put them out), and he told Eric

*Perth Collegiate Rugby Team 1930. Champions, Lanark County, E.O.S.S.A. Semi-finalists. Back row: James McParland (I.W.), A. Smiley (F.W.), H. Lehigh (I.W.), J. Prentice (Snap). Second row: Ken Wilson (O.W.), A. Korry (M.W.), J. Rutherford (F.W.), G. Affleck (F.W.), F. Lee (I.W.). Front row: L. McFarlane (O.W.), F. Vallely (Quarter), J. H. Hardy (Coach), R. White (Vice-Captain), G. Cain (Captain), H. Milliken (Line Captain), Ford Dickson (Asst. Coach), H. Watson (F.W.) Ken Gray (O.W.).*

Sabiston, my boss at the Perth Shoe Company, what a dirty team Dundas had. And Sabiston tracked me down on the phone and told me about how dirty Dundas was, to look after ourselves, and all that. My brother weighed about 185, about 5 foot 8, and I always remember when the first Dundas rush came he hit the opposing guy and knocked him out cold. And they were supposed to be the dirty guys!

On the way back home we went to the hockey game in Toronto; Chicago Black Hawks playing the Leafs. Stayed at the Ford hotel, all on a hundred-and-fifty dollars. But, that Ford hotel was an awful place. Women coming in with men, and we knew they weren't married, and we were having a hell of a time ourselves. On Sunday we came back and I had never been to Ivy Lea Bridge, so whoever was driving, I talked him into going by Ivy Lea and then to Perth. And there was a dance hall down here at the edge of Perth, Hogan's Dance Land, where we ended up Sunday night. We left Perth six o'clock Friday night, got to Toronto and stayed at the Ford hotel, played football Saturday afternoon, went to the hockey game Saturday night, came back Sunday and ended up down here dancing at Hogan's Dance Land. I went to work on Monday—you never missed work—and I played hockey Monday night. You couldn't catch a guy doing that nowadays. But I was only twenty-eight.

I played hockey against Queen's University. Jean Chouinard was the coach, and I remember Donny Murray from Perth played for Queen's and we'd a player by the name of Bud Goodfellow who came from up around Tichborne—oh, a good hockey player. And Chouinard said, "It will be a clean game. You've no need to wear shoulder pads." I wish we had put them on. It was a wild game! But I was always happy as hell because the score was 6 - 6 and I scored three goals. Queen's came to Perth for that game. They used to call it the Van Horn series, and we played at the Jock Harty Arena on artificial ice. That was before we had artificial ice in Perth and it was good conditioning for us to play Trenton Air Force, Queen's, and the army up there. A good league and a lot of good players, but RMC was not in the league. They never had a good team anyway. Funny thing, isn't it?

I get mad at a lot of things now. Course, I'm an old guard, but I came up through everything. Football I played before the forward pass, and then I played when the forward pass came in, and then I coached when the forward pass came in. And interference, I came up through it all. And in hockey—I wasn't seventh man—that was changed by the time I got playing—but the blue lines came in, the red lines came in and I went through all that. What would you sooner see? A guy going up and down the wing at about a hundred miles an hour or a guy with a puck stick-handling through everybody and scoring? I figure that Wayne Gretzky is more of the old guard. He plays like an old-time hockey player. In my day, if you couldn't stick handle there was no use going out because you never had the puck. Like, we'd have a great big patch on the river and if you couldn't stick handle you'd never have the bloody puck. So you learned how to stick handle. Like poke checking. I used to have a great poke check. They couldn't get by me, but then it got that they just fired the puck down the ice. It's a changed game.

In Perth, the football was really centred in the Collegiate. They had a soccer league here in the late '20s and early '30s. I can remember them playing, but I never got mixed up in it. I wanted to keep myself in one piece for hockey.

Basketball. It was invented, of course, over there in Almonte. But they weren't that good. It didn't mean you'd be good just because the game was invented there. Our Olympic Club team beat their town team in the early '30s and some of them were playing in the city league. I could score. In those days in Ottawa, basketball was strictly a high school thing. Maybe there was a Y team. They had a city league there. We played Almonte there and they had a couple of Jewish guys on their team that had played in the city league. They were good, but I outscored both of them. I could score anywhere. It didn't matter where I was.

Our Olympic Club had a fair hockey team, too. What was the Olympic Club? Oh, just a bunch of us got together with the money that was left over from the football and formed the Olympic Club. All men, over seventy members, on Perth's main street there

*Perth Eastern Ontario Baseball Champions, 1923. Front L to R: Kelly King, Ken McEwen, Tom Wilson, Norm Lightford, Les Waddell, Gay "Big Shot" McLaren, Walter McKee. Rear L to R: Bill Furlong (local blacksmith), Jim Kellock, Laurie Thompson (dentist), George Thornbury, Lex Scott. (Taken at the Collegiate grounds, home of the Rideaus and the Mic-Macs. Details in parentheses are Rusty White's.)*

on the third floor. The clubhouse had everything—a mat for wrestling, lockers, a basketball net for practising—but it died out early in the war. We were getting older. The Olympic Club played the Collegiate a lot. And we beat them every time out, and we even beat them at a track meet. We were a good bunch of ex-grads. We beat them in hockey—there was nothing to it in hockey and basketball. This guy was in the shower and I overheard him saying, "Rusty White can score more points than your whole team put together." Next game I scored more points than the whole Collegiate team. I could score and it didn't matter where—in those days you jumped after every basket, and it was different. It wasn't the big scores—it was always 30 to 28 or something, not 130 to 128 like today.

Once I get talking about sport I never shut up. Baseball, I guess, is the oldest game. The rules hardly change. And it's cheap to play and you could pick up a scrub team and play any time, anywhere. Do you know who liked baseball? Farmers. 'Cos they could all play it at their little schools, eh. Oh! They loved baseball. And that's why you saw little schoolyards with little baseball diamonds. When I was young, we used to have three men on a team. And there was a lot of vacant lots in those days and we'd play Saturday mornings. Yes, three men on a team and we had a hell of a time. We'd make the balls ourselves. Maybe put a golf ball inside and wind it with cord.

And here's something else. I often tell young guys this. When I was playing on that good imported baseball team where I was the only Canadian on the team—the rest were all big-league Americans—I lived in the centre of Perth and I'd be going up Drummond Street to the Collegiate throwing the ball up, running and catching it. Could you imagine a guy doing that today? Going to a ballgame? Or I'd get against a barn and throw it and catch it.

Perth had good baseball teams around 1923 when we won the Ottawa Valley Championship. Norman Lightfoot was really good; a catcher from the States, but he lived here. There was a pitcher, Les Waddell; he was good too. I don't know whether he was an import or whether he just came in to work. All the rest were pretty well Perth guys. So that was in 1923.

In 1928, there was a kind of baseball doldrums in Perth. I was sitting on the fence behind the outfielders at practice. When the ball went over their heads, I'd catch it and throw it back. So this night I'm getting over the fence to go home and the coach yelled, "White! How would you like to play tomorrow night?" Well, I was down off that fence so fast. I was only sixteen, very small for my age. The funny thing is my brother was a good hockey player and a good ball player, but he was different than me. I used my head and my speed and he was the big guy. I might play a lousy game of hockey, but I'd score the winning goal or something—I always had that knack of pulling it together at the end. The first game of baseball I played was against Carleton Place. I can remember every play, even today. I was playing centre field. We went into the tenth inning. The bases were loaded, two out, and the batter hits a little blooper over in the infield, and I came charging in, slid along on my belly, stuck my hand out, caught it—and saved the game! I always seemed to be like that, eh? A lucky teeter.

That was in '28, but then Smiths Falls spoiled things. They'd always go for imports and they always had to get the best team. So in about 1929, they started bringing in ball players from Montreal and the States and everywhere. They had two teams there; the little guys were kind of a home brewed team and the big railroaders were the imported team. So that was in '28, '29, maybe '30. The odd time Perth would be proud to beat them. In '32, Perth brought in a bunch of players from Toronto and they were fairly good. The coach also was from Toronto. By that time, Renfrew was in the Ottawa Valley

*Another tradition in Perth sporting life, the Glen Tay Block Race, which began in 1907, the year of this photo. E.B. Code was the winner.*

*Shanty dinners were a Perth Golf Club tradition in the early years. Amazingly, Rusty could remember many of the people in this photo taken in the early 1900s: Robert Burris, James "Gummy" Allan, F.L. Mitchell, Capt. Matheson, James Craig, W.P. McEwen (great golfer), J.M. Walker (owned Perth Courier), Eardley Wilmot (played for Aylmer football, then played first game Ottawa Rough Riders played), Boyd Caldwell (lumbering), T.A. Code (owned Code's Mills), R.S. Drummond, Frank Hicks, C.F. Stone (ran the Perth Expositer), W.B. Hart (owned Hart's Bookstore), Nat McLenaghan, J.A. Ferguson.*

Baseball League—Brockville, Carleton Place, Perth, Smiths Falls, two teams in Ottawa. Pembroke never seemed to be a baseball town. Cardinal had a team. They got guys from the States, eh? Anyway, Cardinal dropped out finally. Those other teams stayed in and, as I say, I ended up the only Perth guy on the team in 1935. All the rest were Americans. I made plays that these Americans never even thought about, no kidding.

The Perth Block Race—marathon—began in 1907. At the Collegiate, they used to have me show them how to start. I could get such a good start, but I couldn't run a hundred yards. The same in hockey. I wasn't a very fast skater, but when I got a breakaway, they didn't catch me. They'd get me to show them how to start the hundred-yard dash. For fifty yards I

could go like hell then I seemed to lose my stride. I was a good pole vaulter and high jumper. I held the record at the Collegiate for a long time in pole vaulting. In the high jumping, it was just the scissors—you just stuck your leg up and over. I could do five-foot-four which was pretty good, since I was only five-foot-seven.

But we used to have track meets on Saturdays in Perth. The people today don't realize how much sport we played. I was going to tell about the Perth road races. From the middle of town at the museum, up Foster and Wilson Streets, you cut up to Glen Tay across country and back to the town centre. It was ten miles and dozens ran it. McNeilly Nichol used to give prizes from the hardware store. I knew all the guys who were running in it. I revived it in

'67 when Ron Wallingford won it. He was an Olympic runner. It's now nine miles long and still run today.

And they used to have foot races in Perth. I'd challenge you to run from James Brothers down to the post office for twenty-five dollars or fifty dollars. All kinds of betting races. Then they had horse races up on Grant's Creek here where you'd bet money. Oh, it was wild! I can remember in '34 or '35, we played off in baseball at Brockville. Oh, geez! They had a good team. If we won the first game that was in Brockville, we had to play another one right afterwards. And we won the first game. We had to play the second game. Holy Geez! And I remember Perth guys at the game with a fist full of money walking up and down the stands waving the money in the Brockville guys' faces. Betting money. A lot of betting went on in those days. Oh, yes. The first year out of school I lived in the poolroom. I had more money than when I was working. I was a real shark. Played money pool.

I have guys stop me yet on the street and talk about when I played baseball. I was playing baseball right field in Carleton Place. The poor people used to sit on the railroad tracks which was just beyond the outfield. They couldn't afford to pay to see the games. That was in the Dirty Thirties—I don't know how we kept going as long as we did—but, anyway, this guy—I still can see him—Hutch Herman was his name, from Carleton Place. He was a good hitter, and he hit a line drive. And it was a sun field—like the sun was shining right in my eyes—and I started back and then I had to come in, and I dove, and the ball hit my glove and I rolled over. My body was to the diamond, and I don't know what made me do it—there were two out—but the ball rolled out. I just stood up, picked it up and lobbed it into second base, and trotted off the field. I can remember Herman coming round first base and he never said anything, he just stood looking at me with his arms folded. I never told a soul that I had dropped the ball. I was in the poolroom about, oh, say, thirty years ago and this old Dan Lee, he lived near where I lived at the time in the Centre Ward, and he was one of the guys that had sat on the railroad tracks at that game. So I was in the poolroom gassing off and he said, "Oh! You're not so smart, White." I said, "What do you mean, Dan?" He said, "I saw you drop the ball that night. Nobody else did, but I did." That was about thirty years afterwards.

# 14

## "For My Grandfather, the 'Short Walk' was Twenty-five Miles"

### WRANGLER HEARTY – Chapeau, Quebec

*Since I began my work collecting the oral/social history of the Ottawa Valley some twenty years ago, I have travelled thousands of miles, met hundreds of wonderful people, and given dozens of lectures and readings to groups ranging from large conventions to small intimate living-room soirées. Out of all this collected data, I think I have enough evidence to support a somewhat tongue-in-cheek theory that as eating-place, drinking-place, and gathering-place for musicians and storytellers, Fred Meilleur's Hotel in Chapeau, Quebec, is one of the most renowned landmarks in the Ottawa Valley.*

*People who didn't know what or where the Ottawa Valley is, or didn't even know they were there, have found their way to Fred's. There they discover liberal portions and low prices that defy comprehension. On the table is a breadbasket that is kept full with fresh homemade bread, thickly sliced, and a butter dish with enough butter for everyone. And then there is Fred, a gentle giant, who may, if they are lucky, recommend which of the many fine wines from his well-stocked cellar would best complement their meal.*

*Pictures have been stolen off Fred's walls and then later recognized by his clients on the walls of other hotels as far away as Calgary and Sudbury. Irishmen from Dublin, following rumours, legends and their intuition, have made their way to Fred's, and I have seen them there shaking their heads over the Irish accents of Fred's local clientele whose ancestors "got off the boat" one-hundred-and-fifty years ago.*

*Like most famous watering-holes, Meilleur's Hotel has a group of "regulars" and amongst these is Wrangler Hearty, owner of his own hunting and fishing camp, brother of Fred's late wife Helen, and a teetotalling storyteller. He has a deep knowledge of lumbering technology, but I think it was his talk of Trout Lake, the deserted village back of Sheenboro, that first fascinated me.*

*Wrangler Hearty's great-grandfather, Michael John Hearty, arrived with a group of settlers at Quebec City in 1835. They walked up first to Calumet Island, but moved on to Vinton, Quebec, where they took up land. Michael John married Julia O'Keefe from County Cork in Ireland and raised three sons and five daughters. Paddy Hearty, Wrangler's grandfather married Margaret Connolly from Sheenboro, whose ancestors also originally came out from Dublin. Then at some point, like a gathering of the Celtic clans, three families of Sullivans, three families of Brennans, families of McCormicks, Dugans, Bradleys, Doyles, Sweeneys, Ryans, Foxes, Bushes—and a Burgomaster—packed up their belongings once again and moved to the shores of Trout Lake, back of Sheenboro, Quebec.*

*Of their church, school, houses, barns, nothing remains today except the rubble of a few foundations reclaimed by the once great forest's inferior second growth. But the descendants of this intrepid Irish community are scattered all over the globe.*

FOR MY GRANDFATHER, Paddy Hearty, the short walk was the walk from Trout Lake into church in Sheen. He was the mailman. He used to walk out with his backpack and pick up the mail in Sheen and deliver it to all the families on the way back. That would be about twenty-five miles return. And he did that every day.

The long walk was when he was courting his girlfriend, Margaret Connelly. She lived on the twelfth range of Sheen and he lived in Vinton. And he used to leave Vinton on Saturday night and he'd walk all night and he'd get to Connelly's some time in the forenoon and he'd have dinner with the Connellys on Sunday, leave after dinner, and walk back to Vinton to be back at work the next day. Fortunately, she agreed to marry him.

There is an old story about my grandfather. He was a big tall man, six-foot-four, and he used to make big long steps, eh? And they say when he was living at Trout Lake, one time he left Vinton in the morning with the kitchen stove on his back and a bag of flour under his arm, and was at Trout Lake in time to cook supper.

A fellow by the name of Doyle kept a post office in there. He was the guy that the Bradleys moved in with before they came out to Sheen in the early 1900s, and then they moved to Demer's Centre. They bought that place from Napoleon LaFrance and that's when the shooting started in 1933. That was when the Bradleys all got murdered.[1]

Back in Trout Lake—they had their own school, and the priest used to come once a month and say mass in there, and they had a little cemetery, too. They supplied the lumbering industry with grain and pork and beef and poultry. They worked in the lumbering business in the wintertime with their horses. They lived well. The only thing they bought was salt and sugar. They had a little grist mill to make flour right on Trout Lake Creek and they had a couple of little sawmills, one owned by a man named Cline.

At that time they would be supplying J.R. Booth and the Gillies Brothers lumber camps. The last families moved out of Trout Lake around the 1920s. My grandfather was one of the last to move out to Chichester. My Grandfather Paddy used to walk from Trout Lake into the church at Sheenboro, have lunch and walk back again. Probably they brought their own lunch and stopped at a little creek along the road to have a drink of water. At that time, everybody knew everybody in the country so, he might go in and have a cup of tea with the farmer. My dad used to walk from the twelfth range of Sheen to home all the time. That's twenty-five miles one way. Lots of times he left on Saturday evening—he was a fire ranger and worked for the Forestry—he'd leave after supper and he'd get home to Trout Lake around midnight and he'd leave at daylight in the morning and go back up.

At that time there was no such thing as special boots. They wore just plain black gum rubbers. With woollen socks. And the woollen socks absorbed the sweat from their feet. And they wore the big heavy woollen underwear, even in the heat of the summer. You see, it absorbed the heat and insulated them and it did the same in the wintertime, and they never had rheumatism or anything else. The mitts and the socks were all made at home. They kept sheep, most of them, and they got their own wool spun and they made their own clothes out of their own wool. They made their own soap. They made everything.

My grandfather used to be, most of the time, buck beaver[2]. He used to make the main roads for the sleigh horses and he used to be the buck beaver on that job. And my father following him in the lumbering business was cut control man for most of his life. Summertime he'd work for the Forestry; wintertime he used to go to the lumber camp to make sure that they didn't cut anything under size and didn't leave anything in the bush. Anything that they cut they had to take out of the bush. Later, he was the guy that made the jammers for the first mechanical logging that they ever had in this country at what they called The Hurdman. In Chichester and Waltham Townships. They dumped their logs in the Ottawa River. Hurdman Lake is where they had the main camp. That was in the middle '30s. And the first logger that had the mechanical logging was Willard Whitmore, and Whitmore bought eight or nine brand-new ten-wheeler trucks that time to do the logging, and he logged there for the one winter, and my father built the jammers.

The jammer worked on the same principle as loaders do today: it used to pick up the logs and the horses would go ahead with the pulley and they'd lift the logs up. And then they'd cant it out over the truck and they centred the main pulley block and the jammer on the centre of the truck, and there was two "bull" rope men and they placed them logs on the truck wherever they wanted them. They could drop them in the exact place. See the horse used to back up and let the log down, eh? And it was all done with cables and pulleys and horses. They did a lot of line loading. He used to send the lines with a decking-line[3] when they loaded the sleighs before the jammers were ever built. But they couldn't load the trucks with the decking-line because the trucks were too high off the ground compared to the log sleighs. So they had to build a jammer and the jammer would be, maybe, somewheres between twenty and thirty feet to the top of the jammer so that they would get enough clearance with these pulleys to put a full load on the trucks.

I don't know if my father invented it, but he was the first guy that built the jammers for the

Old wooden one-way bridge at Chapeau, Quebec, c. 1890, leading to busy stores, to St. Alphonse Roman Catholic Church, to Fred Meilleur's Hotel.

*The horse jammer used to hoist logs onto the load. A horse (out of the picture) hauled the log up the skid by means of a chain running through a block and tackle atop the A-frame.*

mechanical loading in this part of the country. The cat's crib? Well, the cat's crib was like a raft of logs all fastened together. There was like a wagon wheel hub in the centre with a long pole on it, and you'd put a horse on that, and the horse would walk around in a circle. The guys would pull this down the lake with a boat, and they'd snub it to the shore with a rope, and

the horse would walk around and he'd pull in the cable. When they got them towed in, then they'd move their cat's crib to the next location and they'd tie it up again and the horse would wind the cable up again and bring the logs into that. And they did that on most of the big lakes—McGillivray, Lake St. Patrick, Big Moose Lake—before they got those alligators[4] to tow the logs, before they got the tugs. I don't know why it was called a cat's crib, but that's what they all called it. I've one at McGillivray. It's the only one I know of in existence.

My father broke his leg one time in the bush. He was hit by a log and it took them four days to get him out with horses and a wagon. Four days and no painkiller. A drop of brandy—if he was lucky.

A cure for the common cold in the lumber camps was a tablespoon of kerosene with brown sugar in it. I've taken it myself. If you were kept awake from coughing, when you took that you went to bed and you went to sleep. You filled the spoon up with the kerosene and then you'd soak it with the sugar to kill the taste a little bit. Terrible taste, but it did the trick. Another remedy for colds was brown paper and goose oil on the paper, and put it on your chest under your shirt.

A lot of people in the lumber camp had different remedies for different things. For infection, what they used to do a lot of times was make a poultice of raw beets and it would draw anything you had out. A raw beet out of the garden—that's one of the old remedies and I've used it myself. It really works. You just cut it in two and put it on raw. And a lot of the old people used to put bread and milk and make a poultice.

There was all kinds of old recipes for different things. They used a lot of lye soap in the bush instead of having fly dope in the spring of the year. They washed themselves with lye soap to keep the black flies and the mosquitoes away. The black flies wouldn't go near that.

Another recipe that still works today for bee stings in the bush: You just take three different kinds of green leaves and you rub the underside of the leaves on the bee sting right away. It's as good as any remedy you'll get any place. I guarantee it won't even

*Men risking their lives trying to break up a log jam on the North Branch of the Petawawa River reputed to be the fastest river in the watershed of the Ottawa Valley.*

swell up. My grandfather would go into a bees' nest and the bees would buzz round him, and the bees would never sting him. I don't know what it was about him. But that's how I learned about the leaves—through my grandfather. Whenever we got a bee sting he used the leaves on us.

In the bush the men used to make salve—I remember this quite well—they'd make it out of Balm of Gilead buds and beef tallow. They used to go to the balsam trees and they'd take the blisters of the balsam trees and they'd take the gum out of that and they'd put that in with the Balm of Gilead buds and the beef tallow and boil that all together. It wouldn't wash off. There was enough gum in it; it would hold right on the spot. They used that in the lumber camps to heal things like infected heels.

Everybody had their salve. A lot of the times they brought it up from home in their little kit for the winter, eh? I remember quite well some of these lumberjacks used to leave home in late August or September, and they wouldn't get back 'til the next May or June—they'd be gone all winter. So they took whatever they needed for the winter in their pack, first aid remedies from home.

My father was more at the timber cruising than on The Drive and he used to peel hemlock for some of those outfits. They used hemlock bark to make medicine. Different drug companies used to buy this hemlock bark. And they'd peel it off and ship it to some pharmaceutical company, eh?

And, a lot of times, the old people, when they used to catch the bears, they used to render the fat off the bears and they'd rub that on their hands and knees and it would protect your joints for the winter, so they wouldn't get rheumatism. It worked—I used it. I tried them all.

The Indians showed the early settlers about medicines and salves, and how to make birch vinegar.

*Logs being piled at the skidway preparatory to The Drive down the tributaries of the Ottawa, to the Ottawa and thence to market in Quebec City or Montreal.*

They took the sap from the wild birch and they made vinegar from it. The Indians made drinks, but not alcohol. They made drinks out of different barks like sarsaparilla, but no sugar in it. They used to make a kind of tonic out of alder bark. They'd boil that and drink it if they were run down. They used to make a physic out of poplar. And they used a lot of fish oil for some of their sores. They used to say that eel oil was the best. They used to catch the eels and they'd hang them up on the branch of a tree and put a little can underneath to catch the oil in the sun. I seen my grandfather do that. And they used to use that eel oil for different sores.

I worked for Gillies and I worked for Consolidated Paper and I worked for Whitmore in the Park. We cut logs there in Algonquin Park and we walked four miles from camp every morning to the woods, and we cut logs for fifteen cents a log, cut and skid, and we walked back the four miles that night. The camp was right up on the Bonnechere River. I hauled pulp and I hauled Hydro poles and I tagged roads and I did mostly everything that was done in the bush. I made roads with bulldozers and I skidded logs with bulldozers and I drove a truck for a Hull company and I also hauled logs for the Austin Lumber Company at Chapleau. I hauled ties for the CPR by piecework and I worked in a sawmill for M. Kidd and Sons. Then we used to pick potatoes for T.E. McCool at Sheenboro when we were only kids. And we picked potatoes all day. They used to get us because the young lads could stand to bend over all day to pick the potatoes and the older people used to just take the bags and put them in the wagon. Because we were young, we could pick more potatoes than the old fellows—fifty cents a day, ten hours a day.

I went into guiding in the forties. I guided for the Buckhorn Fish and Game Club and I guided for the Pontiac Fish and Game Club and I bought my own outfit in McGillivray in 1963. One day I took this American tourist out fishing on McGillivray Lake and he caught a fish so big that he had to put it back so that the lake would go down to its normal level. They were always talking about big fish and we always fished in this big deep bay, and if there wasn't any fish there, we used to go to this big shallow bay and this American caught this big fish this day, and he was so big we had to throw him back out of the boat to get enough water to row ashore.

I've never heard of wolves killing anybody yet in this part of the country. The wolf is the cowardliest animal in the bush and he's one of the smartest animals in the bush. If there's humans around, he won't come near you at all. It would have to be a sick wolf or something like that that would come near humans or attack them. They're more scared of humans than any other animal in the bush.

In mating time, the cow moose stays in the same place and she bawls and the bull moose goes to her. You can hear them bawling for three or four days, starting in late August. Before the bull makes it through the bush, they can be a hundred miles apart. It depends on the terrain. If it's flat terrain, sometimes the sound doesn't carry very far. If it's in the valleys, the call will travel a lot further. The cow usually gets down in the swamp in the rushes and then she'll call from that mash[5] and the echo will follow the creek bed for a long, long way and then it will follow the mountain. Through the valley and all the way up.

When my hunters kill a moose they have to eat it. That's compulsory. There's a fine if you leave the meat to waste. What we usually do, if there's a bunch of people in camp, all the hunting parties get together and pull the moose out. If we can't reach it by vehicle, we take it out by rope.

The Americans are bear hunters—but they are cowardly bear hunters. They have to have a tree stand or they won't go out there. They build a stand up in a tree and they climb up into that and they sit there and they wait for the bear to come to the bait, eh? That's the only way they hunt. They won't hunt any other way.

You've got to be extremely careful with those Americans. They're all psyched up about taking this bear back. They hear so many narrow escapes, and they read so much in *Field and Stream* and *Outdoor Life* about the bears attacking, that they are ready to shoot at *anything*. They wouldn't even go across the road here in broad daylight without bringing a gun with them; that's how much they're scared of bears.

I have some great bear stories. This old guy used to come to my place every once in a while to have a beer. One time he said, "Would you like to come up and spend a weekend at my hunt camp? Lots of bears there." I said, "Sure, I'll go." When we got to the camp he said, "I'll make the fire and you go out to the woodpile and bring in an armful of wood for the night." So I'm getting the wood and I look behind me and this big bear is coming right at me. I dropped the wood and started running for the shack, and the bear running close behind me. Just before I got to the door of the shack, I tripped on a little stump and the bear sailed clean over my head

The Fishing is Excellent Here.

AT WALTHAM, Que.

right into the shack. And I got up. I closed the door on him. "Skin this one," I yelled to the old lad. "I'm going back for another!"

Here is my best recipe for cooking bear and moose. To tenderize the moose or the bear or the deer, you marinate overnight in water with salt. You can put whatever kind of spices you want in it. You clean all the fat off it then. Then you can roast it, or fry it, or whatever. I've cooked moose and deer hearts—not bear hearts—and ducks. Usually with ducks, we put the duck in a pot of water and put a teaspoon of soda in it and bring it to a boil and then pour the water off, and then bake it. That takes the grease out of it and it takes the wild taste out of it.

The first thing you take from the moose is the tenderloin. That never gets to the butcher shop. That's the choice part. And before the end of the moose season, everybody comes to a party and we have the tenderloin—I usually cook it.

My father was a taxidermist. The deer heads in Fred Meilleur's Hotel, my father did them, before 1927. I have a copy of his diploma. He used to make his own snowshoes, too. He'd take a cowhide or a bullhide and, to take all the fat off he scraped it with a hoe, a real dull hoe so it wouldn't cut the hide. And he'd cut it in strips, and after he cut it in strips, he used to soak it before he laced the snowshoes with it.

When they trapped at that time, they had a dog team because they had a long way to travel, and they used to feed the dogs the beaver meat. Oh, I seen them tanning. If they wanted to change the colour of the deer hide, they used to smoke it. They'd make a fire and when the fire was just about down to smoke, they'd put the deer hide in a barrel upside down and put the barrel over the fire and the smoke would stay in there and that changes the colour of the hide.

This lad was building this house, and he wanted some money from the old guy he was working for, and the old guy wouldn't pay him. The lad left without his money, and then he died. But before he died he told the old guy, "There's nobody will ever live in that house." And the house stood on the

*The second bridge to Chapeau, still single lane. It was finally replaced by a two-lane bridge in 1996.*

*Streetscape in Chapeau just up the way from Fred Meilleur's Hotel.*

*Logs ready at the skidway with men working for jobber Meehan of Sheenboro on a Gillies limit, Black River, 1912. The oversize postcard is addressed to Miss B. Evans, East Templeton, Quebec, and says, "How do you like the Old Boy when he is amongst the Wild Woodsmen?"*

highway hexed in Waltham for years and years, and nobody lived in it. I heard different stories—if they'd move a chair from one room in the house to another room—the next time they came back the chair was back where it used to be. There was all kinds of strange noises, and people walking at night. At last they tore the house down. Nobody could live in it.

The first lake when you go over the mountain at Hayes Barn is Trout Lake. Back there, they always said that when the Bradleys moved in with old Doyle—now this would be Nick Bradley's grandmother—and old Doyle went missing and they never found him. They said that old lady Bradley had killed old Doyle and buried him in the stone fence. And they claimed that every year in the full of the August moon they would see old Doyle walking up and down that fence with his coal-oil lantern, looking for old lady Bradley.

There was a fellow by the name of Bushe went missing, too, in Trout Lake—Bill Bushe's brother—and they figure he was murdered in there, too. And there was a Dinny Nickabeau and he was murdered.

And they figured that McAuley shot McLeod. And one Bradley shot the other Bradleys—Mick and Tom and the two girls and the old lady and the old uncle. They lived with old Doyle at Trout Lake for a while until old Doyle disappeared. It was 1914 they moved out of there, bought the farm from old Napoleon LaFrance. After Jack moved in—that's when the trouble started, fights and arguments, and that's when Mick really went haywire and shot the whole bunch of Bradleys.

The Brennans from Trout Lake moved to North Bay. Some of the Keons and Slatterys moved to Saskatchewan. A lot of the Trout Lake people moved to Saskatchewan. One of my great-uncles—a conductor on the Michigan Railroad—got stabbed by a bum and killed there. Great-uncle Pat. Great-uncle John went out West and we never found out really where he was.

I've done a lot of playing for the Lumber Kings and other teams. We used to play hockey on the river here with Professor Allore from Chapeau. The forwards and defence used the sales catalogue for shin pads and the goaltender had the winter catalogues. They were a little bit heavier. We made our own hockey sticks and we weren't too well equipped for anything else, and if we hit the old professor with the hockey stick in the shins, he'd chase us home. That was it. End of the hockey game.

This trapper and his buddy were sitting in the bar and this other guy came in and he was talking to the trapper about beaver scent for animals and different things they used to attract the animals. So the other guy was sitting there and he said to the trapper that was looking for the scent, he said, "Get Doreen to piss in the bottle." And the other guy said, "And what good is that for scent?" "Well," he said, "it has to be a real good scent. It once drew a trapper from McGillivray Lake to Nickabeau over the mountain on snowshoes."

This story had to be in the late forties. The Swisha Bridge broke and these guys went into the Ottawa River. And the bodies were in the eddy— that's the one that Colton went into before the dam was built.[6] Anyway, the bodies went into the eddy and they weren't coming out and, on Sunday morning, they had a mass here. Father Dinny John Harrington said the mass and then after the mass he jumped in his car and he went to the Swisha and he took the bread and he blessed the bread and he threw it in the whirlpool and the bodies came out. That's true. I knew everybody that was drowned that day—Edmund Peacock, Riel Remo, Romeo Chapeau, Val Bertrand and another guy was from Pembroke. I don't know what his first name was, but he was deaf and dumb. His father used to be chief of police in Pembroke.

Grandmother Venosse had an old white horse. She lived in Chichester, and she used to leave there seven o'clock in the morning about five miles from our place, and it took her five hours to get to Trout Lake on her old white horse. And when she got there with the old horse, she had to tie him to the little Manitoba maple so he wouldn't fall asleep, fall over and break the shafts in the buggy. And then she'd never be able to get back home. He just suited her fine because he just went at one tenth of a mile an hour, and he'd even fall asleep on the road—if she didn't watch out. He'd just stay there tied to the old tree all day long while she visited us.

This is about Fred Meilleur and Dorion Beland. Dorion was here at Fred's on the drunk for about three or four days, and he hadn't eaten anything, and the cook had some good stew on. So Fred said to Dorion, "Would you like a plate of stew?" And Dorion said, "Sure." So Fred went and got Dorion a plate of stew. He put it on the table in front of him, but Dorion just sat there and looked at it. And Fred said to Dorion, "How come you're not eating your stew?" "Well, Fred," Dorion said, "at home lots of times we didn't have very much to eat, but we *always* had salt and pepper." Fred never said a word. Typical Fred. But he never brought Dorion any salt and pepper.

Did you ever hear the story about the two old farmers? They were in Meilleur's Hotel having a few drinks. They each had a horse tied up in Fred's yard. The first farmer said to the other farmer, "I would like to buy your horse." The second farmer said, "I can't sell you that horse because the horse has two faults." So they had a few more drinks and the first farmer said, "You'd better sell me that horse." The second one said, "I'm not going to sell it to you because you'll be mad at me later on. That horse has two faults." So they had more drinks and the first farmer finally negotiated a contract and paid for the horse. Then he said, "Would you tell me the fault of the horse?" The second farmer said, "Well, when you get him out in the pasture he's hard to catch." So they had a couple more drinks and the first farmer got up ready to go home and said, "You may as well tell me the other fault in the horse." And the second farmer said, "He's no damned good when you do catch him."

---

1 Five members of the Bradley family were murdered at Demer's Centre, Allumette Island, July, 1933. Michael Bradley was tried in both Chapeau and Hull in trials attracting overflow crowds and described in details by the *Ottawa Journal* reporters. Bradley was found guilty and sentenced to life.

2 Assistant to the foreman in charge of clearing and building bush roads.

3 A chain run through a block and tackle and, with hook on one end, snagged into a log so that a horse could haul it up on a sleigh load or atop a skidway pile.

4 A flat-bottomed amphibious barge invented by John West of Simcoe, Ontario, and generally used to pull booms of logs downriver.

5 Swamp.

6 For further details of Colton's drowning in the whirlpool at Des Joachim, see *Tell Me Another Story* by Joan Finnigan, McGraw-Hill-Ryerson, 1981. Chapter 24.

# 15

## "Sing and Be Happy"

### RUSTY LEACH – Chapeau, Quebec

*Russell D. "Rusty" Leach of Chapeau, Quebec, had ancestors who went back to the 1820s when they took up land where the present city of Pembroke stands on the Ottawa River. The Leaches and the Quaits came from England shortly after Pembroke founder Peter White arrived at the site, and, on the riverfront at Mirimachi, they, too, established farms. Rusty said that when he was a child, the old Campbelltown Hotel was right behind their riverfront house. "When I was about four, we lived in that hotel while a new house was being built for us, and the old hotel was filled with shantymen then. How I wish I had been listening in!*

*Rusty Leach spent eight years collecting the old songs of the Ottawa Valley, published by the Shawville Equity in 1984, an incomparable treasury of our heritage that, but for his dogged determination, would have been all lost when the old shanty lads died off.*

*Over the past twenty-five years the Shawville Equity (Dickson Enterprises) has performed a unique and invaluable service to the Pontiac community, the Ottawa Valley, the Province of Quebec, and to our country by publishing books, such as Wyman McKechnie's*

*What Men They Were, Venetia Crawford's Pontiac Treasures, J. Lloyd Armstrong's Clarendon and Shawville, and Rusty Leach's Upper Ottawa Valley Shanty Songs and Recollections. These books and many others have functioned singularly to preserve and record the history of the Anglo-Celts in Western Quebec since their first settlements around 1800. The Equity also acts as one of the few, if not the only outlet for the sale of books in the English language in Western Quebec.*

**N**OW, AS FAR AS collecting the old songs is concerned, that began right here at Freddy Meilleur's. We used to sit in the back room with the guitar and a fiddle and a piano, and we'd play here for hours on end. Mike Berrigan used to play the piano, Joanne Tallon the piano, Leonard Marchildon the fiddle, Claudia Turner the fiddle—we'd stay from maybe one or two o'clock in the afternoon right through till daylight the next morning.

Somebody came in one afternoon and asked if I knew the song, *The Black Steer*. I'd never heard it before, eh? They said, "Well, it's one that old Hughie McParland wrote and used to sing." Afterwards I got thinking, "What the hell? All the old songs these people wrote, you hear people talking about them all

*Rusty Leach, 1931-1994, in a photo taken at the White Water Hill on the Ottawa River about four miles from Chapeau, Quebec. Song collector, storyteller, musician, unaccompanied singer, artist, poet, Rusty made his living by hunting, fishing, guiding and trapping.*

the time but they only know one or two lines." So I got the idea that I should collect them because, if the old people died, the old songs would go with them because they were never written down.

I believe it was the spring of 1978 when I started collecting these old songs in the Ottawa Valley here, the old logging songs and poems that people had written around here, eh? I didn't know how to go about it at the time. I just wrote them all down and I got permission from the people to use their names. It took six years to collect them. I thought I'd do it in a couple of months. I could still do another six years of songs.

Every time I wrote a letter to somebody asking if they knew something about a song, I'd also include in the letter, "Do you know any other songs of the Ottawa Valley? The songs they used to sing in the kitchen? If you don't know them, do you know anybody who does?" And I'd get either a name or two or three lines from a song and it would give me a start, a clue. I wrote to England—even to people who had gone from here. I'd write to Calgary, and phone. I was even in Saskatchewan looking for songs. They'd gone West on the Wheat Excursions of the '40s. I'd heard of two or three poems and nobody knew who'd wrote them.

One day I was in the old age home at Marionhill, Pembroke, and somebody said, "You should see old Tommy Fitzpatrick." So I went up to see old Tom and I got the song, *Raffle at Tierney's Grove*. He told me the whole song, right from start to finish. It took about an hour to bring back memories, eh? And some of the words might be a little changed. Shortly after I got the song, old Tom died. But nobody had heard that song in years and years and years. It was written around about the turn of the century by, they say, Hughie John Cosgrove. He was one of the ones who put a lot of music into this country back then. He was a singer and he wrote all these songs about certain people. Every time they had a party down there—and they had one about every week, eh?—there was a big fight. And it winds up that the *Raffle at Tierney's Grove* turns into a fight. The stove was worth about four dollars and there was about a hundred dollars' damage. Back in the 1900s, that was a lot of money. You can see in the song where they were just waiting for the next weekend for the party at the guy's place

that caused all the shit that night, eh? They were going to raise hell over at his place next week.

He doesn't mention who won the stove, but he tells about the fight and the black eyes and the women in it. He could identify all the people in the song. Amazing.

### RAFFLE AT TIERNEY'S GROVE
Last Tuesday I attended a raffle for a stove
Of a gentle wife and family, Bill Tierney's in the grove.
At eight o'clock that evening, the raffle did begin,
And Donny Toner jumped and cried
When Cotnam made the win.

The Ryans and the Gallaghers, they all came in a drove
To shake the dice, shake them nice,
And try to win the stove.
Forward four, go allamand left, the music it began
With bowlegged Willy Ryan, just a drummin' on a pan.

#### Chorus
*I never laughed to hearty, in the course of all my life*
*To look at Paddy Culleton, waltzing with his wife.*

Tom Leary and Ned Murphy came to play a little jig,
Two fiddles just a squeelin' like Paddy's Irish pig.
The boys and girls a jumpin'
Like they all were run on steam
But I know the bloomin' difference,
It was Willy John's poteen.

Meg Allen sang of Donegal, Ned Murphy called a reel.
Outside the feathers flying,
Some chickens they did steal.
The bouillion's on and boiling, just grab a cup and plate
On drinks or eats at Tierneys, nobody has to wait.

They danced all night and hollered
And everyone had fun.
They figured it was over with the rising of the
  sun.
The gang that came so early, and landed in the
  grove
Now were sleeping neatly, all 'round the kitchen
  stove.

At five o'clock in the morning, the raffle it was
  o'er.
While Charlie Ryan, staven drunk,
Broke the bloomin' door.
Laronde, with a bottle, had all the windows
  broke,
Cosgrove caught him by the neck,
Oh boys I thought he'd choke.

Cosgrove poked Laronde and bloodied up his
  nose
While Murphy hit poor Duffy, several dandy
  blows.
Mary Jane Maguire tripped Joe Daniel with her
  cane
And beat up on his noggin' just to liven up the
  game.

Now Mrs. Paddy Culleton tripped on Ryan by
  the stove
And landed on poor Toner whose wife began to
  shove.
You never heard such language,
Even from the great Cosgrove.
It sounded like Napoleon
Led a charge through Tierney's Grove.

Now that the party's over and the drunken crew
  away
I hope they have a party at their home next
  Saturday.
We'll go and get rip-roarin' and kick and yell
  and bite.
We'll fight with all the rowdies and sing away
  the night.

All the windows they are busted
The door is hanging loose.
It's Bill's own hens they pilfered,
They could have ate a moose.
There's a hundred dollars damage
At Bill Tierney's in the grove
And all because he raffled off a four-dollar stove.

Oh, sure if you go ask the old ones they know all
the old songs and the people in them. And names like
Bowlegged Willy Ryan—that's an uncle of old Frank
Ryan's[1]. Frank talked about old Willy Ryan making
poteen. They never bought brew to go to these
parties; it was all homemade stuff. Everybody had
their own still. Homemade wine they used to make
with apples or potatoes and they'd make it in a big
crock and when it was done fermenting, they'd set it
out in the fall—the end of October or so—when it

*Mr. and Mrs. Joe Poitvin of Chapeau in their later years. They are the subject of Joe Potvin's Song collected by Rusty Leach and, according to his notes, written by Sandy Kennedy, c. 1920. It is a celebration of the marriage of Adolph Joseph Poitvin and Valerie "Giddoo" St. Cyr, October 29, 1912.*

was cold and ice crystals would form on the top, and they'd take a little scoop and scoop the ice crystals off and throw them away. Alcohol won't freeze, eh?

There are two songs and one poem about the party at Tierney's farm at the foot of Allumette Island. The song here was written by Hughie John Cosgrove, as was the other one that is called *Bill Tierney's in the Grove*. The poem is called *The Battle of Tierney's Grove*. This version was given to me by Thomas Fitzpatrick, born in 1901. He said that the party occurred about the time he was born and that he learned the song from his father as a boy. When Mr. Fitzpatrick recited this song to me, he thought there were about two more verses, which he had forgotten. Both Hughie John Cosgrove and Thomas Fitzpatrick were descendants of the early Anglo-Celt pioneers in Western Quebec.

When I was working on collecting the old shanty songs of the Ottawa Valley, Rosaleen Dickson of the Shawville *Equity* put a letter in the paper asking for more information about songs or any old ones, and *The Hunt on the Egan Estates* was sent to me in the mail unsigned. To this day I don't know where it came from! I get a number of things in the mail with no name, no information at all. I don't know why people do that.

I found out that for a lot of these old songs, too, there's two versions, one the lads sang in the bar and the other one too. the *Maganisippi Maid*, well, there's two versions of that one and one of them is a nice version and it's in my book. The other one that they sang in the bar, I finally got it but I won't tell who from.

The version of the *Maganisippi Maid* which I published in my song collection—the public version—I got from the Ottawa Valley singer Loy Gavan, late of Chichester, Quebec. The song was written around 1920 and is supposedly true and has come down the generations in various versions.

These were all loggers and shantymen and they'd spend months in the bush, so they're not going to come down and sing *The Old Rugged Cross* in the bar, you know. They were singing about *The Tart from Turtle Creek*—that's back over on the Picanock Road, that's Turtle Creek. And *Bess the Blacksmith's Cross-eyed Daughter* and *The Black River Whore*, and *The Red Light*

*Saloon*. They'd sit in the bar and they'd hoot them, and make up verses probably as they went. *The Red Light Saloon*, that's a song that I have found references to in all the northern states—Michigan, Minnesota, and in Quebec, Ontario, and Manitoba. It's claimed that there must have been a Red Light Saloon at one time. I've read a thing on it done by a collector of old songs back in the 1800s, and he says that he has references that there was a Red Light Saloon, but he just can't pinpoint where it was, you know.

I found that whatever the story of the song is, there's always a basis in truth for it. Like *Foreman Young Monroe*. That song is as old as the hills and they're trying to place where that is. In the ones I have in this book, it's mentioned as Eganstown. Now, that's a tough one because Quyon was at one point called Eganstown, and so was Eganville. Gerry's Rock is mentioned and sometimes the song is called *Gerry's Rock*, but I have searched that Bonnechere River for anything that could be called Gerry's Rock, and I've never found an old riverman who could tell me where that was. And I've travelled the Bonnechere quite a bit by boat and canoe myself.

There's lots of graves on the streams around here. I think there's twenty-seven at the Rollway Rapids on the Petawawa. They don't have little crosses left on them, but they're there. At the time to get to a cemetery—it was miles downstream to any place where you could get a road, and you'd have to carry the body through the bush. Often they just buried him where he died.

The Gareau Shanty, that's back here at a place called Sheenboro Lake where they drove logs by sleigh down and let them go in to McGillivray Lake, and somebody got killed in there. The wrapper chain on the load broke and the logs started to roll, and he went under. And all they did was wrap him in blankets and bring him down to Pembroke. The song that came out of that was *Gareau's Shanty Band*. It's in my book as well. There were people still alive around Chapeau and Pembroke who could identify the men in that song.

*Rusty Leach was fortunate in that he collected his songs while there were still old-timers alive in Western Quebec who could identify many people in the songs. (Gareau's Shanty Band) is a great example of this. Gareau was thought to be a sub-jobber in the bush for the Pembroke Lumber Company. The shanty was near Long Lake, Quebec, and the logs were dumped in Chute Bay on McGillivray Lake. Rusty rhymes off the names of many of the Anglo-Celt families who settled Western Quebec generations ago.*

Michael Hayes was from Sheen, Victor Fitzpatrick from Allumette Island, Dick Salter from Westmeath, Angus McNair from Renfrew, Black Bob Primeau from Chichester, Weston from Pembroke, Sam Desrochers from Calumet Creek, Des Tanner's last name was blurred on the original sheet—could be Toner or Turner—Christy Tallon from Sheen, Robert White from Nickabeau, Tom McCrea from Sheen. I can't find out who Stan was. It is not known who wrote the words of this song, but it is thought that Hector Perrault (of Sheen) had his hand in it.

I hear lots of stories about how wonderful the old timber barons was. They were the most hypocritical, money-grubbing bunch of bastards that you ever seen in your life. J.R. Booth or whoever. And when you died in the bush! There's stories of loggers getting killed on the job in the middle of the winter, killed by a team of horses or a runaway with a load of logs or getting hit by a "widow maker"[2] and they just wrapped them up in a grey blanket and pulled them up into a tree and let them freeze, 'til somebody was going down. Or put him up on top of the stable, up on blocks to keep him.

They always had a gun in the camps for bears. Bullets were worth more than dynamite. Dynamite was thirty cents a stick, so they just blew the heads right off the "done in" horses. They'd take a quarter stick of dynamite and lead the horse away out in the bush, tie him there with a rope, tape a piece of dynamite to his head with a ten-inch fuse and light it. Oh, I've heard that so many times! It was the boss that was running the camp that told them to do that.

Rusty said that "whatever the song is, there is always a basis for truth in it," and he was close enough to the events which inspired some of the songs to be able to document them. In his notes for the song **Jim Whalen**, he tells the tragedy of Whalen who, in 1878, "was drowned off Pete McLaren's raft" when two rafts collided coming out of Cross Lake at King's Chute. This is a Topley photograph of Pete McLaren in his later years when he had become a Senator and before he died at Perth, 1910.

No room here. Can't eat the oats if you're not putting in your time.

*The Shantyman's Alphabet*. Well, a lady, around eighty, wrote me a letter from Renfrew and asked me would I put *The Shantyman's Alphabet* in my book. She said her father, Alfred Vincent, sang it when he was in the shanty camps and she remembered him singing it to her when she'd sit on his knees. Vincent was born in 1888 and he'd made shanty work his life from fifteen years of age. He's been dead since the early seventies.

One of the stories I remember from early years happened up on the Schwyan River, which comes out into the Ottawa just above Chalk River. This year the men were in the camp up 'til October. They had their logs all cut, but before they could start to haul them out they had to have snow. They all left the camp to come down to Pembroke to wait for snow. They'd go down the Schwyan by the hand ferry, or boat, or whatever the hell. They'd walk into Chalk River and then catch the train to Pembroke. There must have been about twenty or twenty-five of them coming down, but only three or four of them got past Chalk River. They all were at the Chalk River Hotel when the foreman met them there with their pay. The men said the only damned way they would have got on the train to Pembroke was if the train had come right into the bar and picked them up! They had fiddles, and there were girls and all that. That bar never closed—and some of the men were still there when the snow came! A few of them left after four or five days, home to families and that. But when they got back to Chalk River on the train, some of the ones that came out of the bush with them were still in the bar! They mentioned some names of ladies that are grandmothers now, or dead and gone.

*Fred Meilleur addressing the crowd at a roast in Almonte for retiring lawyer, Mike Galligan, in 1996.*

Old Henry used to get so drunk in Chapeau they'd carry him out and put him in the back of his vehicle and tie the reins up and the horse would go home. He'd walk until his nose hit the door of the stable and old Henry would wake up in the morning and put the horse away. When you got drunk, the horse had more brains than anyone! Once horses get to know the route, you don't have to say, "Whoa," or nothing.

At this point Fred Meilleur himself joined in.

CHUM (radio station) from Toronto phoned me one time at six o'clock in the morning and they asked me, "How come a Frenchman with the name of Meilleur in Chapeau celebrates St. Patrick's Day with such a big party?" And I said, "If you were married to an Irish girl for thirty-five years, you'd learn how to celebrate St. Patrick's Day."

One of our biggest St. Patrick's Day celebrations ever was when we brought the mule into the bar. Jim McCool—that's Tom McCool's son—brought the mule into the bar for St. Patrick's Day and the mule was all dressed in green with a green hat and Jim McCool had green hair, and we took it all around the bar, and the Donnelly brothers rode it. And I got on the mule and this man said, "Isn't that a disgrace to see a Frenchman riding the mule on St. Patrick's Day?"

Oh, we had good fiddlers here in Chapeau! Johnny Morin, O'Connor, Thompson—we had good fiddlers in Nickabeau—Lawrence Ranger, Leonard Marchildon. We had parties every Saturday afternoon organized by singer and storyteller Brian Adams, and Joanne Tallon would be playing the piano and they would all sit in the back room and enjoy it, every Saturday afternoon. Spontaneous fun. We had a gentleman who lived here back in 1941 when I first came here, Tom Sauvé—he could play the fiddle and he was a great stepdancer—he lived down the hill here one mile.

We had good singers that came: the Brennans sang, Loy Gavan did a lot of singing here in his younger days; Lennox Gavan used to come. Then we had all the men that worked on the ICO, and they'd come down here for the weekend. Walk in from the boom at the head of the Island and back again. In the bar we have the bench with their initials carved on it that came from the boom, went to Waltham, then to Fort William, then Pat Keon kept it in his hotel in Sheenboro for years until it burned in 1987. They saved the bench from the fire; names there from 1911—Stevie MacDonald, T.E. McCool, Lou Miller, Alphonse Labine, a Brazeau.

Around the tenth-fifteenth of September every year, the Chapeau Fair kept us busy here. And all the jobbers, like T.E. McCool, Zaddow, Consolidated, Clouthier, would come to the Chapeau Fair and bring one of their best teams to compete in the draws at the fair. And at the same time they'd hire all the men for the bush right here in the hotel. The men would go to the bush from September to around the fifteenth of March. Some would come home for Christmas and some would stay the run. If they stayed the run, they made more money. Then the jobbers would come back to the hotel here after March and hire all the men for The Drive. They wouldn't all stay here, but they'd eat here. We had specials on for Chapeau Fair.

The shantymen would say, "We'll meet at the Chapeau Fair and we'll settle all the scores."

My dad bought this hotel in 1940 from Emmett Gray, who went to Renfrew then. Before that, it was owned by Maloney from 1852. Think of all the great Valley hotels that have burned—the Renfrew Hotel, the Copeland Hotel in Pembroke, Moorhead's, Proudfoot's in Shawville, and one at Desjardinville, the hotel at Luskville, the hotel in Arnprior, Lebine's Hotel in Fort Coulonge, the hotel at Portage, Zikorsky's at the Allumette Bridge.

The shantymen used to come down from the bush at Christmas and say that they had cut logs thirty-six inches—that's a yard across—but when they got down to Chapeau on The Drive, the logs had shrunk to twelve inches across because they had run them on the water and the water had shrunk them. And the biggest loads of logs in the history of lumbering were pulled right in this bar.

In this hotel here there was a Merchant's Bank and a telegraph office and we used to have a taxi service here for years run by Wilf Dedeen—his real name was Nadine but he called himself Dedeen—started with a Model T Ford. When Maloney run the hotel, he didn't have a cash register; he had a slot in his counter and a drawer under it and if there was four of you, it cost you twenty-five cents, and if there was two, it cost you twenty-five cents, and if there was five, you got five shots for twenty-five cents.

RUSTY: The Pontiac Club started in 1890 and they used to unload supplies for all those hunting and fishing camps at Fort William too. They'd park their cars in Sheenboro or somewhere like that and somebody would come out by horseback and take them in—a lot of Americans, but doctors from Toronto, too.

FRED: We had a famous hockey team here in the Depression. There was no work, so they called themselves the Chapeau Millionaires. That was in 1934. The cup was bought in Pembroke by Bob Allard in a second-hand store. They could only afford to go as far as Pembroke to play. Carmen Keon played on that; Christy Kelly, Mervin Kelly, and Mainville, and Argenault Daniel, Wilfred Dedeen, Maurice Beaudry. There's a picture of them sitting beside Kelly's store, taken in 1934, when there was no snow in that wintertime, and they called themselves the Chapeau Millionaires—but for different reasons from the Renfrew Millionaires.[3]

RUSTY: In old Pembroke on McKay Street, across from the post office, there used to be a huge building owned by a family by the name of Hunter. They turn up in some of the old songs—Hunter's Team and so on. Well, Hunters out of Pembroke used to supply all the depots and they used to send it on the train from Pembroke to Moore Lake. The Moores had a farm at Moore Lake and the little station there was called Moore Lake Station.

Yes, they used to hide back in the bush here during the World Wars. Most of the shacks, like the shanties, are gone now, but they just found one when they were working with bulldozers back in the bush near Indian Creek. It was used by draft dodgers, then by trappers, then by moonshiners. They were bulldozing into this pile of sand and they realized they were running into a log building with a door, all carefully hidden under a big pile of sand, and a spring run into it for the water for the moonshine.

And two little bunks were there even yet. And they took the old still out of it—an old homemade still. Should have gone to the museum in Pembroke, make a live exhibit. But some guy named Deneau got it. The ghost of the moonshiner may still be running around there on Indian Creek, looking for his lost still.

When the Big Fire went through, it started up around the John Bull Depot, around Sand Lake, and it came out just north of McGillivray Lake, around Schwyan Lake and Lake St. Patrick. I was working for the Forestry there at Ackeray in Algonquin Park on the CNR, and they came in and asked us to help because the fire was running out of control. So a bunch of us left, got in a taxi in Pembroke, and went up to the fire. We loaded up the wagons, got a team of horses, and went in to the camp we would be staying at. About three days later, they asked three of us to stay in the camp until nine a.m. because they were going to drop supplies off on a little lake. So we started out walking, but we heard the airplane land and leave before we got there. And when we got there they had this Jesus baloney piled there between two spruce trees and it just looked like a goddam cord of wood—baloney piled four feet by three feet to feed us!

These paintings I did for Fred's Bar were called the *Twelve Apostles, 1972.* Ronald Reginald—everyone called him "Jingle Balls"—he played the guitar, tore up hell, sang in the bar. Beside him is Red Carroll—he used to be here in the bar. He done a little bit of bush work, bulldozer work, hung around the bar. Left on bottom is Wrangler Hearty, sixteen years ago; we change quite a little in sixteen years. Beside him is Philip Chartrand— he was in here all the time, smoking a pipe, drinking. On the other side of the moosehead is Dorian Beland—he was known as "Roaring-eyed Torn-down Dorn Beland." Great old lad, great bar-room character. His brother is Russell Beland. Next is Eldon Chapeo—he's quit drinking and is living in Arnprior—up once in a while. And one picture is missing: Gordie Lavallée. It's in Ottawa. And the one of Gerald Dunn is in Sudbury; the one of Fred is in Edmonton in a bar. They disappear off the wall.

Stolen, but you don't say that. Just gone. Somebody walked in here one day and said, "Fred! I seen your picture in Edmonton on the wall." Leonard Marchildon—I don't know where he disappeared to—he's probably in some hotel in the Yukon. And Silver-tailed Burnet, his name was Silvio and he had silver hair. The bottom right one is Tommy Sullivan, the boxer. He is in the Boxing Hall of Fame. He taught the Canadian Olympic boxers.

A great bar! Great decorations! A moosehead, wolf head, antlers, an American flag, Quebec flag, old beer trays pegged on the wall—one of them Sudbury Silver foam. A jackalo—that's a rabbit with horns—a cross between a rabbit and an antelope, shot around Chapeau, rare breed. There is a whole family of jackaloes around Cobb Lake. One of Fred's big bar clocks keeps time and the older one beside it runs backwards. In Fred's bar, time stands still.

*Storyteller, singer, song collector, song writer, Rusty Leach was also a poet, as evidenced by this creation myth of The Ottawa Valley, 1980.*

The chill winds blew from the Northern coast;
Grew cold through the Caribou passes,
And picked up the damp of the tundra flats
And touched on the beaver rushes.

And the grasses twisted all dry and brown,
And turned to a rusty grey,
And the brown earth heaved, as the fiery cold
Came down on the land to stay.

The waters in on the nesting holes,
Froze down to the blue clay rim,
And the wild geese came in their circling flocks
To look for their northern dream.

And the skies burst forth, in a ceaseless storm
That battered the dying land,
And ice and snow to the heavens piled
That ground the rocks to sand.

For a thousand frozen snow-clad years
And aye ten thousand more,
In icy blasts from northern vasts
To hold all this land in store.

And out of the coldness a sunray grew,
A dim small gleaming spark
It grew and cut like a burning sword
And hacked at the frozen heart.

And the magnitude of the glacier's hand
Began to wane and wither,
And the little drops of water grew
From a run to a raging river.

And the bleak and desolate mantled land
Cast off its cloak of crystals,
With its burden lost, the brown earth tossed
And threw up its craggy vestals.

The emerald waters filled each lake
And the hills with pine and maple,
While the deer and moose and the beaver came
To feed on its boundless table.

As nature moved through the verdant stands
With a diamond pen took tally.
She smiled and said, "'Tis my best so far,
'Twill be called the Ottawa Valley."

---

1  The Ryans were amongst the first settlers in the almost one
hundred per cent Irish bailiwick around Sheenboro, Quebec.

2  Widow-makers were dangerously hanging broken tree limbs
which fell and sometimes killed shantymen, like Harry Dunn
from New Brunswick, the subject of the ballad *A Wild
Canadian Boy* "who leaves his happy home, and longing for
excitement to Michigan will roam." Harry was swamping out a
trail one day when a hanging limb fell down and "crushed him
into clay."

3  A famous highly paid Renfrew hockey team of the 1920s,
funded by M.J. O'Brien, Renfrew millionaire.

# 16

# "From the Head to the Foot of the Island"

## GERALD GRIFFIN, PIERRE SCOTT – Calumet Island, Quebec

*Gerry Griffin's great-grandfather, Martin, emigrated from Tipperary, Ireland, in 1846. They fled the famine and met the plague on the way over. Seven Griffins died on the boat, two went to the States and were never seen or heard of again, while Martin Griffin made it up the Ottawa River and landed on a sand bar on Calumet Island. Today, right off Calumet, there is a little island named Griffin Island in honour of the area's first settlers. The Griffins "pulled stumps, made land and married," Martin to an Island Gallagher. Gerry's grandfather, William, married Ellen Donnelly from The Island, moved further in and took up more land. His father, Martin, married Clara Cahill from The Island, originally from County Mayo, Ireland. Of eight children, seven were girls and Gerry was the only boy. "So I got the farm," he says. "I had to buy it. You didn't get too much in them days for nothing. I worked hard for it." Gerry's father was Secretary-Treasurer of the Municipality of Calumet Island, Pontiac County, Quebec, for thirty years (1910-1940). Gerry followed in his father's footsteps, was secretary-treasurer the next twenty-five years. In 1941, Gerry married Loyola Butler from the Anglo-Celt settlement at Wakefield, Quebec. Their children and grandchildren are scattered*
*from Chile to China. One son has stayed on the farm where they live and, in the Griffin tradition, still keep Open House for everyone.*

FATHER ENRIGHT from Douglas was instrumental in getting the Roman Catholic Church on The Island, St. Anne's, renovated away back in the twenties with the permission of the parish priest. He was a young man then and one of the few priests who had a car, so that made it handy for him to get around. He listed all the people he knew that had a dollar or so, visited them, and asked them to buy a window for thirty dollars. He said, "If you buy the window, I'll put the plaque there in memory of your deceased relatives, your father or your mother, or whoever." Anyway, he went all over The Island and all around the church and he got thirty dollars from the Walshes, McCarts, Donnellys, Griffins, Carrolls—you could go on and on. They all bought a window. There was some French people that was able to buy, but the majority was all Irish.

The Lamothes, of Ottawa's Morrison-Lamothe Bakery, originated right here and Dick used to come and visit my dad for hours on our farm—he was the same age as my father. Dick Lamothe donated the money for the main office in the church—five hundred dollars in the 1920s! They built the power plant in Bryson in 1922, and the Bryson Hotel flourished during those years. There was seven hundred men worked here for four years and there was only one hotel in Bryson owned by a Mrs. Poisson. And she became, well, pretty big, and she donated two altars on the side in St. Anne's. They were two hundred dollars a piece, which was a lot then. The names of the first settlers were all on the windows at St. Anne's. But in the 1940s, when the church had repairs, they took them all off, took all the Irish-Catholic name-plaques off and discarded them.

I was thirteen years old when we used to take the trains down to the hockey games. It was four miles to Campbell's Bay. I had a horse to go to school every day.

I had the horse to go to Campbell's Bay for the hockey games and I used to pick up a couple of people down at the village. In Campbell's Bay in March they had the play offs. To preserve the ice they used to cover the entire rink with snow, and then they'd scrape it off just before game time. There were three hundred on the train down to the game, six coaches put on for the games.

There was two trains a day, Canadian Pacific, that went right up to Waltham and turned around there at

*Martin Griffin's tombstone laying flat in St. Anne's Churchyard, Calumet Island. He came out from Tipperary in 1846.*

*A Lawn tombstone in St. Anne's Church graveyard. The Lawns thought they had discovered gold on The Island. The Reeders from Texas developed the site into a working mine producing lead, zinc and gold.*

the roundhouse. On hockey nights the train then came down to Campbell's Bay and picked up the fans from Waltham, Campbell's Bay, Bryson, Shawville. The hockey match would be over at eleven o'clock. After the game the train would *back* all the way to Waltham! The next morning the train was already turned around and headed for Ottawa. It got steam up all night.

Bryson wasn't in the Pontiac League play offs. There was Quyon, Shawville, Campbell's Bay and Fort Colounge. They all played off and then the last two games they played off in Fort Colounge on the open rink. When it came to play off time, Shawville had a covered rink. There was lots of arguments about soft ice, "We would have won the game if it hadn't been soft ice," and so on. Who went with me? I can remember the McNallys from Calumet Island, Cecil McNally and Bernard McNally—they were playing off at Campbell's Bay. And the teams used to be able to pick the best from the other teams when the play offs came. Shawville could pick a fellow from Quyon, Colounge could pick a fellow from Campbell's Bay to play, so they'd have the best—that's why it was such good hockey.

My wife came to The Island to teach school and that's how I met her. On the Griffin farm, here, my neighbours were Pigeons, Sicards, Jolicoeurs—two families—Lepines, Chevaliers, Meilleurs, St. Germains, Turgeons, 'til you came to the Lamothes, Tom Lamothe's place. Big Tom he was called. I did learn French because most of my close neighbours were French—so I had to. When I started school, I had to go to the Mine Road Roman Catholic French School. The Protestant English school was at Dunraven, ten miles up. The Ivan Thomsons[1] were Orange, but they lived at the foot of The Island (south). They had to start in separate schools and then went some place else to finish—Campbell's Bay, Shawville—I don't know where, but some of them got a business education. You see, the Thomsons were able to do that because their father was a slidemaster and he "made bucks;" he didn't have to farm, he had money. The Thomsons and the Cleggs were big people around there, and they intermarried. The Thomson house is still there. The Thomson and the Reeder house is the same. The Reeders came after the Thomsons left.

I knew Big Jim McQuaig of Bryson. A great athlete. He played on the first football team that Ottawa had—I don't think it was the Rough Riders. They had a football team in 1902 or '03, when he was a young man. He lived up in the bush where he was a bush cruiser and forester, but he went down and got some good jobs in Ottawa. They never seized the first line, the McQuaigs, and they were back on the second line, and they lived in the same old house. He was a great man for taking pictures.

I didn't finish my schooling at the Mine Road R.C. French School. I went to Dunraven because they had the Ontario education system, not the Quebec one. But, when I first went to the Mine Road School, they all called me "l'etranger." Four miles from home and I was "the stranger!" But at the Dunraven school I had all my cousins, the Irish settlers, the Roaches, Donnellys, Maguires, Heaphys, Sheas, Cahills, Needhams, Nevilles, Letts, Murphys, Durrells, Lawns, Carswells, O'Hares, Ryans, Newells, McGraths, Kellys, McArts, McKellehers, McGees. So I went to school two years at Dunraven and got my exams, my Ontario ones. There really was no Scottish on The Island; a few Stewarts at the head of The Island, but I don't know of any others.

I was just saying last week, what a great mix they were. All the people around, they'd come to the United Church Strawberry Festival every year. That was by horse and buggy and you tied your horses along the fence and you had a great feast. They served them in the church, and they served them in the school close by. Then the Catholics used to have big picnics and the Protestants turned out to help them the same way. We got along really good.

There's a family of Stewarts up there and their mother was a Knox out of Shawville and the Knoxes were quite the toffers—money. Old Mrs. Stewart and her husband Mosie lived right across from John Donnelly. Pierre Scott bought their place. Willard Stewart and John Donnelly were great friends—neither of them ever married. Anyway, these Stewarts started raising a family away up at the head of The Island (north) and one time Mrs. Stewart said, "I don't care what they say. There's going to be a Stewart for every Dumouchel on Calumet Island." The

*Two teams in the Pontiac League in Griffin's young days, the Quyon Pets, 1910, and the Shawville Hockey Club, 1927.*
*Top row, L to R: C.L. Dale, W.J.G. Gibson, Ned Cowan, Leslie Dale, A.G. Proudfoot. Middle row, L to R: A. Turiff, Claude Horner, H. Young, M. Hodgins, V. Chisnell, J. Bowles. Front: J. Horner (mascot), —, J. Donahue.*

Dumouchels lived at the head of The Island and they were French—big families. They had eighteen or twenty-one kids. So Mrs. Stewart, a Scot, was going to produce a Stewart for every one of the French Dumouchels. And I think she did. Quite an ambition.

Growing up on The Island, the roads were bad, and it was five miles to Bryson and five miles to Campbell's Bay, a long trip to get to the railway station. If somebody was sick, they had to go to Ottawa on the train and you had to be at the Bryson or Campbell's Bay station at six o'clock in the morning. Generally we travelled by night to get to the station. If somebody got appendicitis—well, there was about four or five people that died because they didn't get there. One lad died on the flat bed on the train, a Leichent boy. And Timmy Merchant died, and somebody else died, all before they got to Ottawa. Anyway that was a big problem, and the Griffins were half-way so there was a steady stream of people through our place—still is. Some of these people were relations and some were friends—they put their horses in and got a meal—and we served meals year round for people until the cars came. Then they put a ferry on and they used to cross to Campbell's Bay.

There is three times as much bush on The Island as there is cleared land. Some of it is original bush. A fellow bought a farm back there where the mine is and

*The Reeder-Thomson house at the south end of the Island as it is today. When Mrs. Reeder owned it, it was much larger and had side wings, one of which was servants' quarters.*

cut stuff one hundred years old. But that's about the last of it.

Lawns thought they had gold, but it was ore, lead and zinc. And the lead was shiny, just like gold. Old Tim Lawn back there was ploughing with his sons, skimming the rock, and he turned up a stone that was shiny stuff. Well, my God, he'd struck gold! It took a long time for news to get out that there was gold back there. I don't know who all came up. But, anyway, the first person was Mrs. Reeder—she got interested in it, and she bought the land off them. She came up here from Texas and they built the mine the year I was born, 1913. Mrs. Reeder raised some money around here, but very few on Calumet Island bought.

I've seen it spelt Reeder in the old Calumet Island records. It was in the record books that my father had when he was secretary-treasurer of Grand Calumet Municipality from 1910-1940. The separatist movement got them and they didn't want any English records, so they threw them in the dump. The Catholic Church here was established by the Irish the same as the United Church at Dunraven was established largely by the Anglo-Celt Protestants. And all the names of the first settlers were on the windows. Then in the graveyard, the Anglo-Celt tombstones—they bulldozed them all under. The only reason I know this is that my great-great-grandfather had a tombstone there—he was from Tipperary—and his tombstone, because it was lying flat, is the only one still there.

Anyway, the Lawns sold out to Mrs. Reeder and it was called the Reeder Mine. Then there was some man from England put money into it, and the first shaft that they sunk that year was just a hole in the ground and they called it Longstreet Deep Shaft. When it started operating, it was so rich that they could put the ore in bags, take it by horses and wagons to the station and ship it to England for processing. There was dozens of teams on the road at the time in 1900. My father told me that, and I used to have pictures of all the wagons going to the railroad station at Campbell's Bay. All burned in a fire. The Reeders had a big building for servants' quarters and they furnished their house from all over the world. Mrs. Reeder spent money like crazy. She bought property all over, including all that line of Big Jim McQuaig's[2].

I was told personally that they were firing for smelting and they were losing fire, that somebody put the fire out three times and somebody else was setting it. Finally the mill burnt to the ground. I know where it was because we used to go back there and play. It was a wooden mill and when it burnt, Mrs. Reeder got the insurance and disappeared overnight. Then in 1936, '37, the sound of coming war was in our ears and the government was back here because of the lead and zinc. I worked there in the summertime. And they did get a good load from it. Then in 1939, the war broke out. The mine went from Dr. Armstrong—called Ventures—to a man by the name of Jack Dunlop. He reorganized and called it Blue Calumet Mines and it ran for twenty-five years. He went down four thousand feet and he got mineral rights. People moved in to Calumet Island, and they had jobs. And they shipped the ore from the mine to the States. But there's gold in it. There's lead and zinc, but there is some good traces of gold. I forget how many millions of dollars they took out of that mine, but it was a hell of a boost for Calumet Island.

I worked in Sudbury in the mines in '31, '32, and '33 with International Nickel. I knew Toe Blake there. He had a summertime job in the mine, but he was playing on a team in Timmins. When they won the Allen Cup, they went from Timmins and Schumacher out West to play, and we followed that on the radio like crazy. They beat the Trail Smoke-eaters! When they came back, International Nickel was getting big and they wanted to have the best hockey players and they hired the Cook brothers—Bun Cook and Bill Cook—Toe Blake from Timmins to make the team—and the Cooks came from Noranda. Noranda had been the good team the year before. They all came to Sudbury and International Nickel was going to win the Allen

*Val D'or hockey club in the mining country, c. 1940s.*

*"Oh, in the mines it was hard work!" Unidentified miners underground in a Timmins mine.*

Cup. After so many years, I went on to work somewhere else and Toe went on to bigger things, like playing in the NHL with the Canadiens. I knew Murph Chamberlain, again in the International Nickel in Sudbury. All the hockey players worked in the summertime and played hockey at night.

I went to Kirkland Lake in 1939 because I didn't like farming and I had lots of money saved from Sudbury when I worked for International Nickel. I worked underground there. I moved from Sudbury to Larder Lake, Ontario. I came home in the summer then to work because my father wasn't too well and it was busy here in the summertime. Then when I got married, I couldn't do it anymore in the mines; it was too hard on the lungs and I might not have lived to eighty-three. I couldn't work because there was spots on my lungs—it was on the X-ray. In Ontario they'd let you work if you had spots on your lungs. They had

my record. The first time I'd be X-rayed would be 1932 and I got a job in '33. Then they X-rayed you every year that you worked in the mines so they had a record of my spots. But in Quebec, they wouldn't accept me with spots on my lungs.

Oh, in the mines it was hard work! It was slavery. First of all, we were supposed to be working eight hours a day—that was before the unions came in. I had to get up to go to work for seven. I got a boarding house in Sudbury, and then you went out and caught the bus, and went two or three miles, changed clothes, and you'd stand in a line then and wait for the cage to go down. When I started, the mine was 2,600 feet deep, and I worked on level twenty-six. At six o'clock, I'd change clothes, catch the bus home. They made damned sure to get you in there for seven so that you could work more than eight hours. We used to stop for lunch, half an hour.

*In the Mining North young men could get a job during the Depression; therefore, the exodus was northwards. Many of this 1937 group, No. 5 Shaft, Noranda Mine, were from the Pontiac. Back row, L to R: Joe Cooke, Mike Metro, Jerry Walsh, Woodrow Stevens, Frenchy, Alex Beaton, Gordon Stevens, Andy Allen, Jim Young. Kneeling, middle row: Carl Horner, Jack McDonald, Collie Miller, Clayton Summers, Laughie McLean, Jamie Amm, Norman Smith. In front: Alex McDonald, Reg Bagsley.*

I was there when the King and Queen came down. They decorated the tunnel for them. I don't know why they let the Queen come down the mine because it was bad luck for a woman to go down. Mind you, the mining superintendent of International Nickel, his wife was a woman from Timmins and they said she was the one that really ran the show. She laid out the mine, but she never was allowed to go down. She wanted to but her husband, the superintendent, said it wouldn't be proper. So she figured when the King and Queen came over she'd get the Queen below. They fixed up a new shaft, the most modern in this country and when the Queen went down, the superintendent's wife made it, too.

I worked in "the drift" they called it. It was about two thousand feet long. I worked on the project for about two years. That's where I became a miner—I did everything.

Frank Finnigan from Shawville, the star of the Ottawa Senators, had a big heart. He used to be in here often. He owned land on Calumet Island and he'd be here to pay his taxes, doing business. And he loved to talk. One time he said to me, "It's too bad, but sometimes you just can't help people who need help."

We had some really poor families at the Head of The Island (north) and Frank had met a little girl there in one of those families who had real potential. "She should be in show business," Frank said, "she can really sing. And I offered to put up some money to send her to school and educate her, give her some singing lessons. I love singing, you know. If I could have been a singer, I wouldn't have been a hockey player. But I offered her family help, and do you know what happened? They turned me down. The parents turned me down."

After Frank told me all about this case I asked my wife about the girl. My wife said she was so poor she didn't have lunch at school, but had the gift of putting on "a good front."

I was the tax collector for the municipality, secretary-treasurer for twenty-five years, so I had the chance to talk to all kinds of people who came in here to do business. When the township records were taken to the dump by the separatists, they only kept the last twenty years so, if you need anything before that, tough luck.

I've told you about taking the records to the dump and about removing the Irish name-plaques from the windows in St. Anne's. If you go into the graveyard, you'll see some stones with Irish names that have been pushed into a gully at the side of the cemetery.

There's two stories there. The church goes back 150 years and it's an old cemetery. People moved away and the years went on and the graves weren't looked after. The church never notified the people, the descendants or relatives, to come and look after them. They "cleaned up the graves" and any old stones that had fallen over, they removed them and threw them into the gully—their way of "cleaning up the cemetery."

Then there's another factor. Many big stones were set on clay ground and they wouldn't stand long; they fell over. When they fell over, people "cleaning up the cemetery" piled all the fallen stones like slab wood at the edge of the cemetery. People would come to visit looking for their roots, doing genealogy study. They would turn the stones over and further damage them. So more were pushed over into the gully. There were Frenchmen on the tombstones, but mostly Irish. My great-grandfather Martin Griffin is there. His headstone is flattened, lying flush with the ground and the grass is growing over it—my grandchildren come and clear it off every year. It says 1814-66.

This family has always held open house. Donny Gilchrist, the Ottawa Valley's greatest dancer, often came into this kitchen here and danced the night away. He danced so hard the floor would be blackened from his dancing shoes and my wife would have to get down on her knees the next day and scrub the floor. Donny died young. He danced himself to death. At his wake, according to his wishes, all the mourners danced on his grave. We all did that.

*One beautiful day in the 1980s, I was moseying around Calumet Island working toward my secondary goal in recording the history of the Ottawa Valley—photographing all of its heritage log buildings. I was shooting at the bottom of the hill on the old Sullivan place when Pierre Scott, out of curiosity about the stranger or to engage me in conversation, came strolling down the* hillside lane. When I talked to him, I realized he was an integral character in the history of The Island. Not only was he part of the Anglo-Celt settlement of Calumet, but the Scott-Vinet de Souligny connection had made real commercial contributions through the fox farm and the sawmill. I returned in 1986 to verify his tape for this book. Still an avid student of and researcher into Ottawa Valley history, he showed me a treasure he had just found in the Calumet Island dump: A History of the Jesuits published in 1631. After Gerry Griffin's report of the Calumet

*The tombstone of Father Lemoyne, Pierre Scott's grand-uncle, at St. Anne's cemetery.*

Island municipal records all being thrown into the local dump, it made me wonder if a trip there might not be worthwhile for a social historian. Pierre Scott died in 1998.

The Scotts came up to Calumet Island with Father LeMoyne. On my father's mother's side, her brother was Father LeMoyne. He was a priest in the 1880s at La Passe and he used to live there and invite his sister, my grandmother, and her little monsters, my father and uncles, to spend the summer there. And eventually they would come across to Calumet Island to Tom Sullivan's farm where the priests had built what they called a "priest house"—sort of a place where they could come and hunt and fish and rest. And it belonged at the time to Father Ferrari from Vinton. Eventually Father LeMoyne, my grand-uncle, inherited the place and the little kids like Father and his brother, they got older and, in the First World War, both my father and uncle were majors in the Canadian army.

And they were wondering what a professional soldier does when there's no more war, so eventually in 1916 they bought Sullivan's place in order to have a sawmill and a farm to live on. In 1912, my mother got married to Maurice Scott, my father, and we've been around The Island since.

In 1930, my father started a fox ranch—a fur farm they called it. On that fur ranch we had silver foxes which were very fashionable then, and minks. My mother had invested fifty thousand dollars. In the Thirties it was a fortune. At that time a man would work for twenty-five dollars a month—if he could get a job. Eventually we lost everything—sawmill, farm, fox ranch.

My mother was Beatrice Vinet de Souligny. Her father was rich and owned what was considered a seigneury near Montreal. My Grandfather Vinet went for holidays in Europe for two years with his whole family. The Grand Tour. He was well enough off to do that. On the ship going over there was a bunch of young Canadian athletes (directed by my uncle, Henry Scott, then living in Montreal and teaching gymnastics in colleges and schools) going to the Olympics in Rome in 1912. And that's how my parents met. On the boat. Of course they went to Italy—that was the site—

*Pierre Scott's mother, Beatrice Vinet de Souligny, and his father, Maurice Scott, met on an ocean liner going to Europe, she with her family on The Grand Tour and he as a young athlete going to the 1912 Olympic Games in Rome. The photo of the Olympic athletes was taken on board ship and includes Pierre's father and uncle.*

and the pope of that time was one of the spectators and one of the judges. And my Uncle Henry, instead of singing the national anthem, asked the Pope's blessing. The Canadian athletes won two prizes—a laurel crown, and one big medal about ten inches across. I still have that. Sadly, Uncle Henry drowned in the Ottawa River in 1926.

William Scott, my great-great-grandfather married to Catherine Ferguson, came to Canada in 1805 from Scotland with at least one son, William Henry, and one daughter, Barbara. William Henry, my great-grandfather, came at age five to Montreal. Eventually they went to live in Saint-Eustache where he got involved with a French-speaking girl, and a Catholic, Marie Maragrit Paquette. His father told him, "You don't marry French and Catholic." William Henry was a well-off merchant and they lived together—imagine this—for twenty years, had five children, and he became the deputy of the County of Two Mountains.

He was involved in the Rebellion of 1837. I have a poster with "Dead or Alive, five hundred pounds reward." I have it here somewhere and he was arrested, so was one of his brothers, Neil, and the father, William, had to pay twenty-five thousand for each one of them in order that they wouldn't be sent to Australia as punishment to do hard work and fourteen years for high treason. They were Scottish people, you know, and yet they were on the French side in the rebellion of 1837. My old Aunt Lucy, who lived to be seventy-four and with whom I lived for a while, refused to talk about the Scots.

My great-grandfather, William, was a heavy drinker. When he was fifty-four, he decided to get married legally. He said, "I think my time has come." In fact, he died three days after they were married. Of course one of his sisters, Anne Scott, decided he was in delirium tremens when he married, that he didn't have his head straight, and she contested the marriage and the will. And it went from one Court of Law in Canada all the way up to England, and she lost. She was a drunk also. She never married in order that her nephews not have any money from the inheritance. She gave her land and money to McGill University in Montreal and the Royal Victoria Hospital.

When Champlain came up the Ottawa, he was talking about the seven terrible rapids of the Calumet where the Indians used to find stone to make pipes, smoking pipes. Champlain described it as like alabaster. It must have been a soapstone of a sort. Blue-white. I've looked for it and I can't find it because likely it's all flooded out now.

My wife, being part Indian, wanted to do some genealogical research but one has to remember, if you were an Indian with an Indian name, you didn't get into the registers of the church unless you got baptised, and then you changed names and you would become Ryan or Paul or St-Jean. There was no more mention of you being of Indian descent. Very, very seldom, although at Lake St. Patrick way back behind Fort Coulonge, there was a colony of Métis. They moved their cemetery and I looked at the record book and I saw Father LeMoyne's signature there. As part of his parish, he would go to Lake St. Patrick and very likely with my Aunt Lucy, who was my father's sister, the oldest sister, because he was a bit fussy about the food. So Lucy went along and they used to go there with a buggy. And they would unharness the horses, put the harness up in a tree so that the wolves wouldn't eat it, or something wouldn't eat it. Then they would go on horseback to the shanties for confession, communion, and she would do the cooking for him. Of course, Father LeMoyne used to have quite a beard and whenever he'd come back he'd have to shave everything because he was lousy. Why? Because confession was done under a blanket. There was no privacy in the shanties so the two men had to go face-to-face under a woollen blanket and exchange confessions and forgiveness, and of course the blankets were crawling with lice.

The Indians traded furs at Fort Coulonge and Fort William. One day of paddling in between. Golden Point is a big point and there were campsites there because my Aunt Lucy told me. She lived over there with Father LeMoyne and she said every year some Indians would paddle back. Some of those that were too old to travel stayed at home and Father LeMoyne would feed them. She told me about one old Indian lady that wouldn't even live in the house. She wanted to stay out in the tent and she boiled the fish because she had no more teeth.

I returned here from Montreal. Home to the Valley. Recently. I wanted to help a friend of mine who had a contract to pick up deadheads on the Ottawa River for the Consolidated Bathhurst, so much a log.

We pick them up and beach them and somebody else picks them up and our job is done. But it has to be good logs. It's not to clean up the river. It's a salvage operation. We make a lot of money doing it and we don't spoil anything. We just pick up dead logs dangerous to people boating on the river. Everybody's been complaining about them. Also, you have all kinds of things in the river, trees that have floated down and have sunk and are a real hazard. The river has really

*Beatrice Vinet de Souligny (1893-1980) in a photograph taken in Montreal. It was her money that financed the fox farm on Calumet Island, but in this photo she appears to be into chinchilla.*

been a garbage disposal for years. I've walked half the length of The Island on both shores and I picked up all kinds of things people have discarded—old stoves, wire, tires. So they shouldn't blame the company for all of it. Many of the logs go back to before the ICO was on the river, back almost to the square timber days. There are thousands upon thousands of logs there, sunken to the bottom, and they're still good, and still serviceable. I asked somebody the other day, "How long is the salvage going to last?" He said, "For the next twenty years or more." There are accumulations of logs, sixty, maybe eighty, feet deep, in some places.

We're paid ten dollars a log. If it's a cull, it's five dollars, but we can keep it and do whatever we want with it. Sell it. If it's good lumber, maybe only a fifth of the log is damaged. If you're well organized you can make two, three hundred dollars a day. That's a small operation. A small motor boat, a small outboard motor and two men, that's enough. We can pick up sixty logs in no time at all.

Strangely enough, we're back using the old river-driver's peavies[3]. You need leverage sometimes. Some of the logs are twenty-five, thirty inches across and sixteen feet long and sometimes some are stuck in the mud so you need a long, long handle and a lot of elbow grease to roll them into the river. Sometimes you have to put buoys on them in order to float them to somewhere on the beach. They soak up water after so many years. They're heavier wet.

During the First World War, it wasn't just the French who took to the bush to keep out of "the English war." Some of the Irish from The Island did, too. Across from the small creek in front of our fox farm is an island where the dodgers used to hide. From there they'd watch all the partying going on at our place on the Barrie River. You see, they were lonely hiding in the bush. They wanted to have a good time, be with people. But some people said to them, "You can't come because, if you do, we're going to have to report you. It's our duty. You're putting us in a terrible position." They wanted to help during haying time, for instance, to do anything, to be with somebody, not to be shunned. But after the war, there was no bad feelings between them. They were good friends and were forever.

There are still three cottages left there at our fox farm. The ranch was three storeys high and there were twenty-five big cages for foxes. You can still see the cement foundation of the fox cages, huge fox cages,

*The fox farm in operation on The Island.*

twenty-five feet long by twelve feet across and six feet high. Each cage was double, one for the male, a small cage, and one for the female with her pups. At the time we were the only ones who had the telephone, direct line to Fort Coulonge, and we had electricity in the house. We had to have people working for us. Six, seven people at a time. Mostly Island people. They had room and board there. We had the farmhouse for the employees.

I remember a story. At the time we used to feed the foxes on horse meat, so we'd buy old horses. One time this man walked from Vinton, Quebec, with his old horse to sell it to us for five dollars. But we didn't want it. So the man told Mr. Lambert, our manager,

*The Island has always attracted many fascinating summer visitors like Major Gus Mainville who wintered in Majorca and summered on Calumet for many years.*

"Keep the goddam horse. I'm not going to walk it all the way back. Just give me a square meal." Just one square meal for a horse! Imagine how tough it was! It was 1930, '31.

The Duvals, three brothers, worked for us, doing anything, as handymen. And eventually my father had no more money to pay them and he said, "I'm sorry I have to let you go." And, you know, those Duvals had to walk four miles to get to work at our fox farm and back home every day. Eight miles a day. The Duvals said, "Listen, if you want to give us our tea and tobacco we'll come and work for just that. Don't let us go." So my father said to my mother, "I cannot do this. I cannot take advantage of somebody like that. They need the little bit of money they make. So we'll find the money to pay them." You see tobacco and tea were the two things they couldn't get without cash. And those are the grandparents of the Duvals that are still here on The Island. At the time our ranch was a bonanza for a lot of people. With the sawmill and the ranch, we were the only ones hiring people. The cottagers would take advantage of people like that. Just like a rich man that I've heard about in Fort Coulonge who used young girls as maids, had them work for him for one month and then kicked them out—if they didn't want to sleep with him. That was told to me by a lady who worked for him as well. Have them work for one month and save the salary if they didn't come across.

---

1  For more on the Thomson family, see *Giants of Canada's Ottawa Valley* by Joan Finnigan, General Store Publishing, 1981.

2  McQuaig was a renowned Island character, a forester, a storyteller, and a member of the first Ottawa Rough Rider football team.

3  A long handled pole with a metal hook to move logs.

# 17

# "They Used to Put Us All on the Top Floor in the Vankleek Hotel"

## DAVID HAYES – Ottawa, Ontario

*David Hayes, forty years a Bell man, is second generation in Ottawa. Right after the First World War, three Hayes brothers came out from Castlehill in Ireland, including David's father, William, who joined the Royal Canadian Air Force and was stationed at the old seaplane base on Victoria Island. David's mother, Fanny Ryves from the north Midlands of England, was a war bride. After the end of World War II in 1945, William Hayes organized the Department for Continuing Education for all the vets coming back home to Canada and anxious to catch up on their missed schooling. David Hayes was in the navy during World War II, ending up as a gunnery officer attached to a British unit. He has been part of the musical scene in Ottawa for many years, including serving as an active member of the Orpheus Society since 1959. He retired from Bell in 1984. Lately, he has been singing with the Ottawa Police Chorus, performing solo, and doing musicals with various senior citizens' groups. Recently he sang* Old Man River *at the Ottawa Ex. He says that only lately has he "turned old."*

*There are today in Ottawa and area many descendants of the three Hayes brothers who came out to Canada in 1919. But they say they are not related to the Hayes of Western Quebec, the Anglo-Celts who settled Shawville and the Gatineau. David Hayes' life story as a Bell telephone man is a truly remarkable record of the pioneering days when working in the field was an exciting, challenging and dangerous adventure. I first introduced David Hayes in* Tell Me Another Story, *McGraw-Hill-Ryerson, 1988. This is the second half of that same interview.*

IN MY DAY, Cornwall used to get some of the worst sleet storms in the whole world. People don't realize that to go to work on the lines in a sleet storm is the scariest thing you ever got involved in. I went to Kingston one time in a sleet storm and we were working, and trying to be careful, with this line foreman. Everybody was pulled off because it was raining so hard, but the minute the last drop of rain fell, this foreman had his men back out to work. In those days the backs of the trucks were open and everything was sopping—hand lines and everything. He took his men to a location where everything was down and they had to start trying to restore service. And I don't know exactly how it came about, but one of the fellows took a hand line and threw it up and over, and there was a high-voltage power cross about five miles down the road and it killed him. It killed two of them, and the others ran to help them and then there was five of them dead in the ditch. So the foreman just kind of went over the edge. Later on in the morning, he got into the big construction truck and he drove into town to the bank.

It was payday, so he had all the paycheques and he gave them to the girl to cash. That's what the foreman used to do and then each one went into a little brown envelope. They weren't supposed to, but a lot of the foremen wouldn't give you the time off to go and cash your cheque, so one Bell man would go in and the rest would be out there working. When the girl went to cash them, she realized that none of them were signed. She said, "They're not signed. Get the men to sign them." The foreman said, "They can't." She said, "Why not?" He said, "They can't sign them, they're just lying there."

The conversation went along this way, so she went and got the bank manager and he tried to talk to the man, and got nowhere. So he called the police and they talked to him and they said, "Well, where are they?" So he took them out there and these fellows were all lying there and they realized they didn't dare touch anything until they got a bunch of Hydro crews out.

Two of them were electrocuted and the others went to help them and, of course, if you touch them the current goes through you too. But they couldn't *see* anything wrong. They discovered the cross-arms about five miles away. This is why I say it's the scariest, most dangerous thing when it's wet because water is a conductor. Actually, a lot of Bell stuff has insulation on the outside. So it really wouldn't matter too much if they're bone-dry. But, when you've got a

*T.W. Bouchard's gang at Brockville, Ontario, c. 1932, in front of Bell repair truck. L to R: C.W. Dennie, J.P. Brady, M.R. Rundle, J.M. Brontmeyer, Foreman T.W. Bouchard.*

half an inch of ice and water on top of that, it doesn't matter if there's insulation underneath—you're going to get it anyway.

I remember I was working as an installer in Ottawa when the foreman said to me, "Ever work on an ice storm?" I said, "Yes." He said, "Do you want to go to Cornwall?" I said, "No." He said, "Why not?" I said, "There's not too much that I'm afraid of in this life, but I want to tell you I'm scared to death of a sleet storm and I don't want to go." He said, "Every foreman in the city has to send two men and a truck. Do you want to go?" I said, "No." He said, "Okay. Any volunteers?" Nobody would volunteer. The foreman, his name was Joe Leduc, said, "Okay, I'll put all the names in a hat and I'll draw two. Is that fair?" And everybody said, "Yes." He picked my name and then came up to me and said, "Here, pick your mate."

I picked the one guy, Ernie Houston, who'd just been transferred to our crew from the office. In later years he was my best man, but he wasn't an outside working man, and this was the guy that I picked to go work on this terrible . . .

You really have to trust the other guy. You're a team with your lives in each other's hands. You have to have a lot of confidence in your mate. Ernie Houston, a nicer man you never met in your life—but every time he started in to work, it looked like it was the first time he'd ever handled a screwdriver or a pair of pliers in his life.

While I was up in the air working I'd yell at him, "I can't keep watching you all the time. Don't get out of the truck." Then I'd call him and say, "Send me up this or send me up that." Now our trucks were closed, so my hand lines and everything were dry, so I would throw a hand line down to him and say, "Tie on this tool or that," and I'd pull it up—I was doing all the bull work.

Everything was in such a mess in this Cornwall storm that after we got the major storm damage cleared up, we were just doing odds and ends. We were at the last pole on a street. And a lot of the wires were sagged and stretched very badly because of the weight of the ice, so I put block and tackle on these and I pulled them up until they were fairly respectable looking. I cut out all the slack and I spliced them back up and I'd take off my block and tackle and get ready to come down and, gee whiz, there's still a lot of slack in that line. So all right, I'll do it again and I'd rig up the block and tackle and I'd pull the lines back up. There, now they look fine. I'd cut the slack out and splice it and I'd go to come down and I felt awkward on the pole. So I looked down and what I'd been doing was I'd been pulling the pole over, and this is where the slack was coming from—the pole was bending over and the wires were going lower and lower. If the poles haven't been put in deep enough, they will move when it's wet out.

Ernie had the truck running and the heater on and the defrosters going, so I start to yell for him. I couldn't move then because if I moved the whole works was going to fall down. I yell and yell and nothing happens. Finally I threw a pair of pliers and bounced them off the hood of the truck. He rolled down the window and he said, "Geez, man, you really get nasty sometimes," and he started to roll up the window and I said, "No, no, don't!" He said, "What's the matter?" I said, "Get out of the truck." He said, "It's raining." I said, "Get out of the truck." And he gets out and he looks at me and he didn't realize I'm on a forty-five-degree slant! He just looked at me and couldn't see anything wrong with that! He said, "What do you want?" I said, "Do you know what pipe poles are?" He said, "Kind of." I said, "There's three of them on the truck. Will you get two of them?" Then I had to explain to him what to do with the pipe poles while I'm hanging up there; how to block the pole up so I can climb down it.

There was one very famous picture in the *Bell News* of Ernie and I. When you first go on a storm, they give what they call rural route maps; they don't have roads drawn on them, they just have the telephone lines drawn on them and each line has a number—like there'd be an RPR one-two-zero, rural party route one-two-zero. Every fifth pole is numbered, so if you've got a rural route map you can go anywhere. Anyway, I drove down this road and I had a tough time staying on the crown of the road because it was so desperately slippery, everything was ice and the road was rounded and I was having a hell of a time to drive along it. And I'm being very careful and I came to a T-intersection—there's no other traffic around and I looked and there was no lines going so I turned to the left—all the poles had snapped off right at the ground! As far as you could see, they'd all done a complete turn! They were standing top of the pole down and the bottom of the pole straight up in the air with all the cross-arms still on. I didn't twig when first I looked at it. <u>Then it just took me a moment to realize that the cross-arms were all at the bottom!</u>

This was just outside of Cornwall. And our foreman on that particular little jaunt was a chap from Nova Scotia named Walter Bezanson. Walter came back with Ernie and I and the three of us, we had loaded up two trucks with all these great big reels of wire that was insulated and we replaced all the wire that was on those poles. We replaced it with insulated wire and hung it all along the fencepost all down this country road, for I guess about a mile and a half, and we hung all the stuff along the fence and at each end spliced into the wires on the pole to connect all your circuits. That was all long-distance wiring.

In those days, Killaloe-Eganville-Douglas area belonged to the Davis Telephone Company, a private line. If they got into a lot of difficulty due to a bad storm and they had got a lot of damage, they would

*Bell construction crew, Renfrew, Ontario, 1922. L to R: Jerry Armstrong, sub-foreman; Bill Klabundy, lineman; W. Clark, clerk; S.F. "Happy" Empey, lineman; Felix Seguin, lineman.*

apply to the Bell Company for a repair man. The last time I worked up through Pembroke, I was a cable repairman. You see the smaller companies couldn't afford to keep a full-time cable splicer and maintain all his tools and equipment, so Bell would send me out, the same as they did in Chapeau across the river from Pembroke.

The whole town was out one time when I was sent over there. It was all cable trouble. I met Sheldon Davis after that and I used to go and work for the Davis Telephone Company. I made a lot of extra money on the side because sometimes Sheldon would phone and say, "I want such-and-such a job done. Do you want to do it or do you want me to call the telephone company?" "When do you want it done?" "I want it done by such-and-such a date." So I was moonlighting.

Douglas had only the poles with the cross-arms and the open wires right on the streets. They had no telephone cables as such. So Sheldon Davis got a construction crew going to put up all the cables throughout the town in those steel grey boxes you see on the poles. Sheldon hired me, so I made up the records and I did all the splicing in all the cables in the whole town for him. Obviously I didn't have a truck. I couldn't take the Bell Company truck over. I took a week of my holidays and I worked over there day and night. I would sleep in the back seat of my car and I got the whole town cabled and everything finished right through to the telephone office. That would be '53, '54.

Anyway, I'd do all this to make some money. Bell never did pay very well; Sheldon was always very good to pay. When he sold to the Bell Telephone, part of the deal was that Sheldon got a job in the engineering department with Bell.

Bell men used to do a lot of things when we didn't make much money. In Maniwaki they had a great big Bombardier snowmobile and I used to use it to drive taxi at night for the lady who owned the hotel in Maniwaki. When people who lived outside of town got off the train and wanted to go to their farms, I would drive that for pocket money. In those days, Bell only paid your way home every second weekend and on the other weekend you sure didn't have the money to get home, so I used to go and cut wood for Elmer Brannigan in Pembroke, and Eric Fisher. It was cut and I split it.

For many, many years, I was doing semi-professional wrestling. I used to do stand-in bouts up the Ottawa Valley and in Gananoque and all along The Front. I went to the Olympic Trials, but I didn't make it. Jimmy Flockhart was my coach so he'd be in whatever town I was working in, and he'd have his own car there with a blanket and a pillow, and I'd crawl in there and go to sleep and he'd drive me to whatever town, and I'd get out and do the stand-in. If somebody was hurt or sick I'd do that, and then we'd go and have something to eat, and I'd crawl into the back of the car and he'd drive me to the next town and he'd waken me up and I'd stagger out and go up to bed and fall back to sleep.

So I got a call from Bell boss Bill Purcell to come to Ottawa on a Friday morning. This was when I was working in Buckingham. And he started all this baloney about, "You're a pretty tough guy, eh? Nobody wants to mess with you, eh?" (I'm trying to think back. I haven't been in trouble and I haven't hit anybody.) So I said, "I don't know what you're talking about." He said, "What were you doing in Kingston on Thursday night?" I said, "I was earning some pocket money. How do you know?" He said, "I saw you." It wouldn't have done me any good to lie then, would it? He said, "You move pretty good." I said, "Jeepers, considering the size of the guys I'm up against most of the time, if I don't move pretty good, they're going to murder me." "Anyway," he said, "it's none of my business, but how much money did you get paid for last night?" I said, "Twenty-five dollars." He said, "Do you do it very often?" I said, "Maybe twice a month sometimes." He said, "What am I paying you right now?" I said, "You're paying me twenty-one-fifty a week!" He chewed the fat a little while longer and then he said, "Do you want to fight or do you want to work for the Bell?" I said, "What do you care, so long as I do my job?" He said, "No. Bell policy won't have it. You've got to do one thing or the other." I said, "Well, I guess I'll work for the Bell." But I still used to wrestle and then I got into judo and I got into competition judo. Then when I

was in Pembroke, I opened a judo school and I ran a Judo school in Pembroke for five years. Moonlighting.

Shawville and Quyon had the Pontiac Line, private. One time I went over there because they panicked. Jack Dixon wouldn't even let me put my truck on the Quyon-Fitzroy ferry to take it across the Ottawa. They were taking Coca-Cola trucks and all kinds of trucks and he wouldn't let me put my Bell truck on there and I had to go down and drive all the way around on the Quebec side. Well, anyway, I got there and I saw the Pontiac man. He wasn't too pleased that I'd been sent for and he hadn't too much to say to me at all. I said, "What's the problem?" He said, "We've got a cable trouble." I said, "Are you sure it's cable? Did you check the fuses in the office?" He said, "I checked everything." I said, "Do you mind if I go and have a look?" He said, "Do what you like."

So I went in and every line in the office has two funny little fuses that they call heat coils and they were all fine. But back of the heat coils there are two other little rigs they call carbons and the carbons were all horribly burned. It's another safety feature that if you get electricity on your line, it'll burn your little heat coils and any excess will go through the carbons and then go to ground rather than going into your telephone office and burning the place down. So I replaced I don't know how many carbons and put half the town back in service just changing the carbons. The Pontiac man was so disgusted he just got in his truck and drove off.

Now, your grounding systems are better and your cable makeup is different. The cable used to be covered with lead and now it's plastic. But I know that in one span—which is what we call the distance between two poles—right on the main street of Chapeau when I opened the cable in twenty-three places—it was burned in twenty-three places in that one span! If it were in Ottawa, you'd have a crew in to replace that section of cable. But I was just there to get the phones working again. It doesn't matter what it looks like, just so long as you get it patched up and repaired.

I worked out of Pembroke at Round Lake and Alice and in through there. Somewhere back in that country there's an emergency landing field for the Department of Transport and I know that whenever there was a really bad storm with high winds, a lot of sections of tarmac wires would come down like a pile of straw. There were two lousy little wires going out to that emergency landing field that had to be restored, no matter what happened. You'd go out there and start swinging an axe all day. I was up on a big pile of rocks and there was a couple of these small trees and they had the wires pulled down to about a foot from the top of the rock. Like a dummy I was swinging the axe and I guess I finally cut through; the wires sprang back up, and they snatched the axe right out of my hand. And I was in an awkward position with one foot up and one foot down and I'd no place to run, so I put my hands over my head and hoped to hell the axe didn't come back down on me. It landed in the middle of the road.

There was a man up there named Ellard Popp and he was an installer in Pembroke. A very, very strong man. When a pole was broken, I'd want to take the pipe poles and jack it up but he'd say, "No, no, we ain't gonna do dat dere. We're gonna fix dat." And he'd dig another hole right beside the butt and grab the pole with everything still on it, and move it over and drop it down in the hole.

When I was young, I was a splicer's helper and we went to do a cable splicing job in Petawawa Military Camp. I went back another time on a temporary help basis, when I stayed at the Hotel Pembroke for ten months. And then the last time I was sent to Pembroke, Bell was looking for people with experience and qualifications, and they couldn't find anybody to go because of the difference in wages. Pembroke was Zone E. Ottawa was Zone A. You're not going to take a cut in pay like that voluntarily. When push came to shove I had to go and I said, "You know, that's not fair. I've been up there a couple of times already." They said, "Yes, but you know the district, so away you go." I said, "Send somebody else." They said, "We've got to send somebody that's single." I said, "I'm getting married in three weeks." "Well, you're not married now."

So I went there on October the third, 1958. Five years to the day I worked in Pembroke with the low rate of pay the whole time. I had the top-rated job and I still was making about sixty-five bucks a week less than any two-bit installer in the city of Ottawa. That's why I didn't like working in Pembroke.

My cousin Dennis Hayes worked up in Pembroke for Bell for a while, and then later on went to Maniwaki. One time he'd gone on a toll trouble between Petawawa and Chalk River, and he was right on the highway by the military camp and found out the reason there was trouble was because one of the wires was shot down. The soldiers were firing right across Highway 17! And Dennis, up the pole, fixed the trouble and then was afraid to come down the pole. He phoned his wife from the pole and said "goodbye," because he figured he was going to get killed. Why he didn't phone someone at Petawawa and say, "Get these fools out of here," I don't know. I guess he was going to eventually, but he wanted to phone his wife first. He didn't figure he had that much time left!

But part of Petawawa Camp was their own telephone company. The "married" patch was Bell. So once in a while they'd phone and have a repairman sent up. Their telephone man's name was Frank Atkinson and he'd say, "I've got trouble on such-and-such a line and I can't seem to find it." First thing I'd do was go and see the range officer and say, "I've got to go to such-and-such a section and I don't want to get shot down." "Oh no, no, they're not firing over there," he'd always say. There was so much shrapnel and stuff in the grass that you couldn't drive a Bell vehicle in there, so what they used to do was give you a military driver and a bren gun-carrier and they'd drive you up there and you'd do your testing. I have pieces of shrapnel that I've taken out of the poles. And yet the military would turn round and swear up and down that they don't do any firing in that area. Chunks of shrapnel ten or eleven inches long that I'd pull out of the pole.

Anyway, one time at Petawawa I get out with a fellow and Boom! Boom! Boom! it starts. The soldier that was driving the gun-carrier says, "Come on, we've got to get out of here." I said, "They're not supposed to fire over here." He says, "Get the hell down that pole and let's get out of here!" I came down and we hadn't gone half a city block when the shrapnel starts whizzing around us. We did some moving then! I said, "You take me back to the range office."

So I went back—and I guess he was a major—and I stormed in there screaming curses at the top of my voice and he says, "Who the hell are you talking to?" I said, "You, you dumb toque. You bloody near killed me." He still swore up and down they weren't firing anywhere near us. I went back out and I said, "What's this? What are these? Is that shrapnel or is it a can of peas?"

Anyway, I went back to the telephone office and I told Frank Atkinson where the trouble was, and then some Petawawa officer who had driven down to Pembroke came into the Bell office and saw me there and said, "We need a cable repairman right now." So I went up and saw the communications officer and I said, "Haven't you got a cable repairman?" He said, "Yes, we have, and he'll help you and give you any assistance that you require." And I said, "Well, if you've got your own cable repairman, why doesn't he fix the trouble?" He says, "You've got better equipment and you can find the trouble."

So I get busy. In the telephone office at Petawawa Military Camp there's a big trapdoor in the floor, and I lift the trapdoor up and there's a foot-and-a-half of water! There's not much headroom, so I'm down on my knees sort of sitting in the water and I look at what they call the central office splicer—it's where all your sections of your switchboard come together—all those cables are joined together in one big splice and then one big cable leaves the telephone office and goes out and up the pole and spreads out in different directions. Somebody had been messing with the central office splice or looking for trouble sometime, and they hadn't bothered to close the main splice. And, as I said earlier, the insulation used to be just paper. Well, this was only six or seven inches above the water, so you couldn't touch any of the paper because it was so dry it would just come off on your fingers like a little bit of glue.

I said to the Petawawa guy, "Have you got any desiccant[1]?" He said, "Oh, yeah." I said, "Well, you'd better get me as much as you can." He said, "Well,

you don't need it." I said, "The splice is open." He said, "I already checked it and the water's not touching it." I said, "How long were you in cable repair school down in Georgia?" He said, "Two years." I said, "Fine. Get me some desiccant."

So I made a little trough with some bandage and filled it full of this desiccant, and then I was doing this and holding it up to the splice to get all the paper dry and then it got to the point where I could pour desiccant in and wrap it all up and let it stand for an hour. And then I opened it and dumped all the desiccant out and did it over again and kept doing that until it was dry enough that all the telephones worked again. This is five feet from the main switchboard in the camp. The Petawawa fellow didn't like all this and started giving me a bad time and I said, "Look, don't run off your mouth at me. You're only a sergeant. Back off. I don't have to take any abuse from you at all."

I was trying to figure out a way to get around blaming him and he was so frigging obnoxious that, when the communications officer came galloping in to say that everything was working, I said, "Well, not all of it. It's coming. It's going to be all right." And he looked and he said, "Sergeant, do you know what the trouble is?" He said, "No sir." The officer said, "Fine. Leave and go about your business." As soon as the guy was out of the office the officer said to me, "What's the problem?" I said, "Well, I really don't want to say." He said, "Well, I've got to make a report on it anyway, so what was the problem?" I said, "Your main splice was open and it was soaking wet. Look down there." He said, "Look at you!" By this time I was standing up. He says, "You're soaking wet. Have you been in that water all afternoon?" I said, "Yep." So he called for pumps and stuff like that and then he lay down on his stomach and looked underneath and I showed him and he said, "How's that supposed to be closed?" So I told him and he said, "Oh, I've seen him doing that. You put a lead thing over it and solder it up on the end." I said, "That's right; that's the way it's supposed to be, but there wasn't anything over it and all that paper insulation was sopping, wringing wet." He said, "Wa! Wa! Wa! Wa! We've got a new private."

I have a good party-line story. I married and we went to Pembroke and I got a lot of good breaks because several new jobs opened up and when a new job opened up, I got it. It didn't make me very popular with the local troops, but so what! Finally I ended up as the tester—you get all the trouble reports and you test them and you dispatch men on them and so on. So I got a trouble on a rural line and at that time I think the most people you had on a rural line was about eight, and the most you can possibly have anywhere now is four. I was trying to test and trying to test and I just couldn't locate it. And it was right up the main highway towards Petawawa and I had done a lot of work on the records and the cable drawings, so I knew the area on paper pretty well and I sat there and listened and listened and listened and I thought, "Jeepers, as true as I sit here I can hear a canary!" I could hear this cotton-picking canary singing away like blazes. And I yelled and I whistled and I hooted and nothing.

Rural lines—the way they're made up—you may have four of them but not every next-door neighbour is on the same line. You stagger them. So I picked another rural line in that area and I phoned the lady and I told her who I was and explained my problem and I asked her, "Is there somebody that lives near you who has a canary in the kitchen that sings like the dickens?" She says, "Oh yes, Mrs. So-and-So." So I sent a repairman out there and he went out and there was nobody home and he climbed the pole and had a listen on the line and he could hear the canary. He disconnected that lady's line—she'd left her receiver off the hook—so once he disconnected her wire, everybody else was back in service. Then I get a very irate lady phone me in the afternoon saying that her phone didn't work. "I want it fixed right now." I said, "Are you the lady with the canary?" She said, "How did you know I had a canary?" So I told her what had happened and she said, "Oh, my God, my neighbours are going to kill me." I said, "I didn't tell your neighbours." So I sent the lad out and he hooked the line back up. People are funny, you know.

There was another man and his daughter worked in the Bell office and I got a trouble call to fix their phone. And I'm just starting to drive down out of the laneway of the Bell Telephone office when the girl came out of the office and stopped me and said, "Are you going to such-and-such an address?" And I said, "Yes, I am." She said, "Well it's very embarrassing; be very careful of my father." I said, "Why?" She said, "Well, he ripped the phone off the wall and he's been drinking. So be careful because he'll hit you." I said, "Well, not twice he won't,"

So off I go. The mother was home and they were all embarrassed with this bloody idiot. He'd ripped the phone off the wall all right—ripped it off the wall and broken it in half. I get a new one and stick it on the wall and I call in to Bell and I get a test call back and I'm just going to leave and the son of a gun walked in. So he started to rant and rave and curse and swear. Drinking, he was, and he was uglier than sin. And he ran off his mouth at me and I said, "I'm sorry you're upset. However, your phone's working and I guess you must have dropped it." (You say garbage like that just to try to keep everything smooth and give him an out, you know?) But he's not going to go along with that. He said, "I broke the so-and-so and such-and-such and I'll break this one too." I said, "Go ahead and break it. I'm not going to keep replacing them for you and, besides that, Mr. Man, we're going to start billing you." So he hauled off and punched me. So I say, "Enough's enough."

I was right beside the front door and when he punched me I just gave him a push and then put my tools out the door. He came after me and gave me another punch. So I took him by the scruff of the neck and the seat of the pants and chucked him off the front porch and out onto the street. I said, "We're not on your property anymore. Now what are you going to do?" So he went around the house and in the side door.

I got back to the Bell office and his daughter arrived and she said, "Are you all right?" I said, "Sure, I'm all right. Why?" She said, "My father hit you." I said, "Aw no, not really." She said, "My mother saw him." I said, "Don't worry yourself about it." She said, "Are you going to call the police?" "No, I'm not going to call the police." She said, "Well, you'd better because he called the police and reported you for hitting him!"

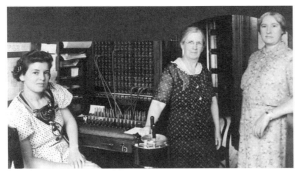
*Bell Telephone switchboard operators at Maxville exchange, c. 1939. L to R: Agnes McEwen, Rachel McEwen, Manager Bertha J. McEwen.*

If you get an order to take a telephone out for non-payment, there is a little code number on one side. I know that, but you're going to go knock on the door and say, "Good morning. I'm from the telephone company. You ordered your phone removed?" Anyway, this guy got very abusive and nasty and said, "You're the third one that's been here and they didn't take the phone out and you're not going to take it out either. The last guy went down those stairs." I said, "Well, I'll tell you what: if anybody goes down those stairs today, it sure isn't going to be me." He says, "Did they send a tough guy?" I said, "They just sent the meanest son-of-a-bitch in the whole telephone company, so you put one hand on me and I'll throw you down there and you want to hope you hit the stairs before you hit the street." He said, "Do you mean that?" I said, "Yes, sir. I'm not going to stand here waiting for you to hit me." He said, "Get in there and get it and get out." So I went in and took the phone out, wrapped up the cord, put it under my arm, and said, "Thank you very much. Good morning."

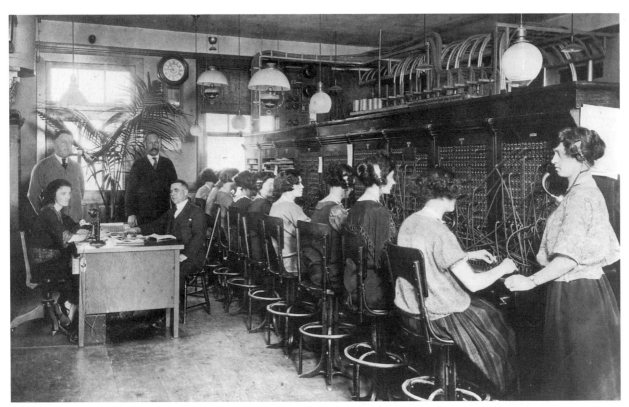
*Bell operators at #1200 Magneto switchboard, Smiths Falls, Ontario, c. 1923. Seated at table: M. Faughnan, Chief Operator, John J. Gardiner, District Manager. Standing: P. Faughnan, Wire Chief, J. Lowe (right).*

The Bell operators, you couldn't date them because they wouldn't shut their mouths. It would be all down the line. They talked to one another. It was a lonely job. And especially the operator that was on in the evening or at night. She knew everything that was going on in town. And she told it most of the time. They had eight different rural companies coming into the Bell switchboard in Cobden—the Queen's Line, the Acorn Rural, I don't know all the names of them—eight of them. And it was in such terrible shape that when there was a storm on, if you'd ring in, the number would flap down and the operator would yell at you—she'd be standing against the wall on the other side of the room—"I'm not going to answer the phone." She'd be afraid of getting a shock because there'd be a bad storm and it would be Zap! Plop! Zap! Plop!

We were just a bunch of working guys; there were no standouts in the Bell men. It was a team, in a manner of speaking. I used to chum with the Bell men in the different towns I'd go into. Later on, when I got to be on my own and had my own truck and would travel all over by myself, I'd do my day's work, come back, and check into the hotel, get showered and shaved and changed and go and have supper. I'd go into the tavern and somebody'd say, "Hey, hey, Dave." Bell men got transferred hither, thither, and yon but, no matter where you went, there would be one or two Bell men that you'd worked with somewhere throughout the company. So there was always somebody around that you knew and you'd have a beer, "Where's So-and-So? How's So-and-So doing?"

In Vankleek Hill there was a big, tall, blond fellow called Slim McDonald. He was on the Kingston police for a good number of years, but then he was a lineman in Vankleek Hill. At this time it was my second stay in Vankleek Hill, but I wasn't a splicer anymore. I had my own truck and what they used to do was put all the Bell people on the one floor, the top floor, in the Vankleek Hotel. So somebody comes along and yells "Bell men, downstairs to the tavern." I was reading and I jumped up off the bed and opened the door and said, "What the hell's going on?" "There's a fight in the tavern!" And McDonald jumped right over the top banister and landed right down in the hall in the main lobby. About six feet in front of the foot of the stairs was the door that led into the tavern. So he went roaring through and we all go charging after him—and a couple of Bell fellows had gotten into a row with a couple of the locals and there was a big fight going and the local boys were beating them up pretty good. All the Bell men go charging in there and Gunner Laconde says, "Lock the doors! Don't let them out! Don't let them out!" Oh, it was a wonderful brawl!

The Bell men paid for that brawl and we also paid at the Château de Grace[2]. There were three or four construction crews got into a drinking party one night in the Château de Grace in Gracefield. I know that that night, the Bell men stuck together. But the next day the owner called us all in and told us that if we didn't pay the damages he was going to call our head office in Montreal. They worked it all out and it cost everybody twenty-five bucks—darned near a week's pay in those days. We had even swatted the light fixtures off the walls with brooms and we had ripped the doors off the washrooms and were racing them downstairs like toboggans.

In Hawkesbury—this was a little later on when everybody was getting a little bit more money—one of the Bell men whose name was Roy Honeywell, his father bought a new car and gave Roy the old one. And Roy was very, very good in that, instead of having to take the bus or the train every Sunday

*Bell telephone operators at #105-B Magneto switchboard, one local position, one toll position, at Kemptville, Ontario, 1939. L to R: M.P. Bowen, U. Patterson, M.J. Leeson, G. Hogan, Chief Operator.*

*Bell Telephone men on and around Bell Telephone Company truck, c. 1922 at Hawkesbury, Ontario, including foreman Emile Hout.*

afternoon to get back to wherever you were working, Roy would come and pick you up wherever you were, and run you up to whatever town you had to work in. He'd even come Monday morning, so you could stay over Sunday night.

Eddie Desjardins, Paul Campeau, Roy Honeywell, his daddy was the superintendent. Des Wales and myself, one time were working for a foreman by the name of Charlie L'Abbé in Hawkesbury. We all went back early to the King George Hotel in Hawkesbury Sunday evening and then we went to the hockey game. I'm not much of a hockey fan, but I went along and it was Ottawa that was playing Hawkesbury. We all got hooting and cheering and yelling for Ottawa, and got in a punch-up with people from Hawkesbury, and we all got thrown in jail—the whole gang of us. Well, then, first thing Monday morning, Charlie L'Abbé came down into the dining room and was sitting there having his breakfast and he keeps looking around and nobody

appeared. Finally he went out to the lobby and the owner was at the desk. Nobody liked Charlie L'Abbé. He was from Arnprior. The owner wasn't going to tell him anything. L'Abbé says to him, "Did my men check in yesterday?" "Oh, yes." L'Abbé says, "I suppose I've got to go up and look through their rooms and see what the hell they're up to." So finally the owner broke down and said, "Well, you won't find them in their rooms." L'Abbé says, "Where are they?" The owner says, "At the police station. They were all arrested last night." It was all over town. The Bell men were in jail! And we weren't those roughneck linemen; we were all installers—a cut above, you know!

Well, anyway, L'Abbé was mad! He came and asked us if we had any money and we all said, "No." And he had to get all his expense cheques together to go and get the money to bail us all out so we could go back to work.

I know another time they locked us all out of the King George in Hawkesbury one night. But there was a little balcony upstairs and there were posts and the posts were all carved so we climbed up the posts. They hadn't locked the balcony doors and so we got into our rooms that way.

Then there was some kind of an affair and we all decided we should have something to drink. And we took some cases of beer up to our rooms and we were drinking in our rooms. And then we began bowling with empty beer bottles. I guess it wouldn't have been too bad—except we stood them up along the stair railing, so all the broken bottles were smashing and falling into the lobby. We were having a pretty good time, but then Paul Campeau got just ridiculous. He put on his climbing spurs, and proceeds to climb up the door of my room on his spurs. We had a hell of a mess! Oh, we used to have some laughs!

The Bell men used to get off the train or the bus and head into the Ritz Hotel in Ottawa, and there'd be as many as sixty linemen down one whole side and all the tables pushed together. But you know, nobody ever got mean, generally speaking. There was always spiffs and squabbles, but it was always a laugh. "Do you know what So-and-So did? Ha-ha-ha!" Everybody in the place would knock themselves out laughing. And I'll tell you about Bell camaraderie.

*Another group of intrepids: telegraph linesmen in Glengarry at the turn of the century.*

If you're building a new pole line, first of all you'd dig all the holes and put the poles up and there's all these naked ugly poles sticking up in the air. Then you go along and you put the cross-arms up, and then you string the wire. Now, you know the poles have those round glass insulators on them and there's a ridge in them and it's up there like this and the wire coming has to lie in that ridge. Then you have another piece of wire and you put it around the insulator and tie it—you twist it around the wire that's going this way to keep it up in the air and keep it in place. Well, you stretch your wire from pole to pole to pole to pole.

In my early days as a Bell man, I'd get a farmer with a team of horses and I'd have all these wires on the whippletree and he would pull this tight with his team of horses. So what I would do is I'd climb this pole and tie my two wires in. I'd be doing it on one; Eddie'd be doing it on the next one; Paul would be on the next one. So on the days you were going to do this, the foreman would say, "I've got to make up my expenses," or "I've got to make up my time sheets," or "I've got to order material," and he'd stay at the hotel because he knew darn well what would happen . . . You had a whole bunch of these tie-wires and you'd fold them over like that and stick them over your belt down the back of your pants and then you'd go and you'd just wear your climbing spurs—no body belt, no safety strap, no hard hats in those days and most of the guys wouldn't wear gloves—so you'd go out and you'd climb the first pole and tie your two in. And it was a thing of pride to see how few steps you could come down the pole, and it came to the point where you could jump down twenty, maybe twenty-five feet and hook your spurs back in and just step off. If you could do it, and hook back in the pole just about a foot above the ground, and then just step off like King Tut, then you were something else! But then what you had to do was run past the other pole to get your next pole. If you slipped and fell and somebody passed you, it cost you the beer that night. So what you were always trying to do was run like hell to lap somebody, but everybody is laughing like a bunch of fools and you're laughing like stink. I'm telling you, you climb a lot of poles and you tie a lot of wires. The foreman was smart enough to know, "I'll get it done if I just stay away."

It was an honest-to-God friendly competition, and everybody would be laughing and, by the time you got to the end, everybody would just be lying in a heap laughing. But some of them could do fantastic things. They'd run up a pole and run right up past the end of it and do a back somersault, and come back down, and cut their spurs into the pole again.

---

1 A substance, such as calcium oxide, that has a high affinity for water and is used as a drying agent.

2 Ottawa journalist Tom Van Dusen documented the Château de Grace. "During the Depression my uncles—Gerald, Father Tom, Wilfred, Raymond Grace—decided to build a hotel. Château de Grace was erected on the Main Street of Gracefield where the old store had been for years. A new store and a barber shop were opened on the ground floor of the hotel, probably the first village "mall" in the Gatineau." Destroyed by fire.

# 18

## "The Lads from 'Paradise Springs'"

**JIMMY CUTHBERTSON, KEITH HOWARD** – Shawville, Quebec

*In 1818, the sailing vessel* Camperdown *made the ocean voyage to the new world with sixty families on board—amongst them three related Hodgins families—all bound for the Talbot Settlement in Western Upper Canada. But the long tedious journey of thirteen weeks, plagued with considerable sickness and insufficient food, caused considerable friction amongst the travellers. When Montreal was reached, there were many desertions from the Talbot party, including "Daddy Tom" Hodgins who then met up with John Dale and made the trek into Clarendon, Quebec.*

*In 1823, Thomas Hodgins brought in his wife and family, and started to clear a farm near Dale. It was about this time, too, that Thomas began writing to his friends and relatives in Ireland glowing accounts of his new-found land. One clearing in his second lot he described as "the nearest approach to Paradise to be found anywhere." For many years afterwards, this little field at the north end of the Hodgins farm was always called "Paradise."*

*In quick succession, other Irishmen followed Hodgins to "Paradise:" McDowells, Brownlees, Sparlings, Hobbs, Richards, Pearsons, Eberts, Telfers, Halls, Armstrongs, and Starks. Together, they, their descendants and all kinds of other newcomers cleared the rich land rolling riverwards and established the Anglo-Celt communities of Western Quebec.*

*Jimmy Cuthbertson is the fifth James Thomas Cuthbertson at Shawville, Quebec. His family was part of that early 1820 Scottish enclave on the Front Road at Bristol, Quebec, a settlement which included the McFarlands, Cowleys, Armstrongs, Orrs, Umsteads, Drummonds. His mother was Elsie Mary Hobbs, daughter of Robert Hobbs, again a family of earliest settlement in the Pontiac. As was usual in those days, the families were large and descendants numerous, his father's family having eleven and his mother's eight. Jimmy Cuthbertson spent his working life on the family farm just outside of Shawville. An abiding interest in, knowledge and love of horses threads itself through his interview. Now in his seventies he lives in retirement in the village with his wife, the former Maisie Richardson of Wakefield, Quebec, whom he married in 1946.*

**B**EING SCOTTISH, I was always taught, "It's not what you make. It's what you save." Mother was Bella Starks from Starks Corners. And her mother was a Cuthbertson.

And I have often wondered, did they marry for love in those early days or did they just marry for a mate? Somebody to do the dishes and the laundry, or whatever? For instance, out in the Yarm settlement back of Shawville, the Richardsons all married the Hodgins and the Hodgins all married the Richardsons and that's as far as it went because they had to walk to court.

Eldred Mee's father used to drive to Ottawa where he courted and married a Pettapiece girl. He didn't have a good "road horse." He had what they used to call a "third horse." You see, in those days they drove three horses abreast on a grain binder, and this and that machine, and they always called it "the third horse." The other two horses would probably have weighed seventeen or eighteen hundred pounds.

*A proud and stalwart group of the County of Pontiac Agricultural Society, 1909, representing many of the Anglo-Celt pioneering and founding families of the area around Paradise Springs. Front, L to R: William Thompson, James Steele, James Amm. Second row, seated L to R: Andrew Grant, John McVeigh, Thomas McDowell, William Hodgins, Hamilton Taber, R.W. Hodgins. Third row, standing, L to R: Dr. John Armstrong, G.F. Hodgins, Edward Thomas Brownlee, William McFarlane, W.C. Young, John Caldwell. Standing at rear, L to R: Andrew Sly, Joe Brownlee, Thomas Edes, John Stanton, Joe Kelly, Fred Thomas, Otto Bretzlaff. Inset photo of William Clark, first president in 1856.*

The "third horse" was also the driver. They'd hitch him up to go to town with the cutter and the buggy. They put him on to help the other team draw the binder. They took "the third horse" to court a girl. It was a little lighter. Anyway, Eldred Mee, he'd go to Ottawa for a day and he'd court for a whole day 'til his horse rested up because it had to go fifty miles home again to Shawville. When he went down to court her in Ottawa, the first thing he asked her, "Do you want to be buried with my people?" And she said, "Yes."

My dad told me that when he was a small boy, when they lived on the farm at Bristol, they used to cut down the trees, but you could hardly sell the logs because they were worth peanuts. Hemlock bark was worth more than the good lumber was. You could sell the hemlock bark—if you cut it in four-foot lengths and bundled it—to people that had apiaries, eh, and for smoking and for making smoked meat. I guess there was a factory someplace in Ottawa that bought it for smoking things, too.

He also told me that they used to cut down the trees to get the land to work, eh, and you'd take timothy seed and clover seed—that was the only two, there was no alfalfa then—just timothy and clover seed and you'd sprinkle it on the leaves. And he said the next year there'd be timothy as high as your head.

And he also said then the next year you had to scythe that, because there was about as many raspberry canes as there was hay. And he said they used to coil the hay on top of the stumps—there was no such a thing as rakes of any kind. And they drew it in with a cart—but he never told me whether they used a horse or an oxen.

His job on Saturday was to get in there and pull the raspberry canes out of the hay because the sheep would have the wool all pushed back on their necks trying to get at the hay through the prickly raspberry canes. So that was his job—to pull the raspberry canes so the sheep could get to the hay, and so the wool wouldn't be damaged by the prickly raspberry canes. Fred Rose was an old German guy—his dad used to go with one of my aunts—but Rose used to go down to Grandpa Cuthbertson's place to court one of the girls. There was a big flat rock there and Grandpa said to him, "Lookit, young lad, if you're going to

stay here all night, pull your buggy in front of the flat rock so the sheep can get to the grass."

The gypsies used to steal the hens, but they had a technique. Everybody's hens were running loose in the barnyard and they would soften a grain of corn and put a string through it, and then they'd dry it so it wouldn't pull out, and they'd throw it out to a hen that was passing, and she'd grab that, and they'd reel her in like a fish. A hen can't bring anything back up again, you see.

I was talking to this fellow, Walter Moffat, one time and he had this nice little "third horse," but it had the heaves. And Moffat said to some of the guys here in Shawville on Saturday night, "Let's go down and trade horses with the gypsies." So away they went and traded horses with the gypsies, and they got this nice chestnut. Oh, man, that was a real horse! And the next morning they got up and hitched him up and oh, what a circus! You couldn't drive him. He was crazy.

He was doped you see. Old Bill McDonald had a mix, eh?

And with those heavers, well, he'd shove fat pork down their throats. It would block them for a while— twenty-four hours— 'til he sold it. Then it was somebody else's heaving. McDonald was a horse trader. At one time he had racehorses. He had about eighteen head of horses. He was well-to-do. He was an extremely good veterinarian, but they said he was in partners with Dr. Bell from Kingston[1]. He sold his share out to Dr. Bell and Bell took off from there and made a fortune. But Bill could mix medicine for a horse like it was going out of style. But then Bill, after his wife died, got into the alcohol, and race horses, and everything, and went broke.

Now Harper Rennicks was the blacksmith in Shawville for years. He knew horses, but he wasn't smart enough for Bill McDonald. Bill had this nice driving mare, Standardbred, pretty as a picture. Bill would travel with ten or twelve horses coming behind him tied to a wagon—he went to "gypsy" after he sold to Dr. Bell. So anyway, he came into town with this nice brown mare—Doll he called her. And he'd go in to Harper's, and scout around, talking to Harper. Harper hit him up for a trade—he had this old scab horse in the back shed there. He said, "Bill, I'll make

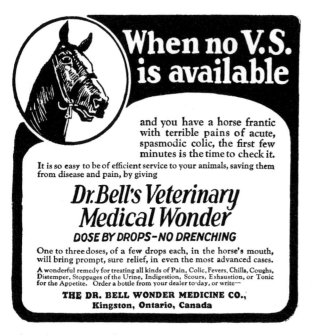

*An advertisement from Dr. Robert Bell's 1934 catalogue. Running to sixty pages, it contained advice for the "prevention, diagnosis and treatment of common diseases of livestock," with illustrations, lists of medicines available with prices, and testimonials. Amongst his clients Bell counted: J.R. Booth Company, E.B. Eddy Company, Col. R.S. McLaughlin of Oshawa, M.J. O'Brien of Renfrew, Silverwood's Dairy in Toronto and the University of Alberta.*

you a trade." Bill said, "No, you couldn't drive this mare." And he drove off, and wouldn't talk to Harper. But a few days after McDonald came back again to see Harper—what he was doing—and Harper hit him up for another trade."Oh, no I don't want to trade Doll," McDonald said. Harper said, "Come on, trade horses." McDonald said, "You can't drive this mare, Harper." "By the living Jesus, if you can drive her, I can drive her." "Well," McDonald said, "Give me a hundred dollars and I'll trade you." So Harper gave him the hundred dollars and Bill put Doll in the stable and picked up this old scab and went away. And he didn't come back for a couple of weeks.

He came in and Reuben Harris was working there and he said to Reuben, "How's Doll this morning?" Harper's blacksmith's shop was front and the stable was behind and Reuben said, "Go and look at Doll. She's the full length of the stall." So just then Harper came in and he was hopping mad and raising Cain. He said, "Look at this horse. She's got sore feet." So McDonald said "Well, give me fifty dollars and I'll trade back. I told you two or three times you couldn't drive her."

So, anyway, to make a long story short, Old Bill McDonald went out into the stable and got in alongside of Doll, and pulled a needle out of his pocket and he needled her right in there and sewed

*Entrance to one of the great agricultural fairs of the Ottawa Valley, c. 1910.*

up both her feet. Then he said to Harper, "I'll be back in twenty minutes." He came back in twenty minutes, put the harness on Doll and she took off like new. How many times did he trade Doll and take her back? Nobody will ever know. All across the country, Old Bill McDonald made a fortune on a crippled horse.

I remember, too, one time I was showing horses at the Shawville Fair. Kundle from Renfrew had a nice black-brown, a chocolate pair of roadsters. My!

*One of the many "Sheriff Sloans of Vinton," Pontiac Sheriff Joseph Dominic Sloan drove his nationally famous covered wagon to Expo '67 with his prize horses. The paintings of the Father of Confederation, Queen Victoria and County Buildings on the two sides of the wagon were done by Mel Kensley of Campbell's Bay. The provincial crests around the body of the wagon were printed by a "guest," who spent some time in the guardianship of Sheriff Sloan. He is flanked by Campbell's Bay Centennial Queens, Sheila Bowie and Joanne Smith.*

they were a snapping pair, Seven Up and Wings of the Morning. He said they had both been runaways. They were on the way to Scott's fox farm on Calumet Island when he got them. (In those days, they bred foxes for the fur and they'd buy horses for meat for the foxes, so that's what they always used to say, "Ship them to the fox farm.") But anyway, he had this nice little horse, Wings of the Morning, a beautiful horse. In the stall he'd always have a blanket behind his horse, and the horse was always lying on the straw, and he'd say that the horse was tired. But anyway, he never would bring that horse into the road class—it was a road horse—until we were just about ready to judge. But before he'd bring him in he'd needle him, froze its feet. Then he could go, boy!

But the judge caught on to him this time, and the last time I saw Wings of the Morning he made about three or four trips around the barn and the judge kept shouting, "Drive on. Drive on." And the needle wore off, and the horse fell right down on his knees, and they had to run to him, and take the check off, and he hobbled out the gate and I never saw him again.

Clive Smart had some nice horses, road horses. There were quite a few nice horses around in those days. Lawson Corrigan used to have a good horse and Larry Hynes. My dad bought a nice little black mare from Larry Hynes. Hiram Strutt used to race horses at Aylmer and different places. I think he went as far as Toronto with one. What they're showing today for road horses are not road horses. They're rejects from the racetrack. A horse on the racetrack today has got to go about 156 or he's just a hayburner. If he's in fourth place he gets no money for it, so, they get rid of him. Mennonites buy those horses; they come up there to Connaught, bring a truck, buy all these horses, drive them back down to Kitchener-Waterloo.

My dad used to raise Percheron horses. He always used John Horner's horses.[2] Well, ninety-nine per cent of the time it was John's horses. He was Irish, eh? I remember, in those days they led the stallion around to different farms. Those days you'd get a colt for, say, six dollars—service fee for the colt, eh? But my dad and John, they had a special thing going for themselves. Fee was ten dollars and, if your mare had a foal, you paid ten dollars and, if the mare didn't foal, you didn't pay anything, that was their terms.

Some of them was kidding John Horner one time in the barber's shop and they said, "You're doing pretty well with Jimmy Cuthbertson." "Oh, yes," John said. But then John decided he wanted to advertise his stud horse. So I remember John Horner coming down to our place—we were cutting corn at the time—and he got after my dad to bring his colt out to show her. But my dad wasn't interested in showing horses. So John Horner told him, "I want to advertise my horse. We'll have a class where you bring in your mare and foal, and my stud horse will be there to show the results of good breeding." And it was good advertising.

I can hear John Horner yet. He talked loud. I remember the first car wreck we ever heard tell of. Horner came to our place after our mare proved to be with foal by his stud to get his ten dollars. And, you know, they'd stand and talk for an hour-and-a-half, maybe two hours—time wasn't too valuable in those days. Anyway the story went on and on, they were talking about the car wreck and John took my father for a drive. And they went off the road—and I can still hear John saying in a very loud voice, "YOU COULDN'T SEE NOTHING FOR BLUE-BERRIES!"

My grandfather was ninety-seven when he died. And he was only sick about two weeks before he died. Fifty-one years ago I went over the mountain to Wakefield to court a girl. I came round the corner there at that little brick house and I saw this road going up to the right, so I thought, "that's the road I'll take." So I took off in there and, when I come to, I was right up against a barn. I didn't know where I was, but I said, "I want to get out of here before the farmer gets up." I didn't know who it was. It was past midnight. Anyway, I got out of there and I thought, "I turned right in here so I'll turn right again when I go out." So I kept on going 'til I came to a road. It was a terrible road. Crazy. And the stones and the rocks! I was driving a '30s model Durant. There was

*Shawville's Main Street, c. late 1920s. This photo must have been taken on a Sunday, because on Saturday nights you couldn't move on the streets.*

one part I went over was still corduroy. And when you went up over this hill there was sharp rocks sticking out of it, and I'd lose a tire every time I crossed it. It was terrible. But it was worth it all! And I thought, it was you wanting to get buried with my people!

My dad had steam-engine papers. James Cuthbertson was running the electric plant in Shawville up there round where the fire hall is now. There was only the two men. I don't know who the other guy was with him, but my father said when it started up there was no voltage regulator—it was before they came in—he said when they started up the people would have bright lights. But then he said it got darker and darker and darker, the more people turned on their lights. He said the people at the far end of town only had a red light that was wavering up and down. The fellow beside the power plant, he couldn't keep bulbs in, and the fellow at the other end, he only had the red light. It would get red as the juice faded. He said they'd come down to him and raise Cain because they weren't getting enough power—but the machine wouldn't put out any more power, so what were you going to do?

Oh, yes I remember in W.A. Hodgins' store in Shawville there used to be a box stove at the back and there was a tin shield around it to keep your trousers from running up against the stove. He had benches at the back of that. The farmers would come from Ladysmith or wherever with a load of wood and they could bring in their lunch and they'd have a tin pail—that's what they had their tea in—and they could put it on the stove and have it warmed. And W.A. would make sure to have a good fire on when he knew they were coming. They'd sit in there. Oh, the place would be rolling! You see, in this country around Shawville, there was never too much bush—it was all cleared—and it was great farmland with good crops and a lot of hay. But the old farmers back of Shawville—back of the tracks we called it—the farms weren't as good and they used to bring wood down to Shawville and sell it or trade it for hay to feed their cattle and horses. Now on Saturdays, I've seen it there in W.A.'s yard on Saturday when you could hardly get through for sleighs and horses, and wood, and hay, and—you name it. That's when the sheds were all around the store. Yes, I'd say fifty-five years ago things were booming.

*Keith Howard gives us a memorable picture of "growing up in the village." Shawville was English and Orange entirely, a service centre for Pontiac County. Mr. Howard was born in 1922, of prolific and productive Anglo-Celt first settlers in Quebec. His father, Henry Howard, married Lila Horner; his paternal grandfather, Sam Horner, wed Ambrosina Murphy. On his maternal side he descends from Hodgins.*

*In 1949, Mr. Howard married the girl with whom he spent a hazardous night in a terrible snowstorm on Highway 148, the former June Wheeler of Ottawa. He is the cousin of that great Shawville character who appears in* Laughing All the Way Home, *G.A. Howard, master of spoonerisms and one-liners. After several decades of service with Electrolux and London Life, Mr. Howard moved G.A. Howard's old office from Shawville to Sand Bay, Quebec, transformed it into a lovely cottage on the Ottawa where he and his wife, now both retired, live for six months of the year.*

I grew up in the village. My father was a stationary engineer, served in the First World War. I went to school in Shawville and I went off to do mining of the Ottawa Valley in 1939 when I was seventeen years old. Oh, I didn't work in the mines; I worked around the recreation centre in Duparquet, Quebec, thirty-five miles from Noranda. I swept the bowling alley, but I found the country a little bit too wild for myself. At seventeen I was protected pretty well by my mother's apron strings, and I didn't know whether a bowling ball was coming down the alley or a green beer bottle. There was every nationality in that recreation centre. So I decided I'd better come back south again. I worked on a farm over at Rupert, just outside of Osgoode, in the Gatineau for a couple of summers. Then I came back to Shawville. I drove

Ralph Hodgins opened his brickyard in 1888 and thereby put his imprint on the whole Pontiac, even today dotted with dozens of the large sturdy brick houses so characteristic of the area. Frequently, sleighs were loaded with Hodgins bricks and taken across the ice of the Ottawa River to the Ontario side so that people there also could "move up to brick." Very little remains of the brickworks, but "Brickyard" Hodgins' big house stands solidly today on Centre Street, Shawville. Hodgins' first grandchild, Frank Finnigan, was born there.

One of Shawville's great brick buildings, Proudfoot's Hotel on Main Street. For many years it was the stop-over for the Valley's travelling salesmen who showed their wares in upstairs display rooms. Destroyed by fire, 1980s.

a truck delivering slabs for Bert Horner, son of Big John Horner of Radford, Quebec.

Then I left Shawville, went to Ottawa to live with another sister, Eva Howard. I was breaking ice on the sidewalk on Bank Street in January 1942 when I said to Gerry Sutton, my friend from Shawville, "Insect,"—they called him for a nickname—I said, "There must be an easier way to make a living than this." "Well," he said, "what do you suggest?" I said, "Let's join the army." He said, "Let's." So we left all the tools lying right on Bank Street, the axe and the shovel and the pick-axe, and we went up to the corner of Metcalfe and Sparks and we joined the army.

He went to Petawawa and I went to Cornwall and we never saw one another for five years. I served four years overseas in the army and it wasn't all a rough time. It was a good time, too. At my age of nineteen, I needed discipline and I got it. The army just gave me exactly what I wanted, what I needed at that time. Discipline was the answer. When I came back from overseas I stayed drunk for about five months. I tried to find myself at Sand Bay, with my sister Eva, who had a cottage there. I went up and down the river many times hooting and hollering. Then I took a mechanic's apprenticeship at Myers Motors in 1946. My brother-in-law was the service manager there and he helped me try to get re-established. And I guess I had some mechanic's blood in me. I liked it and it liked me.

I remember when G.A. Howard and Byron Horner brought a train car load of wild horses and they arrived in Bristol, Quebec, at the railroad station there. And G.A. and Byron never had a hold on them, never had any kind of harness on them. And they chased them from there to the Pontiac House in Shawville and they got them into the stable in different stalls. I guess they were sold to the local farmers. G.A. was smoking cigars and Byron Horner had a big Sifton hat on. And the two of them were out in the yard with this one wild horse, and he was jumping. He was going up in the east and coming down in the west. I guess one horse wouldn't jump very much—I didn't see this happen—but I think G.A. or Byron, one or the other, put the whip to him inside the stables. Now they didn't mark him at all

because they had a blanket on him. They put a blanket on him first; they didn't want to mark him. But I'll tell you, when they took the blanket off him and took him outside he was raring to go.

I remember one time my brother Wellington and I—he's dead now—went picking potatoes up at John Ellard Horner's, just past Radford. The potatoes were planted right on the front of the house between where the highway is now and the house. I always think of that when I go by. But anyway, I was getting twenty-five cents a day and we picked potatoes all day long and that night my brother and I were walking home to Shawville, a little better than three miles. We went to go by the old school in Radford and, so help me God, there was a mother bear and two cubs—they'd been eating the crumbs I guess from the students' lunch. Anyway we stopped in our tracks and my brother said to me, "Don't run. Whatever you do, don't run. Turn and walk away very slow." I did what I was told; my brother did likewise. We walked back not very far to Big John Horner's and we had to tell him the story inside the house and he said, "Well," he said, "I guess Lloyd had better drive you down to Shawville." So Lloyd took the harness down from the nails and drove us to Shawville.

Walter Corrigan lived down the Seventh Line a few miles from Big John Horner's. Corrigan had a bush on the Seventh Line, a maple bush, and he used to tap his trees there, and he had an evaporator. There was a gang of us from school and on Sunday, regularly, we used to walk up the railway tracks and then we'd go back to the Seventh Line and fill up our bottles. We carried liquor bottles tied with rope over our shoulders, and we'd fill up the bottles with maple syrup. I don't know if Corrigan knew that we were doing this or not. Maybe he tried to catch us but he never caught us.

As you know, Shawville is a very English town. It's a very Protestant town, and there was about seven Protestant churches when I was a kid, and they were all active. So, on Sunday morning when everybody'd be in church—the odd time I wasn't—I used to go down to Tatterson's Hill, just down in the gully below Shawville, by the millpond there where Reuben Smith kept his bees. They had big fines then. I think twenty-five dollars for disturbing the bees. We used to sneak up to the box of bees and very quietly lift the lid off the box, take out the comb section of honey, both sides of the box full length, and then we'd put the lid back on, very quietly. Everything was done very slowly, and we'd walk into the bush very quietly, and we'd eat honey until our eyes would stick out. We'd be sick. We'd be sick. And then we always put the section back in the box, and I don't know if Reuben to this day (he's deceased now), ever figured why one section of honey was always short in the box.

I was only stung once. A honeybee can hit you as many times as he likes, but he hit me once between the eyes and, so help me God! I turned flat on my back! I fell down flat on my back, just like being hit with a sledge.

*An important historical memorial stone erected in Litchfield Cemetery near Shawville.*

The first day I went to school in Shawville I got a trimmin' from Rita McNair, my teacher. I think she lined up six of us on the bench and we all got a trimmin'. For stinking feet. I was wearing gum rubbers at the time and my feet were stinking—so she said. Everybody got it. I don't know what the reasons were for the other fellows. There were six of us. Alan Crisp was one of them. He used to run Dewbury's Stick-With-Us store where Norris Horner had his first clothing store on the main street. Right near where Fraser's are now. I didn't like school after that. I was smart. I used to win the spelling matches and I used to win the reading matches, but I never liked school after that.

I learned to speak French at Shawville High School. Thanks to Reggie Scobie, now deceased. He taught me French in the days before it became fashionable, or compulsory. The inspector used to come round to Shawville and he used to say to Reggie, "Who's that little French fellow down there?" That was me. When I went overseas, I was the one who helped the fellows in Belgium because I could speak enough French to get by. As years went by, I used to visit Reggie on my way to Sand Bay at Portage-du-Fort where he lived, and just talked French once in a while. He got a great kick out of that. There was three of us left Shawville being able to speak French. One was Leslie Dean, who used to be the postmaster, Alan Young and myself.

G.A. Howard was an amazing character.[3] My father was better educated than G.A. Howard was. He didn't have the way with him, he couldn't handle orders the way G.A. could. G.A. was a born natural. He sold Model T Fords. With "rubber bumpers" and "self commencers." "baboon tires." Now I used to ride a bicycle all winter. It was a girl's bicycle, so it had a small sprocket on it, and it had lots of power. I had a ski on the front wheel and rope on the back tire, like a chain, wrapped around the tire to give me more traction in the snow. G.A. used to hide in Caldwell's Hardware, and he'd try to catch me. Of course, I was past before he'd time to come out the door. He didn't approve of me riding on the sidewalk. It was a danger, he claimed.

I was still drinking in 1946 when Goldie McDowell was the mayor of Shawville. Anyway, there was Bud Hynes, Willie Harris, Jerry Strutt and I, and you couldn't buy any beer in Shawville. You could buy porter, but you couldn't buy any beer. So we went down to Quyon and we bought twenty-four. We came back to the old Clarendon Inn and we threw the twenty-four underneath the table and we proceeded to drink. So Percy Russett—now deceased—he was there, and Clarence Hodgins—we used to call him "Gypsy Clarence"—he had a broken arm in a cast. So

he was standing at the counter and Percy was talking to him and, I guess, he started roughing him up a little bit. So I jumped up quickly and said, "Maybe you'd like to try somebody who hasn't got a cast on his arm?" So anyway, as the story goes, we wrecked Hodgins' drinking spot, the Clarendon Inn. And Mrs. Erskine Hodgins, who was a Smith from Constance Bay, she came out of the kitchen and she blamed it all on me, but I said I wasn't guilty. Mayor Goldie McDowell was in there, but he hid on his hands and knees behind the bar. Yes, on his hands and

*Shawville Hockey Club, Champions of the Pontiac League, 1932. Back row, L to R: J.H. Stewart, B.C. "Bert" Horner, J.H. Findlay, C.A. Horner, C.H. Horner, G.A. Howard, G.G. McDowell. Middle row, L to R: U.S. Hodgins, H.M. Dale, J.A.W. Hayes, E.G.W. Chamberlain. Bottom row: K.E. Sereney, R.A. Carson.*

*Like McCool's great frame summer hotel at Fort William, Quebec, and Scobie House at Norway Bay, Burnham Hall at Norway Bay was the destination for half a century of travellers and summer holidayers. Leta Finnigan Horner remembered a trip, late 1920s, all the way from North Bay to Burnham Hall with sisters, brothers, girl friends, and boy friends. "When we got there, my oldest brother, Frank, told us all exactly where we would sleep," she recalled. Photo late 1920s, early '30s.*

knees behind the bar, his head covered up with his hands. And Larry Hynes was in the fight, too, but he disappeared, and then he came back and he threw a lawn mower—a real lawn mower—through the coloured glass, through the window of the front door. We made a shambles of that place for sure.

So the next day I came downtown and Al McKeague, the barber, was doing a shaving job on Percy Russett. He was lying in the chair and I walked over and I said, "For very little I'd hang one on you right now." And he said, "Hold on, hold on. We'll go and have a beer together." So that's what we did, exactly what we did, back to the old Clarendon Inn.

I remember years ago Steve McCoy and "Redtop" Dale used to fight rough-and-tumble in the Pontiac House yard, every Tuesday and Saturday night. That was the entertainment for all the town. They all ran down the street to witness it. Steve was

a trained boxer. Oh, yes, he was a Golden Gloves champion. He used to be scientific with his boxing and "Redtop" Dale was a rough-and-tumble guy, no holds barred. Many's a time they went down, but they always came up still fighting mad, and then they went and ate hamburgs together in Smart's restaurant. The only man that could cook hamburgs without a big fire. Asa Smart. His father, "Buck-sharner" Wellington Smart, had a meat shop beside the restaurant. I won't say if he used to invite various women into his walk-in freezer, but he used to be accused, lots of times, of holding his hand on the scale.

But Asa Smart always had fresh hamburgers. "Judas priest!" That was his favourite saying. And he could make a hamburger—so help me, God, I ate hamburger overseas in Holland that weren't near as good as Asa Smart's hamburgers. I often thought of

Asa when I was eating Spam. But Asa Smart's restaurant didn't pass the cleanliness inspection. One night, "Redtop" Dale, down from the skating rink, gripped a big knife and hit a pile of buns on the counter at Asa's, and the cockroaches, so help me Jesus! they all flew! and they all went up the wall and Asa said, "Oh, Judas Priest! Did you have to do that?"

Somebody told me—and I think it may have been Bob Horner—he said that one time the pea soup had black spots in it, and he asked Asa what they were, and Asa said. "Judas Priest! Those are just dark peas."

I wonder how the Canadians ever won the war because there was so much shenanigans going on. I'm very fortunate in that I have a reunion every two years now—it used to be three. The 45th General Transport Company. We organized in Camp Borden in 1942 and I went overseas with the unit and stayed with them all the time and, in 1961, a bunch of the fellows got together just outside of Camp Borden at Barrie, and then the following year we had a reunion. I guess the first reunion was 1963, with about a hundred guys there. We had been through England and we stayed in England together for a couple of years. Then we went into the Spartan Scheme, the biggest scheme that was ever held on the continent or in England, and we trained for the Dieppe Raid. We didn't go on the Dieppe Raid in 1942. Why didn't we go? There was too many troops. Then on June 6th, 1944, came D-Day. So I went in not so long after D-Day.

In the Spartan Scheme we transported the South Saskatchewan Regiment. They were the ones that were almost wiped out in the Dieppe Raid. But we also did some fun things. We were sent on a scheme to waterproof vehicles so they could go in the water at the landing at Dieppe. We were up in the north of England, involved with some "ducks" and "weasels"—they call them that—they're mechanical machines. But we got a little bored at night so we went around to see if we could find any chicken houses in the north of England. We found some chicken houses and we stole some chickens, and we put the stolen chickens up the trees. But the cops came after us. The cops came and searched all around the bivouac area that we were camped in. They couldn't find the chickens, and later we had a chicken bouillon. Better than bully beef, I tell you!

And I remember being once with the American soldiers in northern England. It was the blackout, pitch dark and the Americans were playing crap on the streets of England using flashlights. We could see the flashlights, that's all. They were Negro-Americans playing crap in the dark on the streets of England and you could see their white teeth now and again in the gleam of a flashlight.

Hughie McHenry, my driver mechanic, used to drive the last truck in our section. One time when he had a load of the South Saskatchewan Regiment in England on the Spartan Scheme, he drove right into this jam factory, the only wooden building in England. Yes, right into the middle of a jam factory and the whole South Saskatchewan Regiment yelled out, "Hit it again, Canada! Hit it again!" I was at the front and I went back to see what it was all about. It was a big shambles. A lot of English jam all over the place.

I was out West in 1979 when I decided to look for Hughie McHenry, my driver mechanic. I went to the Legion in North Battleford where he lived in Saskatchewan and I asked a girl bartender there if she knew Hughie McHenry. She said, "I don't know him, but the two fellows sitting there would know." So I went over and introduced myself to the two fellows at the table and I sat down and they said, "Well, before you start talking about Hughie McHenry, maybe you could tell us some stories of World War II." So I told them about Hughie ramming the jam factory. One of them said to me then, "Oh, yes, we've heard that story before. You are in the right place. But Hughie has moved up to Prince Albert from Battleford." To this day I never saw him again.

I can go down the Main Street of Shawville and just tell you every place as though it was still there. Like the old blacksmith shop, Harper Rennick's, down where the Kodak Express Company is now. At the corner of Victoria and Main Street. The old post office is the town hall now. And Proudfoots' huge hotel burnt down. The Canadian Tire used to be Clark Caldwell's Hardware and Joe Him's Restaurant.

Lloyd Hodgins furniture department, that's in now where McKinley's used to have a freezer building. The Hynes funeral parlour was at the corner of Victoria and Main Street. Old George Hynes had a vault up in the village cemetery across the road from my home. So we used to play in that vault. We used to take the lid off and get in.

The old swimming hole? Well, we had built a dam, Billy Hodgins and Teddy Morrison, Gerry Strutt and Ronnie Masson—now they're all gone. Ronnie was killed in the war. He was the first Canadian killed. So when the June exams would be out in the old school, the Victoria Street School, we used to run from there down to the old swimming hole. We used to run a hundred yards, maybe less, and we'd start to shed off the clothes and, by the time we'd hit the water, we'd be in bare skin. Then the girls would come and pick up our clothes, and run, and hide them all in the bushes. We had a hell of a time. Oh, it was cold! It was all spring water. It was a toss-up whether to call us Angus or Agnes when we hit the water.

When I was a kid growing up in Shawville, on Hallowe'en night the favourite pastime was to see how many outdoor toilets you could pick up—some of them were two-holed, some of them were one-holed, and the odd one was three-holed. And we used to take them off their footings and pile them at the corner of the banks and the post office and the grocery store—right in the middle of Main Street. The odd time we'd set them on fire. And then people would have to come the next day and pick out their own toilets, and get them home again.

One Hallowe'en night they were putting the water works in in the back street of Shawville near the old curling rink. They had all the ditches dug, and right beside me in Shawville was where Fred Richardson lived and the old Scholastic—I guess it used to be a school at one time—Jim Caldwell lived there. Jack Storey lived there, right beside the Anglican Church. It's tore down now and that's where Lloyd Hodgins' garage is now. So, now Fred Richardson was a great guy to raise pigs. The place was so clean you could eat off the floor, no fooling. Anyway, Hallowe'en time came along and we let the

pigs out. And we chased them. We chased them down the street and we chased them into the ditch on the back street next to the curling rink. One pig ran from there, and he seemed to know his way home. We ran him up towards the Anglican Church and the Anglican Church which had a fence, an iron fence right across the front, and it was made like a cross and in the middle was a white thistle head. And the pig ran into that thing with great gusto and it turned its four feet up. Knocked it out colder than a nit. Fred never did find out who let his pigs out that Hallowe'en, but we didn't kill any of them—just gave them a good run for their money. They lost a few pounds, no doubt.

"King Billy" worked for Harold Hayes on the outskirts of Shawville; he was a farm helper. I forget his real name now, but he rode the white horse and he rode him well and he could beat the drum, too, I'll tell you. He could beat the drum with both hands—no trouble at all. But, much to everyone's surprise, he was a Roman Catholic.

For years and years they kept the Catholics from building a church in Shawville. Well, they still don't have one. They threatened anybody that would sell property to them. Lee Hodgins, I guess, was the owner of some property and he was told by the town council, I understand, that anybody who would lease any property or who would sell any property to the Roman Catholics to build a church, he'd be tarred and feathered right on the main street of Shawville. So I guess there was no Catholic Church in Shawville and there still isn't.

You know, that old Jake Dunlap[4] story. He met this guy at the Quyon Fair and this guy was bugging him; he wanted to come and see him or meet him somewhere or have a visit with him, have a talk with him, and finally Jake said, "Well, okay, we'll make a date. Meet me in front of the Roman Catholic Church in Shawville on Sunday."

I think I can tell you a story about the late Dr. Bruce Horner. It was when they were building the new skating rink in Shawville, covered. The old one belonged to Ebert Richardson. And they were building a new one in the Exhibition Grounds. So I guess the rumour was around that the money collection wasn't going very good. They had a big thermometer in front of the town hall, a homemade job, and, as the money came in, they raised the thermometer and the mercury was getting only a little bit higher and a little bit higher. So, anyway, the story goes that the Sisters of the Grey Cross were going to contribute quite a bit of money to the building fund for the rink. So Dr. Bruce Horner said, "Over my dead body." And he opened up his wallet, and that was the end of any R.C. contribution.

Now I'll tell you about New Year's Eve, 1948. With my bride-to-be at that time coming up from Ottawa. We drove as far as Luskville into a big heavy snow storm. I was driving a '31 Oldsmobile Coupe, had chains on the back wheels. Just about the R.C. Church at Luskville, we went to come through the snow and we met a gang from Shawville coming down, so we helped them through the snow. I got out and helped Ray Hobin and the gang of fellows that was with him. After they left, it came our turn to come through there and we got halfway through and we got stuck. So we spent all night on the road at Luskville. In the car. It was storming so bad you couldn't see out at all. I shovelled the car out three times during the night. You could hear the wolves howling at the foot of the mountain. I told my wife-to-be that they were just dogs. I had a brand-new suit on and a brand-new felt hat. I lost the felt hat.

Well, Ralph Gordon was ploughing the roads at that time. We got out of the car before he came along—in the morning about eight o'clock. We got out of the car and we ploughed our way through deep, deep snow, up to our waists, and the wind was still blowing, so I had my top coat over my wife-to-be, her head, and we went up to this Lusk house. They had two chickens on the table and I got a pair of dry socks and fresh underwear, all dry clothes. The next day the Lusks decided to hitch up their horses and try to pull my car out of the snow. But we discovered it had got wet, wouldn't start. So we pulled the car up as far as the Lusk house where, with all my mechanical experience, I got the engine all dried out. We were all in the Lusk house when Ralph Gordon came by, and ploughed the road. He covered our car completely, and shoved it right over to the fence. He didn't see the car for snow! So now we were really buried.

How did we survive the night in the car? Well, it wasn't real cold. It was one of those big heavy storms where it isn't really cold. We were lucky. We ran the engine, off and on, 'til four o'clock in the morning, 'til it wouldn't turn anymore. It was all snowed in. We'd have been found dead in the morning. If I hadn't got out and shovelled us out, we would have smothered.

Anyway, the next day we put about a gallon of Prestone in the rad and took off for Shawville. We got up as far as Charlie Hodgins, now deceased, on the old highway, and the snow banks were at least twelve feet high. More than horses had been down, cut a path through the snow. This D.P.[5]—we called them D.P.s at the time—he was running horseback. So the horse and the rider were coming towards us and the horse jumped into the side of my car. So I wheeled quickly to the right and ran smack into the back of another car buried in the snow. Jesus Christ!

Anyway, we got to Shawville about four o'clock in the afternoon. We'd started out from Ottawa about nine o'clock the night before. My mother was lying on the old couch in Shawville and she was pretty sick. She didn't know that we were coming and nobody knew at the other end that we hadn't made it. So nobody was worried about us. We were on our own. Anyway, in July, the next summer, somebody found my hat down on the shores of the Ottawa River.

I was overseas a year-and-a-half when I finally discovered the joys of liquor. On my twenty-first birthday. The boys took me out. Oh, yes. I was down in Reigate, England, and I started to smoke and drink at the same time. I tried to straighten myself up when I came back because I knew I couldn't possibly live the same kind of life as I'd been living in the past in the army. Not in Shawville. I didn't know where the stills were but I did know where the bars were. The only still I knew was that bootleg place up near Wakefield.

I had no licence to drive until I came back from overseas in '46, but I learned to drive an old Model T Ford that Bert Horner owned—an old Chev

Sedan—they're good on the road. I learned to drive when I was thirteen. I could drive anything at all. So, anyway, I was driving a truck for Bert Horner. Bert wanted me to go down and see about this big stud horse that he owned down in Beechgrove opposite Merrifield's store. I said, "Okay, whatever you say, Bert." So a Henderson fellow was coming with me, not Sherwood Henderson, but his brother. Anyway, Bert said, "If this horse is down in the stall, just shoot him and leave him there." I wouldn't have anything to do with shooting a horse, so this Henderson fellow came along with me. We got down there, told the guy who we were, and so on. He said, "Well, the horse is lying down in the box stall." We went out to the barn and sure enough the horse was down. Very, very thin. All you could see was ribs. I stepped outside. I heard a shot inside, and that was the end of the horse. Henderson shot the horse and left him there. So the guy said, "Don't tell me you're going to leave him there." I said, "Yes, he was there when we came and he's still there when we're leaving."

So we were coming back and right at Beechgrove, right on the crook in the road there, we side-swiped another truck. I didn't stop. When we got home and went looking for Bert in the Clarendon Hotel, I told him all about the accident I had had. He said, "Did you stop?" I said, "No. I didn't stop." "Well," he said, "that's the right thing to do. Whatever you do, don't stop when you've no licence to drive."

I remember when Bert Horner was a policeman in Shawville. He used to take Big Tommy Watts and put him in the cell. Watts was a big man. But Bert had big hands, very, very strong hands and he'd just tighten his grip until he could see Watts flinching a little bit and then, no trouble at all. "Come along. Come along," Bert would say, and he'd take him to jail. The cell was in the fire hall. It probably still is. I've never been there. I don't know. Why'd he take him? Oh, he was drunk and disorderly. Disturbing the peace.

I remember when Bert Horner used to travel and sell horses and breed horses. A gang of us used to get together and Bert would bring the mares—somebody would bring the mares—and Bert would always have Nigger, a big black stud, and these mares needed to be bred, you know. I remember Bert very well putting lots of Vaseline and grease or whatever it was on the stud's dink. And I'm telling you, we were a bunch of kids, we were sitting watching this. That was a big performance. Far better than Eaton's and Simpson's catalogues. Bert used to try and chase us, but . . .

---

1  Dr. Robert W. Bell, born near Kingston, 1858, a veterinarian world renowned for his Wonder Medicine. For more references see *Tell Me Another Story* by Joan Finnigan, McGraw-Hill-Ryerson, 1981.

2  John Horner, referred to in Ottawa *Citizen* accounts as The Strongman of Radford, was a prosperous farmer and horse breeder. See also chapter on horses. In the winters, he took men and horses to the Rouge River on contracts as a jobber for J.R. Booth, King of the Timber Barons.

3  For stories from and about G.A. Howard of Shawville, Quebec, see *Laughing All the Way Home* by Joan Finnigan, Deneau, 1984.

4  An Ottawa lawyer, in his youth a renowned Ottawa Rough Rider player, and still a popular after-dinner speaker in the Valley. For more of Jake Dunlap see *Tell Me Another Story* by Joan Finnigan, McGraw-Hill-Ryerson, 1988. Chapter 13.

5  Immigrants from war-torn Europe were called Displaced Persons.

# 19

# "An Indian Guide and His 'Garnets' at Quinze Lake"

## DAVE LEMKAY – Douglas, Ontario

*When I met Dave Lemkay at the Petawawa Forestry Institute and he gave me the names of some of the great storytellers from Douglas (like Larry Moriarity and Hilary McHale), I realized as I listened to him talk that he himself had a lifestory full of Valley interconnections as well as interesting ancestry in Ottawa, Burnstown and the Petawawa-Pembroke area. Although Dave had been born in Saskatchewan, he always seemed to be making his way back to his roots in the Valley. He did just that in 1967 as a young man returning to immerse himself in Valley history and his own fascinating genealogy. He worked in various places with Acme Seeley, Barry Breen Insurance, and as marketing manager for the ill-fated Timbertown, a proposed historic site on the Ottawa River near Farrell's Landing, to be devoted to the lumbering saga of the Valley. In our interview, he gave me a history of the rise and fall of Timbertown. As I listened to him, I remembered some correspondence between myself and John Grace, then editor of the* Ottawa Journal. *In my letter I had said, "Why in the name of God in heaven would you uproot historic buildings and drag them to a site on the Ottawa for which thousands had been paid when you could spend all that money on the preservation of the Opeongo Line, a natural historical site lined with the log original buildings built by the first settlers from the first timbers?" John Grace agreed and I quote from his letter, "Why would we make another 'Upper Canada Village' when we can preserve the real thing on site?" Investors in Timbertown, both private and government, lost their money and today the beautiful site on the Ottawa River sits as a painful reminder of our lack of care for our unique history.*

*In 1970, Dave Lemkay married Dolores Seigel of Rankin, Ontario, and they have two children. They bought and updated the old manse in Douglas where they live.*

WHEN TIMBERTOWN was in process and faltering, the Dicks of Balaclava offered the whole site, five hundred acres with waterfront, as a "lumbering village" in its place. Can you believe they were turned down? It was an "instant site"—log buildings, ice house, old mill, storehouses, old general store, classic houses—all on Constan Creek, which had been used to run logs in the old days. The mill was the only one of its kind in Canada.

I can give you a brief on what happened. I spent three years with Timbertown and we raised a million dollars. But it wasn't enough and then it got all bound up in politics. For one thing, the Conservative Mulroney government wouldn't give money to a Liberal riding, etc. So in 1982, we decided we needed to create a new structure and we branched off to form the Ottawa Valley Heritage Foundation. It

*Lloyd Rochester standing in doorway of Maplelawn, 1921, in a period of his life when he was leading the clan north to the mines for development and investment. He is surrounded by four generations of family from great-grandmother to grandchild. L to R: Lillian Catherine Cole Rochester, Lois Catherine Crabtree, Hilda Cole (Rochester) Crabtree, Phoebe Cole (Schryer). Built in 1830 by William Thomson, Maplelawn was lived in by various members of the Rochester-Cole family until 1989.*

was a charitable foundation and we thought that that way we might get more money out of the government. Timbertown would simply be one of the projects within that foundation. Through the foundation, we acquired a number of old buildings, including the MacKenzie Schoolhouse. As it turned out, the government did give us about three hundred thousand dollars, but they bypassed the Heritage Foundation and gave it to Timbertown Incorporated. It was the vehicle that raised all the local money, but it didn't seem to be viable to raise the huge amount of government money needed to build Timbertown. About this time I became disheartened, realizing we were not going to make it and I withdrew. The project went down the drain after years of work and effort on the part of many, many people, mostly volunteers. The buildings and the site were eventually sold to a camp-site company. Can you imagine what might have been done if they had taken the Dicks up on their offer of Balaclava? Not only did the Timbertown site fall into ruins, but Balaclava is falling into ruins as well. As a dévoté of the Valley, as a person with history going back generations into the Valley, all this loss of our history pains me.

Lemkay is a German name that should be spelled Lemke. And on that side of the family, during the First World War, there was a lot of persecution one way or another, even right here in this part of the country, along the Opeongo and around Petawawa. Not just Kitchener-Waterloo. But as much here. I think there was a stronger enclave here, more concentrated. If you read the book *Harvest of Stones*, it's all there. German immigration in the 1850s and '60s was about the third wave after the Irish and the Scottish and others who came to the Ottawa Valley. I think there was a lot of hoodwinking going on in attracting these people from Central Europe. They were told we had fertile land and people were farming and making a living. And, of course, they came here and found that along the Opeongo Line and in and around Petawawa Township, they couldn't grow a damned thing.

Anyway, by the time the First World War came round, the Lemkays were third generation. My

*The Cole-Rochester clan pose in the doorway of Maplelawn, one of Ottawa's great heritage stones, 529 Richmond Road, c. 1907. Back row, L to R: William Alanson Cole, 1861-1921; Elizabeth Donalda Cole, 1877-1914; John Edward Cole, 1864-1949; Mrs Holland, Lillian Edna Rochester, 1887-; Harry Willan Cole, 1872-1959; Norris Cole Bryson, 1890-1948; Lillian Catharine Rochester (Cole) 1870-1954; George Hamilton Rochester, 1856-1925; Hilda Cole Rochester, 1889-1950. Front row, L to R: Thomas Bertram Cole, 1872-1946; Mary Ann Morgan (Cole), 1859-1922; Lucy Helena Rochester (Cole), 1866-1957; Gordon Hamilton Rochester, 1894-; Phoebe Cole (Schryer) 1833-1921; Olive May Cole (Learoyd) 1883-1966; Minnie Ross Bryson (Cole), 1868-1945. Children, L to R: Robin James Bryson, 1900-1963; William Laurence Rochester, 1901-; Bertram Cole Rochester, 1899-1953; Lloyd Baillie Rochester 1893-1982.*

paternal great-great-grandfather, August Lemkay, came to Canada in the 1850s as a sixteen-year-old, and married a lady by the name of Ida Hardiman—she was only second generation. They settled in Petawawa Township, had eleven children on the family farm, which is still owned by a grandson of August Lemkay. But I moved back to the Valley in '67 because my roots on the maternal side—Coles, Rochesters—are here in Ottawa and Burnstown and, on the paternal side, the Lemkays around Petawawa. At eighteen I packed the car one day, and my mother had said, "Where are you going?" I said, "I'm not sure where I'm going, but I think I'm going up towards Ottawa. I'll phone you whenever I get to wherever it is I'm going." And I landed in Pembroke and went out to the Lemkay farm, the homestead. And I was home to the Valley, home to my roots.

On my mother's side the Coles and Rochesters are entwined in the early history of Ottawa and the Valley. Renowned Ottawa heritage residence Maplelawn was owned by the Coles since 1878 and then bought by the Rochesters. My great-grandfather, Thomas Cole, came to Canada from England in 1822, took up a large tract of land outside what was then Bytown. To maintain the holdings, gather the crops, tend the livestock and market the produce at one time required twelve to fifteen permanent farm hands, plus uncounted domestic help, all living in residence. For their education Thomases' four sons and four daughters daily made the five-mile walk to and from Model School, Lisgar Collegiate, Miss Harmon's and Ottawa Ladies College. School was AFTER chores and one of the sons reported late in his life that he could still remember "all the fireplaces in the house and five of the various-sized stoves, their pipes running here and there through rooms and hallways" that constantly required carrying of wood,

*Woodlawn in the days when it was a gracious estate, a centre for social and cultural activities in Ottawa.*

stoking, attention. Sometimes "good old Dad" would hitch a team in the cold weather and go with his buffalo-robe laden hay wagon to the Hintonburg toll-gate to pick up his brood. But by the time they all reached the teens, they found ways to "miss him," much preferring to walk home with girlfriends and boyfriends.

My great-grandmother was Lillian Catherine Cole. One of her brothers, John, became owner of what was later McLaren Industries in Masson, Quebec. John "stayed on the farm," became a major figure in his community as the school trustee, the lodge member, the worker on behalf of temperance, the advisor on commercial and municipal affairs. His establishment of Pinecrest Cemetery was largely conceived to give employment during the Depression.

Good Old Uncle Bill, the bachelor of the family, became auctioneer, assignee, bailiff, real estate agent, broker. Much of his business brought him in contact with "the poorer classes" in Ottawa with the result that his was the first planned approach to "low income housing." With his brother John in the first decade of the twentieth century he established a settlement of "small purchasable houses" in the Hillson Avenue area—ten dollars down and ten a month.

Thomas, as a young man, was the idol of his clan, particularly with his nieces and nephews, for his athletic and gymnastic abilities. He not only brought to Maplelawn an array of medals and trophies, but as a musician he attracted the musically accomplished to its great drawing rooms. As a mandolin player, he was a disciple and great friend of George Peate, master of the strings.

For several years annually Ab Thomas, the then famous Welsh harpist, was a special guest at Maplelawn "invited to the house for a fortnight and

THE HARMON SCHOOL FOR YOUNG LADIES

still welcome when a month had passed." In later days, the wandering minstrel fallen on evil days, aging and in need of solace, was still "maestro of the strings" at Maplelawn.

Thomas served for a number of years as private secretary to George H. Perley, later Sir George, lumberman and one-time Conservative member for Argenteuil, Quebec. When Perley's appointment as Canadian High Commissioner took him to London, Thomas became Assistant Secretary to the Prime Minister, Sir Robert Borden. During his later years, he extended the rose beds and peony plantings in the walled garden at Maplelawn, still "sights to behold" decades after his death in 1946.

Harry went much further afield to die far from home in San Rafael, California, in 1959, widely known and respected throughout the entire lumbering industry on the west coast of the US. After matriculating from Lisgar Collegiate in Ottawa, "that venerable institution that nurtured and inspired so many great men and women," Harry went to McGill, "one of Canada's great universities." It is said that one of the hobbies of his youth was "soldiering as a commissioned officer in that famous old cavalry regiment, the Princess Louise Dragoon Guards."

After graduation, Harry read an advertisement for a young man to work as private secretary to the president of the Bronson Lumbering Business at headquarters in Ottawa. Upon application, Harry was accepted immediately. At that time the president, Honorable E.H. Bronson, was a minister in the Ontario provincial government entailing many absences from Ottawa to attend sessions at Queen's Park, Toronto. This opened the door for Harry to assume increasing responsibilities and to place him in line to become Secretary of the Bronson Lumber Company. When Bronson purchased and decided to develop a large tract of redwood timberlands in Humboldt County, California, Harry Cole was dispatched as manager, 1909. For the next forty years he remained a force in West Coast lumbering.

After Harry's death in 1959 foresters found that the tallest redwood trees in the world were the redwoods of Humboldt County, and Harry was honoured by having the second tallest one of these named after him. It was also intended that, by drawing attention to these gargantuan trees, a movement would be set in process to preserve them from logging companies.

It might be said that the Cole sisters "married well." Except for Mary Ann who married a farmer from Shoal Lake, Manitoba, the other girls married lumbering and mining men and two Cole sisters married two Rochester brothers, my great-grandmother, Lillian Catherine Cole to George Rochester, then of Burnstown but married in Rochesterville, and Lucy Helena, who married Daniel Rochester of Rochesterville. Lucy Helena and Lillian Catherine, as wives of men both engaged in lumbering and later in mining, saw many pioneer fronts in Eastern Canada and the Mining North while accompanying their husbands: in the early years on visits to centres of lumber operations, Eagle Depot and further reaches of the Gatineau, Ostobonning, Magnasippi, Dumoine, Grand Lake Victoria and the Quinze Country, Mattawa, Kippewa, and other tributaries of the Ottawa River; and later around the early 1900s, in another chapter of pioneer life when their husbands followed the discoveries of silver at Cobalt and gold in the Porcupine.

About this time, the sale of the Hull Lumber Company's limits around Kippewa Lake relieved Daniel Rochester of his responsibilities as bush manager. He moved into mining and at Cobalt became fourth member of a mining syndicate composed of Perley, Reid and Avery. When the group wound up a successful silver project he was appointed managing director of the Cobalt Lake Mining Company. Its holdings comprised the mineral rights under that lake purchased by tender from the Ontario government for the incredible sum of one million dollars raised by public subscription from a deluge of interested investors. A new company was formed to develop Cobalt Lake. Rochester had to establish headquarters in Cobalt and the family was in continuous movement between Ottawa and the Mining North.

In the meantime, George Rochester, to supplement his lumbering and mining activities, established himself in the hardware business on Lake

*The legendary Sandy McIntyre staked the ground for the McIntyre Porcupine, one of the richest gold mines in Canadian mining history. It is said that Sandy found nothing for himself at Red Lake "but a good time." However, after Sandy's discovery, southern capital flew north and many people with already familiar names accumulated wealth, M.J. O'Brien of Renfrew, the Gillies of Arnprior, J.P. Bickell of Toronto, so long associated with the NHL. Percy Hopkins was one of the original geologists in the area, c. 1926.*

Temiskaming in the town of Haileybury where the family lived until his death in 1925.

During those many years when mining history was being made and they were part of it, the Rochester families made many friends and either knew or knew of many important and colourful characters in the history-making: people like Henri and Noah Timmins of the Larose discovery; John Rankin of Mattawa; J. Lorne McDougall, auditor-general under seven prime ministers; Judge Brown, the bearded one-meal-a-day man; Foghorn Neil MacDonald[1], his voice and exploits known from coast to coast; Dr. Henry Drummond, poet of Habitant verse; Norman Fisher of the Temiskaming; Logan in his Bank of Commerce tent; Hersey, the delightful English remittance man and authority on liquor; Sheriff Caldbick; the Langs (Dan and his

brother); George Smith[2], the mining recorder; Captain Henry Toke Munn, the Artic explorer; Cyril Blacklock who, on a Rochester et al grub stake, staked Gillies Lake adjoining Hollinger in the first rush. Later he became the British general leading the Highland Division, the Fighting Fifty-First of World War I.

But the Rochesters go back further in Valley history and further afield in the Valley. My great-grandfather, George Hamilton Rochester, was born in Burnstown, 1856, as were his brothers—Daniel, John, Francis, James and William. And they have a close tie with Archibald, the Last Laird MacNab of White Lake and Waba who for twenty years, 1820-40, held his settlers in a feudal system. It was the settlers on the Madawaska at Stewartville and Burnstown—the Duffs and Stewarts, the Millers and McIntyres—who spearheaded the movement to overthrow MacNab's tyranny.[3] When MacNab was finally banished, the settlers in the area decided that they needed some improvements, including a grist mill. The nearest one was at Perth, a distance of two days' walk away from the Madawaska settlements.

I do not know how but they found their way to Bytown to George Rochester in Rochesterville. With his capital and the settlers' labour, they built at Burnstown their much-needed mill. George Rochester had come from England with both education and money and around 1850 he bought the millsite, three hundred acres of land, one hundred on one side of the Madawaska and two hundred on the other side where Burnstown was to arise. There he built a log house to which in 1851 he brought his bride, Marion Baillie of Scotland, and there they raised their family. In 1876, they

*In the 1930s and '40s, Ottawa was still a small town with each of its districts boasting a representative gang of boys who entertained themselves, generally on Saturdays with "recreational violence" or gang wars. From an* Ottawa Citizen *feature, here, grown to adulthood and achievement, are three well-known Ottawa figures of the 1940s acknowledging their memberships: Ottawa's one-time mayor Stanley Lewis as a Grinder from around Gilmore Street; Jess Abelson, member of a leading Jewish family, as a Sandy Hill Snowflake; and renowned hockey star, Punch Broadbent, as one of the Pipefield Boys from Centretown. The Rochesterville Gang was renowned as the most daunting of all. In a 1937 interview, Broadbent said, "We were tough enough, I guess. But we weren't crazy enough to set foot in Rochesterville and run into the Riopelles and the Latreilles of the Rochesterville Gang."*

sold and moved back to Ottawa, the newly-appointed capital of Canada. The stone mill stood for many years, but was eventually allowed to fall into ruins. No one in the Ottawa Valley could be convinced to preserve that history so, in 1939, the millstones were removed to a government-owned park in—of all places—Niagara Falls, there marked with a plaque.

Meanwhile, the Ottawa Rochesters were busy with their real estate holdings in Rochesterville, expanding Maplelawn's farm, and other business enterprises. One of the pre-Confederation landmarks of old Rochesterville was the famous Rochester Victoria Brewery at the corner of Rochester and Wellington, built by John Rochester in 1829 and famous for its "Double Stout" and "Indian Pale Ale." The Rochester Tannery at Confederation was then the largest in Canada.

In the beginning, Rochesterville was one of the choice residential areas in Bytown but, in the Great Ottawa Fire of 1900, Rochester enterprises and residence were destroyed as were the residences of the Lumber Kings—Booth, Bronson, Eddy—who also lost much of their vast complex of mills on Victoria Island and at the Chaudiere.

But back to mining. It went down into the next generation of Rochesters and particularly to Lloyd, son of Daniel Baillie Rochester. In the Valley he was one of the revitalizers of Hilton Mines at Bristol, Quebec, until a few years ago one of the big employers in the Pontiac. Born in 1903, Lloyd Rochester was another one of those outstanding graduates of Model School and Lisgar Collegiate in Ottawa. He enrolled at McGill in 1913 but joined up in 1914 as a gunner with the 27th CFA Battery, saw active service in France. He transferred to the Royal Flying Corps, 1917, and became one of its senior flying instructors. He also was a graduate of Smith-Barry's School of Special Flying at Gosport and then a flight-commander in 87 Squadron, RAF. After the war he returned to McGill and graduated with a Bachelor of Science degree in Mining.

He signed on as a timber cruiser on the Quetico Park limits of the Shevil-Clarke Company for the Ontario Timber Investigation and later on an extensive cruise of the Blanche and Nation limits for the Singer Manufacturing Company. He then turned to mining and spent the next forty years in mining exploration. He was one of the early pilots who helped to incorporate the use of airplanes into mining explorations and he was one of the first bush pilots in Canada. Leo Springer, his partner, and Lloyd Rochester were the team which staked Opemiska Copper Mines in Northern Quebec.

In Lloyd's retirement, he bought Maplelawn from the last of the Coles, hired an Ottawa architect and upgraded the wonderful old house, living in it until his death. Prior to that, in his retirement he expanded the gardens, entertained the clans, collected and collated the genealogy of the Coles and Rochesters, gathering all kinds of fascinating documents and letters including one of the most fascinating of all—his own letter to Sydney Johnson, Westport Point, Massachusetts[4], dated 1959. In a previous letter, Johnson had referred to Joe McKenzie, the Indian, and his "garnets" on the shores of Quinze Lake[5], and this evoked a whole long wonderful procession of memories from Lloyd Rochester, memories paralleling the history of lumbering, mining, camping, exploring in the Mining North of the Ottawa Valley.

Again your remarks about Joe McKenzie and his "garnets" somewhere north of Quinze Lake brought back many interesting recollections of that whole area and that small, wiry, interesting character who accompanied Jim Mawdsley and me on a claim staking trip into Boischatel Township to the west of Rouyn, Quebec, between Christmas and New Year's, 1922, following the finding of the Horne Mine, now Noranda Copper, by Ed Horne in the summer of that year.

In the later autumn of 1922, "The Dad" (Daniel Baillie Rochester—you may have known him in early lumbering and mining days—Cobalt from 1903 onwards) and his faithful henchman, Ronald Dickson, an old timber cruiser, and I went up to New Liskeard and in to Klock's Farm on the Quinze where we were outfitted with canoe, etc. (J.B. Klock was an old friend of Father's.) Klock's motor-powered pointer boat, if I remember right, took us to the mouth of the Ottawa River from where we took off on our own to look over a 50 square mile timber limit through which the Kenojevis River flowed to the Ottawa. "The Dad" had either purchased this limit or proposed doing so.

We picked up an Indian from a family tenting at Sturgeon Falls and proceeded on our way for a week's tour. After almost completing our inspection we sent the Indian on his way with some pals of his who chanced along the river; gave him most of our surplus grub and tin stove, expecting to follow down river in a day or two. The next day the weather turned— and the next day a fierce storm dumped snow, rain and sleet onto us and, with no food, no stove and a leaky tent, we were not too comfortable. Ed Horne (discoverer of Noranda), paddling back to Rouyn with his newly-acquired wife to add some further claims to his previous stakings of the summer, told us of his find, and also of the great Haileybury fire which had swept the whole countryside in his absence.

With Mother having come to Haileybury with us to visit her sister, Mrs. George Rochester, while we were away, we couldn't get back fast enough. (The Rochesters had survived the fire by spending the night in the lake, their silver tea service wrapped in bed sheets.)

I had thought of going back and getting in on the copper rush to Rouyn which had gained some mild momentum. It meant travelling to Dane on the TNO[6], into Larder Lake by indifferent road, then walking forty miles or more along old tote-roads—and in the face of winter just around the corner—I abandoned the idea for the time being and we all returned to Ottawa.

But I still had an "itchy foot" and felt that I was missing a possible good bet so got in touch with an old classmate, one Jim Mawdsley, ex-Princess Pat, ex-Royal Flying Corps WWI, now Dr. Mawdsley, Prof. of Geology and Dean of Engineering, Saskatchewan University, who was taking post-graduate studies at Princeton. He was all for hitting the trail but could only get away for ten days between Christmas and New Year's.

Came that time we packed our kit and equipment, entrained for Dane on the Temiskaming & Northern Ontario Railway, having picked up our trusty Indian, Joe McKenzie and his husky dog at New Liskeard. At Dane we ran into an old First World War General—whose name I can't recall—who, hibernating after some financial reverses, had a small trading and transportation business. He roused up a team and a good old hay sled to take us to Larder Lake. The driver, the local bootlegger, was a typical Drummond French character and one of the funniest chaps I think we had ever run across. His stories and exploits, if written up, would have made a Book-of-the-Month. At Larder we said good-bye to our character—Joe Mufferaw I'll call him—and started to mush into Boischatel Township around Lake Fortune some thirty miles or so away to the east along an old Booth tote-road which would all over the country.

A large granite porphyry stock or boss in the northwest corner of this township which adjoined Rouyn Township to the west was our objective as around the borders of such occurrences were likely places for ore deposits. The whole venture was a theoretical bet in the manner of "shooting first and investigating later." Joe McKenzie proved to be his weight in gold. We had an Arctic sled, skis, snowshoes and enough kit and equipment to stock an expedition to the North Pole. Making camp, cooking, and generally looking after all the chores which descend on one in the bush, Joe took it all in his stride and without him we would have had a "hell of a time." Furthermore, the weather turned to provide real Christmas atmosphere, a wonderland of

snow and temperatures which never went above 15 below. At one time we were staking in 30 below weather and thoroughly enjoying it. The bottle of scotch which we got from our bootlegger friend to prevent "snake bites" proved to be of the rawest kind and we could only drink it well camouflaged with snow water and honey.

We arrived at our destination finally after staying over the third night after leaving Larder Lake with two trapper lads. They gave us the lowdown on the topography of the country as it was on their trapping ground and they knew it intimately, giving us tips about where to pitch camp, get water, wood, etc., and were very helpful. They were Leo and Karl Springer who later wrote their names in broad letters in mine-making achievements from coast to coast. They became my great friends, Leo being my close associate when we were part of the team which found and staked Opemiska Copper Mines, one of the great Canadian mines in the Chibougamau country of northern Quebec. Leo was killed in a flying accident in 1936 and Karl is now one of the great mining moguls.

Well, we finally staked out 1000 acres comprising five claims of 200 acres each, having a wonderful time doing it. On the way out the Springer lads offered to trade a few mink skins for our sleigh and grub (they were against it as far as funds were concerned until a little later). We were only too glad to do so. We told them that they might be well advised to take a few claims around us and showed them how to do it and where to procure licences and record. This they did and later in the winter when the rush was really taking on wide proportions, they were offered a good sum which they accepted. This was their first introduction to things mining. Today Karl could write a cheque for a million with ease.

While mushing our way back who should we meet on the trial but our bootlegger friend and his team taking a load of supplies into one of the jobbers. We left Joe McKenzie off at Haileybury and I kept in touch with him for many years afterwards. I believe he died a few years ago. What a small world it is that involves him with you and "garnets" on the Quinze and us with claims in Boischatel, with years intervening and a chance remark that prompts this whole story.

Now back to the Lemkay side. I grew up in a small town called Grimsby. My dad grew up in North Bay. He had an uncle who was the United Church minister in Niagara Falls. So my dad and two of his chums bicycled to Niagara Falls to visit his uncle. Can you imagine coming down No. 11 in the 1930s from North Bay to Niagara Falls on a one-speed bike? Anyway, my dad went through Grimsby, right past the manse that we eventually lived in. It's reported that he said, "Some day I'm going to live there." And he did. My dad studied at the Royal Ontario Conservatory, piano and organ under Sir Ernest MacMillan, got his doctorate in music and then he went into theology and got his BA. My parents married in '43 and their first charge was out in Paradise Valley, Alberta. In '48 my dad answered a call from a church in Hamilton. I came across the country as a two-year-old on the train. I remember quite well the night before we moved in there was a major snow storm in Hamilton and the snow had blocked everything. We had a little Austin car, but there was no way that Austin was going to make it anywhere. I remember my dad chopping open a can

*Lloyd Rochester encouraged the use of aeroplanes in the Mining North. Prospectors started using aeroplanes soon after the Red Lake Gold Rush of 1925. Here, George Campbell (staker of the Red Lake goldmine property) stands on the pontoon of a Norseman aircraft to greet his canoeist friend, Jacob Hagar, 1943.*

of beans with an axe because we'd no can opener. Then my dad answered a call from the United Church in Grimsby. And so we ended up in the very manse that he had noted when he rode his bike from North Bay to Niagara Falls. He knew he would be coming. That was his fifth call. He was thirty-three and he died in '56 at thirty-nine.

When my great-grandmother, Lillian Catherine Cole Rochester, died in Ottawa, we took the corpse on the train to Haileybury. At that time we had a lot of family in Haileybury because the Rochesters and some of their descendants were all in the mining business. Also my great-grandfather, "Kitty's" husband, was buried there. We had a room at the Haileybury Hotel. And I remember—I would have been seven—finding my way down the back stairs to the kitchen. My dad would have been busy with funeral arrangements as the clergyman and I remember sitting there amid all the pots and pans having breakfast with the chef of the Haileybury Hotel surrounded by the ghosts and the passages of all the people, humble and famous, who were part of my history and part of the mining history of Canada; people like the Springers, the Timmins, Foghorn Neil McDonald, Henry Drummond, J. Lorne McDougall, Princess Maggie, Indian guides like Joe McKenzie, remittance men from England, Rochester ancestors . . .

1 Foghorn Neil MacDonald was a flamboyant character renowned throughout the Mining North. Legend has it that he could make his voice heard across the English Channel.

2 In 1904, George Smith was appointed first government mining recorder. His office was in Haileybury with bilingual services.

3 See also Henry Taylor interview, Chapter 2. The Stringers of Burnstown were also part of the rebel group.

4 By coincidence Westport Point, Massachusetts, is where the Devlins of Chapter 4 live today.

5 Quinze Lake is near the headwaters of the Ottawa River in Northern Quebec.

6 In 1902, the Temiskaming and Northern Ontario Railway was begun at North Bay with government funds. Mining discoveries like that of McKinley and Darragh at Long Lake gave immediate impetus to the building and extension of the line.

# 20

# "We Crossed Twenty-two Tracks to Get a Loaf of Bread"

## VELMA FITZGERALD FRANKLIN – Glengarry County, Ontario

*Velma Franklin of the Maxwell area in Glengarry County was born in 1927 at Parent, Quebec, into a clan of Fitzgeralds who had decades with the E.B. Eddy Company. Rare and important are her glimpses of growing up in Parent on the CN line, in the northern wilderness of Quebec, above the headwaters of the Gatineau and Lièvre Rivers on whose raging waters the Fitzgeralds for so many years were overseers for the running of the timbers to the Eddy mills of Hull, Quebec.*

*Mrs. Franklin attended St. Helen's High School in the Eastern Townships and graduated with her Bachelor of Science from McGill University in 1948. She married in 1950 and moved to her large Glengarry farm where she raised her family, was a correspondent for the* Glengarry News *and the* Cornwall Standard-Freeholder. *For a period she was curator of the Dunvegan Museum where, ironically, she functioned as the keeper of the Scottish relics. She represents, in a very feisty way, the Irish in Glengarry County, an area so preponderantly Scottish I have dubbed it "The Scottish Holy Land."*

WHEN WE LIVED in Parent from 1924 to 1948 the McLaren's limits would almost go to Parent and the E.B. Eddy men and the McLaren men could hear each other working in the bush, but neither company was going to open the road between. They felt that if they opened the road between the limits, the public would have the right to travel through and you couldn't bottle them up. It wasn't until 1971, that they actually got a road to Parent.

Well, I never knew my great-grandparents. They died long before I was born. But they came out from Ireland at the time of the Famine. All the Fitzgeralds came out. My great-grandparents came out in 1846. I did get to talk to an old man—Pat Delaney— and they and the Fitzgeralds were distantly related, in Ireland, he thought. Delaney's father came out at the same time. Pat had a lovely accent and he lived to be nearly a hundred. He was the one who told me about his father taking him off to Treadwell to see Lord Monck, the governor general, coming up the Ottawa River. Their farm was on a ridge overlooking the river at Treadwell and the Delaneys walked over to see Lord Monck on his way to Ottawa. John thought it would be very educational for Pat to see this. So I said, "What did he look like?" And Pat said, "Sure, I don't know, at all, at all, at all! Abner Hagar was having the first four-wheeled wagon with four iron wheels unloaded off the boat that day and nobody paid any attention to the Governor General of Canada."

The Delaneys and the Fitzgeralds may have come out together. There was a large settlement from

*Loading supplies at the E.B. Eddy cache in Parent for a trip up to the depots on CN rail, c. 1938-40.*

Tipperary and most of those came out together. They took land back in from the rivers, sand farms, not very good land. By the time the Irish came out here all the good land had been taken up in Quebec and Ontario. And what they got was the little river valleys—the Rouge and the Lièvre. The Lièvre—that's where McLaren's limits went straight up to Parent. The road goes up that way, but it was a river we never travelled on because The Drive at home came down the Gatineau to Eddy's. Eddy's limits were exactly north of the Lièvre, but they came down on the Gatineau. McLaren's came down the Lièvre and Eddy came down the Gatineau. And Eddy also had limits on the Coulonge and the Dumoine.

Well, the Fitzgeralds came out to lands on the ridge between Plantagenet and Treadwell near Plantagenet. The English settlement was on the Nation River, good farm land there, and my husband's people—the Franklins—settled there with Smiths and Fletchers and Johnstons. But, the back settlement again was Irish—Fitzgeralds, Delaneys, Muldoons, McCranks, Shanes—I can't remember all the names.

The first thing they did was cut the solid bush. Actually it belonged to Abner Hagar from Vermont—Albert was the son's name. Abner came up from Vermont and he was a contemporary of Philemon Wright and he owned all the land around here so the Fitzgeralds, for sure, and I imagine most of the others, bought their farms from him. They had a hard time when they came out; you don't get over a famine like you do a head cold. A lot of them died *after* they got here. Also, there were crop failures and a depression in the 1870s here in Canada.

I remember seeing some of my uncle's papers. He had a little shoe box with his very valuable papers in it and there was a half a dozen rolled up little slips and on them was the payment for the farm sometime in the '70s, and the payment on the farm for several years was three bags of potatoes. And this was all they paid. And Grandma had kept these little slips of paper so that some day they would know if it was paid off.

The Fitzgeralds' farm was just north of Plantagenet, on the hill north of the village. When the farms petered out—they were very good there for a while, but there was no fertilizer and after they took a few crops off it, it was just light sandy soil—nothing left. They cut wood all over the place, but then they went across the river to Quebec and into the bush for E.B. Eddy on their Rouge River limit.

My great-grandfather, William Fitzgerald, eloped with Katharine Saxton of Dublin and came to Canada in 1846. When I was in Ireland I looked up Saxton. They were a family in Dublin, spelled Sexton, and they were very well off. But William and Katharine left Ireland with nothing at all. One old lady, Mrs. McAuley, knew her and she told me in the raspberry patch one day, that she used to visit my great-grandmother and had asked her if she ever heard from her people in Ireland. But Katharine said

*E.B. Eddy's "Old 37" depot, thirty-seven miles from Parent on the Pine River, a branch of the Gatineau, c. 1926.*

that her family didn't want good news and she wouldn't send them bad, so she never heard from them again.

Pat Delaney referred to her as Aunt Kate. She was very interested in gardening and great-grandfather was the gardener on her father's estate. From the dates, she was about twenty-six when they eloped. This was no child bride; they were people who knew what they were doing and conditions were so horrible in Ireland at the time that they didn't want to stay. But Pat said they were always homesick for Ireland and if you read that very sad book on exiles and emigrants—over seven million people have left Ireland since 1600, and none of them ever wanted to emigrate—or very few of them—it was always circumstances.

And if you go across the Ottawa River and up the Rouge River road, you'll come to the little community of Avoca. I always drive up along there in the fall, and it's all blowing sand there, and low brush, and cut-over bush. And two years ago I was through the Vale of Avoca in Ireland and it was so lovely, so green, almost semi-tropical. Beautiful! And I thought, "How they must have missed their homes." All they had that was similar was the name.

So my great-grandparents eloped and they came to Plantagenet. They had a family of seven and my

*Some of the senior E.B. Eddy Company employees at Duck Lake, forty miles from Parent, beside a plane from Laurentides Airlines, c. 1940. L to R: Ernie Fitzgerald, assistant superintendent; Jimmy Patterson, Woodlands, Ottawa; Dean Folkes, depot clerk; Jerry Fitzgerald, boss; Pickering, pilot. Altogether the three Fitzgerald brothers put in about one-hundred-and-twenty years service for Eddy.*

grandfather, John, was the youngest and he married Melissa Erratt—a neighbour and another family that had come across from Ireland, too. And my father and his four brothers were born. The oldest Uncle Bill—he was a marvellous fiddler—and then Uncle Abbey—the one who stayed on the farm. Then my father, James. When he went to work for Eddy's there were already four men named James in the office, so they called him Jerry because his name was Fitzgerald. Then there was Uncle Ernie. There was two years between all the brothers. Then much, much younger was Uncle Percy. He didn't work too long for Eddy's.

My mother was Stella Graham from Pembroke. Her grandmother came from Plantagenet, though, a Hughes. They were married in Ottawa. That was quite funny. They didn't want any great big fuss over it and they decided to get married on the First of July. It's a holiday now, of course, but they didn't think much about that because in those days most people were working all the time and they didn't celebrate all these official holidays. Anyway, they had made arrangements with the minister and they were married in Ottawa and I think there was some trouble getting witnesses or a ring or something because everything was closed. Dad had told Uncle Bill to come to Ottawa. He wanted him as a witness, but he didn't tell him why and Uncle Bill thought he was going to write his scaler's exam. So he came in bush clothes to the wedding!

Dad had been through what they called Continuation School, the equivalent of high school. And he had worked in the bush over on the Rouge for an old fellow called Asa Young who had camps all through the bush, and the Fitzgerald boys would go and work in these camps in the wintertime to earn some money because the farm wasn't bringing much in. Dad wound up as company clerk for one of Eddy's camps on the Rouge. In 1914, they drove up to L'Assension with a team and buggy and they drove up the old sand road. It's still there along the Rouge where there's white-water rafting.

Hawkesbury was a very important business centre then and the only river crossing. Eddy's had a limit on the Rouge up in what is now Mont Tremblant Park and, when that was cut over and finished, they sent Dad in, temporarily, to take the place of the chief clerk who was leaving. He had to go by rail. There was no road. It was on the height of land, so they had to go from Montreal and rail in all their supplies.

We were exactly on the height of land, fourteen hundred feet. Much later in the '60s, there was a radar base there, but in the '40s we used to climb up to a little wooden tower on the mountain. It was three miles from Parent and we would climb up the mountain and then climb up the tower. Then the radar people came along and put up this *huge* concrete tower and then tore half of it down. It's an eyesore. It's still there. We can make the most ugly modern ruins and we burn all the old ones. This

*The Bald Head fire ranger tower at "Old 37" depot, c. 1926. Yes, that is a man at the top! Probably a Fitzgerald.*

hideous eyesore, I forget how many millions and millions it cost.

Uncle Ernie had been working with Dad, so it sounded like a real clique, but Eddy's appreciated their loyalty to the company. Back in those days, Dad wrote a letter to Ottawa every Saturday night to tell Eddy's what he was doing with nine hundred square miles of bush and seven or eight hundred men.

The Fitzgeralds were all big men, big-boned men. Uncle Abby was the shortest and the fattest. Abby was just round. He lived longer than any of the others, but Abby never worked in the bush. Abby stayed home on the farm. Dad was superintendent and Uncle Ernie was assistant superintendent, and Uncle Bill was chief scaler for a long time, and they always worked together and always got along all the

years they were there. They knew what they should do. And then Uncle Percy had more mathematical ability and he took his accountancy by correspondence course, failed twice and the third time he made it, came first in Canada, so he went to the Donnacona Paper Company in Quebec. But all together they put in one hundred and twenty, one hundred and thirty years for the E.B. Eddy Company.

Parent was fun in the summertimes. Most of the men went home in the spring. The limit was thirty miles, you see, from the town. Some of them in the summertimes built dams and cleaned the camps, did road work. I was listening to Pierre Berton talking about growing up in the Yukon; he thought everybody had a deserted village to play in. Parent was one single village and it had twenty-two tracks in

*The stable's best at Parent, c. 1940. Henri Boyer, and on the right, Teddy Legault who knew so much about horses Jerry Fitzgerald always used to take him to the sales at the Bodnoff Horse Exchange in Quebec City. The deal was a certain amount per horse, buyer's choice, sixteen to a carload. Bodnoff always complained that Legault invariably took the sixteen best horses he had in his sale.*

the centre as a divisional point, and we crossed those to get a loaf of bread, and I thought everybody did that. And, I remember the hobos in the Depression. There was always somebody at the door looking for food. I remember going to get bread and the hobos would be camped at the end of the town, at the edge of the mountain near the tracks, and they had these little fires in these little hollows in the hill, and we'd hike along the edge there going by just to get our bread. I thought every kid did this kind of thing. We used to go and play in the big cache where they had all the supplies and everything and we'd take out all the cook's supplies, the tin plates and tea dishes and big iron spoons. Tea parties with the cook's stuff. We thought everybody lived like that. We would fish all over the place. The company land was off limits to the public you see.

I learned to drive when I was eleven years old. Well, there was only a few miles of road in Parent—and it went nowhere! It was a 1931 Ford and that was one of the ten best cars ever built. It had over three hundred thousand miles on it at the end. It was all brass underneath. It had been welded and welded and welded, but the thing was still running. My father sold it to somebody for more than he ever paid for the thing, and the buyer ran it for another twenty years. The second last time I was up in Parent, somebody had it. I remember seeing it in somebody's yard.

Parent was a CNR village. The E.B. Eddy Company was twenty-two miles in the bush and spread all over the limits. They had a depot in Parent and some of the men worked there. We lived in town because we had to go to school. Dad went to the bush and stayed for the week and came back on the weekend, but the rest of the men went in and stayed all winter.

And there was a coal chute and a big roundhouse and everyone in the town worked for the CNR. Either that or they were storekeepers or something like that. We had our own English public school and there was a big French school. There were only about eight English families in the town. I don't remember learning to speak French. Everybody talked French. It just happened. Back in Plantagenet, the Fitzgeralds were bilingual, too. You see, there were a lot of French people living in Plantagenet along the river there. Fitzgerald's neighbours there were French and the Irish learnt French easily, as a second language—no problem.

Parent was named after a surveyor. He probably laid out the railway line. M.J. O'Brien of Renfrew built the railway. It was an election promise of Sir Wilfred Laurier to open up the mines around Noranda, Rouyn. And, I think Laurier went out of office in the early 1900s and the railway didn't get to Parent until 1917 or 1919. There was a date on one house in the town and I think that's when it started. When the railway was being built, they put a divisional point every one hundred and twenty miles. They had a terrible time. The CNR was formed from a collection of bankrupt railways—a terrible handicap. People say the CNR can't make any money, but when you start out like that! It wasn't like the CPR— from the beginning a going concern.

I remember Dad saying that the CNR engineers used to book off their runs and go moose hunting to feed their families. There was no money, there was nothing. This was during the Depression because all the hobos travelling through Parent were going north to look for work in the mines. The line went then from Parent to Rouyn, it really did go to the mines—from Montreal and Hervé Junction.

There were a few Scotsmen in Parent, among them one of our many town drunks. He was a kindly old fellow except when on the occasional spree, when he would tend to get violent and shout at his neighbours. The neighbours who realized that it was his illness and not any ill will that brought this on—and there being half a dozen boys in the family—used to cabbage the old Scotsman and tie him to the only piece of furniture in his house that he could not move—a good heavy piano. When he recovered his wife untied him. This practical accommodation to an emergency went on for many years.

Dad came down with arthritis and the doctor told him he had to move further south. He bought the house in Maxville and then wrote home to Parent to tell us that he had bought this house. I remember running upstairs and looking at the map in the hall to see where Maxville was. Mother didn't know either.

That was his way to tell her. Dad had an air of authority, eh? The family were quite in awe of him and, every once in a while, he'd come home and he'd lay down the law—we were going to do this, and we were going to do that, and nobody would dare say a word to him—except me—and we used to have terrible fights. He was lots of fun to fight with, too. You don't hang up your crown like a hat just because you come home.

Dad couldn't get over the standard of living in Glengarry. It was below everything he had had in Parent. He thought he was living in the bush at the outposts of civilization. As I said, the Scots are the dirtiest people. John Galbraith mentions that in his book, *The Scotch*. And it's funny. I remember going down to the museum when that book came out and somebody said something about it and the curator looked down his long nose and said, "I hear Galbraith thinks we're dirty!"

Another shock my dad got when he was meeting the local inhabitants; like the habit of not bothering with being clean. This concerns the blind adherence of the Scots to the commandment, "Honour thy father and thy mother," even to the ruination of your life. When he moved here Dad found a nice small barn on the property and decided to raise a couple of pigs. Somebody had advertised pigs for sale in the local paper, so he went off and found the place, trotted up on the verandah and knocked on the door. A very old man slowly opened the door. My father said, "I understand you advertised some pigs for sale. I'd like a couple, and how big are they and how much do you want for them?" The very old man looked at this stranger and said, "The pigs? Oh, you'll have to wait until I ask my father about them." He returned presently with a very, *very* old man and my dumbfounded father made the deal with him. Ninety-five and still in complete charge!

My husband, Keith, and I met through friends of mine. The Franklins had come out into the English settlement originally. Their farm originally was where the Scotch River flows into the Nation River. So what Keith actually did when he married me was just move up river from near Riceville to St. Elmo.

1834—that's when the Franklins came out. Great-great-grandfather, they came out and settled on the ridge near Riceville. He had a trading post there. Henry Ben was his name. There were eleven sons in that family. That gave the family a great start in life. The family's scattered all over now. That's a very good farm even though it flooded. They didn't mind it too much then. They didn't worry about their carpets. Everything just floated around on the wooden floors of the house and they cleaned all the mud out after. The fences, woodpiles, chicken coops got wrecked with the ice and floated away down to Montreal every spring if they weren't tied down. But very, very rich land. They're fertilizing now. It's rather sad; most of the Valley is owned by another absentee landlord.

The first surveys were always from the rivers inland. Now there was always the Seigneury of L'Original and that's at a different angle from everything else that was in there. L'Original —the only seigneury in Ontario—runs back in long narrow strips at right angles to the Ottawa River. The rest of the counties of Prescott and Glengarry were surveyed in the usual English two hundred acre rectangles. And then the French farmers had settled towards Montreal, always along the river, and they had their fields running perpendicular to the river. Glengarry, in the first survey in 1790—we have a copy of the map at the museum—and they just ran the lines north to wherever because they were getting the disbanded regiments and the Loyalists settled along the St. Lawrence. They were moving north after the American Revolution.

This county was empty you see. It wasn't good farmland. The Quebec people—that's good farmland down there—and further west towards Dundas and up along the river is better farmland there. So here in the centre was Glengarry, a sort of No-Man's-Land. It was terribly swampy—tile drainage is what the Ag reps have been talking about for the last fifty years. In Glengarry, the second generation didn't have to go far to get land. They just went north to the next township. They had settled around Hawkesbury early on so that all had to be surveyed. There were early roads from Williamstown and

*A vintage letterhead of one of the first lumber companies in the Valley.*

Martintown up to St. Elmo and the road ended at Athol at that time. And there were roads from Plantagenet to Riceville, of course, because the Franklins were there and they wanted a road through to Maxville and south so that people could travel through. But none of the Scottish townships were in the least interested in anything outside their own boundaries; they were busy at their own little thing. This petition was signed by everyone around Riceville in Prescott including one Benjamin Franklin—he signed with an X. And the Cyrus Thomas history deals with Prescott. St. Isidore is in Prescott. Just on the other side of Highway 417 you are out of Glengarry. Just totally different.

I talk English until I get to the next road and then I can talk French from there on. The French people didn't settle there until much later because that was clay and nobody wanted that. The Scots were offered that clay land around St. Isidore, but they were offered that clay land because it was empty. My insurance man told me he was doing his family history and I said to him, "When did your people come out here?" He said, "1880." I said, "Where were you?" You know this was all empty and they came from Dieppe and Dieppe is very similar farmland. It's that heavy clay land and they knew exactly what to do with it. The theory of the Scots being a buffer between the French and the Germans only applied to the borders of Stormont and Charlottenburg in the south.

But, the Scots, they were offered those lands at St. Isidore there—good land—but they hadn't a clue so they fled into Glengarry where their familiar stones were. The man who had the store where we have the Star museum now, in Dunvegan, he was happy to sell them land at forty per cent interest. A real usurer that's what he was. And, with his own clansmen! His name was McIntosh. He had a store, the Star Inn. He was a Scot taking his own people. They did that all the time. They'd sell their grandmothers.

Bonnie Prince Charlie's pot was in the museum long before I became curator in 1974. Shows how some Scots preserve their heritage. It's a large iron pot with three legs. It only has two now and a hole in the bottom. But it was given by, I think, a MacDonald from Cornwall. Bonnie Prince Charlie ate out of this pot when he was fleeing across Scotland. He sheltered with the MacDonalds—they should have turned him in, you know.

I told you there was an Irish family in every single settlement around here. One Irish family. The Hartricks in Dunvegan, the Quigleys at Locheil, and there were Fitzgeralds on the third of Kenyon. A little leaven in the lump, a little salt, you know? I keep telling people this. But anyway, like I said, the pot sat there and Bonnie Prince Charlie ate out of this. It was quite heavy and everybody ate out of the same pot in those days. Anyway, one time I was looking through a couple of filing cabinets at the museum and I turned up a metallurgy report. I thought it was a funny thing to find. It was for an iron pot. So I read. I could only understand some of it, but it went on for five or six pages. Somebody had taken a little bit of filing off this pot and sent it off for analysis. The report came back that it was indeed a very fine old pot, 1745, or possibly considerably earlier. So it could indeed have been Prince Charlie's pot. The MacDonalds brought it out with them on board ship when they came out.

With the Scots it's just clannishness. But this Irish, the only reason there's any of us here is because they just disappeared. Reading back in Irish history—this race has been divided from the day one—no two could ever agree on any one thing. Total individuals? They never could muster a firm stand against any foe and the English could never quite conquer them because there was never any large united group to attack. Have you ever heard of the Irish Highland Games, the Fitzgerald or Delaney or whatever gathering? In the long run, it is safer to quietly disappear into the bog until the troubles are over.

Just before Christmas in Montreal, I found this lovely little bookstore and I got a copy of *The Irish Literary Times*. They did an interview with an Irish writer. She'd gone back to her ancestors and she had this enormous sense of history. And I thought it was just priceless because apparently there is a terrific revival of interest in Celtic culture, and they kept referring to the last seven hundred years of oppression and famine and genocide as "The Interruption." Isn't that marvellous? The Interruption! Seven hundred years of interruption!

My mother never saw a white woman the first winter she went into the bush at Parent. She was a teacher and she'd taught at Dunrobin and a few other places. And all of a sudden she's in the bush with the Indians. They were going up on the Dumoine River for Eddy's—which wasn't too far from Pembroke—and then, all of a sudden, my father was sent to Parent. Mother had her curtains and everything made for the house she thought she was going to move into on the Dumoine—which is closer to civilization. But, Parent's away, way up and away, way up she went. They had had a bush fire, too, and when she got off the train that morning in Parent—it was the 11th of November, 1924, in pouring rain, and everything had been burnt around the town. Two big fires; one went by on the north one year and one went by on the south the next year. She said that if Dad hadn't been there on the platform she would have taken the next train back to Pembroke.

My dad had an early camera. He was getting thirty dollars a month from the E.B. Eddy Company and he used to clerk and look after the men and keep the books and everything to eke out his salary. When the Great War started, the company cut down to twenty-six dollars a month and to eke out his salary he sent to Kodak in Rochester and got a kit—a nice folding camera, postcard-size thing, and rolls of film, and a developing kit because you couldn't send your pictures away—and he used to take pictures of the teamsters and anything interesting around the camp and sold them for a quarter a piece and made far more money than he did from Eddy's.

My father actually went on recruiting trips to recruit workers for E.B. Eddy. To New Brunswick and to the Gaspé, and a lot of men came from the Saguenay because they were lumbering there as well. And a lot of them from across the Ottawa River. The old fellow in charge of the stables north of Montebello came from Saint-André across the river.

Teddy Legault went to work in the bush when he was nine years old as a water boy. He wound up with a fantastic knowledge of horses so Dad always took him along when he went to Quebec in the fall to buy a couple of carloads of horses at the Bodnoff Horse Exchange for the winter's work. In accommodation to their different standards, Teddy always chewed gum instead of tobacco when they stayed at the Windsor Hotel in Montreal.

*Jerry Fitzgerald, as superintendent for E.B. Eddy at Parent, periodically sent in reports to his company. This account from the Eddystone Lighthouse, published by the company in the 1930s, gives a graphic and fascinating picture of the problems involved in moving supplies from depot to depot. This was done in the wintertime because it was so much easier to travel while the snow was on the roads.*

I have been pretty busy for the past week. We had some trip up the first time with the new tractor. It arrived at Parent on Wednesday night. Ardell and I went out that afternoon, the expert arrived the following morning. We unloaded on our own siding, rigged up a platform and took it off without any trouble, the lighting system was not installed, they claimed they would have had to hold up shipment for another day. The expert installed it here. We left Parent at 3 p.m. with two sleighs with three tons on each sleigh. Then our troubles started. The expert was driving, he said he would drive for the first trip and we let him go to it. This tractor is about one foot wider than our old one, the expert not being used to the road, and not much of a driver even

if he were used to it—was either cut off the road on one side or the other. We would have to unhook the chains to let him get back on the road and then hook up again. I had them cut the hind sleigh at three miles, from then on we went a little better, arriving at Twelve Miles at 12.30 a.m. We hadn't had anything to eat since dinner at Couvrette's.

After lunch we decided to go ahead to Twenty-two where we would have a decent place to sleep for a few hours. I had them leave the sleigh and come with the tractor alone to break the road and we could come back for the sleigh in the morning. Snell went to bed at 12 Miles as he was tired out, Ardell got on the tractor with the expert and I took Plante in the Snow-Mobile. We went ahead from there arriving at

"The Big Dump" on the Gatineau River, c. 1926. This pile of lumber was considered to set a record and you can tell by the fur coats on the men in the photo that company "big wigs" have come to see it. It is very unlikely that Eddy's ever did this again, for the mountain of logs would be nearly impossible to dislodge and send to market.

Twenty-two at 2.30 a.m. I waited up until 4 o'clock and at that time I thought I could hear it coming and went to bed. Woke up at seven and no tractor. Called Twelve Miles and found they had slid off the road at 14$^1$/$_2$ Miles in the sand cut. They were very lucky it did not roll right down to the river. We went back with chains and cable and took a good snub to a stump and the upper track, chopped away the ground from under the high side, got it canted back and with a few skids it came out on its own power. We got going again at 4 p.m. when to Twenty-two pretty good. Went back in the morning for our sleigh left at 12-Mile at 11.30 a.m. and got to Forty-one at 2.30 Sunday morning.

We were damn near all frozen. It was 42° below when we arrived. Sunday afternoon they started back, Plante driving. They went to Twenty-two in four hours and forty minutes and had a cup of tea out of that time at 30-Miles. Monday morning they went out to Parent in five hours and ten minutes. That afternoon the expert opened up the machine and explained everything he could to Plante, Gow and Ardell. This morning Plante left Parent with six tons on two sleighs at 6.45 and

arrived at Twenty-two at 3 p.m. passed 30-Mile at 5.15 and we expect him here around 8.30. This machine looks very good to all of us, our only trouble was widening out the road the first trip. Even Plante cannot find any fault with it. The only thing he wanted to know was that if it ever stopped with him where would he look for the trouble as it has no spark plugs.

*Even his notes are interesting:*

This hauling of supplies is a 24-hour job and is done whatever the weather may be like.

"Twelve Miles" is an old depot, disliked by all except a man and his wife who keep two or three buildings habitable and who can furnish some kind of a meal. "Twelve Miles" is a non-stop station whenever possible.

"Lunch," in the second paragraph, refers to the meal consumed at one o'clock in the morning.

"Twenty-two" is the normal halfway stopping-place when travelling in a rig. This is one of the Company's depots. From "Twelve Miles" to "Twenty-two" one travels through burnt-over country which is very bleak.

# 21

# "There is Truth in Every Legend"

## A Miscellany of Stories, Ancestral, Hockey, Lumbering, Humorous

*Composing an oral/social history is somewhat akin to creating a sculpture: you start with a great deal more "clay" than you are actually going to end up with when the work is finished. You prod and push and mould and indent and cut out and add on until voila! you have a pleasing and completed entity. Some interviews "work" and some interviews "don't work." Some "work" but don't fit into my conception of what this book should be, and they are set aside for the next book. Some "don't work" at all, but have good sections that should be preserved for the record. In my last three oral/social histories of the Ottawa Valley,* Laughing All the Way Home, Legacies, Legends, and Lies, *and* Tell Me Another Story, *I established a precedent for including a chapter of miscellaneous stories and excerpts from interviews that "didn't work." This book continues the tradition of providing a laugh at the end.*

*Carl Jennings of Sheenboro, Quebec, was one of the major storytellers in my second oral/social history of the Ottawa Valley,* Laughing All the Way Home.[1] *It was on the shortlist for the Stephen Leacock Award for Humour that year and I still get countless requests for it. In her review of the book in* Maclean's *magazine, Gina Mallett described Carl Jennings as a "wit, a sage and a master of imagery." You can imagine my surprise and delight when just recently working on this book I went out to my storage to dig through research papers and found more stories and one-liners from Jennings. Carl died June 21, 1995, at the age of ninety-four and is buried with his ancestors in the Sheenboro cemetery. At his death the last Ramblin' House in the Ottawa Valley was closed to the singers and drinkers, dancers and storytellers.*

THERE WAS ALWAYS great but friendly rivalry between the Chapeau Fair (in Catholic country) and the Shawville Fair (in Orange country), two of the oldest country fairs in the Ottawa Valley. Carl was one time asked by his friend Goldie McDowell to go to the Shawville Fair with him. Carl replied, "The Shawville Fair! What's there but a band? And it's so bad it's like listening to the band on your hat."

Another time Carl remarked, "Yes, Goldie McDowell, I took him in back of Nickabeau looking for maple syrup in places where there isn't a maple tree for five miles."

Clemmie Hayes of Sheenboro had a bottle opener on every stall in his barn.

251

The night Sheriff Sloan of Vinton shot Sullivan they buried him right away. But he had all his keys in his pocket so they had to dig him up again.

To be Irish is to be pagan wild overlaid with meek gentility.

There's good in every kind—except the Irish.

You can give a man an education but you can't give him brains.

In his store at Chapeau, Conroy has weigh scales for meal that give ten per cent off for senior citizens. But there is also a built-in lie detector on it because so many senior citizens lie about their age.

One time Jack Courvrette, one of the greatest characters that ever lived around here, was eating in the old Leland Hotel in Pembroke. He was served a very, very rare piece of beef and, you know, he always talked to himself, so he was overheard to say, "Fart and bawl if you like, but I'm still going to eat you."

Twenty years ago, Fort William, Quebec, was the scene of annual regattas which became riotous, orgiastic, and involved motorcycle gangs. The cottagers were outraged by the antics, horrified by the noise, and angered by the debris left behind for days after. After one of these orgies, Carl said, "I don't think we should call it the Fort William Regatta any more. It's the Fort William Regretta."

*Journalists from England interviewing His Excellency the Governor General of Canada, the Marquis of Lorne in his study in the vice-regal residence, Ottawa, 1880. In 1881, wishing to know something of the conditions facing immigrants to Canada, he undertook a wagon journey by prairie trails from Portage la Prairie, then the end of steel, to the Rocky Mountains.*

I knew the Duke of Connaught when his sister was the wife of the Marquis of Lorne, then Governor General of Canada[2]. When he came to Canada, the Duke and Colonel Buller, his chief aide, came many times to our Ottawa Rowing Club with Borden and Laurier, and they would sit on the verandah. Later, 1917, the Duke returned to his country seat at Bagshot, Berkshire. At that time the Canadian Foresters had a large forestry operation on his estate. At the same time I had been placed in charge of all the CFC operations in England with my headquarters at Egham. From my window I looked over Runnymede Common at Windsor Castle.

Well, the group of officers at this camp on the Connaught Estate were the limit! Good chaps but booze hounds. The famous Fog Horn (Neil) MacDonald[3] of mining fame was commanding officer, along with Percy Jory[4] of Ottawa, and several others. When I took over, I had decided to break up that combination. One day an officer from the King's Household at Windsor Castle called me up and came over to see me, saying that the Duke of Connaught would like me over at any suitable time to have a spot of tea. Right away I figured what he wanted. So a day or two later I went. He asked me, "Is it possible to arrange a change in the officer personnel?" I assured him that was already in my plans. When it took place he was most pleased. One officer of that group (of booze hounds) was a brother-in-law of Beaverbrook's—Von Ribbentrop. He had been in Ottawa in 1914 and was a member of the rowing club with his locker right next to mine. He was quite a pal of Princess Pat's. During the Hitler regime, he was German ambassador in London and one of the people most responsible for bringing to premier Baldwin's attention the danger of his association with Eddie of Windsor (the Duke of Windsor).

It was through the late R.M. Anderson of Ottawa and myself that Grey Owl—Art Belaney—was taken up by the National Parks Branch. Henderson and I had many the chuckle over that. This Belaney fellow was an Englishman at Mattawa, Ontario, and later worked with Freeman Daniels who ran a hotel that John Lumsden built at the foot of Lake Temiskaming. There he worked with the Indian guides. Had a pal there, Alger Smith, who fell off the CPR bridge across the Ottawa at Mattawa and was drowned. A third pal, Badham, was a veterinary surgeon for a time with the NWMP and a most talented musician. All three were squaw men.

*The late Lloyd Gavan, of the famous Gavans of the Pontiac was a renowned singer, storyteller and character. A first cousin of Carl Jennings, his stories appear in* Laughing All The Way Home, *the first of my oral/social history collections of the humour of the Valley.*

One day at the Gavan farm near Chichester, a priest from Chapeau, Quebec, came by and asked for a donation to pray for rain. It had been a very dry summer, back in the early 1950s. Gavan asked the priest who else gave money around there and the priest told him that McDonald on the adjoining farm had made a donation. "Well, then Father," Lloyd replied swiftly, "Why should I give? If it rains on McDonald's place, surely to Christ it will rain on mine!"

*Bob Horner, former MP for Mississauga, told this story at a recent clan wedding up the Valley.*

I was visiting my old home town, Shawville, Quebec, and dropped in to see my uncle, Frank Finnigan, who then owned the old Clarendon Inn in town. He had had matches made with his photo as a young NHL star on the back of them, and gave them away as promo. I took some off with me and had them when, shortly afterwards, I went to do some business with Conn Smythe. I put the matches down in front of him with Uncle Frank's face up, looking at him.

"Do you recognize that guy?" I asked Conn

Conn looked at the face on the matches.

"Indeed, I do," he said. "And if I were picking an all-star team of all my time in hockey, this guy'd be on the right wing."

*Ebert Richardson, Anglo-Celt descendant of first settlers in the Pontiac, a neighbour of the late Frank Finnigan's in Shawville, Quebec, was an avid hockey fan with some stories to tell.*

I kid them all the time. I say, "You have this new rink in Shawville since 1972 and you've never sent a pro hockey player out of it yet. The old covered rink fell in 1972 and you sent three great ones from it, Eddie Finnigan, Murph Chamberlain, Frank Finnigan—and pretty near Charlie Bowen." I only saw the one NHL game in Ottawa. Frank Finnigan's team (the Ottawa Senators) was playing Toronto and they beat Toronto 9-1. I remember Harold Cotton was playing. But I usually went to Montreal to see the games.

Walter Smith—the harnessmaker here for a while—was in the air force during the war. And he said, "I'm going to make up an exhibition team with a team of lads just something like myself." And then he brought up a team from Ottawa made up of the commandoes, and the air force team, and lads retired from hockey, like Harold Starr and Frank Finnigan— and they slaughtered us. But we had a good time.

And I'll tell you why we don't send great players anymore to the NHL. There isn't one of them can stickhandle. The rinks have got too big now—they just shoot it, and skate after it, and knock everybody down on the way. In the old days when they had smaller rinks, a player had to earn his way up the ice by stick handling.

We used to have a rink in Murph Chamberlain's back yard on School Street. Old Anson Murphy, the grandfather, kept the rink up for us, and we used to have pick-up games all the time. And not all of us had

*Raising the old Smiths Falls rink, 1912, destroyed by fire 1947. Measuring 230 by 74, it was one of the largest ice surfaces in Canada at the time. The New York Americans trained there in the 1930s.*

*Old Pros vs Shawville Juniors. Back row: Leslie Dale, J. Wilkinson, P. Morrell, Frank Finnigan, Bill Cowley, Sid Howe, Hugh Proudfoot, Eddie Finnigan, Selly Langford, Bill Gibson, Bill Boucher. Middle row: Bruce McTiernan, Doug Powell, Sterling Hobbs, Kervin Burman, Bev. Corrigan, Nelson Angus, Arnold Garrison. Front row: Don Carson, Jim Martin, Lee Devine, Vaughan Harris, Bill Horner, Ray Young, (Buckie) Dalton McKay.*

skates either. And I remember one time Hughie Proudfoot came over—he was a little bigger than the rest of us— and he said, "Ebert and I will take on the rest of you"—maybe three or four other lads. And we were just in our boots, you know. And I got hold of the puck and Murph Chamberlain was in goal and he dropped down on his knees, and I shot it and hit him on the head, and he's lying there and Mrs. Chamberlain comes out and yells, "Ebert Richardson, you get home and don't come back to this place." Murph was just lying there. But he got up to play again.

Frank Finnigan's grandson, Roderick MacKenzie, a few years ago when a partner with McCarthy and Tetrault, Toronto, was about to begin business with a client named Kehoe. Making some preliminary small talk and exploring backgrounds, MacKenzie asked Kehoe where he grew up.

"Oh, a small town in Western Quebec you've never heard of," Kehoe said.

"Try me," MacKenzie said, smiling to himself at the thought of all the time he had spent holidaying in Western Quebec with relatives, indeed, with whole ancestral clans there.

"Ever heard of Shawville, Quebec?" Kehoe asked.

"Well, I guess so! All my mother's people come from there and my grandfather is Frank Finnigan, the hockey great who used to play for the old Ottawa Senators and who just recently helped them get their new franchise."

"Oh, my God!" Kehoe exclaimed. "I can tell you a story about Frank. I remember some years back they staged an old-timers game at the Shawville arena. When Frank got the puck, nobody could get it away from him. So they called the game. They actually ended it there and then—and he'd be at least fifty at the time."

*I taped Reno Ramsey of Low, Quebec, in 1989. As well as being a descendant of first Anglo-Celt settlers in the Gatineau, he was connected to the Nesbitts, Kirks and Brooks of Brooks Hill. As a young man, like hundreds of other Valley men, he had worked on the Paugeen Falls Dam Project in the 1920s.*

I had a wonderful team of horses at Paugeen Falls, Sam and Cora. I did a lot of horse trading, get an old horse and trade it here, and trade it there. Horses wasn't that cheap you know. I bought this team. They cost me three hundred and fifty dollars. They had been in logging camp all winter and they looked bad. They hadn't been looked after but they were good horses. I took real care of them for a couple of years and then I took them to Cedar Rapids in '27 to work there putting in cement. My dad liked that team so much he offered to trade with me. You see, he was afraid that, as an old horse trader I might trade them to someone else. To keep him happy, I traded the team for Sam and Cora, my favourite team forever.

There used to be Jews that peddled along the road here in the Gatineau. The Assyrian pedlar never had a horse. He walked and carried two bags on his shoulders. But the Jews had a horse and an express and they'd draw tomatoes from Ottawa to here and sell them for ten cents a basket, six quart. Just imagine, eh? And I used to trade horses with the Jews, make a deal.

I did some wild trading. One time I had a bicycle and Cecil Keller wanted it, but he had no money. This is when we were just young lads, eh? But Cecil

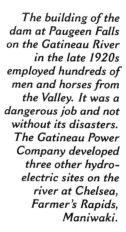

*The building of the dam at Paugeen Falls on the Gatineau River in the late 1920s employed hundreds of men and horses from the Valley. It was a dangerous job and not without its disasters. The Gatineau Power Company developed three other hydro-electric sites on the river at Chelsea, Farmer's Rapids, Maniwaki.*

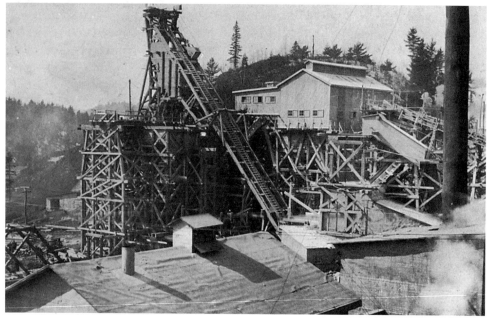

had a little steam engine, a real three-hp steam engine. So I said, "I'll trade the bicycle for that." The steam engine was of no use to me, but it was worth much more than the bicycle. So we traded. Well, then, this Bouchard had a sawmill at Venosta and he had O'Rourke working for him with his team of horses but the work finished. O'Rourke decided to go to Detroit—there was lots of work there—and he didn't want the horses, so I traded the steam engine for that team, my first team of horses.

*Norman Mahoney was also taped the same day on his farm back of Low.*

Oh, there used to be an awful gang of Irish around here at one time! But they're getting scarce now. Old Brennan came out from Ireland, the first farmer, and he built just off the road there, and the whole bunch of his sons, they all bought farms around there, and it became Brennan's Hill. Oh, there were some stories about Brennan's Hill, I tell you. Some people made out there was a fairy hole there with fairies all around it, and the little people sitting around at night, but I never believed it, honest to God. They frightened us as youngsters and when we got a bit older, they told us all those things to keep us off the road and at home.

I was about fifteen when I went to work in the bush for Mick Hendrick from Chelsea with my team for two dollars a day and my board. And I worked for Conyers and McDonald, a company that was in the limits going across towards McLarens of Buckingham. Their limits joined CIP. I'd go with all the neighbours around here, maybe twenty-one men and their teams. And the Muldoons from Quyon, they'd cross the Ottawa over to here, and Neeleys, and a big bunch from Fitzroy Harbour, and we'd all go into the camps for Conyers and McDonald.

Now Jack Heafey[5] was a very nice man, but he was also a terrible man to curse. Jack Heafey used to take his wife and family in to the lumber camp, the wife to cook for them, and the children to help. And the priest used to go in once a month. The young Heafey lad was carrying in wood for the mother, and piling it, and the priest said, "Now that's a great

little boy helping his mother like that. A smart lad, too."

"You're goddamn right I am," the lad replied.

Whereupon Jack Heafey yelled at his son, "Shut your mouth you little bastard! Don't you know that's the priest!"

I remember John Holmes. He never drank. He used to say, "Many's the night I put away five teams of horses for my neighbours. They'd all be drunk. You know it was a terrible failure with the Irish. Although I am one escaped it. I'd be sober and I'd have to put away all their teams of horses so they wouldn't freeze to death around the Low Hotel."

Old Mr. Burke from Cantley used to draw the potatoes in to town. There was no railroad then. And they used to draw them into the lumber camps, too, hundreds of bags. And they never froze on the sleighs going maybe eight miles an hour for hours.

If you kept going, the potatoes wouldn't freeze. That's what they used to do in Poltimore; load up and go right through to the market in Bytown. I asked old Joe Pink—he used to grow a lot of potatoes—and I said to him, "Cripes! If you stopped for dinner the potatoes would freeze." He said, "We didn't stop for dinner. We went right through to the Byward Market and, as long as we kept going, the potatoes didn't freeze, even if it was forty below."

*When I was in the Gatineau in 1988 I taped Ruth Dunnigan at Mayo, Quebec. She was descended from Burkes on both sides, Irish who came out pre-famine in the 1830s.*

My grandfather was the first man in Mayo. The men came over first, six weeks on the ocean, to take up crown land here. Then the women and children came; six weeks on the boat coming over to Quebec City, then another boat to Montreal, then another boat up the Ottawa River to Thurso, Quebec. The men met them there, and it was all bush and they carried the babies. My grandmother on my mother's side and my grandmother on my father's side each had a baby. On my mother's side, the baby died on the boat within a few days of reaching Thurso. Well, she didn't want to throw the baby overboard, so she kept it hidden in her long skirts and petticoats until they landed, and it was buried then.

My mother always said her mother told her again and again, "We left our cellar full of potatoes in Ireland." Trouble was there was no famine in Ireland. The potatoes failed and that's what they were living on. It rained all summer and they rotted but, in the part of Ireland that the Burkes came from—that's the West—the English took everything from them. So a million starved and a million emigrated and a million stayed. Only for France and the United States and Germany shipping in food for them, they all would have died. All his life my father was very bitter about this. He used to say, "I hate an Englishman, dead or alive." And then he would tell about what happened to them when they were coming out, how they carried with them all that they had—a bag of rolled oats, maybe twenty pounds—and they left it on some

steps at the port in Ireland, and when they came out it was gone. That was their supply for the voyage. I don't know what they ate. I guess God was with them. My grandmother was nursing her baby and I suppose she had no milk for it, so it died. Some people on board must have shared with them or they all would have died.

Our parish priest, Father Braceland, told me one time that sometimes the parents died on Grosse Ile, leaving three or four little children. Some of them even left a baby. Of course the French were living along the shores of the St. Lawrence and they took those children in and they became French, sometimes with Irish names. Father Braceland told me we never thanked the French enough for what they did.

Mayo was called St. Malachy until about 1900, when we got an Irish priest. We'd always had French priests before that. And this Irish priest came and he

*Portable sawmill for cutting firewood at local farms and homes, c. 1912.*

said, "Everybody in this parish comes from Mayo. This is going to be called Mayo."

My husband's grandfather—that's the Dunnigans—the eight boys he had were the biggest men you ever saw. I saw three of them and they were giants. I asked our parish priest, Father Hughes, "What do you think they ate to make them that size?" And he said, "Potatoes! There's a lot of iron in potatoes."

*Harold Richardson, descendant of first settlers in the Pontiac around Shawville and Radford, Quebec, was taped at the age of eighty-seven just a few months before his death in 1995. He was connected to the old families of the area, the Brownlees, the Gordons, the Armstrongs, the Johnsons, all Anglo-Celt first settlers in Quebec.*

I even knew my great-grandmother Mary Brownlee of Radford. She was the first one over here from England. There was a big family of boys and she left home and went to live with some aunts. And Mary had a boyfriend, well-to-do, and he'd a yacht. One time he was on the ocean, and it was dark, and he was coming towards the dock. And Mary went to the dock to meet him. But when he landed, he had another woman on board. So Mary settled "his" right there and then, and while she was still mad, and walking up and down the dock, she decided she wouldn't go home to the aunts and tell them the trouble she was in. And as she was walking up and down she saw this boat loading with emigrants for Canada. She booked passage on it, went back home for her baggage and the next day left England for Canada. It took a month or so to sail over, and there she was all alone. But on the way she met this Nathaniel Brownlee—he was some kind of a captain in the Irish army—coming to Canada. Before they ever got to the Ottawa Valley, they were married in Montreal.

Of course the Horners were neighbours of ours at Radford, Big John and his sons Arthur, Earl, Bert, Lloyd and all those good-looking girls. I could tell a lot of stories . . . The great Frank Finnigan went courting at the Horner farm. I could go back

to the winter I went to the lumber camp. Big John Horner took men and supplies into the camps every year. Silas Armstrong was a kind of foreman for him and he'd get young lads to help, maybe drive a team. The year that I went up, Big John's son Earl was along, too. And, boy! It was tough going for greenhorns, young lads! It was cold and rough and we were sleeping on the floor, and Earl Horner was always complaining. We loaded everything—men, supplies, horses—off the train at Ascension, Quebec, then loaded the sleighs and went up river to the lumber camps on a tote-road that was only the width of two runners on the sleighs, with snow piled six feet high on both sides, and travelling through the wilderness, miles from any human or any place.

I was on the sleigh with Big John and Earl. And Earl was in really bad humour, jawing away about how cold it was and how hard the work, and we all were pretending we couldn't hear him when suddenly he announced in a big Horner voice, "I'm going to jump!" Well, Big John, his father, just turned his head around and looked at him.

"Jump where, you crazy fool, jump where?" he roared back at him.

My grandmother couldn't hear anything. She was completely deaf from six years old. She'd read your lips. She could talk to any of the family all day long and never miss a word—until it would get dark. On dark nights she'd go and light the lamp and set it out on the table so she could see the lips around her moving.

I can go back to the big Horner fight. The Horner mother had trained them to fight to protect themselves. George and Ralph. Oh, they were boxers, but not bare knuckle—they'd have gloves on. Anyway they got too rough with her so she quit. And she put one against the other and she refereed, and she trained them until they got to be the two best boxers in the country.

By then George had the store there at Radford. He was going to Aylmer once a week or so for supplies with a team of horses. That's the only transportation they had. And this time he went down to Aylmer one night, and loaded up. They only came back as far as Quyon when Moran, the best man in North Onslow, was waiting there for Big George to try him out. But Big George didn't know anything about it. He went in to Gavan's Hotel and had his dinner. And he was late getting eating—it's a long way from Aylmer up to Quyon by horse. Somebody came in and told Big George, "Moran, the best man in North Onslow, is waiting out there to fight you." "Oh," he said, "I wish you'd have told me sooner. I ate an awful big dinner." So he walked round the hotel in circles to get down his big dinner, and they kept coming in to see if he wasn't going to come out and fight Moran. They thought he was afraid to come out. When he got kind of worked down again he came out. They had the sleighs ready in a square all around the hotel yard. Moran had his man picked for his second, and George had to pick a man out of the crowd for his second, and they went at it. I think forty-five minutes they fought. And they went to the sleighs to rest.

And Moran says, "Horner, I'm an all-day man." "Oh," George says, "I'm a two-day man." And they went at it again. And they fought, and they'd rest. They'd get on the sleighs, and rest, and then go back at it again, until at last George started knocking Moran down. The last time Big George knocked him down, he put his hand up, "Horner, you're the better man." And George said, "I knew that." And he put on his shirt and went home. Drove all the way up to Shawville, and then drove up to Radford with a load of supplies for his store.

I knew Frank Finnigan. He'd come in here and we'd have a chat. Frank was quite a man. He was a small man. He didn't get his greatness from his size. It was his quickness. He was the smartest man I ever saw on the ice. He'd go down the ice there, and he'd leave the opposition lying on the ice and never touch one of them. He'd just sweep them off their feet. Just leave a row of them lying there behind him on the ice, and he was gone with the puck, and if he couldn't get by any other way, he'd shoot it straight at them. I saw him play several times here in Shawville, and I saw him in Toronto.

One time I went down to the States with my uncle and aunt, and I was coming back just the time there was a hockey match on, and when I got as far as Toronto I went to the game, and I saw him there playing for the Leafs. You know, he put our first telephone in for us. About 1920. That was before he was famous.

*Journalist Doug How spent a number of years "On the Hill" in the Press Gallery, and collected these hockey stories.*

Lionel Conacher was an early hero of mine. I had grown up in this little village in New Brunswick and we'd have these scrub games, pick up sides. And we loved to use the names of the hockey stars! One was known as the Big Train and his brother was known as Chuck Conacher. I fancied myself as a winger. Before a game we named ourselves, Old Poison Stewart, the Chicoutimi Cucumber—Marvellous nicknames. So years later out of the Press Gallery in Ottawa, I still hadn't got over living with the myths of these giants. Anyway we used to have an annual assassination called a softball game when we, the Press Gallery, would play the Members of Parliament. And the Members of Parliament suddenly realized what a terrific advantage it was to be an athlete. Bucko MacDonald was there, Lester Pearson, Bob Winters and Lionel Conacher, who then was a member for Toronto. I just played in two games; one was '51 and one was '52, and that would be the last one before I left the Gallery. In 1951, I had gotten on the front page of the *Journal* because I thought these games were jokes, so I took a great big waste-paper basket and I caught a fly ball in left field in my waste-paper basket, and I was on the front page of the *Journal*.

Well, in 1952, we were terribly short of talent—God knows we always were—we'd get slaughtered. They put me on second base and Lionel Conacher comes to bat. He was a terribly intense man. He knew only one thing to do—win! I'm standing on second base and I suddenly see him swat what was really a single. He hits first base, and I suddenly realize, my God! he's not stopping! He's coming at me. And I looked at him, and that nickname flashed and I said to myself, "My God! that's exactly what he looks like! A Big Train!"

He's coming at me and his legs were flying and his eyes were big, popping out of his head. And he came to the second base, and I stood there and I didn't even say a word to him, but I said to myself, "Oh, my God! Here I am! If the boys back in Dorchester, New Brunswick, could see me now! Side by side with this legend!" Well, Conacher looks round and my team is still fumbling the ball, so he suddenly takes off for third. And same thing all over . . . his legs flying and his elbows flying and his whole body hurtling. He wasn't playing ball. He was making war. And he got to third. I was in my thirties and I'd never gotten over my hero worship. I was so awed by being with him that I even forgot to tell him that I used to take his kid brother's nickname as a kid. That was one or two years before he died. I thought that day on Parliament Hill, "That man is going to die out here." And that's exactly what he did. He had no brakes, no gauge. What the heck

difference did it really make whether he hit a single or a triple in a fun game? And they were leading by about 18-1.

A friend of mine, Dave McDonald from Jerusalem, one time did an article for some magazine on King Clancy, and he loved his Ottawa Valley stories. Dave said to King, "What is the roughest hockey game you've ever played in?" King didn't have any hesitation. He replied, "One time, two religious orders, Catholic religious orders, had an annual game in Ottawa. I was smuggled in by one of them as a winger, that was the dirtiest hockey game I have ever played . . . elbows, pucks, sticks, high-sticking, tripping, slashing, fighting. It was unbelievable. And they were all priests."

Somebody asked Charlie Conacher one time about Clancy and he said, "The worst thing about Clancy,"—he was just a small man—"was he'd get in these fights and he'd always lose them. He'd be down underneath the other guys, and they'd be beating the daylights out of him. So I'd pull them off him, and

*In this rare 1918 photograph the young bucks of the Shawville area who were lucky enough to have first motorcars line up in front of the freight sheds at the old Shawville station, now moved and kept as a museum. Note the lone horseman to the right. Probably afterwards some of them, looking for further amusement on a boring Sunday in Orange country, would seek out the excitement of visiting the girls, finding a church with a good choir, or even a still in the back country.*

turn him over and put him back on his feet. And I'd look back and King was right back down where he'd been, on the bottom again. But he was a character."

*The late Elizabeth Lusk Hay of the House on Ghost Hill6 told some amusing stories from the Quyon-Beechgrove-Luskville area of Western Quebec. Luskville, of course, was named for her ancestors.*

I remember our first radio. My grandfather Isaac Lusk was listening to it. I would have been eight or nine. He was listening to a political speech and, I guess, trying to be sophisticated, I said, "Is that a Liberal or a Conservative?" (Those were the only names I knew, anyhow.) Well, Grandpa's chin whiskers just shot straight out, and my mother said, "Come here, Elizabeth! Your grandfather would NOT be listening to a Liberal!"

My grandfather when he was a young man went to a wake around the mountain near Young's Corners. A crippled man had died. His legs had never matured at all, just shrivelled. So to get him into his coffin they had had to put rocks on his legs. It was a real Irish wake and the drinking and the dancing started. They danced so hard, they jiggled the stones right off the dead man's legs. The corpse suddenly sat straight up in his coffin in the midst of all that revelry. Grandpa said he went out the door, but he said most people went out through the windows. Can you just imagine!

George Hetherington—another great area character—kept a store in Breckenridge, Quebec. He had a goose he was fattening for Christmas and he kept it a big secret because he knew somebody would likely swipe it from him. He had it over in Joe Ferris's stable where Joe was feeding it for George. Joe was very careful about it all, but word got out anyhow, and somebody swiped the fattened goose, cooked it and had a great big do. Howard Wright, my cousin from Aylmer, my father—oh, the whole group were in on it.

Now, George was secretary of the school board and he was always having parcels come in from the States, American textbooks, of course. So after the big party Howard Wright was going to Syracuse and

he said, "Give me the goose bones and the head and the feet," and they did, and he wrapped them all up and mailed them from Syracuse back to George. George even had to pay for the parcel, which he did, thinking it was textbooks. He was so mad when he opened it up he threw it all out his front door, and the whole thing lay there in the snow, the bones, feet, and head of George's fattened goose.

And my father was going in to George's store one day, and there it all lay, and Father saluted it solemnly and said, "Indeed, we've met before."

*Wyman MacKechnie was born at his ancestral family farm, "Bonnieshade," at Wyman, Quebec, in 1898. There today, on over a thousand acres, his children and grandchildren carry on the outstanding reputation he gained at the forefront of the farming community of Canada. Before his death, MacKechnie added to his life achievements by writing two excellent memoirs of Anglo-Celt pioneers in the Pontiac of Western Quebec,* What Men They Were *and* So Well Remembered.

Oh! The Shawville Fair! We showed—and won—every year.

It was in the year 1927 that they built the old highway from here to Shawville and trucking was a very new thing. G.A. Howard[7] in Shawville, was one of the first men to have a truck. It wasn't a stock truck by any means—like you have today. It was too high off the ground and I had to make my own ramp at home, and his racks around it were just about two-and-a-half feet high—not high enough for cattle. But G.A. was an obliging fellow and he said, "I'll truck the cattle." He came down with his 1927 Ford truck and we spent the first hour or two extending these sides. We had six animals to take. We felt sure it would take three and we put three in. We went up the road with three in, and they were just bawling, and I had one favourite cow—I was trying to divide the weight—but even so they were too tight. And some of them started mooing and bawling, and before they were half a mile from home, one cow had burst through the side and was hanging out by the halter. I had a jackknife and I cut the halter and we stopped, and we went ahead with two, after some more fixing up of the wreck. Then we had to come back and get two more and the last time we got back, they had the chores done at home. It was dark and we had supper. By this time it had started to rain and the road along the Maple Ridge area, just above the town hall, was mud, mud everywhere. It was raining hard and the hill was slippy and we had to break branches off the trees and lay them under the tires and we finally got to the fairgrounds at twelve o'clock at night. After that year, one lady wrote a letter to the editor of the Shawville *Equity* and said they should make me president of the Shawville Fair for perseverance!

In my day, the schools weren't too well heated; they'd be too cold in the morning and too hot in the middle of the day. And to get there, we had to walk along country roads, so all the girls wore long underwear, same as the boys, and they didn't like it. They were getting to the age where they wanted their legs to be nice and neat. After a few washings and a few pullings on, the underwear would get stretched around the ankles so, do you know what they did? At night they used to soak them in water and dry them behind the stove and they'd shrink a little. They'd be a little tighter around the ankles to go to school the next day!

*And there's always another Harry McLean[8] story. The late George Roy of Bristol, Quebec, had this one.*

Harry McLean came up to the opening of the Swisha (Des Joachim) power plant. I remember he flew up in his private plane and landed on a little lake out on the other side of Mattawa there. Somebody, an old fellow, lived on the lake and had a car—an old car—and he drove McLean up to the Swisha opening. So, on the way up to the job, McLean said

*Harry McLean had his own private plane and flew throughout the Mining North and in to all his construction sites like the Flin Flon Railway and the Abitibi Dam. In a country of remarkable characters he is remembered as one of the most remarkable characters who ever stayed at the old Empire Hotel in Timmins. He well might have attended the Timmins Silver Jubilee, June 28-July 1, 1937, or been present when this Timmins-to-Ottawa courier dogsled team set off in February, 1937.*

*Charlotte Whitton would have come and gone from this Renfrew railway station many times, and sometimes down to Queen's, c. 1930s.*

to this old lad, "Look it, on your way back, run your car into the ditch and I'll send you a new one." Of course, the old lad didn't pay any attention. God! If McLean didn't phone me the next day to find out if the old fellow had run his car into the ditch. McLean remembered! If that old fellow had run his car into the ditch, he would have got a brand new one from Harry McLean!

*And there is always another Charlotte Whitton story. This one from the late Lillian Handford, Renfrew, Ontario.*

When I was down at Queen's University in the 1920s, I was very active in extra-curricular events and athletics. I was on a number of teams there, some of them championship. But one time I was on the senior basketball team and we were beaten by the juniors.

Well, Charlotte Whitton came into our dressing-room afterwards and she gave us a short tough scolding from her diminutive height.

"Imagine, letting those young ones beat you! I think I should douse you all in the swimming pool."

And I was a very tall girl and I walked over to her and looked down at her and said.

"Yes, you and who else?"

*The late Kate Miller of Renfrew, painter, creator of folk art, member of Renfrew Council for seventeen years, recorded memories of Renfrew and area at the turn of the century. And, once again, Charlotte Whitton stories.*

Oh, don't talk about Charlotte Whitton! We went to school together, the old Renfrew Collegiate. We were good friends in the sense that we helped each other out. I was dumb in maths and she couldn't draw a line but, if I helped her first with her drawing, I never got the help with my maths. I learned early that I had to get my maths done first before I did her artwork. That was my impression of Lottie always. She used people. And tough! You should have seen her playing baseball! She was the umpire, the manager and everything else. I would say she was best at seizing opportunities—even then.

I was the first lady councillor for Renfrew. Charlotte Whitton was Mayor of Ottawa when I was on council because we wrote back and forth. And, if anything bothered me on council, I'd call her and she was very co-operative. She always had good advice. A problem with Renfrew's bad water was one time I asked her for help. Our engineers here didn't seem to be able to correct it. Well, you could smell the odour when you turned the tap on! So I called Charlotte.

"What can we do?" She sent up one of her engineers and he went out to the filtration plant and put everything right. No more smelly bad-tasting water, and no expense to the town of Renfrew.

My one big early disappointment in life was that I got a two-year scholarship to the Ontario College of Art, and I couldn't take it. The eldest of such a big family, I had to start earning money. So I started teaching right away. I taught at Horton and then I went two years to Killaloe and they were the best years of my life. They were always having sleigh rides or parties or picnics or dances—the young people of Killaloe were terrific. Killaloe was a Catholic and Protestant community and school separated them, but they all came together after school. They were the kindest people I ever knew. But then the war came along and took the young men. The family I remember most were the Stringers.[9] The Stringer

## COUNTIES' COUNCIL FOR THE YEAR 1898, United Counties of Stormont, Dundas and Glengarry.

### DONALD McDONALD, Warden.　　　A. L. MACDONELL, Clerk.

| MUNICIPALITIES | NAMES OF REEVES | P. O. ADDRESS | DEPUTY REEVES | P. O. ADDRESS |
|---|---|---|---|---|
| CHARLOTTENBURGH | WILLIAM MACPHERSON | Williamstown | D J McDONALD / ANGUS A McDONELL | Munro's Mills / Martintown |
| LANCASTER TOWNSHIP | DUNCAN C. McRAE | Bridge End | JOHN B. SNIDER | Bainsville |
| KENYON TOWNSHIP | *JAMES FRASER | Loch Garry | DONALD A CAMPBELL / JOHN A CAMPBELL | Dunvegan / Loch Garry |
| LOCHIEL TOWNSHIP | A. B. McDOUGALL | Glen Norman | JOHN A. McRAE / R. F. McRAE | McCrimmon / Lochiel P.O. |
| ALEXANDRIA VILLAGE | D A McARTHUR | Alexandria | | |
| MAXVILLE VILLAGE | JAMES BURTON | Maxville | | |
| LANCASTER VILLAGE | NEIL McGILLIS | Lancaster | | |
| OSNABRUCK TOWNSHIP | ALEXANDER FRASER | Sandringham | THOMAS DEY / JOHN CRAWFORD | Moose Creek / Gravel Hill |
| FINCH TOWNSHIP | F. D. McNAUGHTON | South Finch | SIMON HUFF / HUGH A. McMILLAN | Berwick / Berwick |
| OSNABRUCK TOWNSHIP | JAMES MARTIN | Newington | JAMES O SHAVER / GEORGE KERR | Farran's Point / Farran's Point |
| CORNWALL TOWNSHIP | DONALD McDONALD | Cornwall | JAMES GROVES / JAMES MYERS | Cornwall Centre / Eamer's Corners |
| CORNWALL TOWN | WILLIAM HODGE | Cornwall | ROBERT CONROY / PETER E CAMPBELL | Cornwall / Cornwall |
| WINCHESTER VILLAGE | MAHLON BAILEY | Winchester | | |
| WINCHESTER TOWNSHIP | FRANK ELLIOTT | Morewood | JEREMIAH F. CASS | Cass' Bridge |
| MOUNTAIN TOWNSHIP | GEORGE W. STEACY, M. D. | South Mountain | ISAAC KINNEY | South Mountain |
| MATILDA TOWNSHIP | CARMI LOCKE | Dixon's Corners | EDWARD FOSTER / SAMUEL SMYTH | Strader's Hill / Dundela |
| IROQUOIS VILLAGE | CHARLES E CAMERON | Iroquois | | |
| MORRISBURG ON VILLAGE | JOHN H MEIKLE | Morrisburgh | | |
| CHESTERVILLE VILLAGE | WILLIAM B. LAWSON | Chesterville | | |
| WILLIAMSBURGH TOWNSHIP | CHARLES T. WHITTAKER | Morrisburgh | RILEY M BECKSTEAD / ROBERT CUNNINGHAM | Morrisburgh / Archer |

*NOTE.—James Fraser, Reeve of Kenyon, having died since January Session, D C CAMPBELL, Esq., of McCrimmon P.O., was elected by acclamation as such Reeve.—COUNTY CLERK.

**20 Municipalities.　　　20 Reeves.　　　23 Deputy Reeves.　　　Total, 43,**

*This rare archival 1896 photo of the Counties Council for the United Counties of Stormont, Dundas and Glengarry would have included one or more members of every Scottish clan and sept that went that day to North Lancaster to greet the Prince of Wales.*

boys all went to war and they all came back.

One of my loveliest Killaloe memories—it was back of Killaloe, way back in the hills, a whole load of us, on the sleighs—we drove away, away on the sleighs to a big log house with a nice warm kitchen and crowds of people, mostly Polish. What I remember most is this young man coming into the kitchen with a whole keg of wine and this John Joe Turner turning on the tap. And after that it wasn't just one glass of wine that went around, it was a whole barrel, and then another one after that, and then another one—they just kept bringing in the barrels and we just kept on dancing and singing, and I didn't get home until dawn. We danced all night, yes.

*From 1780 onwards, the Scottish clans, by the boatload, by caravan, in disbanded battalions, singly on foot, filled up the glens of Glengarry County and there took up the good lands and the bad lands. Paradoxically, in droves they made their exodus out of Glengarry to the universities of North America, the outposts and trading routes of the Hudson Bay Company and the North West Company, to explore and survey the wildernesses of Canada, to the goldfields of the Yukon and California, to follow the beckoning light to the United States, to Australia, to New Zealand. It was almost as if, having survived the experience of migration to Canada, they hungered for more adventure.*

*A.M. Sutherland, formerly of North Lancaster, Glangarry, was ninety-one when he penned from the U.S. letters to A.J. McDonald, a relative of the MacDonnells of Beaverview Farm, Glengarry, who retain these letters today. With a great sense of comedy, Sutherland describes in 1935 from Menominee, Michigan, the donnybrook visit in 1860 of the Prince of Wales, later Edward VII, to North Lancaster, Glengarry.*

The visit of the Prince of Wales in July 1860. It was under the management of the Duke of Newcastle. The party consisted of the Prince, the

Duke and several lords. They went west as far as Hamilton by rail and returned to Montreal by steamer down the St. Lawrence. I think that the name of the steamer was the *Banshee*. For a week or ten days prior to the date of the visit, notices was sent throughout Canada giving the time of the arrival of the royal special train at each town and village.

The time of its arrival at North Lancaster was eleven a.m. It was a bright hot day and from midnight until ten o'clock, there was a steady stream of farmers' wagons, buggies and other vehicles coming in the village and the vacant lots were filled with farmers' wagons with the horses tied to the hind wheel eating hay out of the wagon boxes. Visitors came from all over the county. It being quite clear that the three barrooms would not be able to supply the demand for Molson's proof, the hotels and storekeepers laid in a supply of flat pint bottles, which they filled, corked and had all ready for delivery.

There were several lunch stands set up for the sale of coffee and sandwiches. A good many of the men began to visit the barrooms soon after their arrival and as eleven o'clock drew near were feeling pretty lively. The train was a few minutes late but, when it did arrive, the platform and the ground on the north side of the main track was crowded with people. There were many farmers from the back concessions, mostly elderly men and women who had never seen a locomotive and when that monster came puffing in to the depot, they were somewhat nervous. But when the engineer shut off steam causing the safety valve to let go with a loud explosion, they were terror-stricken. Women screamed and grabbed their husbands who were as badly scared as they were. A lot of old fellows crowded in the front of the depot doors and out of the back doors and stood trembling until the train passed and they did not even see the royal coach. It was expected that the train would stop for a minute or two and the prince say a few words to his loyal Glengarrians. But it did not stop at all. It just slid along at about five miles per hour. The prince and the duke stood on the rear platform and the prince waved to the crowd until he passed. Then when he entered the coach, the engineer picked up speed and away they went. Well, if there was ever a red hot mad lot of

Scotchmen, it was right there and then. They yelled after the train. They cursed the Prince of Wales, the Queen and the entire royal family in two languages. I saw men throw their hats on the ground and jump on them, they were so mad. They went for the flat pint bottles and being in just the right temper to fight, they fought. They had to. It did not take much to start a fight. They fought in the barrooms and in the streets. They used no clubs or other weapons, just their fists, but they did such good work with them that it kept Dr. McLean pretty busy patching up cuts and bruises. Of course they did not all fight, but quite a lot of them did. A man came in the store with one eye in deep mourning and said that he had a blue eye. He said that he was not fighting and did not want to fight. Mr. Stewart said that he must have been too near a fight and he said that he guessed that was so.

A good many who had a long distance to go left the village soon after the train had passed and there was as big a rush going out as there was coming in and the crowd was thinning out fast. Things quieted down and, by four o'clock, there was a general hitching up and leaving. It was getting toward dusk when a team drove up to the door. It was owned by Rory McIntosh and by his side on the driver's seat sat Alex McRae. Mrs. McIntosh sat on a barrel of flour that was blocked against the tailboard. Rory was not drunk, but was pretty well lit up. He jumped off the seat to the platform that was about as high as the hubs of the hind wheels and came in the store with a gunny sack in one hand and said that he wanted three dozen schens (herring). I took the sack and went in the back room and got the herring. They were covered with brine and I had to take them out with a hook. They were very wet herring. I handed them to Rory, who slung the sack over his shoulder and kept on talking to Mr. Stewart. Rory delayed so long that Mrs. McIntosh, who was sitting on a barrel of flour that was blocked against the tailboard and could not see Rory, got up and went forward to the back of the seat where she could see him and began to call him in a very loud voice, but he paid no attention to her but kept on talking to Mr. Stewart.

Now as there was a puddle of brine forming on the floor that was running down Rory's back and off the end of his coat-tail, Mr. Stewart began gently shoving him toward the door with Rory talking all the time. He got him out at last and then he became very active. He jumped on the seat, grabbed the reins from McRae and brought the whip down on the horses' backs, which so surprised them that they started forward with a jump. Mrs. McIntosh, who was a tall raw-boned woman, was backing up to resume her seat on the barrel of flour, took a couple of steps backwards, sat down on the barrel and went on over backward, landing on her hands and knees on the road. We thought that she was hurt, but she was not the least. She jumped up, straightened her hat and took after the wagon. Rory did not see what had happened but McRae did and he grabbed the reins from Rory and stopped the team. Mrs. McIntosh climbed over the hind wheel and was giving him a piece of her mind until they were out of hearing.

When the royal party arrived in Montreal, they learned of the trouble at Lancaster and the Duke tried to smooth it over by chartering a train and five coaches and inviting the Glengarrians to a free ride to Montreal and return. Quite a good many accepted the invitation, which the people from the far back concessions could not do.

*Tommy Van Dusen, now retired in Russell, Ontario, had a long and distinguished career with the Ottawa Journal, the National Film Board, the Press Gallery, as speech writer for Allan McEachern, and executive assistant to John Diefenbaker. When I interviewed him, he also told some wonderful ancestral stories.*

Muddy, my grandmother, Elizabeth Doyle, came from Low, Quebec, about fifty miles below Gracefield on the Gatineau River. When Thomas Grace, "Pappa," was toying with the idea of taking a wife, he wrote the parish priest at Low asking for what really amounted to a character reference on Elizabeth. Years ago I saw the letter the priest wrote back saying Elizabeth "came from a fine family, highly respected on the Gatineau, was a young lady of great integrity and high character." And so they were wed.

My Irish clans were invested with great characters like my mother's aunt, who started out as Mary Jane Doyle and never married. She was a daughter of Black Mickey Doyle from Low, considered by many to be the King of the Gatineau. At the old cottage on Blue Sea Lake, there was a red-painted cabin known as Grandpa's House where Black Mickey Doyle spent his declining years. What persuades me of the prowess of Black Mickey is that, according to my father, he stood well over six feet and, when he was well past his eightieth year, it took two carloads of Ottawa police to get him out of the Canada Hotel in Byward Market. That was a man.

*Tommy Van Dusen's great-grandfather, Black Mickey Doyle from Low, Quebec, also known as King of the Gatineau. When he was well into his eightieth year, it took two carloads of Ottawa police to get him out of the Canada Hotel in Byward Market.*

My father himself was a character who could call wolves. Lac Mer Bleue was a beautiful isolated lake in the Cayamant country. My father liked to go down to its shores when the timber wolves gathered under the moon. First he would howl like a wolf to get their attention. Then he would call them in a series of low plaintive barks and howls. Finally the grey forms would move closer and closer to him through the forest.

During prohibition, my father went to Chicago to work for H.H. Mills, boss of Mills Novelty Company, manufacturers of slot machines, Wurlitzers, juke boxes, even an automatic violin player. He felt there was a bright future for all his machines in Canada and the Juke-Box Czar wanted my father to be his "front man." My father had an apartment on North Kedsy Avenue from where one night he heard a wolf howling in Chicago. He dressed and went out into the snow, walked for several miles, using the wolf howl as a guide. Other wolves joined in. My father walked until he hit a sign which read CITY OF CHICAGO ZOO. He marched up to the night guard, told him he wanted to talk to the wolves. At first the dumbfounded guard refused entry, but when my father told him he was a Canadian he said, "Well, I guess it should be okay. These are Canadian wolves!" So my father went in and talked to the wolves in the Chicago Zoo. I imagine they were glad to see and hear a friend.

*Dr. John Murphy, now retired in Ottawa, grew up in Timmins, Ontario, part of a family of Doctors Murphy. When I interviewed him he told this unforgettable story about a Gatineau character, now a legend.*

This story involves a Quebecois who lived up near Thirty-one Mile Lake. He'd lived there all his life; name of Jacques Laplante. During the Second World War, the government was trying to conscript men from Quebec with—to some extent—the blessing of the church because the church saw Hitler as an anti-Christ. Well, anyway, Jacques was up there in Gatineau; in the spring he opens up cottages, and he does general handiwork and he's been doing this

all his life with his wife and his family. Anyway, Jacques gets this letter saying that he's got to appear to enlist in the army. Jacques doesn't even know that much about the war and he says, "What's this all about?" They said, "Jacques, we want you to go over to Europe and fight the Germans." And Jacques said, "I've got nothing against the Germans. They haven't done anything to me. I don't know that I want to do this." So, anyway, they say, "Jacques, you're going to go down to Hull and be processed." Well, down he goes and the more he talks to people the more he decides that this thing is totally idiotic. "I don't want to get involved with this country I know nothing about, and people who never did me any harm. What would I go and kill them for?" They managed to get him on the train, but he jumps the train at some point and works his way back up to his shack in the Gatineau, and goes on living.

Everything's quiet for a while and then next thing you know the RCMP gets notified that Jacques is a deserter, and they've got to go and bring him in. So, of course, they pick two RCMP guys who can't speak a word of French. Typical, eh? These two RCMP guys head into the Gatineau. But Jacques' friends and neighbours get wind of it—that these two RCMP are coming up to get Jacques—and, of course, he is warned.

So the next thing that happens, the two RCMP officers get up into English-Gatineau community and find out they have to get an interpreter. So they advertise they are looking for somebody that can speak the patois, joual, whatever. They interview a few people, one of which is Jacques. They like Jacques so much that they hire him as their interpreter. By this time everybody in the countryside around knows what's going on. Off the RCMP go with Jacques. Well, Jacques goes and starts talking to people. "Have you seen Jacques Laplante, the deserter?" he asks in French. "Well, the last time I saw him, he was on his trap line up near Maniwaki." So the RCMP guys say to Jacques, "Can you take us there?" So Jacques takes them on this wild goose chase to Maniwaki. And then the rumour comes that Jacques has been seen in Parent. So up they go. And ask about Jacques in Parent. "Oh, yes," the people say, "he was here two weeks ago, but he went south." So they head south. Anyway this goes on for a whole friggin' summer and still no trace of Jacques. The RCMP finally have to report back to headquarters that they've made this exhaustive search and that Jacques has just disappeared into the woods. They pay Jacques, their great guide and interpreter, and head back to town, and that's the end of it.

Except I got this story from Jacques himself.

1 Deneau Publishers, 1984. Four printings.

2 The Marquis of Lorne, 1845-1914, Governor General of Canada, 1878-83. In 1871 he married the Princess Louise, fourth daughter of Queen Victoria. While in Canada he founded the Royal Society of Canada and helped to establish the Royal Canadian Academy of Art and the National Gallery.

3 Foghorn Neil MacDonald, see reference in Lemkay chapter.

4 One would assume Jory was a mining prospector.

5 For many years Jack Heafey worked in the bush as a jobber for the Boyle Lumber Company of Davidson and the Gatineau. See Chapter 21, *Tell Me Another Story*.

6 For further stories of Ghost Hill see *Witches, Ghosts, and Loups-Garous* by Joan Finnigan, Quarry Press, 1995.

7 For a full chapter of stories from and about G.A. Howard, see *Laughing All The Way Home*, Deneau Publishers, 1994.

8 See *Giants of Canada's Ottawa Valley*, General Store Publishing, 1981, for full chapter on McLean.

9 See more of the Stringers in Henry Taylor and Lemkay interviews.

*Faithfully every summer the Ottawa River drivers from their house on Boom Island would come in their pointer boats with their pike-poles and clean up the stray logs on the beach at Sand Bay, Quebec. c. 1930s.*